FROM THE JAGGED PIECES OF A PUZZLE, A TERRIFYING PICTURE OF BLACKMAIL AND TREASON WAS EMERGING

A nightmare sexual orgy in a German castle . . . the suicides of a man in Paris and of a woman in England . . . a trail of subversion and sabotage in the halls of the U.S. Congress . . . a strange and savage rivalry between the British secret service and the American F.B.I. . . . a quasi-military organization spawned within the Ford Motor Company . . . a secret network of traitors across America . . . an ex-newsman turned lone Nazi hunter and a beautiful young Jewish woman forced into the role of hostage . . .

All were part of a horrifying picture—as fearfully dangerous as the photos with which a brilliant, ruthless, monstrously resourceful Nazi agent could destroy the President of the United States—and the last great hope against the rising threat of Hitler. . . .

THE NIGHT LETTER

"HAS EVERYTHING: SUSPENSE, FINELY DRAWN CHARACTERS, A MARVELOUS ENDING!"   —*Arizona Daily Star*

"Imaginative . . . vividly fleshed-out . . . You'll enjoy the Hitchcockian spirit of the telling!"
                                        —*Kirkus Reviews*

Big Bestsellers from SIGNET

THE NIGHT LETTER

PAUL SPIKE

A SIGNET BOOK
NEW AMERICAN LIBRARY
TIMES MIRROR

AUTHOR'S NOTE

The Night Letter is a work of historical fiction, what has recently been described as "faction." Its central plot is, of course, my own invention. But a number of characters and most of the political background in the novel belong to history. A good deal of effort has been made to portray them accurately.

Roosevelt and Missy LeHand were lovers; this is a fact. So, too, is it a fact that Roosevelt's decision to run for a third term in the White House was not announced until the last possible moment, after weeks and months of public uncertainty and suspense.

But David Hayward and his camera are creations of my own imagination.

Throughout the book, facts and creations stand side by side. Senator Wheeler was a well-known isolationist whose links with the Nazis in 1940 are now public knowledge. But there was never anyone named Anthony Benet on Wheeler's staff, for Anthony Benet is wholly fiction. Fiction, also, are the careers of Sir Roland, Rona and Holtzer. But Reinhard Heydrich was the wretched chief of the Nazi's dreaded *Sicherheitsdienst*; and Harry Hopkins was the President's close friend and Secretary of Commerce. Those are historical facts.

Having written the above, still I doubt if such distinctions will prove all that valuable. My intention was not to provoke the reader into constantly wondering "*Did* this actually happen?" If there is any question I would wish my reader to ask, it would be "*Could* this have actually happened?"

Reader, it is for you to answer.

To my wife, Maureen

Meanwhile, the mind, from pleasure less,
Withdraws into its happiness:
The mind, that ocean where each kind
Does straight its own resemblance find;
Yet it creates, transcending these,
Far other worlds, and other seas;
Annihilating all that's made
To a green thought in a green shade.

—Andrew Marvell

I

WARM
SPRINGS

MARCH 22, 1936

A child had lost its mother in the crowd. It was shriek-
ing. Standing on the platform of the Southern Rail-
way depot, the good ladies of Meriwether County began to
murmur with disapproval.

"Who does that poor baby belong to, Claire?"

"Honey, ah can't imagine."

A young farmer in faded overalls lifted the little boy
into his arms. It promptly ceased its yowling and the mur-
murs of the ladies changed to appreciative sighs.

The President's Special was a mile to the north, throt-
tling down to 40 mph in a forest of scrub pine and black-
jack oak. As the armor-plated locomotive clattered onto a
trestle above a dusty creek bed, it exhaled a shrill blast of
steam that cut through the scrawny trees and into town.

The crowd, which had been gathering at the depot since
the damp hours before sunrise, turned and fixed its eyes to
the spot where the train would emerge from the woods. It
was barely ten o'clock in the morning but the sun rode
high in the Georgia sky. The ladies, those who could afford them, wore new sunbonnets, while their husbands had
shed their jackets and rolled up their sleeves. The middle
of March, in New York City they were still wearing their
overcoats. But here in southwestern Georgia it was going
to hit the eighties. A spurt of filthy smoke rose above the
distant treetops. "That's the Boss!" shouted someone. "He's
just crossed Taffy's Crick!"

The sun caught the stainless steel of the wheelchair.
Hayward dropped the Leica from his eye, momentarily
blinded.

It was empty. Pushed by a dignified black man in a stew-
ard's jacket, the wheelchair rolled slowly down the ramp
from the back of the train. Hayward was unable to take

his eyes away. The glinting spokes, worn leather backrest, thin black tires: Hayward was transfixed by the sight.

The crowded depot erupted in cheers. Someone began to scrape away on a country fiddle, sending a shiver down Hayward's spine. He forced his eyes to return to the train. While he had been watching the empty chair, the President had suddenly materialized on the platform at the rear of the last car. Holding the railing with one hand, waving the other jauntily over his head, Franklin Delano Roosevelt was offering the crowd one of the genuine revelations of the twentieth century: his smile.

"Friends, neighbors and honored guests," began the polished Yankee voice. "I'm not down here to bore you all with one of my speeches. I just thought I'd borrow a phrase from my old friend Bun Wright."

There were whoops of delight. Hayward had the impression that Bun Wright was the old man with the fiddle standing just outside the area roped off for officials.

"You don't mind, do you, Bun, if I borrow a few of your words?" teased the President.

"No, suh," called the fiddler. "S'long as you can find a few that ain't too dirty."

Roosevelt led the crowd in laughter. "Don't worry, Bun. The phrase I had in mind isn't dirty. Actually, the last time I heard you say this, you'd just finished off your third plate of Daisy Bonner's famo's barbecue. You remember what you told Daisy on that occasion, Bun?"

The old man wrinkled up his eyes in concentration, oblivious to the 150 people on the platform who were straining to get a look at him. "Ah do recall," he said at last. "Miss Daisy, ah told her, you do me proud."

"Indeed you did," said Roosevelt. "And that's just what I want to say to everyone who came down here this morning just to welcome home a neighbor. People of Meriwether County, my good friends here in Warm Springs, *you* do me proud!"

Hayward got a lift back to the Foundation in Dr. Irwin's new Buick. The chief resident physician of the Warm Springs Foundation asked him, "What did you think of the speech?"

"Jolly good," said Hayward. What he'd wanted to say was rather different, closer to "jolly convincing." As an

Englishman, he'd found the scene at the depot quite extraordinary. What a strangely mixed crowd! Almost as many black faces as white ones; the majority of the men were obviously dirt-poor farmers or common laborers. And mingling with them were all the men and women, plus a heartbreaking number of children, who sat in wheelchairs or stood stiffly in heavy metal braces. These were the patients who had come to bathe in the spring-fed pool on the grounds of the Foundation which Roosevelt founded here in 1927. The institution where Hayward now was an "honored guest."

Dr. David Sherborne Hayward was forty-four years old, the third son of one of London's wealthiest merchant bankers and the grandson of an ex-Prime Minister. A Harley Street specialist, Hayward was also a director of the National Orthopaedic Hospital. A graduate of Charterhouse and Abingdon College, Oxford, he had married the daughter of a marquess, was a member of White's and half a dozen other exclusive clubs, with a private income of well over ten thousand pounds a year to supplement the high fees his patients were only too happy to pay him. Happy to pay because, when they came to Hayward, it was not for the treatment of a cold or advice about a diet. Hayward was Britain's leading authority on infantile paralysis. A disease which, despite its misleading name, did not confine itself to children. In private, Hayward often called it a "very democratic" disease.

In Hayward's opinion, this disease was one of the nastiest jokes ever sprung on the human race by a God whom Hayward refused, utterly, to believe in. Let alone worship. Hayward was not just an atheist, but a devout one. As a child, he had revealed himself to his nanny as a stubborn perfectionist who would launch himself into the most frightful tantrums if his hands couldn't accomplish what his precocious mind dictated must be so. He was brought up as a Christian like all English boys of his class. But the concept of faith and the ritual of prayer never really suited his character very well. Still, he didn't completely give up God until, as an officer with the Welsh Guards, he had survived what seemed a thousand days in the mud, amidst the sniping and the star shells of 1915.

Both of his brothers had died in the war. Hayward's father had expected young David to begin where they had left off just as soon as he returned from France. There was a seat waiting in Parliament, his grandfather's seat once upon a time. His eldest brother's seat . . . once upon a time.

Hayward had refused. Instead, he had returned to Oxford and started from scratch: in medicine. Later, when his wife was pregnant with their first child, he'd taken a close look at children's diseases. That was when he had first encountered infantile paralysis: twenty-six little girls on a wretched ward in Middlesex Hospital on Mortimer Street. For some reason, this disease triggered an anger in him a hundred times greater than anything he'd ever felt in the war. To savage a child, without warning, by turning its limbs into unfeeling, clumsy wooden sticks; to reduce a life of promise to absolute zero: this was worse than killing. Death had its fair share of dignity. But a crippled child? A crippled child, to Hayward, was intolerable.

David Hayward had not been raised to avoid the intolerable things in life, but to change them. Yet because of his natural obduracy, his traditional upbringing, his frightful war experience, Hayward gradually came to view himself as a failure.

Very early in his medical career, he realized that there was almost nothing he could do to help a child crippled by infantile paralysis. It would have been easier if he wasn't such a proud man. But when he had, in a personal sense, "discovered" this disease, he had vowed that he would devote his life to conquering it. That was back in the early twenties. Now, in 1936, they knew as little about "polio" as they had fifteen years before.

If Hayward had been a scientist, he would have gone into the laboratory. But he was only a doctor, a very upper-class doctor with a demanding family, a rich and social wife, living in a society where very little was lacking so long as you were English, a gentleman and a Tory. To Hayward's credit, he demanded far more of himself than others of his class. He divided his time, equally, between his luxurious practice on Harley Street and the charity wards at the National Hospital. Yet it was never enough. As he grew older, richer and more respected, his idealism turned increasingly sour. It had begun in the war; it had intensified the first time he walked onto a ward filled with paralyzed children, and gradually it came to encompass al-

most everything in his life. Whatever it was, it had turned
Hayward into a fascist.

Dr. Irwin parked in front of the six white columns
which adorned the portico of Georgia Hall. What were the
Englishman's plans for the rest of the morning? Hayward
said he had some letters to write and then he intended to
visit the pool. That was fine with Dr. Irwin, who had a
number of patients to see before lunch. Hayward shut the
door of the Buick and turned to walk the few hundred
yards through the pines to his bungalow.

Irwin had told him that Missy LeHand, the President's
personal secretary, had said she would drop by and speak
to Hayward that afternoon. Hayward assumed she was the
tall, handsome woman with prematurely gray hair who
had stood just behind Roosevelt during his brief speech at
the train. It was Missy LeHand who had answered Hayward's letter back in October when he had first written the
President about his desire to visit Warm Springs. Not just
as a private doctor, but as a representative of His Majesty's
Government.

Missy LeHand had written back at once. The President
would welcome a chance to meet Dr. Hayward, of whose
work among infantile-paralysis patients in London he had
heard remarkable reports. Unfortunately, Roosevelt's plans
to visit the Foundation were not yet definite, as no
President's plans ever could be. But Missy LeHand would
keep in touch, for Roosevelt would very much like to have
the opportunity of showing Hayward around Warm
Springs personally.

In February, she wrote again saying the President was
hoping to visit Georgia for a week in late March. He wondered if Hayward would be free to come and meet him in
Warm Springs at that time?

So it was that Hayward boarded the *Queen Mary* on
March 8 and, after a stormy crossing, arrived in New
York City to catch a Pullman for the South.

The day before Hayward left England was the day Hitler ordered his troops to reoccupy the Rhineland. Hayward
read the news in the *Times* over breakfast in his
Southampton hotel. The German "invasion" was a direct
violation of the treaties of Versailles and Locarno. It was
a blatant threat to the national security of France. But

France had done nothing more than issue a few nervous protests. In London, the government led by Stanley Baldwin followed the French example and said even less. Certainly there was no reason why anyone in the American State Department would have seen a connection between Hitler's move into the Rhineland and Dr. Hayward's visit to Warm Springs. And certainly no one thought to warn Roosevelt to be wary of his handsome and distinguished visitor.

It was near the end of lunch when Dr. Irwin came and whispered in Hayward's ear. Hayward pushed aside his slice of rhubarb pie, rose and followed the doctor outside. They went down a corridor and turned into Irwin's office.

"How do you do, Dr. Hayward," said Missy LeHand. She was standing in front of Irwin's desk, a most attractive woman, with a gracious confidence in her smile. She had changed out of the tailored suit she'd worn on the train into a cotton skirt and a simple plaid blouse. "It's wonderful you could come. Have they been taking good care of you?"

"The royal treatment, I'm afraid. No doubt it's the accent."

She laughed. "I'm glad to hear it."

"Dr. Irwin has kindly shown me all the grounds and I've had two baths in these extraordinary waters. How is the President? Exhausted from his journey?"

"A little tired," she confessed. "He's in the pool right now. It's always the first thing he wants to do when he arrives. After a week in Warm Springs, he'll be completely rested. All set to go back to Washington and get tired out again, unfortunately."

"Well, I don't wish to tire him with my own concerns," said Hayward, "but I do hope we can—"

"Of course," she interrupted. "And so does he. Can you come to supper tonight? Dr. Irwin will be there, and a few other friends. He can drive you up."

"That's very kind of you. Of course I can."

"Good. Supper is at six-thirty. Now I'd better go and fish him out of the pool. He's going to have a nap this afternoon whether he likes it or not." She laughed with such a girlish sparkle it eclipsed the oddly faded color of her hair. Hayward was aware of the rather voluptuous figure under her plain country clothes. She gave him her hand.

After she had let herself out of the office, Irwin sighed and said, "Missy LeHand is quite a gal."

"Very charming," agreed Hayward. "How long has she worked for him?"

Irwin gave him a strange look. Then said in a very quiet voice, "That's a little hard to say."

Dr. Irwin was in a talkative mood that evening as he drove Hayward up to Roosevelt's Little White House. "You know who first discovered our springs? The Creek Indians. They used to bring their sick and wounded to lie in the waters, which they, quite rightly, assumed had magical powers."

"They are magical, aren't they?" said Hayward. He was enjoying the drive. Dusk was settling over the valley below. The ivory flowers of the magnolia trees flared amidst the dark green of the forest.

"The Creeks regarded the springs as a holy place," said Irwin. "Even enemy tribes were allowed to bathe here without fear of attack."

Hayward sighed. "I suppose he's changed this town quite a lot since he came."

"Yes and no," said the Georgian. "But then I guess that's one of his greatest gifts, isn't it? Knowing just how far he can go with people."

Hayward said nothing. He was eager to meet Roosevelt and judge for himself. It was his conviction that what the world demanded at this moment were proud, self-sufficient nations led by strong, visionary men. Was Roosevelt to be one of these men? Hayward had serious doubts.

After five minutes' drive, Irwin turned off the highway onto a dirt road and they suddenly left the woods. On either side were fields of freshly tilled soil awaiting their spring planting. Then they entered a meadow where a herd of brown-and-white dairy cows grazed in the twilight. A hundred yards farther, a young man in a dark suit stepped into the middle of the road and raised his hand. They stopped and the man came over to Irwin's window. He recognized the doctor and asked who Hayward was. Satisfied, he told them to proceed and "enjoy your supper."

"One of Colonel Starling's boys," said Irwin. "The Secret Service."

"He's fairly well protected then?" ventured Hayward.

Irwin laughed. "Not if he can help it. When he's down here he likes to roam as free and easy as he can. It drives Colonel Starling crazy sometimes. But they let him do pretty much as he pleases. After all, he's the boss."

Another three hundred yards of gradual uphill climbing and they were on a ridge near the summit of Pine Mountain. An open meadow stretched down the slope to Hayward's right. The view was spectacular. He could see the lights in Warm Springs coming alive like a small constellation on the floor of the valley. Above to his left, he glimpsed the side of a modest white house with green shutters.

The road ended in a large gravel yard. Four other cars were parked there. Irwin pointed out a battered Model T Ford which, he said, was rigged so Roosevelt could drive it around his farm.

Two agents sat in a darkened Packard, their cigarettes glowing orange like fireflies. One of them extinguished his smoke and got out of the car. He shone a light into their faces and recognized Dr. Irwin. "I assume that's the other doctor with you, sir?"

Hayward offered to show his passport but the agent waved it away.

They entered the Little White House, as the press had christened the place, across a patio trellised with red rambler roses. It was a warm evening but the door was closed. Irwin knocked once gently. A moment later, Missy LeHand welcomed them in an emerald-green frock.

"Who is it, Missy?" called out a familiar voice from inside.

"It's our two doctors."

"Well, bring them on in," called Roosevelt. "You've got some drinking to do, gentlemen, if you're going to catch up with us."

Suddenly Hayward found himself standing inside a warm, cozy sitting room which reminded him of his maternal grandmother's house in Dorset.

Roosevelt was in an easy chair next to a large stone fireplace. The first thing Hayward noticed were his legs. Seated, it was impossible to hide their frail condition, contrasting so strongly with the muscular upper torso and the famous head, at once powerful and generous.

The President introduced Hayward to the three other men in the room. There was a judge named Revill, who was extremely plump. Then a man whose name Hayward didn't catch: the editor of a local newspaper called *The Meriwether Vindicator*. And a local farmer who was called Otis Moore and who, said Roosevelt, managed this place for him.

Missy LeHand offered the newcomers drinks. Dry martinis, which she said were a specialty of "The Boss." Hayward couldn't very well refuse a cocktail personally mixed by the President of the United States, although he detested gin. When it came, four ounces of iced alcohol with a green olive floating on the bottom, Hayward forced himself to swallow.

Judge Revill was in the middle of a story. It concerned a recent possum hunt and Roosevelt kept laughing uproariously. Hayward had a chance to examine the room more closely.

The walls were lined with shelves on which were displayed about twenty very elaborate ship models. There was a large map of the South on which the most important crops of each state were pictured. The mantel was littered with giant pine cones and porcelain statues of roosters and hens. A huge ship model hung suspended on wires above the mantel. The largest piece of furniture in the room was the comfortable brown leather couch on which he now sat wedged between Judge Revill and the newspaperman.

Over by the door a red armchair was placed within easy reach of a walnut radio console. Here Missy LeHand had just sat down. Hayward felt her staring at him and met her eyes. They exchanged tentative smiles. As the only stranger in the room, he was acutely conscious of being under observation. He sensed a strong protectiveness in her, the only woman in the room. The way she had answered the door, and moved about ever since, getting drinks, checking on the kitchen, made it clear that her position in the household was rather more than that of secretary.

Hayward was aware of Roosevelt's eyes. They never rested, but flickered with an intense nervous energy from face to face, always returning to Missy, where they lingered for a moment longer than anywhere else.

During the first lull in the conversation, Roosevelt turned and directly addressed Hayward. How had he found life at the Foundation so far?

Hayward claimed to be most impressed. Everyone was being extraordinarily kind and helpful. Of the patients he'd spoken to so far, all were unanimous in their praise for the treatment they were receiving. And, above all, he found the hot springs an experience unlike any other. It was as if the water was alive, he said. Fifteen minutes in the pool, Hayward joked, and he'd imagined he was fifteen years younger.

Roosevelt smiled. "I've often wondered if Warm Springs wasn't what old Ponce de León was really looking for when he was hiking around down there in the Everglades. Somebody should have slipped him a map of Meriwether County, don't you think, Otis?"

The farm manager blinked, then grinned, obviously unfamiliar with the reference. "Ah reckon," he said.

"The Fountain of Youth," teased Roosevelt.

"Yes, suh. Ah . . . ah almost forgot."

Roosevelt smiled and shook his head, indicating it wasn't important. He turned back to Hayward. "You know, I took my first plunge in the springs back in 1924. After about an hour, I suddenly got this amazing sensation. It was my right foot. For the first time in years, I suddenly felt my own toes. For a man who had reconciled himself to the probability of never again feeling his own toes, that afternoon seemed like a miracle."

A few minutes later Missy got the signal from the kitchen and called them all to the dinner table. They started with baked grapefruit topped with brown sugar. The second course was introduced by Roosevelt as "Miss Daisy's famous Country Captain." Miss Daisy herself brought it to the table. A small, serious Negro woman, she piled their plates high with chicken, French beans, rice and salad. The chicken was delicious. Hayward detected a slight curry flavor in the batter. There was also a basket heaped with the tastiest hot biscuits Hayward had ever eaten. The only thing missing, he noted, was a decent wine. Instead, everyone drank coffee throughout the meal.

The newspaperman raised the topic of the coming elections. What did Roosevelt think of Senator Borah's chances of winning the Republican nomination?

"He's entered all the primaries," said the President. "But Bill's always been more of a Washington figure than a national one. You know he's not very popular with the professionals on the Republican National Committee. All his talk over the years about the so-called 'bosses' hasn't been forgotten. But I wouldn't want to underestimate Bill Borah. He definitely has a chance and he'd make a tough opponent in November."

Judge Revill was eager to draw Roosevelt out on the current political situation in Washington. But the most he was willing to say about Washington was that the Congress was proving far less cooperative than he would have hoped. Hayward gathered Roosevelt was looking forward to the '36 elections for more reasons than one.

By the time Miss Daisy produced a rich chocolate soufflé for dessert, Hayward had begun to form a strong impression of Roosevelt the man. It was, in some ways, contradictory.

The President was intelligent, warm, a good listener and obviously a consummate politician. He seemed to draw on vast reserves of self-confidence. In fact, Hayward guessed he was vain. Yet by no means was he a snob. His dinner guests made that clear. Did he enjoy his awesome power? Undoubtedly he did. Could this man be ruthless? Hayward wasn't sure. But he did sense in Roosevelt a stubborn streak, which, if coupled with anger, could prove extremely dangerous to anyone who was his enemy.

What were Roosevelt's weaknesses? Hayward's instincts, which were the result of an upper-class English education and an unashamedly masculine culture, detected something slightly feminine about the man. Not soft or effeminate, it was just his impression that Roosevelt was less of a "man's man" than he was a "ladies' man." Along with this, Hayward guessed that part of the President's charm was due to a certain immaturity. Every now and then, Hayward got a glimpse of a little boy who had never completely grown up; who loved to tease, build ship models and collect stamps.

Missy LeHand had said no more than five sentences during the entire supper. Seated at the end of the table opposite Roosevelt, she rarely took her eyes off him even when others were speaking. And whenever Roosevelt spoke, he looked to her, not so much for confirmation but as if she was his perfect audience. There could be no doubt about their relationship, Hayward thought. Not only did Missy act like the lady of the house, but all the other guests treated her as such.

What about Roosevelt's wife? Hayward asked himself. Obviously this affair was not a secret, at least not in Roosevelt's private world. Surely Mrs. Roosevelt must know about Missy. Hayward was surprised. Not that British prime ministers—or kings, for that matter—had ever been especially noted for their sexual fidelity to their wives. But Hayward had always taken the Americans' Puritan heritage at face value. Now it appeared he had been just as naive as the Americans were always accused of being. He vowed not to repeat the mistake.

As soon as he'd finished his dessert, Otis Moore stood up and excused himself from the table. He wanted to check on the milking, he said, and anyway it was nearly his bedtime.

"Otis is a remarkable man," Roosevelt told Hayward after the farmer had gone. "You may have heard of our American hog-callers? Well, Otis is the only man I've ever met who can call cows out of the woods with his voice. Sometimes I think I should take him up to Washington and get him installed as Speaker of the House."

They all got a good laugh out of that before Missy suggested they move back into more comfortable chairs.

The final hour of the evening was filled with a discussion of the Warm Springs Foundation and Hayward's own work in London. The newspaper editor asked if he could drop by in the next few days and interview the Englishman for the *Vindicator*. Flushed with what the others took as shyness, he tried to excuse his way out of it. But then Roosevelt said, "Nonsense, Dr. Hayward. The local folks would love to read about your work way over there across the Atlantic," and Hayward had to agree to allow himself to be interviewed for publication. Then Judge Revill asked him if he did much hunting in England. Hayward said he'd hunted quite a bit in his youth but had lost his taste for it after the war. The judge looked confused but Roosevelt nodded with understanding. Suddenly Missy LeHand was standing up and thanking them all for coming and making it such a lovely evening.

"Why don't you join me for a swim tomorrow," asked

Roosevelt before Hayward left. "I'll be at the pool about ten o'clock."

The meeting was arranged, good-byes were said and Hayward walked back to Dr. Irwin's car for the drive down the mountain. Irwin was in a less talkative mood than earlier and this suited Hayward. The Englishman had a great deal on his mind.

The large pool was crowded with patients the next morning when Hayward arrived. Roosevelt was already in the water. He waved at Hayward and went back to teaching a group of patients an exercise designed to develop strength in their knees. Hayward changed into his trunks, slipped slowly into the steaming water and gradually made his way over to the President.

After instructing the group to practice on their own, Roosevelt turned and said, "I thought I'd show you some of the exercises I improvised for myself. When I first arrived here back in 1924, the nearest doctor was Jim Johnson over in Manchester, five miles away. I was pretty much on my own."

An hour passed rapidly. Roosevelt had developed half a dozen good and unique body-strengthening routines to be practiced in the pool. In turn, Hayward thought up a new exercise on the spot which greatly impressed the President.

It was past eleven when they left the pool and entered the changing room. "I've got to run down to the Meriwether Hotel and see my friend Jim Farley," said the President. "Business, unfortunately. But Missy and I have arranged to lose our shadows this afternoon. We're going to drive up to Dowdell's Knob for a picnic around one o'clock. Care to come along?"

"I'd love to," said Hayward.

"Wonderful. It's a beautiful spot; just about my favorite piece of landscape in the whole world. We'll pick you up in front of Georgia Hall at one o'clock."

It was closer to one-thirty when they drove up in Roosevelt's Model T. The President was wearing a floppy old fedora; Missy sat beside him with a pink sweater pulled over her shoulders. A great shaggy Alsatian dog sat proudly on the back seat.

"Hope you don't mind sharing the back with Chief?" laughed Roosevelt. "He's very friendly but I can't say that much for his manners. Just give him a wallop if he gets in your way."

"I'll take this," said Missy, lifting the wicker hamper into the front and onto her lap.

They drove the opposite way around Pine Mountain from the road which Hayward had taken the previous evening. This was a new road, smooth and gently curving. About a mile out of town they passed a group of wooden barracks set back in the woods. "That's our local CCC camp," said Missy over her shoulder.

"I'm sorry?" said Hayward.

"Oh, of course. That stands for Civilian Conservation Corps," she said. "They built this road."

"I'd like to take a picture of it on the way back," said Hayward. He'd brought his Leica along and it hung over the shoulder of his brown tweed jacket. "So I can show my family part of the famous New Deal in action."

Roosevelt chortled, as Hayward had hoped he would. He was catching onto the American style of wit. It was a matter of putting your tongue in cheek, but not too firmly.

The road stretched in graceful curves back and forth up the steep, wooded hillside. The forest was ablaze with honeysuckle, dogwood and magnolias. About six miles farther on there was a paved area at the side of the road where Roosevelt turned off and parked. Chief immediately leaped out of the car and dashed into the woods as if he'd spotted a rabbit.

"Crazy dog," said Roosevelt. He opened his door and turned slowly in his seat, reaching back for his crutches. Missy came around to see that he was all right, then walked the ten yards to where a wide, well-kept path descended between the pines. She let Roosevelt pass her, then followed with Hayward bringing up the rear. He tried to take the hamper from her but she wouldn't hear of it.

It was only a short hike down to Dowdell's Knob, a rocky promontory that jutted out of the mountain to give a stunning view across miles of virgin forest. The rocks were placed in such a manner as to suggest that someone had actually designed this spot. Flowers bloomed in pastel confusion everywhere. Missy soon picked out a level piece of ground and spread a blanket. She began to immediately unpack their lunch.

"See that rock over there," said Roosevelt, pointing at a

boulder which towered above the rest. "That's the Pulpit. A farmer who lived around these parts about a hundred years ago, a man named Dowdell, used to bring his family and his slaves up here on Sunday mornings. He'd climb up on top of that rock and preach them all a sermon."

Roosevelt proceeded to give Hayward a brief nature tour of the area, pointing out the rarer kinds of wild violets, the tiny scarlet strawberries, the fragile silver Indian pipes.

When Missy called them to lunch, Chief suddenly appeared out of the woods, his muzzle and paws caked with damp earth.

"Guess who's hungry?" laughed Roosevelt. "I think Chief must have buried at least fifty bones up here over the years."

Sure enough, the first thing to come out of the picnic hamper was a large bone wrapped in paper. Wagging his tail, Chief came up to take it out of Roosevelt's hand and promptly set to enjoying it.

The President, with Missy's help, lowered himself onto the blanket so that his back was propped against a relatively flat boulder. Daisy had packed them a huge lunch of cold ham, turkey, potato salad, tomatoes, pickles, rolls, brownies and lemon meringue pie. There was a choice of iced tea or hot coffee to drink. After the workout in the pool, Hayward was famished and set about loading his plate with thick slabs of neat and a small mountain of potato salad. Roosevelt, however, didn't seem all that hungry. He took the plate Missy had filled for him but then seemed to have entered a kind of trance, staring out at the distant horizon.

In the middle of the meal, Missy asked Hayward how the English were reacting to Hitler's move into the Rhineland. He had expected a question like this, although he'd hardly been looking forward to it.

"Are you asking me what the British people think, Miss LeHand?" he said slowly. "Or what I personally think?"

"Both, I suppose."

"Fair enough. As for the average Englishman, I daresay he doesn't have much of an opinion either way. Unless there is a war on, an Englishman tends to pay little attention to what goes on outside his own garden. Of course, the Germans are not popular in Britain. But there is a certain amount of grudging respect for the way in which they've built themselves up under Hitler."

"You mean Hitler is popular in England?" asked Missy incredulously.

"Not popular, no. But respected."

Roosevelt had been listening carefully without taking his eyes off the view. Now he turned to Hayward and asked, "You don't feel the English people are alarmed by the return of German militarism?"

"No, I don't think so. The Germans paid for the World War throughout the twenties. But now this fellow Hitler has come along and done the inevitable repair job on German pride. And they are a proud people with an old military tradition."

"I take it," said Roosevelt softly, "that we've progressed from the average Englishman's opinion to your own?"

Hayward nodded. "I'm afraid so. Don't mistake me, please. I have no love for Germany nor any affection whatsoever for German militarism. The war in which I fought against the Germans as a young man and in which both of my older brothers were killed has left as strong a mark on me as on any other veteran. However, whatever I may feel emotionally about the Germans should not interfere with my rational view of the world situation. Frankly, I see nothing wrong with a strong Germany standing between Russia and England. So long as it is under the proper leadership. The Russian Communists have rather worldwide ambitions, as you know."

"Let's forget the Russians for a moment," said Missy. "Do you think Hitler is an example of proper leadership?"

"For the Germans, yes. Hitler wants to unite all the German-speaking peoples in Central Europe under one government. He hasn't threatened France or Belgium, or Holland, and certainly not England. It is a question of culture and language. As for the Rhineland, nobody can possibly claim it isn't a traditional part of Germany. No blood was spilled when Hitler sent the army in this month. In many ways, I think it was a kind of publicity stunt. And it turned out rather successfully, didn't it? Yes, I think Hitler is a proper leader. I happen to believe in strong leaders and strong nations. We cannot afford to 'forget' the Russians, Miss LeHand. At least I do not believe we can, not even for a moment."

Roosevelt took a deep breath. "What about Hitler's treatment of the Jews?"

Hayward nodded, as if he'd anticipated the question. "I'm certainly not an anti-Semite. Nor am I a Nazi. If I had to name Hitler's greatest flaw, it would be his recourse to this rather disgusting prejudice."

"It doesn't seem to shock you though," said Missy. It was an accusation.

"I am a doctor. Most of the patients I treat are all but incurable. Many of them are small children. I confess that few things in life can shock me anymore. No, but it does disturb me," said Hayward.

Roosevelt lit a cigarette in his holder and inhaled deeply. "I'll tell you what disturbs me about what you've said so far. You haven't mentioned the fact that Germany under Hitler is a totalitarian dictatorship."

"You mean 'democracy,' sir, or the lack of it? Yes, I suppose I should have mentioned that," said Hayward. "I deplore dictatorships, of course. But I suspect Hitler represents what a democratically elected majority of the Germans actually want."

"Democracy German-style?" quipped Roosevelt.

Hayward laughed, ignoring Missy's glare. He found it interesting that Roosevelt did not seem shocked by anything he'd said so far. Was Roosevelt holding back his frankest views just as Hayward was? The woman's reaction, of course, was understandable.

Missy finally brought herself to say what was on her mind. "Dr. Hayward, I thought democracy was the protection of the rights of minorities. Not just the will of the majority."

The President burst out laughing, then patted Missy's shoulder. "Well done, Champ."

"I'm serious!" she insisted.

Roosevelt lost his grin. The hand suddenly ceased patting her shoulder and gave it a firm, comforting squeeze. "I know you are. And you're one hundred percent right."

Hayward smiled sheepishly. "I *am* sorry, Miss LeHand. No doubt you're right. You know, I think my children would like you very much. They often accuse me of being a dictator at home."

Missy managed a weak smile. Roosevelt pulled her closer to him. She lowered her head against his shoulder.

Well, thought the Englishman, there's nothing like a political argument to bring out the emotions. It seemed Roosevelt hadn't taken any of his opinions personally. In fact, he trusted Hayward enough to cuddle his mistress in front of him.

"Do you know what I think I'm going to do?" asked Hayward, getting to his feet.

"What, good sir?" asked Roosevelt.

"Take a little stroll and explore the terrain. I want to get some photographs while I'm here." He patted the Leica, which he'd slung over his shoulder. "I promised my children I would bring back at least a thousand pictures of what America's really like."

Roosevelt smiled. "A thousand? Then you'd better get busy. I would join you but I think Missy here would have a fit if I started to tramp down this mountain."

"You're not kidding," said Missy. "But I'd be happy to come with you, Dr. Hayward. These woods can be treacherous if you don't know your way around. All the paths seem to cut—"

Hayward raised his hand. "Please. As an ex-officer in the Guards, I reserve the right to get lost on my own. You two stay here and enjoy the view. If I really do lose my way, I'll whistle for Chief."

The dog, hearing his name, opened his eyes, shot Hayward a glance, then fell back to sleep with his muzzle resting protectively on his well-gnawed bone.

"See you in about twenty minutes, then," said Hayward. He walked off in the direction of the boulder called the Pulpit.

When the Englishman had gone, swallowed up among the pines, Missy said, "What do you think of him? He's a fascist, isn't he?"

Roosevelt tightened his embrace around her shoulders. "Perhaps. I don't think he's all that political an animal. These upper-class British fellows are quite different from their American brothers."

"How?" she asked.

"The cynicism which comes from knowing there will always be an England," he joked. "Seriously, I like the English. I even like Hayward. I suspect he enjoys hearing himself talk. Come to think of it, I've been accused of that myself. By you, as a matter of fact."

Missy ignored his teasing. "But the way he seemed to write off the Jews like that. Being a doctor is hardly an excuse."

"How does Hayward know what's going on in Germany?" asked Roosevelt. "The English papers are different from ours. Do you realize that most Englishmen don't even know their King is extremely fond of an American lady named Mrs. Simpson?"

"Really?" asked Missy. "But everyone in the States knows that. Anyway, he seemed to know quite a bit about Germany."

"Let's not quarrel, Missy. I'm really so happy this afternoon."

She lifted her head and looked at him, at his eyes and his handsome mouth set in a peaceful line. It was rare to see him like this anymore.

She was very lucky. Her mind wandered and she suddenly thought of those days back in Albany; of the fishing trips on the *Larooco* in the warm Gulf of Mexico. She felt again the exhilaration of those trains all over the country in 1932, and much earlier in 1920. Without warning, she suddenly recalled the terrible years after his illness. Even she had suspected (but certainly never admitted) that his political career was finished then. How he had depended on her, on all of them, to keep his spirit from destroying itself. Even as he was struggling, not to walk, but just to crawl.

The strain had taken its toll. She thought of that night in his mother's house in Hyde Park when they listened to the '32 returns. She could vividly recall the expression on Eleanor's face. Even then, Eleanor's joy had seemed somehow apart. Not lonely, but distant. Eleanor. Missy no longer felt there was any jealousy between them. Once, yes, of course. Not for a long time now. Both were equals; both were his wives. One in public, the other in private. And Eleanor had made so much of a new life for herself.

While Missy had continued to give everything to Franklin. She believed she could actually feel his thoughts inside her own mind, feel them as vividly as she could now feel his hand lightly stroking the back of her neck.

Perhaps she had never truly understood Eleanor. But had Eleanor understood her? No, probably not.

She pressed her hand against his broad, powerful shoulder and felt the answer in his warm hands on her back. "Forgive me for quarreling," she said.

"No sorries, my dear. A penny for them?"

"Oh, I was just thinking. How very happy I am today. How much I love you and always have, always will. Silly things like that."

He leaned his head down against her soft hair, soft but sadly faded before its time, and then covered her mouth with his own. They kissed deeply, completely, as they had not for some weeks. A kiss that made her feel young, very young. When it was finished, he proceeded to cover her forehead, her eyelids, her cheeks and the tip of her nose with tiny kisses. She moved closer to him, warmth stirring inside her, the warmth of the sun and of her memories.

Hayward had stood watching behind the cover of the pines at a distance of nearly a hundred yards. Now he began to survey the sloping ground for his best line of approach. He was grateful the dog had not followed him. He decided to go up the hill, to the top of a small ridge in the forest, and then carefully work his way down. That would put him above and at a ninety-degree angle to where he'd left them.

He moved as quickly as possible. The thick layer of pine needles felt like a cushion under his shoes. He was out of sight here, shielded by the boulders which gave Dowdell's Knob that enclosed feeling of a church. At least on the mountain side.

When he reached the ridge, he began to carefully work his way back in their direction. Suddenly he realized a gap in the trees left him open to their sight. But a quick glance told him they weren't looking anywhere near his direction. Reclining on the blanket in each other's arms: how could they be so foolish?

He was only thirty yards away now. Ahead, a fallen tree's decaying trunk would make a good blind.

What had that fat judge asked him about hunting? No, not in England. He had come five thousand miles to America—to hunt. He rolled over on his back and set the Leica on his chest. He took off the lens, put it in his shirt pocket and took the longer one out. It screwed in with that lovely German precision you would expect. Bloody Huns, as much as you hated them, you had to respect them. He checked the film again, then rolled onto his stomach.

Cautiously peering over the edge of the fallen tree, he took about a minute to set the range and the correct exposure. At least he hoped it was a decent exposure. Shooting out of the dark woods into the lighted clearing was tricky.

I'll stay five minutes, he told himself, and shoot the entire roll. Then go back exactly the way I came. It ought to work, provided they didn't turn their faces or, Christ, suddenly spot him. He was shooting down on an angle and getting most of their bodies. If he'd had a longer lens, there would be no doubt at all. He wouldn't have to be nearly this close. But he had to be sure he got their faces.

When Hayward emerged from the woods fifteen minutes later, they were still embracing. He shouted loudly to give them a chance to disentangle. They certainly had no suspicions.

Missy gathered herself up and straightened her hair. Roosevelt grinned and asked if he'd gotten some good shots.

"I found a lovely big patch of those Indian-pipe things," lied Hayward. "Took some close-ups. And a few from below the Pulpit."

"That should please the kids," said Roosevelt.

"I doubt it. I think they're expecting me to come home with nothing but autographed pictures of their favorite film stars."

"How many children do you have?" asked Missy. She had begun to gather up their picnic things and pack them in the hamper.

"Three. Two daughters and a son."

Roosevelt nodded his approval. "I have four of the creatures myself. Three boys and a girl."

It was a more difficult walk for Roosevelt on the way back up the hill to the car. This time Missy let Hayward carry the hamper. She hovered close behind the President until they were safe on level ground. Then she suggested that she drive them back. But the President wouldn't hear of it. "I feel like a million bucks," he said, "to coin an original phrase. Why don't we move the capital to Meriwether County, my dear? It would do wonders for the presidential morale."

"Because," said Missy, climbing into the front seat, "it wouldn't do a thing for the morale of Meriwether County."

"I suppose you're right. As always, my dear, as always."

On the way down the mountain, Hayward had to struggle with Chief to keep the big dog from occupying the entire back seat with his furry body. Then Roosevelt asked if there weren't at least a few Englishmen who held opinions about Nazi Germany and Hitler that were quite the opposite of Hayward's.

"Quite a few, I admit," said the Englishman.

"I thought so," said Roosevelt over his shoulder. "Actually I've got a friend in England who corresponds with me frequently. He believes Hitler is going to attempt to conquer Europe. He feels the man is, I'll phrase it politely, unbalanced."

Hayward had a strong suspicion about the identity of Roosevelt's English correspondent. He spent the next several minutes attempting to implant the notion that most people in England regarded Winston Churchill as a senile old fool. Whether or not Roosevelt believed this, Hayward wasn't sure. He suspected not.

The final moments of the afternoon were suitably absurd. Roosevelt and Missy sat in the Ford while Chief ran madly about the grounds of the CCC camp. This was to allow Hayward to snap photographs of the place with his empty camera. The film, which he'd removed before he left the cover of the pines, rode comfortably in his jacket pocket. Film he was quite sure his children would never see.

II

THE
DISTRICT

JUNE 12, 1940

2

The contact came at eleven o'clock in the morning on Jackson's third day in Paris.

He'd expected the call on his first night. But when it didn't come, he was afraid the waiting game might last for some time. His phone did ring twice on the second day. But when he lifted the receiver there was nothing: a sharp click and the irritating buzz of disconnection. The switchboard was no help, and no messages were left in his box. It meant he couldn't leave the hotel.

His room was on the third floor of the Hotel Ritz. From his large window he could look down on the restrained harmony of the elegant Place Vendôme. His room was very large, expensively furnished, with florid pink-and-gold walls rising to an ornamental plaster ceiling. He could lie on his back and count the plaster arrows in Cupid's plaster quiver.

Through his open window Jackson could hear the distant reverberation of the German artillery to the north. It grew hourly less remote, more confident.

On the tenth of June, the day he'd arrived, the French government had fled to Bordeaux while he was still clearing customs at Le Bourget. Anybody with any sense was leaving the city. The roads to the south were packed solid with refugees all the way from the Porte de Versailles to the Pyrenees. Business at the Ritz was not thriving; its opulent public rooms now conducive to fits of temper and bouts of tears. The staff was sullen, resentful of these foreigners who were about to witness their city's humiliation. Jackson was content to lie on his huge bed and read while he waited for the phone to ring.

When it finally did come, he let it ring four times. Then lifted the receiver and spoke in a calm, neutral voice.

"Either way is fine with me," he said after listening to

27

the man on the other end for thirty seconds. "All right, you come up. You have the room number? Good. See you soon."

After replacing the phone, he rose and went to get his jacket from a padded hanger in the closet, a closet the size of most Left Bank hotel rooms. Two suitcases sat inside on the floor. One was old and battered, its leather straps unclasped. The other was new and expensive. From the old one he removed his snub-nosed S&W .38 Agent in its black cowhide holster. This he slid onto his belt over his left hip.

It wasn't long before soft footsteps were heard in the corridor, followed by a quiet rap on the door. Jackson opened it.

They had never met. Both men were surprised. Jackson stepped back to let the Englishman enter.

He'd been expecting a man on the run. The Englishman didn't immediately fulfill his expectations. The first impression was too smooth, too thin, too handsome. It took several seconds before Jackson perceived that the eyes were anything but calm, that the thinness was undoubtedly due to recent weight loss, that the Savile Row suit no longer fit and had lost its press.

"Please come in, doctor," said Jackson. "Needless to say, I was starting to worry about you."

Hayward's expression implied that any explanation for the delay would have to wait. Carrying his black briefcase to the window, Hayward stood with his back to Jackson and stared down into the empty Place. Without turning, he asked, "When did you arrive?"

"On the tenth," said Jackson.

David Hayward's initial surprise at Jackson's appearance was taking a while to resolve itself. Was this what a high-ranking executive of the Hearst newspaper chain looked like? The American, although of average height and rather good-looking, had the build of a rugby player. And a slightly smashed-up nose, like a boxer's. It gave him an appearance Hayward associated more with athletes or soldiers than with journalists.

"I assume you have some identification to show me?"

"Naturally," said Jackson. "A letter from Mr. Hearst himself." He passed it to Hayward. "As you can see, it gives me final authority to accept or reject as I see fit. And here's my passport and company credentials."

When Hayward had finished studying the letter and the documents which established Jackson as one Frank S. DeMott, a senior vice-president of Hearst Publications, Inc., based in their Los Angeles office, he seemed relatively satisfied.

"Won't you sit down, doctor?" Jackson motioned at one of the plush armchairs. "How about a drink? I can call down and have them send—"

"Nothing, thank you."

"I suppose it is a little early for a drink," conceded Jackson. "We're cutting it close here, aren't we?" He nodded toward the window.

"I beg your pardon?" said Hayward.

"The Germans don't seem to be wasting much time. They'll have Paris by the day after tomorrow, from what I've heard."

"Surely that has nothing to do with you," said the Englishman.

"You're right, I guess. It's still difficult to remember I'm a neutral when I hear those cannons getting closer all night. But you . . ." He paused. "I guess you're okay too."

Hayward's eyebrows shot up. "Despite what you may think, or have been told, I am not a German spy, Mr. DeMott. I am a British subject and a National Socialist. That is all. Whatever I did, I did for Britain. The fact that I am making this offer to you, directly, should imply that I have no wish to deal with the Germans. Otherwise, as you say, it would simply be a matter of waiting two days until they enter Paris. In fact, as soon as our business is concluded, I will be leaving this city."

"No offense intended," said Jackson. "Shall we get down to it, then? Did you bring them?"

"Did you bring the money?"

No denial. Jackson's pulse quickened. He'd never expected Hayward to bring them to their first meeting. The man *was* in a hurry. An amateur.

Jackson brought the expensive-looking new valise from the closet to the bed and opened it. The inside was packed solid with stacks of fifty- and hundred-dollar bills. "I'm sure you'll want to count it, doctor. But it's all there: one hundred thousand in small denominations, just as you requested."

"I'm not going to count it," said Hayward. "If it's not there, I promise you'll never leave Paris."

Jackson frowned. He didn't much care for threats, even if, as in this case, they were obviously empty. "I'd hoped," he said mildly, "that we could keep this relaxed. You don't have to threaten me. I just told you to go ahead and count the money if you had any doubts."

Hayward shrugged. "Relaxation does not carry much relevance in my present situation, Mr. DeMott. I will take your word. Now I suppose you would like to see them?"

It was Jackson's turn to shrug. The question was too obvious to need an answer. The briefcase which Hayward had carried into the room now rested on his lap. He produced a small key and opened it with a muffled click. Inside on top of a pile of various documents was a plain blue envelope.

They were eight-by-tens and he passed them to Jackson in one bunch, without comment. Altogether there were twelve photos.

In each, the figures of the man and the woman took up roughly a third of the picture. Each shot was almost identical, differing only in the slight changes in the posture of the subjects. The background did not change: a rock outcropping behind their heads, a clutter of picnic things, grass, flowers, earth.

They were lying in each other's arms. The woman's head rested on his chest, her face tilted away from the direct view of the lens. The man was on his back, propped up against the rock. In one view, his arm encircled her back, with his hand resting on the full curve of her breast. In another, she was craning her head upward to receive his kiss. In the last four, she had thrown her leg across his. Her skirt had hiked up just far enough to reveal the top of her stocking. In these, his hand lay easily on her hip.

The photographs were intimate and tender. There was nothing vulgar in them. Nothing wanton or salacious.

Yet to Jackson they were the most obscene photographs he had ever seen. The President's face was unmistakable.

He had to curb an urge to rip the photographs into a hundred pieces. Forcing a weak smile, he looked up at Hayward but said nothing.

"You're satisfied?" demanded the Englishmen. "Of course you are!"

"Yes?"

"Of course!"

"Why should I be?" asked Jackson quietly. "Because the man in the photographs resembles Roosevelt? Anybody in the theater, anybody skilled in makeup, could cook up something like these. Especially if the model had a decent likeness to start with."

Scarlet rushed into Hayward's cheeks. "I . . . I hope you are not foolish enough to think you can haggle over the price at this late date, DeMott. I can't believe you would deny these are genuine."

"They're probably genuine, all right."

"Then what on earth are you driving at?"

"Not much."

"Then the deal must be closed," said Hayward.

"Not quite."

"What remains? You seem to find this amusing. Share the joke with me, Mr. DeMott."

"It's not funny enough to share. Not when you stop to think about it, doctor. You haven't given me the negatives."

"What?" gasped Hayward. "There was *never* any question of negatives. We made, or your man Asher and I made, a deal for twelve photographs. The same twelve you hold in your hand."

Jackson frowned. "You can't honestly believe we'd be foolish enough to pay you one hundred thousand dollars for twelve prints, can you? Prints?"

"We had an agreement!" cried Hayward. "*Nothing* was ever said about negatives."

"I'll check on that, of course," said Jackson in a bored voice. "But that's hardly the point, is it? Since if there are no negatives, there's not going to be any agreement. No deal at all. We were supposed to be buying an exclusive. If you keep the negatives, for all I know the *Times* and Scripps and Beaverbrook and *Le Temps* could all have prints by now."

Hayward blanched.

"I'm terribly sorry, doctor," said Jackson with very little sympathy in his voice. "But I'm sure you won't find anyone else in this business who wouldn't tell you the same."

"It's rather late to take a survey of your competitors, Mr. DeMott. I certainly cannot give you the negatives."

"You mean, I hope," said Jackson, "you don't have them with you. You can get them, I trust? Or have you already sold them to another . . . another newspaper?"

"I can't give you the negatives," insisted Hayward. "Not now. Not later. They don't exist." He dropped his eyes. "I destroyed them."

"Is that so?" said Jackson. "I don't mean to sound skeptical, Hayward, but I can't imagine whatever prompted you to destroy them."

"I had no idea! Your representative never mentioned the negatives," he repeated. "I didn't understand."

Jackson smiled weakly. "As I said, I'll certainly check on that when I return to the States." He stood up. In his left hand he held the twelve photographs. Very casually he turned and dropped them on top of the packets of money in the suitcase. Then he closed it, loudly snapping the expensive catch.

Hayward jumped to his feet. "Just what the bloody hell do you think you're doing?"

"Hold it, Hayward."

The Englishman froze, staring down at the blunt threat of the .38 Jackson had pointed at his midsection.

"Do you have a gun?"

Hayward shook his head, more a twitch than a voluntary answer.

"Put your hands over your head. Now turn around." Jackson quickly verified the fact that Hayward was unarmed. "Okay, sit down."

For several moments Hayward tried to cope with this new, this final reality. From the moment he had taken those pictures in the forest in Georgia, guessing how valuable they would prove to Sir Roland and all of them in the movement, until this moment four years later—had it always been a nightmare? Or had the nightmare only begun with Sir Roland's call a week ago in London. "Go to Paris," he'd ordered. "Leave your family for now, they'll manage. It won't be long. Once the Germans take the city, you'll be perfectly safe. I tell you this as a friend." Without thinking, Hayward obeyed.

Yet by the time he'd managed to reach the island of Jersey, he'd begun to think. It all became too clear. Sir

Roland was more than just the leader of the secret Committee of Six which ran the National Socialist Party of Britain, and a man from whom Hayward had always taken orders, both because of his party loyalty and because they were the closest of friends. Now it was clear that Sir Roland must be working for the Germans: a fact he had repeatedly denied to Hayward over the past year. Hayward's distaste for the Germans was well known. It was almost as strong as his distaste for those others: the feeble parliamentarians of both English parties.

It was clear that Sir Roland had used him, lied to him, even as he now wanted to save him from the certain disgrace of arrest in England. Hayward could not obey. He could not go to the Germans. To do so would prove them right back in London. It would truly change him from a patriotic Briton with National Socialist ideals into a traitor.

It took quite a bit of money to convince the fishermen to take him out that night. But no questions were asked once the bargain was struck. It was during those six hours in the dark, bucking spray that he formed his plan. There was no question of waiting for the Germans if he could get out of Paris. As for the photographs, the prints, he'd promised Sir Roland that he'd destroyed his set years ago. Now he knew who they must go to and how they could save him. Just before sunrise, with the plan vivid in his mind, they'd come into Cancale on the tide. The fishermen wouldn't go any closer and he'd had to wade the last thirty yards into France in the freezing surf.

"Your first mistake," said Jackson, "should be obvious." He sat on the edge of the bed with his revolver covering Hayward.

The Englishman's face was drained of color, impassive except for the faint twitching in one of his eyelids.

"Just because Marvin Asher works for Hearst, that doesn't mean he isn't his own man. As soon as you approached him, he cabled Steve Early at the White House. They're old friends."

"I see," said Hayward. "What does that make you? FBI, I suppose."

"Don't worry about me, Hayward. We have some talking to do right now. A little bargain. If you're interested."

"A bargain?"

"Assuming what you told me about the Germans is true, you're looking for a clean break. My guess would be South America, maybe Spain. You need money. But more than that, you need time to run."

"Please understand," said Hayward. "I left my wife, my children, my entire life back there."

"Sorry, you should have thought of that before you started collecting snapshots. Here's the deal. You give me the negatives and I'll let you go. I'll even promise that you won't be followed. You'd have a chance to get out of Paris, make the Spanish border. Or you can stay and wait for the Germans if that's really your game. Not only will I let you go, I'll throw in a bonus. I've been authorized to give you five thousand dollars *and* your freedom. Just give me the negatives."

"You can search me!" cried Hayward, throwing up his hands. "I don't have them. I'm telling you the truth, for God's sake. I haven't had them for years. I destroyed them. You must understand I wasn't working alone. I was afraid the negatives would get into the wrong hands."

Jackson had to laugh, but motioned for him to go on talking.

"I took orders. For example, my trip to the States. The photographs, of course, they were an opportunity that couldn't have been predicted. But it was my duty to take advantage. I was ordered to evaluate him, to make personal contact, perhaps even friendship. When the opportunity came, it was my duty to take those photographs. But I had no great personal antipathy to him."

"Were you ordered to destroy the negatives?"

"Yes."

"You're lying, Hayward."

"I swear I'm not."

"Who ordered you?"

Hayward suddenly bit his lip. Slowly he shook his head and said, "Ask me any questions, but not names. I won't incriminate anyone else."

"How touching," said Jackson. "Bullshit! What happened to your gentleman's code of honor when you took those pictures? Push your briefcase over here with your foot. Don't get up, just push it."

Jackson proceeded to examine every piece of paper in the briefcase. Almost all of it was innocent stuff: diplomas, medical certificates, articles and speeches. There were three bundles of yellowed envelopes: love letters written years before by Hayward's wife. Also several photographs of his family. Finally Jackson probed the sides for a false compartment. Nothing.

"I swear to you," said Hayward. "I destroyed the negatives in 1936. Four years ago. As soon as I was ordered to. . . ."

"I'm afraid I'm going to have to ask you to remove your clothes," said Jackson.

"What?"

"Just do it," he ordered. "You can keep your shorts on."

Hayward slowly stood and began to comply. As each garment came off, Jackson reached over and took it. When the Englishman was reduced to his boxer shorts, he was told to sit down. Then Jackson went over every inch of fabric, all the pockets, fingering the hems and linings for the negatives. For anything unusual. Again, there was nothing. "Where have you been hiding out in Paris?"

"A small hotel across the river. What possible difference does—"

Jackson raised his hand to silence him and reached for the pad and pencil the Ritz had put beside his telephone. "Here. Write down the name and address. And tell me why you waited three goddamn days to get in contact?"

"I wanted to be sure. I used to sit downstairs waiting to follow you or to see who went up to your room. I had to be sure you weren't . . . It hardly matters now. You're exactly what I was afraid of."

"You'd better tell me if you have those negatives hidden in your hotel, doctor. It'll save me time and you a lot of grief."

"Why, oh, God, why won't you believe me?" cried Hayward, bringing his hands up to pull at the slack skin on his face. "No, no, no. I don't have . . ." He didn't finish. His eyes moved to the window.

"Don't try it, Hayward. I'd shoot you first. Just enough to stop you. And that would make a certain major over at the British embassy extremely happy."

Hayward looked up in horror.

"I want you to walk over to the closet. Go inside and sit down," Jackson ordered. Hayward did as he was told. At the closet door, he paused. "Sit with your back touching the wall." When he'd done this, Jackson picked up the clothes from the floor and carried them over to the closet. He threw them inside. Hayward sat with his head resting in his open hands. Jackson replaced the .38 in its holster and removed the other suitcase.

"This is your last chance," he said. "I have the number of a Major Burns over at the British embassy. He's here to take you back to England. My orders were to call him the moment you made contact. I haven't called him yet."

Hayward raised his head.

"Come on, doctor, if I can't find the negatives at your hotel and if you won't tell me where I *can* find them, I'm damn well going to call that Major."

In the dim light of the closet, Hayward's eyes had glazed over and his lips moved fractionally.

"Hayward," said Jackson. "Forget your code."

A sob exploded from the man's chest.

"They're going to hang you," said Jackson. Even as he spoke, he felt the shame. It was the same hard lesson he should have learned long ago. No matter the justice of it, the so-called justice, you could never reduce another man without reducing yourself.

"Do you want the light on or off?" asked Jackson. There was no reply.

Hayward's single sob had not been repeated, but still he didn't speak. Jackson closed the door and turned the key.

If he found the negatives at Hayward's hotel, despite the fact it would prove the Englishman a liar, Jackson would call the hotel desk and tell them to open this door. Hayward could go free. Otherwise it would be the Major. Who would it be, he wondered, a surprised bellboy or Major Burns? Only Hayward knew that, and he was already sitting in the dark.

3

He hung the "Do Not Disturb" sign from the doorknob in the corridor. Then carried his two bags to the elevator and downstairs to the desk. Paying for three nights, he assured them he was not checking out until the following morning. Just paying now to save some time.

Taxicabs were scarce in Paris, since most of the owners had fled south with family and possessions. Jackson was lucky. Just as he walked out into the Place Vendôme, an old Citroën lurched to the curb. Two plump Turkish gentlemen climbed out, paid, and Jackson climbed into a back seat reeking of lemon-scented cologne.

He showed the piece of paper with Hayward's hotel address to the driver. Twenty minutes later, Jackson was dropped on the Rue Delambre in Montparnasse.

The Hotel Marie-Rose shared a courtyard with the local public bathhouse. A typical Left Bank hospice, it was little better than a flophouse. Jackson expected trouble from the concierge, but a hundred-franc note was all that was needed to convince her that the Englishman was a ruthless villain who needed his room searched. She gave Jackson the key and told him it was on the fourth floor.

Thirty minutes were all that Jackson needed to be convinced the negatives were nowhere in the grubby little room. Downstairs, he dropped off the key and answered the concierge's question with a blank stare before walking out the door.

On the nearby Place Edgar Quinet, he found a small bar-café with a telephone on the counter. After obtaining a *jeton*, he dialed Major Burns at the British embassy. Jackson limited himself to a curt description of where Hayward could be found and refused to answer any of the MI5 man's questions. Cutting Burns off in mid-sentence, he hung up the phone.

Half an hour later he found himself in front of the American embassy. Two marines stood at the gate. Did Jackson have an appointment or was he there to be evacuated? "Both," he said, and flashed his White House identification.

The main foyer of the embassy was a chaos of frantic men, women and children. Almost all of them were Europeans who no doubt had very good reasons for urgently seeking the Americans' help. Von Kuechler's elite Eighteenth Army was only seventy miles northeast of the city. Jackson fought his way through the crowd and showed his ID to another marine. He was directed to the third floor.

The door of the naval attaché's office carried three names, of which Malcolm Orth's was the closest to the floor. Jackson didn't bother to knock. A young woman looked up from behind a desk where she was typing on a large black Underwood. She was young, pretty, with bright green eyes and black hair cut in severe bangs. When she spoke, it was with a throaty French accent that made Jackson suddenly wish he'd been in Paris a year earlier, with a couple of weeks to spare and a grand of his own money to spend. "May I help you?" she asked.

"I wish you could. Unfortunately I'm here to see Malcolm Orth. He's in, I hope."

"Your name, please." She rose and stepped out from behind the desk, revealing all of her rather magnificent figure.

"Jackson."

She opened the door to her immediate right, closed it behind her and reappeared less than fifteen seconds later. She caught Jackson's stare and it didn't seem to amuse her. "You may go straight in."

Orth's wasn't much of an office: two metal desks, two old filing cabinets and a photograph of the President hanging next to one of the Secretary of the Navy. Orth's desk was a mess of official government paper, its centerpiece a ceramic cup, obviously child-crafted, full of Eberhard Faber's finest. A man in his mid-fifties, balding and slack-jowled, Orth was in the process of lighting a Viceroy. "I wondered when you were going to show up," he said.

"How are you, Malcolm?"

"Just great. You were supposed to call me, remember?

That limey major has been hounding us for three days. Where the hell were you?"

Jackson smiled and pulled over a straight-backed chair. He sat down and put his feet up on the corner of Orth's desk. "Around," he said.

They'd known each other since 1930. Orth had been in the Albany field office the day Jackson came in for his initial interview at the Bureau. Orth had been less than amused that afternoon at having to take time out from a case to interview another young law-school senior with ambitions of being a G-man. In the end, however, he'd been impressed by Jackson.

After he was accepted, Jackson had gone down to Washington for the full FBI training. There followed his first postings in St. Louis, Birmingham, later New Orleans and finally New York. By then, Orth was number-three man in the New York field office and Jackson was assigned to his section: Alien and Espionage. They'd become good friends.

Although Jackson had quickly proven himself a skillful agent, none of his previous supervisors in the Bureau had been all that sorry to see him leave. For Jackson was not really a team man. A loner, although he was never insubordinate, he had come fairly close to it on many occasions. The FBI was an organization whose basic premise was suspicion. Individual initiative was not against the rules, but it wasn't exactly encouraged either. Two things every agent had to always remember were his own place in the pecking order and to whom all credit for any success was ultimately due: the director.

Nineteen-thirty-four had been a big year for Jackson. The year he'd gone to New York; the year he married Barbara; the year he became friends with Orth; finally, the year he met Al Sheehy.

As far as his friendship with Orth went, it was based on their mutual distaste for some of the more blatantly paternalistic aspects of the Bureau. But, ironically, Orth ended up trying to play the father figure to Jackson much of the time. He'd been with the Bureau for so long that he was always counseling Jackson to take things easy, not to show his independence, to keep his toe firmly on the line. If he was sometimes overbearing, it was only because he saw in Jackson the best natural agent he had encountered in his sixteen years with the Bureau. But for exactly this reason Jackson found it necessary to cool his friendship with Orth at times. Otherwise, he would not be able to function as independently as he wished.

Jackson's relationship with Al Sheehy, on the other hand, began socially. They met at a party. An old Irish-American pol, Al had thrown his lot in with Roosevelt from the beginning and was now a kingpin in FDR's Manhattan organization. In his mid-sixties, a heavy drinker, with a rambunctious sense of humor, he was a fine political operator. He and Jackson hit it off over a couple of glasses of their host's best Scotch and, at the end of the party, traded telephone numbers. Three months later, Sheehy had called up out of the blue for some advice on security at a speech Roosevelt was to make in a few weeks. Later they used to get together in a midtown bar after work for a few drinks. In May of 1936, Sheehy had asked him one afternoon if he'd ever thought of going to work for the President. Jackson didn't know what to say. Al told him to think it over and then give him a call. A month later, Jackson had taken a quiet trip down to Washington. In the end, he took a temporary leave from the Bureau and went to work for the White House as an "advance man" in the upcoming campaign.

They won that one, of course, with FDR beating Landon in every state except Maine and Vermont. When the campaign was all over, it turned out that the President had taken a personal shine to the young FBI agent from upper New York State. With Sheehy's blessing, Jackson was asked to resign from the Bureau and go to work full-time at the White House.

Shortly afterward, he'd heard that Orth had been taken out of the New York field office and sent to Paris as the Bureau's officer under embassy cover. Jackson had never been sure if it meant a promotion or a demotion for Orth. Nor if it hadn't been the Director's idea of revenge for Jackson's "betrayal"?

Now, watching Jackson rest his feet on his desk, Orth looked somewhat troubled. "Come on, Jack. Where the hell have you been?"

"Just around."

"Sure. Major Burns has been shooting migraine bullets into me over the phone and you say 'around.' Where?"

"The Ritz, if you must know."

"Oh?" said Orth. "The Ritz, is it? How swell." He shot a glance at the two suitcases Jackson had left by the door. "So you've checked out? Was the service not to your satisfaction? Vacation isn't over already, is it?"

"Afraid so."

"Just when all the fun is about to start. Why don't you stick around? I could use a little company here when the krauts arrive."

"Why didn't you go south with the ambassador and the others?" asked Jackson.

"Orders, my friend. Speaking of orders, you were supposed to call me."

Jackson resented the implication he was still in a position to take orders from Orth. "Sorry about that, Malcolm."

"Sure you are. Mission accomplished, Jack?" He made it a throwaway, stubbing his cigarette out in the ashtray.

"Yes and no."

Orth looked up. "Want to tell me about it?"

"Sorry again," said Jackson, shaking his head. "You know the way it goes."

"Sure I do. But I just thought that being old buddies and all—"

Jackson cut him off: "We're old friends. I'd tell you if I could. This time, absolutely, I can't."

"What's the big deal?" asked Orth. "White House doesn't talk to the Bureau anymore? I mean, just exactly what did you fly over here for, my friend?"

"Call it politics," said Jackson. "Call it a vacation. Call it anything you want but just drop it, Malcolm."

"Politics, huh? That's a fairly broad term. In your position, I could see that word being applied to a wide range of—"

"You're pressing me, Malcolm," said Jackson, a sudden edge in his voice.

"I didn't think I was pressing you, Jack."

"Maybe you received a directive on me. If so, that's your business. But this time I can't help you. Even as old friends. If the Director wants to know what I'm doing in Paris, tell him to call Steve Early at the White House."

"Steve Early?" said Orth. "Shit. If it's all the same to you, I don't think I'll tell Hoover that."

"Malcolm, if you really want to help, how about finding me a plane out of here?"

Orth took a while to answer, drawing out the ritual of lighting his Viceroy. The phone rang on his desk but he ignored it, letting the secretary handle it in the outer office. "You understand my position, don't you, Jack?"

"Perfectly."

"No hard feelings?" Orth smiled, a little weary, a little ashamed.

"No hard feelings," said Jackson.

"Thanks. Okay, as for a plane, it isn't going to be so easy at this late date. But we'll see . . ."

The pretty green eyes under the jet-black bangs suddenly appeared in the doorway.

"Yes, honey?"

"Major Burns. I told him you were in conference. He insists on holding until you will speak with him."

"Okay. I'll take it," said Orth, watching as she ducked back out and closed the door. He looked over at Jackson. "This is really your call, Jack."

"You're probably right. But if you wouldn't mind, I'd rather not. I'll even say please."

The FBI man rolled his eyes but turned and lifted the receiver. "How are you, Major Burns? What can I do for you this afternoon?" For the next five minutes Orth listened in silence. When he finally thanked the Major and hung up, he turned to Jackson with a deadpan expression which befitted a born cop.

"Well?" asked Jackson.

"So you had a good time at the Ritz?"

"Did I?"

"Maybe you forgot something when you checked out?"

"Like what?"

"Oh, like some guy named Hayward. The Major is rather upset. It seems this Hayward hanged himself with his necktie in your closet. Must have been a fairly unhappy guy."

"Yes," said Jackson quietly. "He must have been."

"You call that politics?"

"No," said Jackson. "I call that suicide."

4

Slowly crumbling onto the beach like some enormous stale pink birthday cake, the Grand Hotel Estoril Palace was almost full. Full of the dregs of the Continent: Jackson had never seen so many obvious charlatans, spies and sloppy drunks.

It had been one hell of a trip. But Lisbon was a relief after his stay in Madrid. The best Orth could come up with had been an Army courier flight out of Paris on the thirteenth.

Madrid had been unbearable. So much of it in rubble, crowds of black-shrouded women and mutilated men on every corner. The largest crowds were always outside the churches. At night there was nothing to do but sit in the lobby of his hotel and listen to the sirens. After five days under Franco's regime of atonement, he'd bribed his way onto one of the few flights to Lisbon. There he'd hoped to pick up the last commercial air service operating between Europe and the States: Pan Am's American Clipper.

It turned out the airline had a waiting list of over three hundred names. Jackson had to use pull, and that meant the embassy. The polished faces of the State Department types held him in obvious contempt. They could get him on the Clipper, all right. But first they'd have to confirm his official status with a cable to Washington. That could take a few days, as much as a week.

On his first afternoon at the hotel, Jackson had gone down to the terrace bar for a preluncheon drink. He was quietly taking stock of his fellow drinkers while pretending to read a two-week-old copy of the *Times*. The noise was incredible, with over a dozen different languages being babbled at various tables. Portuguese, German, French, Dutch, Arabic: to Jackson's ears, it could have been feeding time at the zoo. But of all the voices, the most strident was speaking in an immaculately articulated, well-bred King's English of the type which, for some reason, made the hairs on the back of Jackson's neck stand up like tiny icicles.

The Englishman was tall and rather horse-faced. He wore a well-cut beige suit and a maroon tie and he could have been anywhere between twenty-five and thirty-five years old. It was hard to pinpoint his exact age because, at least to Jackson, it was obvious just how the man had looked as a boy of eight. He had obviously been an attractive child, much fawned over. Perhaps that explained why he was so patently obnoxious.

From what Jackson could overhear, the topic of the bar conversation was not political but gastronomic. In fact, they seemed to be debating the relative merits of a grilled lamb chop versus a tender veal cutlet sautéed in butter, with the Englishman waxing eloquent on behalf of the lamb. Typical expatriate bar nonsense, thought Jackson.

There was something theatrical about the young Englishman, however, which made him hard to ignore. His nose, teeth, blue eyes: all were slightly exaggerated. If he had been an actor, Jackson knew just what parts he would have played. The young dolt who got the girl, only to lose her in Act 3, to the audience's immense relief, when the true hero finally revealed himself.

This impression was not lessened when, without missing a beat in his loud valedictory on lamb, he suddenly cast his eyes in Jackson's direction. Then winked.

Jackson turned to see if anyone was sitting behind him. There wasn't anyone. Whatever the wink was meant to signify, he found the mystery easy to resist. A moment later, he rose and entered the hotel. In the cavernous dining room he found a table and attempted to order lunch. It was then he understood what had motivated the idiotic conversation on the terrace. The hotel's menu was quite short, limited as it was to eggs, sardines and a particular kind of tasteless white beans.

During the next two days he frequently saw the Englishman on the terrace or in the dining room. The group ebbed and flowed around him, one of about ten such groups whose members were interchangeable. Observing life in the hotel was like watching a tank full of tropical

fish. The Englishman was clearly one of the prize speci-
mens of the collection. Jackson began to wonder if the
wink hadn't been a hallucination. Nothing of the sort ever
happened again. Not that he was sorry.

On his third day in Lisbon, Washington's confirmation
arrived at the embassy. Strings were quickly pulled and
Jackson was assigned a seat on the Clipper to New York
due to depart on June 23. All he had to do was kill two
more days.

This he was attempting to do by sitting on a canvas
deck chair on the concrete seawall at the far end of the
hotel property. The afternoon was warm; the Atlantic a
calm, glassy green. There were numerous ships on the near
horizon entering and leaving Lisbon harbor to the east.

He had taken to drinking port mixed with soda. He had
a bottle of the fortified wine on one side and a siphon he'd
borrowed from the bartender on the other. His intention
was to get stone drunk, eat his nightly ration of sardines,
and retire early. Then he heard the soft footstep behind
him on the grass. The next thing he knew, the Englishman
had put another deck chair beside his and was smiling
ingenuously into his startled face.

"I see you're drinking port."

"Very observant of you," said Jackson.

"Allow me to introduce myself. My name is Sir Roland
Plenty. I thought you were an American." He put out his
right hand and Jackson reluctantly shook it.

"John Jackson," he said. "I am an American. Why?"

"You Americans don't drink port as a rule, do you?"

"So what? I'm breaking the rule."

"Marvelous stuff, I quite agree." The Englishman sank
back in his chair with a sigh, his eyes suddenly on the
beach.

Two lean but muscular young Portuguese men had appeared directly in front of where they sat. Clad in brief
swimsuits, they began to kick a soccer ball back and forth
over the sand.

"Is there something you want in particular?" asked
Jackson, eager to discourage any further conversation.

The Englishman laughed. "I hardly blame you."

"Huh?" asked Jackson.

"I don't blame you one bit. I'm not terribly good at this,
am I?"

"Aren't you?" asked Jackson. "Whatever 'this' is, I thought you were doing pretty well at it. Especially if it is annoying me, which it is."

The Englishman ignored this, turned and asked, "The name Sir Roland Plenty means nothing to you?"

"Not really. Should it?"

"In the first place, it's not my real name. You might have known that."

"If I'd been interested."

"My actual name is Greville Leaper. I suppose there's no point in shaking hands again, is there?"

Jackson, calculating the fastest possible exit route from this lunatic, shook his head.

"But I could have told you my name was David Hayward," said the Englishman with a slight smile.

Okay, thought Jackson, that's it. This wasn't lunacy. This was fun and games at the Grand Hotel Estoril Palace. Unfortunately, he had no desire to play, not this afternoon, not when he was looking forward to getting quietly smashed all by his lonesome, blotting out all surroundings until he could board that airplane for home.

"You could have told me that," he said at last, "but then you'd be a dead man."

"Exactly," said the Englishman. "I say, are you FBI?"

"I say," mimicked Jackson, "are you a secret agent? I've always wanted to meet one."

"Come, now, Jackson. You know perfectly well who I am. Seriously, are you one of Hoover's fellows?"

"Sorry to disappoint you," said Jackson, "but no."

"Hardly a disappointment if you're telling the truth. You must realize we're very keen to know what happened in Paris."

"Is that so? Why don't you go satisfy your curiosity somewhere else? I called your lousy major. When I left the hotel, Hayward was okay."

One of the Portuguese ball players had kicked the ball so that it was directly beneath where they sat. He had just come over to retrieve it and was taking his time about it. Leaper frowned and nodded in his direction. "You want to watch your voice, Jackson. Those fellows pick up a few bob on the side reporting anything interesting they've overheard to the local Abwehr."

"Bullshit. They don't speak a word of English."

Leaper just grinned. "Paris wasn't at all clear to us. What were you doing there in the first place? What did you want from Hayward?"

"If they wanted you to know that," said Jackson, "they would have told you."

"We wanted him far more than you realize," said Leaper sadly.

"I doubt that."

"Jackson, all I want with you is a nice quiet chat. Can't you relax just a bit? After all, we *are* allies."

"Excuse me, Leaper, or whatever your real name is, this quiet chat was your idea, not mine. As for being allies, you're a little out of line. We're nobody's ally, mister. We're neutral."

"Obviously I am annoying you."

"Jesus, you're an observant guy."

The two Portuguese ball players had decided their brief game had exhausted them sufficiently. Now they needed a long rest. They had moved over to sit with their backs against the seawall only a few feet below Jackson's chair.

Leaper suddenly rose and stepped forward to the edge of the concrete. In rapid-fire Portuguese he said something which seemed to disturb the two men. They tried to protest, but Leaper shot another burst of Portuguese down into their faces. At that they began to move off down the beach, taking their football with them.

"What did you say to them?" asked Jackson.

"Nothing, really. Simply that I was a British spy and that I was passing secrets with you. That if they didn't go away from here at once, I would see they suffered excruciating pain, perhaps even death. Or some such rubbish to that effect."

"I'll bet," said Jackson.

Leaper sat down again. "We wanted Hayward a great deal. Almost as much as we want Sir Roland Plenty."

"Sir Roland Plenty was who you claimed to be about five minutes ago, correct? Maybe you and I should team up. Like this we're almost as good as Laurel and Hardy."

"I haven't come here to taunt you or whatever you seem to think. I sat down here for one reason only. To share some information."

Jackson thought it would be fairer to read "get" for "share" but said nothing for the moment.

"I'd naturally assumed you were in Lisbon looking for Sir Roland," said Leaper. "Which ought to explain my odd introduction just now. It was meant as a joke, you see."

"Oh, I see. Very funny. Ah, who is this Sir Roland Plenty whom I'm supposed to be looking for?"

"Sir Roland was Hayward's control. Head of the entire network."

"Marvelous," said Jackson. "Head of the entire network. Which network would that be?"

"The English network."

"But of course," mocked Jackson. "The English network. Well, this is my lucky day."

Leaper paid no attention to his sarcasm. "It was an English network working for Berlin. Reinhard Heydrich's organization. Are you familiar with Heydrich?"

"Isn't everyone?" asked Jackson. "The same Heydrich who does those funny reindeer imitations on the radio every Tuesday night? But of course."

"This is serious!" cried Leaper. "Quite serious, and you ought to realize that. Heydrich is head of the Nazi political intelligence group they call the *Sicherheitsdienst*. The S.D. for short. A frightful bastard."

Jackson realized this was far outside his usual field of concern in Washington. This was more up State's alley or the Bureau's. But he could not ignore the connections the Englishman was deliberately planting in his mind. According to him, Dr. Hayward had been lying when he said he wasn't a German agent.

"Let me see if I've got this story right," said Jackson. "Sir Roland Plenty was Hayward's boss in the spy game. They both worked for the Nazis, is that it?"

"Precisely."

"Okay. I admit this is news that . . . it's not all that uninteresting to me." Which was putting it mildly. It meant the photographs of FDR were a Nazi operation. And the negatives could be anywhere, perhaps even Berlin. Which is something he'd been afraid of since the very beginning.

"Sir Roland was Hayward's tutor at Oxford," said Leaper. "One of Britain's leading biologists, the warden of Abingdon College. A brilliant, influential and most respected man."

"And a German spy," added Jackson.

"Frightful, I know. Sir Roland has turned out to be a terrible blow to us. In the first place, he was extremely social, and also, I'm afraid, very political. Great personal charm, above reproach, always ready to lend a shoulder to one of his boys when they needed a soft spot to pour out their troubles. You see, during his years at Oxford, Sir Roland sent scores of young men down to London to fill the ranks at Westminster and Whitehall."

"I thought you said he was a biologist?"

"Warden of Abingdon College, one of our most revered institutions of higher learning."

"A regular Mr. Chips," said Jackson.

"Quite," said Leaper. "The odd thing is he never gave us any of the usual warnings. No Anglo-German Friendship Society meetings, no Moseley connection, no anti-Semitic letters to the *Times*. Nothing but his summer holidays, and we'd hardly got around to logging where men of his stature take their summer holidays."

"I think," said Jackson, "you're trying to tell me something. But you're going about it in a rather peculiar way." What he didn't say was that he was certain Leaper was hoping to obtain something in return for this little "chat." Jackson had no intention of playing a trading game with him.

"You Americans like everything straightaway: meat and potatoes, instant this and instant that. I'm simply trying to give you background on the man."

"Do it your way, then." Jackson sighed, reaching for his port bottle. "Would you like a slug of this?"

"Very kind of you," said Leaper. "But I prefer it with cheese."

Jackson shrugged, reaching for the siphon.

"Four members of the Cabinet," said Leaper suddenly.

"Four members of the Cabinet what? Or do you mean, 'for members of the Cabinet'? Port, is that it?"

"Good God, man!" cried Leaper in exasperation. "Four members of the Cabinet were blackmailed by Sir Roland Plenty. You understand the catastrophe of the appeasement faction in Chamberlain's government? Until Churchill came in, it was difficult to convince the country we'd actually declared war. All they could do in the Cabinet was fight amongst themselves, talk about how to appease the beastly Hun."

"You're saying Sir Roland was blackmailing four Cabinet members? Was Hayward involved?" asked Jackson with growing alarm. How could Hayward have been involved? Why, if he had been, why had he been in such a hurry to get out of Paris? "What about Hayward?" he demanded.

"He must have been," said Leaper. "He was a self-admitted fascist and one of Sir Roland's closest friends. Admittedly, our investigation was just beginning. But we already had enough to intern him. Now do you see why his suicide so disappointed us?"

Jackson nodded, putting the pieces together in his mind.

"Was there something Hayward had that you were trying to collect?" asked the Englishman.

"If you know the answer, why ask the question?" snapped Jackson. This was, he knew, the crucial point of the game.

"Isn't that usually how education is passed on?" suggested Leaper. "And I don't know the answer, in any case."

"But you think you can educate me into telling you. Forget it, Leaper, I graduated a long time ago."

"All I'm trying to do is make you understand the seriousness of a matter which concerns us both."

"Which is?"

"Sir Roland Plenty's blackmailing of the Cabinet was a masterful operation. He managed to turn the Government's war policy into a shambles."

"Then why haven't you arrested him?"

"I told you that. The bloody man was warned in advance. Both he and Hayward just managed to escape Scotland Yard by a matter of hours."

Jackson glanced down the seawall. Not far away, a middle-aged woman he recognized from the hotel sat reading a book. Leaper had almost succeeded in making him see spies everywhere now. Football players, old ladies with romantic novels, what next?

"Look," he said to Leaper, "I'm not going to play your game. If you want information, you'll have to ask Washington. Sorry, but that's the way it's going to be."

Leaper looked momentarily disheartened, then said, "What if I told you Sir Roland had an American contact? Inside your Senate. You must be aware of the problems Roosevelt is having with the isolationist senators."

"Just what do you mean by American contact?" asked Jackson.

"We're looking into that. So should you. I hope you will."

"You'll have to do better than that, Leaper."

"Tell me what you wanted from Hayward in Paris and I might be able to do a bit better."

"Who are you?" asked Jackson. "Exactly what is your position?"

"Let's just say I was sent here to see if I couldn't put a trace on the fellow."

"Sir Roland?" asked Jackson. "Or me? A trace on who?"

Leaper shook his head, unwilling to say more.

"You're not going to get it, Leaper."

"Get it?" asked the Englishman.

"What they sent you for. Not from me."

Leaper closed his eyes for a second. Then stood to his feet with disappointment evident in his attempt at a smile. "I'm afraid I won't see you at dinner, then. But do think about what I've told you. Perhaps you'll see that it's in your interest, very much so, to share with me. In the meantime, enjoy your port, Jackson." He strode off on his long legs across the lawn in the direction of the grotesque pink hotel.

True to his word, he wasn't at dinner. Nor did he appear later in the bar. Unable to sleep, Jackson attempted to put a transatlantic call through to Washington. As usual, the cables were jammed and he never got through. After a restless night he went downstairs and asked the desk for Leaper's room number. They were sorry to report the Englishman had checked out the previous evening.

5

board the *Mithymna*, the Greek sailors smoked their final cigarettes. In a few minutes the feverish work would begin when they reached the wharf. They stood watching the Pointe aux Trembles slide by the starboard rail, talking in loud insinuating voices of their plans for later that evening.

A little apart from them on the deck stood a man who was obviously neither Greek nor a sailor, of average height but heavily built. His gray worsted suit contrasted vividly to the mufti worn by the sailors. His head was impressive, nearly hairless, with a massive brow beneath which two piercing blue eyes stared at the approaching city. It was a head that would not have looked out-of-place on a Roman coin.

Montreal appeared more sprawling than Sir Roland had imagined it. With Mount Royal Park rising in the center above the spires of Notre Dame and St. James Cathedral, it might have been the Seine rather than the St. Lawrence which the freighter was cleaving.

Sir Roland was the sole passenger on this crossing; his name listed on the captain's manifest as Donald Swanson of Cape Town, South Africa. In his pocket was a passport with matching credentials and, if he felt any nervousness about his approaching confrontation with Canadian immigration officials, it certainly wasn't apparent from his face.

At the moment, Sir Roland had far more critical problems on his mind. No doubt Heydrich was furious with him for the way things had collapsed in England. But it would not last. Sir Roland was certain he had made the correct decision regarding the Night Letter. The Night Letter was far more important than anything he had accomplished in England. He would deliver it himself. Then return to Germany or, perhaps, even England by that

time. He would return in triumph, not disgrace, long after
that stubborn braggart Churchill had begun to see the futility of all his "blood and toil."

As he stood thinking of the future, his thumbs gently
slid back and forth along the fine morocco of his belt,
specially made for him at a shop on Old Bond Street. He
had no doubt that its ingenious compartment would elude
even the cleverest customs inspector.

Once more his meticulous mind went over the details of
his escape from England. He was certain it had been perfect, yet he could not help but search for that one error
which might prove his downfall.

The phone call had come at eleven o'clock in the morning. Rogers-Forsythe, his former student who now worked
in the Home Office, had been extremely upset. The
message was clear. Sir Roland, along with seven others,
was about to be arrested by Scotland Yard on charges of
espionage. From that moment, Sir Roland had known
what he must do.

First Mathews was instructed to pack a small overnight
bag for him. Then Sir Roland had immediately called
Hayward and told him in no uncertain terms to get out.
Paris, he'd ordered, and wait for the Germans. Of the five
others, only Hayward had any knowledge of the Night
Letter. It was imperative he not be interrogated by the experts at the Yard. Finally, Sir Roland had fetched the belt
and gone down to the cellar, where he removed the negatives from their hiding place beneath the ancient masonry.

Then he'd gone to find Marion, explaining to her that
he had forgotten all about a dinner engagement with some
London colleagues that evening. He would take the car
down and spend the night at their small flat on Wiltshire
Place. Since there was nothing at all unusual in this, his
wife was not alarmed. She asked him not to forget his pills
and to be sure to pay the quarterly bill from Berry Brothers, which was sent to their London address. He promised,
kissed her on the lips, which was a little unusual for him
before such a routine trip, and went to collect his bag.

An hour later he drove the Rolls into Beaconsfield,
parked on a back street, and walked to the station. He
caught the 1:37 to Liverpool, traveling second class in order to attract as little attention as possible. Since Beacons-

field was south of Oxford, he hoped they would believe he had gone south.

It was after seven when he rang Lafferty's bell on the gloomy row of terraced houses in the Irish quarter of East Liverpool. A two-story house, of which Lafferty occupied the upper floor. After several minutes there was a sound of a door opening and then footsteps coming down the wooden steps. Lafferty opened the door and peered through the narrow space. "Ay!" he said with a mixture of disbelief and fear. A few minutes later Sir Roland was upstairs in front of the gas fire sipping a mug of strong tea and wondering just how long he would have to endure this wretched place.

When he was a boy at school, Sir Roland had often been teased about his soft, pudgy body. It was difficult for him to put a stop to this teasing, since he had an extreme fondness for sweets. Sweets of all kinds, puddings, lollies, ice cream, but there was one candy he preferred above all others. It was a kind of hard jelly that, once sucked, turned soft and gummy in the mouth. It was marketed under the name of Foster's Jolly Jujubes. Sir Roland's fondness for this particular candy eventually earned him the school nickname of "Juju," much to his eternal distaste.

Yet he was helpless to break his addiction. He would always hoard away the last jujube or two, after he'd finished a packet, in a handkerchief at the bottom of his pocket. Although he was a greedy boy, he was also farsighted. Rather than gobble the last few candies, he would save them until he was alone in his bed after lights-out. The raspberry ones were his favorite and he would let them slowly melt on his tongue, believing there was no better way to fall asleep. Unfortunately, even much later, as an adult, he was as addicted to his bedtime jujubes as other people were to their nightcaps or sleeping pills. He only managed to break the habit after his wife firmly chastised him for ruining his teeth.

Lafferty was Sir Roland's last jujube. Over the years, he had been careful to humor him, help him, but never to use him. And now the time had come.

Lafferty was a man of fifty-three years. Short, wiry, with reddish hair and so many freckles on his face he could almost pass for a Latin in dim light, Lafferty was no good. A jailbird, a liar and a thief, everybody's suspect, Lafferty wasn't even good at being no good. Sir Roland had only met him because his father was a servant at the college. On several occasions the old man had come to Sir Roland and begged him to help find a lawyer for his son up in Liverpool. On each occasion, Sir Roland's efforts had helped to either keep the son out of prison or to reduce his sentence. And all Sir Roland had ever asked for in return was a chance to meet Lafferty. This the father had been happy to arrange and his son duly appeared at the gates of Abingdon early one April afternoon. Nervously escorted to the Warden's Lodge by his father, Lafferty had never revealed what had actually been said during his twenty-minute meeting alone with Sir Roland. That had been in 1933.

"I want to stay here for a while," Sir Roland told him that first evening after he'd finished his tea. "I will, of course, pay you well. Shall we say five pounds a day?"

Lafferty nodded. Only a fool would pay five quid a day to stay in this hole, he thought. But Sir Roland was no fool. "You can have my bed," he blurted. "I'll make do on the floor."

Sir Roland smiled, as if that went without saying. Then he proceeded to explain exactly what he wanted Lafferty to do for him. A task for which he would pay him the grand sum of one hundred pounds.

It wasn't easy. It had taken nine days. With the war and the blockade and all those Nazi U-boats lying out in the Irish Channel, security along the waterfront had never been tighter. But in the end Sir Roland and Lafferty were standing in the pub down near Hornstone Lane, a block off the docks, when the Greek captain came inside.

They moved over to the tables. The Greek was all smiles. His ship was due to depart a little before noon and was moored right at the bottom of the lane. All Sir Roland had to do was walk down in twenty-five minutes and stand in front of the chandler's called Dempsy and Piggot, Ltd. The captain would come for him. It seemed the crew was going to create a little diversion, during which time the captain would hustle Sir Roland behind the backs of the customs men and onto a gangway near the stern. If anyone asked any questions, the captain would answer them. When everything was agreed, the Greek rose and stuck out his hand. "No one thing to worry," he said. Sir Roland nodded.

Lafferty said he would escort Sir Roland to the wharf. Since there were still twenty minutes to kill, Sir Roland said they ought to have another drink. He took Lafferty's mug and his own glass to the bar and ordered a pint of Guinness and a double scotch. As the barman was filling them, Sir Roland readied his small chemist's envelope.

Once he'd been paid, the barman quickly departed and Sir Roland poured the envelope's contents into the Guinness. The powder rested on top of the thick brownish foam. He remedied this with one quick swirl of his index finger, mixing the bitter stuff with the bitter liquid below.

At the table, Lafferty proposed a toast to Sir Roland's safe voyage. They both drank deeply. A few minutes later, Sir Roland said he thought they ought to be getting along.

They were halfway down the block when Lafferty collapsed. At least two hundred pedestrians, dockworkers, shopkeepers, sailors and officials were in the immediate area. At least a dozen saw Lafferty fall. Many more heard Sir Roland shout, "His heart! His heart!"

Ten minutes later there was a serious-looking but harmless accident on the wharf which created chaos among a boatload of volatile Greek sailors.

The voyage took thirteen days. Apart from the fact that it was still very cold on the North Atlantic, it wasn't an unpleasant trip. They were in a convoy of twenty-four ships, escorted by British destroyers and corvettes. The only problem was that the *Mithymna*, old and slow as she was, could barely keep up with the others.

This fact precipitated the one unusual, and dangerous, incident during the trip. In retrospect, it was almost funny. At the time, Sir Roland had been hard pressed to find anything at all humorous about it.

They had been about forty-five miles east of Cape Race, Newfoundland. The *Mithymna* was, as usual, a good half-mile behind the rest of the convoy. Suddenly there was an incredible lurch accompanied by a tremendous noise, as if they'd run aground. The bow of the little freighter heaved up twenty-five feet in the air, then came crashing down. Then, as if nothing had happened, they were poking along back on course.

It was obvious to everyone on board that the *Mithymna*

had hit something in the water. Crew members quickly discovered a massive protuberance inside the forward hull. Miraculously, the seams had held and there was no leakage.

Then sailors at the stern spotted an enormous oil slick rapidly spreading in the *Mithymna*'s wake.

Ten minutes later, most persons on board knew the truth. A Nazi U-boat, cleverly surfacing in the convoy's wake to launch a surprise torpedo attack, had caught its conning tower on the lagging Greek freighter. Now the captain was proudly boasting that he was the first and only officer of the Greek merchant navy to have sunk a U-boat in the North Atlantic.

By the time they reached the dockside on the St. Lawrence, Sir Roland had gone below and retrieved his valise. Now, as he stepped over the side onto the iron stairs, he looked down at the two officials in their black uniforms and white caps. One was writing on a clipboard. The other was staring directly up into Sir Roland's face.

Carrying his valise, the Englishman walked carefully down the steps. At the last but one, the customs man made a sudden movement with his right hand. Sir Roland looked up in terror. Then he saw the official was only offering him a steadying hand so that he could reach the dock safely. Forcing a smile, he shook his head and stepped down on his own.

With his head very erect, looking absolutely sure of himself, Sir Roland crossed the noisy wharf to find a telephone where he could place his long-distance call to the United States.

6

It would have been hard to exaggerate the relief Jackson felt as his cab cruised up Fourteenth Street past the Elipse. Through the trees on the South Lawn, he had his first glimpse of the White House. It was midmorning, traffic was congested but his driver skillfully rounded the corner onto Pennsylvania Avenue and pulled up outside the West Gate.

The guards on duty knew Jackson well and waved him past without bothering to look at his card.

"You're back!" cried Norma when he stepped through the door. His office was one of three in a suite on the third floor of the executive wing, the floor where the pressure was less intense, the offices smaller, the secretaries happier. Norma was from Iowa City, hopelessly overweight and happily married to a gym teacher in the District school system. She put her face up to receive her kiss. Jackson rewarded her with three: both cheeks and one peck on the lips.

"I'm so glad you got out of Lisbon at last," she said. "Those idiots in the embassy ought to have their heads examined."

"Thanks for sending the cable so quickly. How are you, Norma girl? Any messages?"

"I'm just fine and they're all on your desk. *All* of them."

"Don't tell me."

"Sorry. Just the chief of Cook County police, a dozen follow-ups on the Chicago arrangements, the National Committee agenda, your May accounts, three or four dozen pink slips, and an urgent one from Mr. Early."

"Is that all?" He walked into his office. Cramped and windowless, at least it was home. He had an old walnut desk, shelves of his favorite books, a well-stuffed armchair with the leather cracked in a thousand places and a Navajo rug on the wall. Hardly the Oval Office, but it beat the hell out of the Spartan accommodations provided by the Bureau.

"Norma?"

Her head shot around the edge of the door. "What can I do for you?"

"Call Steve Early or his secretary and find out if he's ready for me now, please."

She disappeared, only to reappear a few moments later. "Me. Early is *more* than ready to see you now. Don't you want a cup of coffee first?"

"No, thanks. Had it on the train." He picked up the suitcase with the money and walked out of his office in the direction of the stairs.

Steve Early, the White House press secretary, was leaning over his secretary's desk issuing detailed instructions on a press release about to go out. When he saw Jackson, he straightened up at once. With a broad grin he grabbed Jackson's hand.

A large part of the grin, thought Jackson, was Early's relief at seeing the suitcase again. It had been the press secretary who had handed it over fifteen days earlier in this very room.

"Good trip, Jack? Hell, it's good to see you, boy." They entered the large, handsome office with its dark blue carpet and comfortable furniture, the big photo of FDR hanging in a gold frame behind the desk. He shut the door and reached to take the suitcase from Jackson. "Have a seat, Jack. I want to hear all about it."

Steve Early had been with Roosevelt since 1920. As the original "advance man," he had accompanied a young Secretary of the Navy on a whirlwind campaign for the vice-presidency which eventually ended ingloriously for the Cox-Roosevelt ticket. It was on that trip, however, that the foundations were laid for what would eventually become the "inner circle" of the FDR administration.

Early was a big, garrulous Southerner with oceans of charm, absolute loyalty to his boss and a volatile temper. He was the perfect man to deal with the press, who liked him personally and tended to trust him, but were leery of crossing him and thereby provoking one of his famous rages.

He and Jackson, who also had a considerable temper,

got along just fine. Jackson was only thirty-four and a Yankee, but he was part of the Roosevelt "crowd," and that was all that mattered to Early.

Early set the suitcase on top of his large mahogany desk and gave it a little drum tap with his fingertips. He shot Jackson a big grin. "Well, my friend, it *feels* like it's all there. Some people would say we were out of our minds. But then, we probably are, so what difference does it make? Tell me about the trip, Jack."

Jackson shook his head. "Sorry, Steve, but it's not all there."

"It's not?"

"No. I had to dip into the money in Lisbon to pay for my Clipper ticket. Plus the bribe I had to shell out in Madrid so I could get to Lisbon in the first place. You'll find the suitcase about three hundred dollars light."

Early sighed deeply and then suddenly broke into gusts of laughter. "You mean . . . you actually spent three hundred dollars of the money in this suitcase?"

"I did," said Jackson, confused.

"Oh, my Lord, I knew I should have told you."

"Told me what?"

"This here is funny money, Jack. Counterfeit! I got it from the Treasury: stuff they'd confiscated. And not very high quality, either. Oh, my Lord!" He couldn't stop laughing.

"I guess it is funny," said Jackson, not really convinced. "But why?"

"In the first place, it was all for show. Nobody was about to hand over a hundred grand to a skunk like Hayward, were they?"

"No," said Jackson. The plan had called for the money solely to impress Hayward in order to get him to produce the photographs. "But why didn't you tell me it was counterfeit?"

"Psychology, Jack. It seemed to me you'd make a better show out of it if you believed the money was genuine. Well, you sure believed it. Oh, Lord! And so did those boys in Lisbon."

"We're light in another department too," said Jackson.

"How's that, son?" Early was calming himself. "Light in what department?"

"I got the photographs. But no negatives. I think you'd better open the suitcase, Steve."

"I suppose I'd better, if you say I'd better." Jackson tossed him the key. As he was opening it, he asked, "You didn't run into Marv Asher over there, did you?"

"No."

"I don't know how we're ever going to thank that guy enough for . . ." He didn't finish. He'd found the photographs, and the last traces of levity disappeared from his face. Cold and professional, he slowly worked his way through them.

Without a word he reached down and pulled open a desk drawer. Out of it he took a new manila envelope with the White House seal in one corner and "TOP SECRET" in large black letters. He slipped the photographs inside. "Can you hang on a minute, Jack? I want to show these to Harry."

"Of course."

Early took the envelope and walked out of the office, gently closing the door behind him. It was ten minutes before he returned, followed by Harry Hopkins, Secretary of Commerce.

Since Louis Howe's death, Hopkins had been Roosevelt's closest friend, not to mention the chief architect of the New Deal legislation. He had been a handsome, debonair man-about-town in his youth. His wife had died not long before, and now Hopkins himself was fighting a day-to-day battle against cancer, which had robbed him of his once seemingly unlimited political future. That previous May, after his last operation, Hopkins had gone to live in the White House as a permanent guest of the Roosevelts.

He was carrying the envelope with the pictures in one hand, and his face was ashen. Jackson was very fond of Harry. His heart sank as he watched the overly careful way the man lowered himself into the armchair.

"Hello, Jack. A pretty rough trip, I understand."

"It's good to be back."

"And good to have you back. You just managed to get out of Paris before the Germans arrived, I understand."

"About eighteen hours before, yes."

From behind his desk Early cleared his throat. "We've all seen them now. Why don't you tell us the story, Jack.

Just start from the beginning and don't let us interrupt you."

"All right," said Jackson. "It's not a long story. But I wish it had a happier ending." He proceeded to tell them the entire account, from his arrival in Paris until he learned of Hayward's suicide a few hours after he'd left the hotel. The main point, of course, was that the negatives were nowhere to be found.

When he'd finished, there was a long silence. Finally Early said, "Do you believe he was telling the truth when he said he destroyed them, Jack?"

"No." He'd given it a great deal of thought, and that was his final conclusion. "I thought he was lying at the time. I still do."

"The deal was supposed to be an exclusive," said Early. "How the hell did he think he'd get away without giving us the negatives?"

"He didn't know anything about exclusives or journalism, Steve. He struck me as a rather naive, very idealistic, extremely desperate man. He wanted money, a lot of it. I think he was trying to go off someplace and start a new life. In the end, trying to peddle those photos without the negatives, he made a terrible mistake."

Hopkins nodded. "I've been dealing with the British on this. Did you know that, Jack?"

Jackson looked up. "No, I didn't."

"Yes. They're very disturbed about the suicide. Furious at losing him before they could interrogate. Now, nobody's blaming you for that. You had your orders. The Boss set the policy on how to handle Hayward once we got the pictures. But we're going to have to square this with the British before we're finished."

"Speaking of the British," said Jackson. "I was approached by one of their agents in Lisbon. At least, he claimed to be one."

"What did he want?" asked Early.

Jackson told them. What Leaper said about the Germans, the man called Sir Roland and the so-called "American contact" he'd alluded to at the end. "A lot of what this guy said rang true to me, though that's just my gut feeling. But I put him off pretty firmly. I didn't think it was wise to go mouthing off about . . ." He paused, and nodded at the envelope in Hopkins' hand.

Harry nodded, then looked at Early. Early raised his eyebrows. Harry turned back to Jackson and said, "Under the circumstances, you were perfectly correct. The man was a stranger and you haven't been told about the British arrangement. We wanted to keep it restricted to as few as possible."

"We did and still do," said Early. "But I think we'd better tell him now, don't you, Harry?"

Jackson had absolutely no idea what they were talking about.

"Ten months ago," said Hopkins, "the Boss made a decision to allow certain sections of the British Secret Service to set up shop in New York City. A very quiet decision, as you can well understand. By 'sections' I mean, specifically, M15, their overseas counterintelligence branch. They've established an office up in Rockefeller Center under the name of British Security Coordination. There's a man named Sir Ian Fraser with whom I've been dealing up there. When I said we'd have to square this with the British, I meant Sir Ian."

"You must see, Jack," said Early, "that if Congress or the isolationist boys ever found out about this, there'd be hell to pay."

"I certainly do," said Jackson. "And that explains this Leaper a little better. I'm afraid I was pretty hard on him."

"As you should have been," said Hopkins. "You had no idea about the British in New York. Only four of us, plus two people in the Bureau and one man at State, know the score on this. The Boss has gone way out on a limb."

"I'd like to check with the British to make sure this man who contacted Jack in Lisbon was really one of their agents," said Early. He turned to Jackson. "He was convinced that Hayward was a Nazi agent?"

"Yes. Or, more exactly, he was certain Sir Roland Plenty was a German agent and that Hayward was a member of his network."

Hopkins lifted the envelope as if weighing it. "I think before we run off on a tangent, we ought to first talk about these photographs. Just how bad are they?"

"All it would take," said Early, "is one of those damn pictures on the front page of the *Star,* and the President would be finished."

"I'm afraid I agree," sighed Hopkins. "The potential damage is incalculable. The Boss's radio broadcasts have made the people of this country accept him as a member of the family. Their sense of betrayal would be enormous. Plus there is so much affection for Eleanor."

"You're right," said Early. "You'd have every self-righteous hypocrite in the country standing up and shouting 'sinner' at him. Not to mention the Republicans. Think of the smear campaign they could launch."

"Too true," said Hopkins. "These photographs are simply . . ."

"Dynamite!" said Early. "Dynamite that could explode at any minute so long as we don't know where the negatives can be found."

"We have to make a fast decision, I think," said Hopkins. "About the Boss."

"Yes, Harry?"

"Do we or don't we show him the pictures?"

Early frowned, but when he spoke, it was in a level voice that just managed to conceal his annoyance. "I guess that's one decision which will make itself. We can't hide them from him, Harry. He already knows about them. And we'd have no right not to. . . ."

Hopkins had been staring glumly at the floor. Now he looked up and said, "I just know how deeply they'll upset him. With the political situation as it is, how can we tell which way he'll react?"

"Harry," said Early, "I think you're probably right on the political situation. But we're talking about a man's life. His reputation, his family. What do you say, Jack?"

Jackson knew that before Hopkins' cancer was diagnosed there had been much talk of the New Dealer being FDR's successor in 1940. It seemed clear that Hopkins had now transferred all his own ambition to a third term for Roosevelt. Steve Early was being realistic, despite whatever his personal feelings might be. "If I had as much to lose as he did," said Jackson, "I'd never forgive anyone who didn't show them to me."

"I suppose you two are right," said Hopkins.

"Do you want me to be the one?" asked Early.

"Yes, if you wouldn't mind." Hopkins turned to Jackson. "You know the Boss took this personally as a slap in the face from Hayward, whom he liked, and, God knows, admired. In such cases, the Boss tends to react differently than you or I might."

"I know," said Jackson. "Could I say something else? You mentioned squaring Hayward's death with the British? I believe the British know more about this than they've told us yet. I'd like permission to talk to them."

"You mean this Sir Roland's connection with the Senate?" asked Hopkins. "I think you should talk to them."

"We'll have to clear that with the Boss first," said Early. "Before you go talking to the British or to anybody."

"By all means," said Jackson.

"The Chicago convention starts in three weeks," said Hopkins.

Suddenly Early slammed his fist down hard on the desk. "How in the name of God are we supposed to launch a campaign with . . . with this loaded forty-five pointed at the Boss's head?"

"We're not positive it's loaded, Steve," Jackson reminded him. "Hayward may have been telling the truth when he said he destroyed them."

"Do you really believe that?"

"No, I'm afraid I don't." Jackson had never believed it. And after Hayward's suicide, he had even less doubt. The negatives were somewhere, still intact, like live ammunition waiting to be fired.

Early glanced at his watch. "The Boss is free at eleven-thirty. I'll take the photographs in then."

"And ask him about my going to the British?" said Jackson.

"And that too. Anything to add, Harry?"

The Secretary of Commerce shook his head, still staring glumly at the deep blue carpet. "No, sir. I've said my piece."

"Jack?"

"Nothing. Except I'm damn sorry I couldn't have finished this all in Paris." He stood up. "I'll be in my office."

"You know," said Early, "I think the Boss may want to speak to you himself. Better stick around this afternoon just in case."

7

The 1940 Democratic convention was scheduled to open in Chicago on July 15. Although it was by no means certain the President would attend, it was part of Jackson's job to have all security arrangements complete in case, at any point during the convention week, Roosevelt did decide to go.

He had sandwiches sent up to his desk as he worked over the details, taking time out now and then to catch up on his pink call slips.

At two in the afternoon the third White House mail delivery brought him a letter for which he was by no means prepared. The envelope was addressed in green ink, in Barbara's familiar script. Not all that familiar. He hadn't seen a letter from her in two years.

Something made him get up and shut the door to the outer office before he read it.

It was dated three days previously and the heading was the same: 5018 Organdy Drive, Phoenix, Arizona.

Dear Jack,

I hope you are well. You will be happy to hear that Margaret is fine, healthy and even more adorable, if possible, than ever. No doubt you'd be amazed to see how tall she's grown. Her hair has darkened somewhat and I think she's perhaps not going to be a blond for too much longer. I don't know if you know much about five-year-olds, but I can tell you I have my hands full these days!

Of course this letter must be a shock to you, especially after everything I said the last time you were here.

The reason I am writing, Jack, is to inform you that I was married to Mr. Carl Muller here in Phoenix this last month, on June 2, to be exact.

66

Carl is a wonderful, generous and very kind man. We met about eighteen months ago here in Phoenix, where Carl is in the retail furniture business. Margaret is extremely fond of him and vice versa and the three of us make a very close-knit team. At present, we are still living here on Organdy Drive, but in August we will be moving out to Glendale into a new house which Carl is building there.

I cannot emphasize how much Carl loves Margaret and she him. He would very much like to adopt her so that she could grow up with the same name as her mommy and her husband. You know how children can be so cruel to any other child that is at all different! There is nothing personal in this, Jack, believe me, if you can. It is simply something we both feel would be best for the child. I hope you understand and I wish you would write and let us know how you feel about it.

Hoping to hear from you soon.

Sincerely yours,
Barbara

She'd signed it with her first name and he was grateful she hadn't tacked "Mrs. Carl Muller" onto it.

Suddenly he looked across at the door and wondered why he'd closed it before reading the letter. Could it be that he was setting himself up for yet one more fall? She'd been the one to pack and leave. If his stubborn conceit wouldn't allow him to accept a failure as a failure, at least Barbara had marked it correctly and acted upon it.

Perhaps it was his exhaustion, or that look on Hayward's face at the back of the closet which he hadn't been able to forget, but the time had come when he felt he had to take a stand. He'd let it slide, put it all on his own account. nursing the hurt for far too long.

He reached over and pulled his Smith-Corona to the side of the desk. He got just as far as "Dear Barbara" before he ripped the paper out of the typewriter.

On a new sheet he wrote his lawyer instead. The enclosed letter from his ex-wife would speak for itself. He had no intention of allowing Carl Muller to adopt his daughter, ever. On the contrary, the time had come to enforce the custody provisions granted to Jackson in the divorce settlement. Although the distance between Phoenix and Washington precluded the allowed weekends with his daughter, they were still his right. Along with one month every summer. Barbara, however, had refused to even let him see his daughter the last time he was in Phoenix. She had vowed to never let Margaret see her father again, despite the clear terms of the court order. Jackson wished to spend the coming August with his daughter. He directed his lawyer to inform Barbara of this and make it clear that if there was any resistance on her part, Jackson would take all legal steps necessary to secure his rights.

He signed it, sealed the envelope and placed it in his Out tray. Then he picked up the telephone and dialed Steve Early's extension.

Several minutes later, the press secretary came on the line.

"Sorry I haven't gotten back to you sooner, Jack. He does want to see you. But his schedule is tight. It probably won't be this afternoon."

"How was his reaction?"

"About what I expected. The Boss is keeping his own counsel. We'll see what happens. He was adamant on the point of keeping this from Missy. You know she'd never forgive herself if she ever thought . . ."

"Of course, Steve. Look, I'm beat from the trip. I haven't even been back to my house yet. I've got to get some sack time. Could you leave word with Missy that I'll be at home?"

"Of course, Jack. You get some sleep, you hear?"

Ten minutes later Jackson left the White House, walked over to Seventeenth Street and caught the bus. His Ford was at home in the garage on Woodlawn Street.

He had bought the house in Arlington five months before Margaret was born. It had been a little more expensive than he could afford, but the bank, with his White House references, had been more than happy to give him the mortgage. It had been fifteen years old, slightly older than most of the other houses on the block, but honestly built, with a small lawn in front, a screened-in porch and a long backyard. There were two great sycamores, several nice birch trees and enough space to grow their own vegetables if they'd been so inclined. The house was typical Colonial suburban with wood siding, a detached garage, and one unique feature: an outdoor stairway leading up to the second floor on the side by the driveway.

After Barbara left, he couldn't bring himself to sell it. At first in the hope she might return. Later, when it was clear she wasn't coming back, he'd decided to divide it into two apartments.

He had a kitchen installed upstairs and a shower built into a closet next to the downstairs john, and walled off the interior stairway. He ended up renting to two women in their mid-thirties: Nora, a statistician at the IRS, and Millie, an executive secretary to a State Department bigshot. These two ladies, both rather plain, never seemed to go out in the evenings and never entertained at home. Their one vice, as far as Jackson was concerned, was a cat named Basil. A stray which Millie had found wandering in the neighborhood, Basil had an unrequited fondness for Jackson and, especially, Jackson's apartment. No matter what he did, Jackson was unable to keep the cat from finding a way to sneak upstairs.

Aside from that, Nora and Millie were perfect tenants. They even mowed the grass when Jackson was away on long trips.

As he rounded the corner onto Woodlawn, he remembered that the ladies had informed him they would be taking their vacation during the last two weeks of June. Something about avoiding the summer crowds up on Cape Cod. So the place would be empty. Not that it made any difference.

He stopped at the mailbox and picked up half a dozen bills, junk coupons and magazine offers. Just as he'd expected, they'd mowed the front and back yards before they'd left. He'd never exactly been able to determine why the original owners had built this outdoor staircase. Perhaps they'd had young children and the mother had wanted to avoid small muddy footprints on her carpets. In any case, it had certainly come in handy for Jackson. He reached the top and unlocked his door.

Although the room was dimly lit, the devastation was apparent the moment he had the door half-open. In the middle of the chaos, Basil lay curled on a green sofa cushion looking up with a disgusted expression, as if Jackson had some nerve disturbing his siesta.

"Jesus," said Jackson out loud. "Some watchcat you are."

For it was immediately obvious no cat could have torn the room apart that thoroughly. The floor was strewn with broken lamps, overturned chairs, pictures off the wall, the contents of a wastepaper basket, and when he switched on the light, he saw the bottom of every chair had been roughly cut open, the stuffing pouring out.

He dropped his suitcase and walked through the hall. The kitchen was even more of a disaster. In the bathroom: the same havoc, with the tub full of broken glass and various pills and capsules tossed all over the floor. Totally unnecessary, he thought. As if the rest of it had somehow been necessary.

The bedroom and guest bedroom Jackson used as a study were also a shambles. He started to gather up the papers, old financial records, tax forms, letters which dated back over twenty-five years. Then he stopped, realizing the futility of going at it in bits and pieces.

In the kitchen, he kicked aside saucepans and broken glass and reached for the bottle of bourbon someone had left on the drainboard. He found a glass and poured three ounces of whiskey into the bottom. It went down in two long swallows. He poured another.

It was more than a search. This place, these four medium-sized rooms, were the closest thing Jackson had to a private life. He felt much as a woman might feel after being raped. Carrying his drink, he went back through all the rooms just in case they'd left a note. Finding none, he picked up one of the cushions, carried it over to the sofa and sat down.

Whatever they'd been searching for, and he had not the slightest idea, he wondered if they'd found it. Probably not. Otherwise the total devastation would have been unnecessary. They'd not have wanted him to know it had been found. Unless it was much simpler than that: simple robbery.

A couple of kids, hopped up, carried away in the destructive frenzy of the moment? Certainly this was not the work of a professional burglar? Was he reacting like someone who'd spent years in the Bureau, walking the shadowy side of every street? Or should he look at this like any normal houseowner who had just come back from a vacation to find his domicile ransacked?

He really didn't know. His body was exhausted, his

mind bucking uphill in overdrive. Under the circumstances, it was probably impossible for him to draw a reasonable conclusion. Letting out a sigh, he crossed the room, picked up the phone and dialed the police.

"Next time you make sure that window is locked," said the sergeant. "And you let us know so we can keep an eye out." Mazursky was a genial, potbellied sergeant with a vague resemblance to Wallace Beery. His partner, a rookie named Stubbles, had a bored expression and obviously no great affection for his senior partner. They had assured Jackson it had been an attempted burglary. It fit a pattern of recent Arlington break-ins. He shouldn't lose any sleep over it. After all, what had he lost? A couple of mattresses, some glasses, a few lamps.

Once they'd gone, Jackson poured himself another bourbon and began to think about cleaning up. For a moment the alcohol in his bloodstream stirred a vision of his going through the four rooms like a whirlwind of spit and polish, putting the entire apartment back just as it had been. Then the weariness in his shoulders made him realize that was a fantasy as improbable as anything Disney had ever come up with. In the end, he was satisfied to replace the cushions on the sofa.

He lay down with the glass in his hand and the bottle not far away on the carpet. From past experience he knew that the chances of his falling right to sleep were not very good. Not in his present overtaxed, jumpy state of mind.

He drank for several hours, as the room went from dim to pitch dark and, outside in the trees, the birds held their twilight conference, then went silent. It was well after nine o'clock when he finally surrendered to a deep, restless slumber.

He had no idea how much time had passed when the noise brought him bolt upright. He reached for the gun he'd placed under the sofa cushion and sat listening in the dark.

The creak of wood told him that whoever it was had reached the middle of the outdoor staircase. Very quietly he swung around into a semicrouch beside the sofa and then moved to the door.

If they were the same "burglars," they'd chosen a bolder route this time. Their previous entrance had been accomplished by climbing up the boughs of the birch which abutted his kitchen window.

The silence stretched into minutes, broken only by a slight creak of wood on the outside landing.

In vain he waited for the scratching noise that would signal an attempt to pick his lock. He was truly surprised when he heard the unmistakable sound of a footstep, then another, as the stranger began to retreat down the stairs.

Jackson threw the bolt, snatched open the door and jumped onto the landing with the .38 leveled at the descending back. "Hold it right there!"

"Oh!" It was more gasp than word, shocked, female.

"Hands up. Don't move."

"Oh, my God, what are you . . ."

As she turned, he saw two frightened eyes framed by a spill of dark hair, a flash of delicate throat, thin arms holding a pink sweater to her shoulders. He lowered the .38 until it was pointed at the ground. "Who are you?"

"Millie's friend. I'm staying . . ." She paused to catch her breath. "While they're away, they let me use their place. Are you Mr. Jackson?"

"Yes."

"Thank God. I just came back and I noticed there was a light on up here. There hadn't been one before. I was afraid there was . . . a robbery, you know? I came up to listen through the door."

"That was fairly dumb of you. What if I *had* been a thief?" he asked.

"Well, I suppose . . . Did I wake you up? I'm awfully sorry, really."

He realized he was wearing nothing but his boxer shorts. "No, that's all right. How long have you been staying downstairs?"

"Four nights. You see, they're painting my new apartment and I'm allergic. Since Millie was going on vacation, she said it would be okay if I camped out in her place for ten days."

"You work with Millie?"

"Yes, at State."

"I just got back this evening. What time is it?"

"Oh, after one, I think." It was raining, just a summer drizzle, but enough to wet her hair so that the dark strands were sticking to her forehead. He suddenly became conscious of the ludicrous nature of the scene: the gun, his state of undress, the rain.

"You didn't notice anything strange before tonight, did you?" he asked. "Do you want to come up for a second? Get out of the rain?"

She looked at him, then down at the ground. "It's pretty late. Notice anything? Like what?"

"Somebody broke in while I was away. My place is a total wreck. I was wondering if you might have seen a light, heard anything unusual."

"I didn't hear anything. Only just now when I saw . . ."

He reached inside and flipped the switch to light the exposed bulb over the landing. In the harsh glare, she was something quite unexpected. Despite her dark fragility, she had an assurance, a sense of herself as a young, intelligent woman that by no means conflicted with her natural beauty. She might have been a Luxor princess, materialized out of two millennia into that damp Arlington night on the bottom of his stairs.

"This is just terrible," she said. "Awful. Did they take anything valuable?"

"No."

"Believe me, if I'd heard anything, I would have called the police." She looked at his hairy calves and the rain puddling on the wood. "Don't you think you should put something on? You'll catch cold."

The adrenaline had worn off completely, replaced by the dull bludgeon of stale whiskey. He nodded.

"I'm sorry to have woken you. I mean, I suppose I was lucky not to . . ."

"I'm sorry," he said. "The gun is part of my job. I wasn't about to . . . That is, I had no idea there was anybody staying downstairs."

"Millie should have left you a note," she said. "Are you in the Secret Service? Millie said you worked at the White House."

"Not exactly. Look, it's pretty late. And we're both getting soaked."

She nodded, pushing her damp hair off her brow. "Well, good night, then."

He felt an irrational urge to ask where she'd been that she hadn't come home until one in the morning. Not *where* so much as with *whom*? Fighting the urge made his voice come out much colder than intended. "Good night."

He watched as she descended the final steps and walked back up the drive toward the front of the house. Suddenly she stopped and looked up. "Mr. Jackson?"

"Yes?"

"Do you mind that I'm staying here while Millie and Nora are away? I know you weren't asked. Under the circumstances, perhaps you'd prefer me to move to some . . ."

"No, of course not. You're welcome to stay."

"Thank you."

He waited until he heard the sound of the front door downstairs being firmly closed. Returning to the sofa, he replaced his gun in the cranny between the cushions. He was now wide-awake, with a mild pain in the back of his head and a strong desire to pour another drink. That was out of the question. The next day's busy schedule would not tolerate another drink.

There was no way of telling how long he lay in the dark, listening to the windblown leaves and the fall of the rain. His thoughts ranged back as far as his childhood, his father's luck-starved career as a salesman in upstate New York; his mother's long years of silent forbearance; his sister's early surrender to the way it was all supposed *not* to be, but was, goddamn it, it was. The couch was always fatal for him. Too many nights he'd lain on the couch, angry and unable to express that anger, with Barbara upstairs in a deep, unforgiving sleep. Fatal for him.

If only he could have reached back and gathered them all in his arms: father, mother, sister, daughter, yes, even wife, and held them in the magic, impossible circle of a family. But it was too late. And the girl on the stairs. Her face had a delicate beauty which had absorbed the harsh light and transformed it into a softness that wanted to break his heart. That wasn't fair. Not in the middle of the night with a gun in his hand: such beauty. One day he wouldn't know anymore. And if there was a hell, it wasn't little red men, eternal fire, the creak of chains on torture machines, or even memories. No, it was self-pity. Without end, until the end of time.

Sometime after dawn edged up the eastern horizon, Jackson's eyes closed and he slept once more. A solid, rich sleep with no dreams.

8

The telephone went off like a gunner's alarm at ten-thirty A.M.

"Oh, dear, I knew you were asleep! Forgive me?" begged Norma.

"Don't be silly. What's up?"

"I've held them off and held them off. I don't think I can hold out much longer."

"Who's them?" asked Jackson.

"Early, Mr. Hopkins, some Englishman named Leaper. And Missy. Missy has called twice."

"I'll be there in twenty minutes."

"And I wanted you to sleep until noon," she moaned. "But you'd better come. I'll have coffee waiting. What would you like for breakfast?"

"If you could have a bacon sandwich waiting on my desk, it would be a miracle."

"BLT or just bacon?"

"Just bacon. Rye toast, if you can swing it. And lots of butter."

It began the moment he passed beyond the outer foyer in the executive wing. Climbing the stairs, he nearly bumped into Early's secretary. "You know—" was as far as she got.

"I know! Tell him five minutes," shouted Jackson over his shoulder. "Tell him I'll call as soon as I'm upstairs."

Norma had bullied the commissary into not one, but three bacon sandwiches. The coffee was streaming out of the pot and into his mug the moment she heard his voice on the stairs. "You sit down and eat before you do anything else," she ordered, placing the mug in his hand.

"Three sandwiches?" he cried. "What are you trying to do to me?"

"Never mind. Just eat what you can."

He was almost finished with the first when the phone rang. Norma's head popped around the corner and she silently mouthed the name. Jackson lifted the phone. "Hello, Steve. Sorry to have kept you waiting so damn long."

"Jack, you haven't gotten in touch with the British yet, have you?"

"No."

"I thought we'd decided yesterday you were going to follow that up."

"Steve, there was a question of clearing it with the President." In fact, it had been Early's responsibility. But he was a busy man and such foul-ups were commonplace.

"Was there? I don't recall that." Which meant he had definitely forgotten to bring it up with the Boss.

"Well, that was my understanding of it, Steve. What's going on?"

"Don't ask. The British have been raising hell. Been bugging Harry all morning."

"Look, Steve, I still think I ought to talk to the President before I sit down and talk to the British. But I'll tell you what. I'll go ahead and set up an appointment with them. Then I'll make sure I get to the Boss first, hopefully today."

"That makes sense, Jack."

They hung up and he immediately dialed Missy's extension. Missy's secretary picked it up. "Oh, yes, I know she wants to talk to you. Please hold, Mr. Jackson."

A moment later Missy herself came on the line. "How are you, Jack?"

"Not bad. A little frantic this morning, but that's not unusual. And yourself, Missy?"

"Oh, you know, Jack. We heard about your trip. You were lucky to get out of Paris."

"I had a few hours to spare, I guess."

"It's just terrible. And Congress wouldn't let us do a thing. He wants to see you very much, Jack. He's awfully busy today but this evening is fairly open. Are you free?"

"Sure am."

"Good. How about nine o'clock, after dinner. I think he'll probably want to be in the solarium. It's so much cooler up there."

"Nine o'clock," said Jackson.

"There's one more thing, Jack."

"Yes?"

"Please try to cheer him up. You know how he gets sometimes. The past week, with the French surrender, it's been pretty rough. He's more blue than I've seen him in a long time. And it's not just the war. Did you read the papers this morning? About Lindbergh's speech? That man is absolutely impossible. He's actually going around campaigning for the Nazis. Do you think he wants to be the first American fuehrer? Anyway, please do try to cheer up the Boss. I can't get more than five words out of him."

"Count on me, Missy. I'll do my best."

After they'd hung up, there was a brief lull. Jackson managed to get down a second bacon sandwich. There was nothing of any immediate importance in the mail. Finally he asked Norma to call the number in New York where Leaper had said he could be reached.

Leaper answered on the first ring and Norma quickly buzzed Jackson's phone.

"So good of you to call, Jackson," said the unmistakable voice over the wire. "I imagine you're surprised to hear from me again so soon after Lisbon."

"Not at all," said Jackson. "You had a head start on me."

"You know that we've been in touch with Mr. Hopkins and Mr. Early today?"

"Yes."

"Well, then," said Leaper. "There ought to be no problem in your coming up this afternoon. Should we say about six o'clock?"

"No, I'm afraid not. I've got a full schedule today, including an appointment with the President." He wanted to ask why, if it was so urgent, Leaper couldn't come down to Washington. Then he realized that he was supposed to be "squaring" things with the British and said, "Do you think you could wait until tomorrow?"

"I suppose we'll have to, then," said Leaper. "Sir Ian will be most pleased to see you. Three o'clock tomorrow?"

"Three o'clock where, Leaper?"

"Are you familiar with the St. Regis Hotel? Fifth Avenue and Fifty-fifth Street?"

"Three at the St. Regis. Fair enough. If for any reason I can't make it, I'll let you know well in advance."

"We hope you won't have to do *that*, Jackson. Sir Ian is counting on this meeting."

"Does this have anything to do with what you told me about a so-called American 'contact' in the Senate?"

"Absolutely."

"Then I'll do everything in my power not to disappoint Sir Ian."

"Smashing. Until tomorrow, Jackson."

He hung up feeling exhausted and was surprised to look up and see Harry Hopkins waiting in his doorway. Men of Hopkins' stature in the administration rarely ventured up to the third floor.

Hopkins smiled a not very happy smile. "Hello, Jack. I thought you and I might have lunch. Your secretary says you don't have any other bookings. Know a good place?"

"Sure, Harry. I'd love to have lunch." He fingered his calendar. "You'd prefer to go out, then? Not the commissary?"

"Let's go out. Since I've been living here, I get more than my share of White House cooking."

Jackson laughed. "Ever been to the Embers?"

Hopkins shook his head. The flesh beneath his eyes was dark and swollen. "I can't say I have. Let's try it."

They didn't talk much on the way over. Hopkins had the use of a White House limousine and suggested they save time by using it.

The Embers was two blocks south of Howard University, not exactly Embassy Row. It had been carved out of an old cellar in a building which had seen its prime back in McKinley's administration. Long ago it was no doubt a fashionable address. Now its ground floor housed a small grocery with a faded sign in the window which read "Fresh Maws and Chitlins Today." Next door was the U-B-Sure Insurance Co., which claimed to offer the cheapest auto coverage in all of the District. But when they walked downstairs they left the ghetto behind and entered an amazingly elegant restaurant. Waiters in white jackets, black trousers, with velvet bow ties at their throats, were attending to the early luncheon crowd.

The Embers was one of the unlikeliest institutions in a city not noted for its predictability. A favorite gathering place for two irrevocably hostile clans. Sitting at adjacent tables, enjoying the crayfish gumbo and the New Orleans oyster pie, were both the leading businessmen and spokes-men of the District's voteless Negro community and some of the most diehard white segregationist congressmen the Deep South had ever produced. Both groups had declared the Embers neutral terrain.

Dr. Walter Lee, the owner, seated them at a banquette along the wall, gave them two embossed menus and took their drink orders.

It was obvious, from the moment Harry had appeared in Jackson's office, that the older man was in the mood to unload. But it was evidently going to take some time. Hopkins seemed tense, even more disturbed than he had the previous afternoon in Early's office. Both men pretend-ed to concentrate on their orders. But when the waiter fi-nally removed the menus, almost as if it were a signal, Hopkins leaned forward and said, "Jack, I hope you won't take offense if I use you as a sounding board this after-noon. You're a damn good listener and I've got a lot on my mind."

"I certainly won't take offense, Harry."

"Good. What I want to talk to you about is politics."

"Go right ahead, Harry. I doubt if you'd be the first person who ever talked politics at this table."

"No doubt, Jack. No doubt about that."

What was foremost in Hopkins' mind was, of course, the upcoming election. Two years earlier, he would have bet money that the central issue of the 1940 campaign would be the New Deal, just as it had been in 1936. But now the war in Europe had pushed the New Deal right out of the headlines. Hopkins was certain the Republicans were going to fight the election on the issue of the war, billing themselves as the "Peace Party" and holding a strict isolationist line. Once they got in, of course, their chief objective would be to dismantle the New Deal pro-grams as fast as they could. Whereas Hopkins was confi-dent that the majority of Americans still believed strongly in the Deal.

Jackson agreed, remembering the latest polls, which had said that only 35 percent of the American public thought England had a chance of defeating Germany.

"What drives me up the wall," said Hopkins, "is that the Republicans are going to campaign on a platform of fear. And they just might beat whomever we put up."

It was the first time Jackson had ever heard him speak of the coming election as if the Democratic candidate wasn't already certain. Obviously the photographs had badly shaken Hopkins' confidence.

At Hopkins' insistence, they proceeded to run down the list of possible Democratic candidates. As far as the Secretary of Commerce was concerned, each of them loomed, for various reasons, as a possible disaster. Each of them except for one, of course. But his name was saved until the very end.

First there was the Vice-President, "Black Jack" Garner from Texas. Not only a strict isolationist, Garner made no secret of his loathing for the New Deal. His chances at the convention were hardly good, although recently the President's own son Elliott had astounded the press by announcing his personal support for the Texan.

Cordell Hull, the Secretary of State, was about as personally unlike the whiskey-fond, gruff-spoken Garner as a man could be. Hull was no isolationist, but his views on the Deal were not widely known. Sober, honest, he was possessed of an extreme dignity often mistaken for aloofness. Hopkins doubted if Hull was enough of a politician to fight for the nomination, let alone win a tough election in the fall.

Jackson brought up the name of Joseph P. Kennedy, their abassador to the Court of St. James's. He'd recently made some highly unflattering speeches about the British and his isolationist views were winning him a growing political following. But Hopkins said that the Boss had already "faced down" Kennedy in private about his political ambitions. There wasn't much chance of Kennedy running for the nomination.

The candidate who truly worried Hopkins was Montana's Senator Burton K. Wheeler. "He's got John L. Lewis at the CIO behind him now, Jack. And Lewis is putting enormous pressure on the other unions to fall in line. Plus Wheeler's one of the big men in this goddamned America First organization. He's not anti-Deal really. I used to think he was a liberal. No national support a year ago. Now that Lindbergh's made the America First so popular, Wheeler is riding the crest. Wheeler would be the most serious candidate on the party's right. Most delegates would accept him on domestic issues. But a lot of people wouldn't like his blatant isolationism. It might split the convention. But conventions were made to be split."

"So you're afraid of Wheeler?" asked Jackson.

"Damn right I am," said Hopkins.

"So far we've been talking about the conservative half of the party. What about the left?" asked Jackson. "What about Henry Wallace?"

"You've got two problems with Wallace. Wheeler's problem and Wallace's own problem. First, Wallace is hated by the right in the party. It would surely split the convention. And then there's Henry's own problem. He's a True Believer. Not a grandstand artist like Kennedy, but a genuinely modest man. A True Believer, though, and the voters can smell them from miles away. True Believers make people nervous, Jack. Maybe it's jealousy or perhaps just old-fashioned common sense. *I* know I haven't got all the answers. Where does Henry get off acting like *he* gets his straight from God? You understand?"

"Perfectly."

"Jack, I didn't sleep a wink last night. I kept thinking about those pictures and what they could do to the Boss. And something occurred to me. We talked about the dangers of the Republicans getting ahold of the photographs. But what about our own party?"

"Go on," Jackson said.

"Take Wheeler. It's just three weeks until the convention, and suddenly there are a lot of hard men lining up behind Wheeler. John L. Lewis is staking everything on teaching the Boss a lesson by kicking him out. Plus I've heard some rumors about Wheeler being very cozy with the German embassy. Now, you said this British fellow talked of a connection between Hayward's network and the Senate, correct?"

"Yes. He mentioned a 'contact' that they believed Sir Roland, Hayward's boss, might have in the Senate."

"I kept thinking of that last night," said Hopkins, shaking his head slowly. "What if Wheeler suddenly came up with these photographs? It worries me, Jack. Worries me more than I can say."

"I can see your point." Jackson hadn't yet considered the possibility of the photographs being used by a member of Roosevelt's own party. "Harry, what do you want me to do?"

Hopkins smiled, taking a sip of coffee. "Jack, I want you to find those goddamn negatives."

"And if I can't?"

"The Boss will never throw his hat in the ring. And he's the only one . . . the only one who can bring the people to an awareness of what this war in Europe is all about. The only one who can keep Congress from ripping apart the Deal until it has long enough to prove itself. The only candidate who could win on both the war and the Deal."

"So you think he's seriously considering retirement now?"

"Jack, those pictures would finish him off. He'd never get another bill through Congress. Hell, he couldn't get elected dogcatcher in Hyde Park if those photos ever hit the papers. He'd never forgive himself for a scandal that would ruin the Deal and lose the election for the party. He'd withdraw first and try to come to terms with one of the other candidates. Trade his support for certain guarantees in the platform. We cannot let that happen, Jack."

"We won't," said Jackson. "If we possibly can."

"That's all I wanted you to say, Jack." Harry's eyes were moist. He reached out and touched the younger man's arm. Then waved at the nearest waiter for the bill, which, no matter how Jackson protested, he was determined to pay.

9

At a little before nine that evening, Jackson reported to the ushers' room on the first floor of the White House. They were expecting him and quickly escorted him to the private elevator, which he rode alone up to the top floor and the solarium.

On the southeastern corner of the residence, it was a charming room with large glass windows. The Roosevelts had chosen to furnish it with comfortable wicker-backed chairs and a splendid array of tropical plants and desert cacti.

Roosevelt was sitting alone with his feet up on a footstool, a blanket folded neatly over his knees. The view was breathtaking: right down the South Lawn and across the Elipse to the floodlit shaft of the Washington Monument. When he saw Jackson in the doorway, the President closed the leather-bound report he'd been studying and waved him inside.

"Pull up your chair, Jack." He lit a cigarette in his holder as Jackson seated himself. "Sorry we haven't had a chance to talk before now. It's good to have you back safe and sound."

"And good to be back, sir."

Roosevelt nodded. "I've heard a few things about your time in Paris. Why don't you tell me about it? What did you think of Hayward, Jack?"

"In all frankness?"

"Please."

"He was finished. Whatever he'd once been, by the time I saw him he had lost it all. Ideals, self-respect, everything was gone. He was desperate for money, with that look you get when you know you've been suckered but still can't figure out how. He was playing over his head. And he got

83

wiped out. I'm not proud when I think I was the one who gave him that last little push."

"How can you say that, Jack? The man took his own life."

"The last thing I said to him was that they were going to hang him."

Roosevelt met his eyes with a stern glance. "Jack, that kind of thinking will keep you inside that closet with Hayward for the rest of your life. He was a doctor, remember? And every man is born with the right to make the decision he did."

"I understand he was once a friend," said Jackson softly. "Or isn't that so?"

"Not a friend, Jack. But a man who had accomplished a great deal of good in certain areas which mean a lot to me. As you said, he went off the track somewhere. I'm not going to mourn David Hayward. Nor am I going to rejoice. I only knew him for a few days. During that time, he made no secret of his admiration for the Nazis. The Nazis were behind it all, weren't they?"

"I don't know," said Jackson. "He swore to me that he wasn't working for the Germans. But he was part of an organization, no doubt about that. He claimed the photographs were connected with his belief in National Socialism in Britain. Now, how exactly that figures is beyond—"

"The photographs were my own damn fault," insisted Roosevelt suddenly. "There I was fooling around with Missy like a schoolboy in his first bout with spring fever. I hold myself responsible for the pictures, Jack. And now I'm going to swallow my own medicine."

"I don't know about that," said Jackson. "Your feelings may not be any more accurate than the way I felt about his suicide."

"Let's get back to the Germans for a second," said Roosevelt. "Hayward was part of an underground organization in Britain, correct? Was it controlled from Berlin?"

"It seems so," said Jackson.

"I can't help but feel this is just a part of Berlin's latest overall strategy."

"Which is?"

Roosevelt reached over and stabbed his cigarette out in a heavy quartz ashtray. "I wish I knew exactly. At the moment I feel like a child trying to connect the dots when there aren't enough numbers on the page."

"It's the election, isn't it?" asked Jackson.

"Yes. But that's not all of it. Their problem is what they're going to do with England. Do they invade? Or do they try to come to terms? They'd lose a hell of a lot of men on the English beaches. And even Berlin would admit that keeping the British people down would be far more difficult than handling the Belgians or the Danes. We're the key to their entire problem."

"We always have been," said Jackson.

"In 1917 and now again," said Roosevelt. He was inserting another cigarette in his holder, reaching for his gold Dunhill lighter, chain-smoking even more than usual. "Churchill has been putting more pressure on me than I'd care to admit. For someone who's such a formidable politician, you'd think he'd understand that a President can't declare war without the Congress behind him."

"Do you think the Germans are convinced we won't come into it?"

"No," said Roosevelt. "Why would they be sending continual messages to me offering to divide the world between the two of us if I agree to force Britain to the wall? I'm Churchill's last hope. Believe me, he's not about to let me forget it, either. Ever hear of a man named Bill Davis?"

"William Rhodes Davis? You mean the oil man who was shipping from Mexico to Hamburg last year?"

"That's the one. We caught him breaking the blockade and we tried to shut him off. But he's found ways around it. Davis was in my office ten months ago with a message from Marshal Goering. Wanted me to force England into a 'peace treaty' that read like what Lee signed at Appomattox. I kicked him out, of course. Do you know who Davis has teamed up with now? John L. Lewis at the CIO. They're backing Wheeler for the nomination. There's no doubt in my mind that Berlin is behind Davis. I have heard stories about millions of dollars being pumped into a Wheeler bid."

"Why *is* Lewis backing Wheeler against you this time?" asked Jackson.

"Why?" asked the President. "Because John L. Lewis likes to think of himself as the most powerful man in this country. As the king-maker, which means I'm supposed to be the king, I guess. Except he doesn't feel he's gotten enough favors in return for his support during the past two elections. He told me to my face that the only way I could get his support was to come to terms with Germany."

"So you think these millions really exist?"

"I don't know if it's millions. But Bill Davis has been handing out a great deal of money to certain Democrats who don't see exactly eye to eye with me. If we could prove the money came from Berlin, we'd have a devastating case to take to the people. This Davis-Lewis cabal is only part of it, of course. There's the whole America First question. Or should I say 'Germany First.' "

"What do you mean?"

"The FBI is convinced that someone over at the German embassy is secretly running the America First outfit. Again, Wheeler comes into it. But so do lots of other people. Talk to Hoover and you get the impression there are more German spies in this city than there are privates in the Army. Maybe he's right." Roosevelt suddenly stopped and turned to look at the door.

Eleanor was walking briskly in their direction. She was wearing a white short-sleeved cotton blouse tucked into a dark brown skirt. Her graying hair was tied back and her glasses were hanging from her neck on a thin silver chain.

"Hello, Jack," she said, reaching out to shake his hand. "How nice to see you. I'm very sorry to interrupt, but I shall only take two seconds of your time. Franklin?"

"Yes, my dear?" He gave her his full attention, showing no sign of annoyance at having been interrupted.

"I've just come across this letter from the NAACP about their convention next winter. They need to know now if you'll speak or if it will just be me on the dais. Of course"—she grinned—"they'll back you in the election whether you promise to speak or not."

All three of them laughed heartily at that. Then, as Roosevelt reached for the large calendar he always kept near his side, Jackson reflected on the peculiar nature of this relationship.

In the four years Jackson had been in the White House, he'd grown to understand its basically split personality. Either you were the President's friend or you were Eleanor's. The two cliques rarely mixed outside of purely formal social occasions. And Jackson had never seen the husband and wife together when they weren't discussing something practical.

Yet he knew their relationship had to be a deep and, in its own way, loving one.

When they'd finished their NAACP discussion, Eleanor once more offered Jackson her right hand. "Good night, then, Jack. It was good to see you. I wish it could be more often."

The President watched her leave the solarium with a look that was impossible for Jackson to read.

"You were saying . . ." Jackson prompted after a moment's silence.

"I was going to ask you about the photographs. Did they strike you as being as disastrous as they did Steve?"

"Not quite. I think there are millions of people in this country who love and respect both you and Eleanor too much to turn against you."

"That's damn kind of you, Jack," he said. "And I'd like to believe it was true. But Steve is a shrewd judge of the political scene, especially the press. In fact, I'd go even further than Steve. Those photographs, nasty as they might be, happen to constitute a fact. I'm not going to go into my personal life with you, Jack. But I will say this. At no point will I ever try to justify or excuse my private life. My family, my children, Missy, those are facts of *my* life. Not the President's life, but the life of Franklin Roosevelt of Hyde Park, New York."

Jackson nodded. There were holes in the argument. But it was hardly his place to point them out.

"The American people are a funny breed," said the President. "No matter what goes on Saturday night out in Iowa City or Milwaukee, come Sunday morning everyone is on his way down to church and ready to cast that first stone. . . . Take this war. Public opinion is dead set against it right now. But in a year's time, who knows? The only way you can move people is to get out front and lead. Any way you look at it, leading this country is a process of persuasion, compromise and just plain luck."

"So you're convinced the photographs would make it impossible for you to lead the nation?"

"Of course I am," said Roosevelt. His features softened,

as if he were changing the subject. "I saw Harry this afternoon. He told me you two had a delicious lunch."

"Yes."

"He also told me you were going to try to find these negatives. Is that true?"

"Well, I'd assumed that you—"

"Don't assume anything, Jack. Especially about me. Not at this point."

"Does that mean you don't want me to try to find the negatives?"

"I didn't say that," said Roosevelt. He leaned his head back and exhaled a stream of smoke at the ceiling. Then his eyes snapped back down and met Jackson's firmly. "What are your chances, Jack? What are your chances of finding them?"

"I'm meeting with the British tomorrow. They'll be able to tell me a lot more than I know right now."

"The British know about the photographs?" asked Roosevelt.

"I don't think so. And that was one reason I was anxious to speak with you before I saw them. How much do you want me to tell them?"

The President laughed. "Do you think they'd be shocked? Tell them the whole story, Jack. Sir Ian is a friend. For understandable reasons, I'd prefer you explain the situation rather than have to do it myself. By the way, have you thought about going to the Bureau?"

"On what basis? Do you want me to talk to Hoover about this?" asked Jackson.

The President pulled a face that said talking to Hoover was the farthest thing from his mind. "Edgar and I are having a bit of a disagreement at the moment. He's not very happy about my letting the British set up shop in New York. You've never seen anyone more jealous of his own turf than our Edgar. Add to that his profound ambition and that monolithic stubbornness, and you have quite a cop."

"True," said Jackson. "But cops don't always make the best diplomats. An old friend at the Bureau has already tried to pump me while I was in Paris."

"Well, you know how Edgar is if he thinks there's anything, I mean *anything*, that he hasn't already got a full dossier on in that backroom of his. I know my friend

Edgar has his eye on me. But"—and he grinned—"two can play that game. Did you ever meet Stan Peddie when you were at the Bureau?"

"Yes. Close to the Director's office, isn't he?"

"Stan happens to work for me," said Roosevelt. "Believe me, he comes in handy. If you're ever stuck, call Stan. Edgar would jump out of his skin if he knew that Stan and I were old friends. We've known each other since we were both at the Navy Department. So be cautious about any contacts you do make with him."

Jackson nodded, unable to restrain a smile at the thought of Hoover's office being infiltrated by one of the President's men.

"Will you keep in touch with me on this?"

"Of course I will." Jackson realized the meeting was over then. Rising to his feet, he was surprised to see the President reaching out to shake hands. It was a custom the Boss usually overlooked when meeting with his staff. They shook hands staring directly into one another's eyes.

He was almost at the door when something made him turn back. For the first time that evening, Jackson saw Roosevelt with his guard down.

He looked older than Jackson had seen him look just seconds before. And ill. It was so easy to forget he was not a well man. It was the energy in the mind as it flowed out in that rich, familiar Down East voice. But that was gone now. He sat with his hands on the arms of the chair, the gray swirl of yet another cigarette drifting up to cloud the air over his head. Tired and ill.

He must have sensed Jackson's eyes upon him, for his head came erect and his lips broke into a smile. Jackson did his best to return it. Then hurried from the solarium.

Someday he would learn. In the meantime, he had just acquired yet another picture to be filed somewhere in the back of his mind. And a whole lifetime to try to forget it was there.

There wasn't a cloud in the sky and it was already well toward eighty degrees when Jackson left his house the next morning. As he was opening the garage, he heard the screen door slam on the front porch.

She was wearing a sensible light blue summer dress, belted at the waist, with low heels. Her long silky black hair framed her lovely face. In her right hand she was carrying a solid-looking brown briefcase. The other night he hadn't really had a chance to see her, how petite she was, how delicately framed.

"Need a lift?" he called.

"Are you driving into town?"

"I'm going to Union Station. It's on the way to State. I could drop you at the main entrance."

"Thanks a lot."

"Just wait and I'll back the car out." When he had done so, she came around and he opened the door for her. She slid in next to him on the front seat.

"This is really very kind of you. I'm not wild about the bus at this hour," she said.

"Can hardly blame you." He backed out onto Woodlawn and then straightened the car.

In the rearview mirror he caught a glimpse of a tan DeSoto parked thirty yards up the street. No overnight parking was allowed and he had never seen the car before. Or had he? He got a quick glimpse of two men in trilby hats behind the DeSoto's windshield.

"Are you taking another trip?" she asked.

"Just up to New York for the day."

"Do you regularly travel a great deal for your job?"

"Sometimes," he said. "Especially during an election year. Sorry again about the other night. Sorry if I frightened you."

"Oh, no, I understand how awful you must have felt. I'm so glad they didn't take anything valuable. I've been putting the chain on downstairs at night now. It's terrible to think that in this neighborhood . . . I mean, I could understand if it was someplace like where I grew up."

He'd been watching the rearview mirror for the DeSoto since they turned onto Beaumont Avenue. There was no sign of it so far. "Where did you grow up?"

"On the Lower East Side of Manhattan."

"Oh?"

"Yes. My father was a tailor. He had a small shop on First Avenue."

"And what do you do at the State Department?" he asked pleasantly, not at all prepared for the answer.

"I'm Assistant Undersecretary for Immigration."

"What?" He threw her a quick sidelong glance. "But you look so . . ."

"Young?"

"Pretty is more like it."

She blushed, then caught herself and said in a serious voice, "I'm twenty-seven. I got my doctorate from Georgetown when I was twenty-three."

He let out a soft whistle of appreciation. "So I'm driving a genius to work."

"Hardly. I just skipped a lot of grades when I was a kid. That wasn't very difficult considering the New York public schools. I went to City College. Then I got a scholarship to Georgetown. How about you?"

"I'm a scholarship boy myself. Upstate New York. First at Rochester. Then Syracuse Law."

"And what do you do at the White House that makes you travel so much during an election year?"

They were approaching the broad span of the Arlington Memorial Bridge. He wasn't positive. But he thought there was a tan automobile that looked like the Desoto 250 feet behind, hugging the right lane in the thick stream of rush-hour traffic.

"Nothing very momentous," he said. "Odds and ends. I'm sort of an advance man. Which means setting up a city so that when a candidate comes through, everything works fairly smoothly. And I'm assigned enough other projects during the year to keep fairly busy."

"So your work is mostly political. It seems a little strange then . . ."

"What does?" he asked.

"That you would need a gun for that kind of job."

"Well, I used to work for the FBI. I still do a little security work."

"You mean like being a bodyguard?"

He shook his head. It was impossible to explain. "No, there's the Secret Service for that. You're quite right. It does seem a little strange. But enough about me. What are you working on these days at Immigration?" Even as the words left his mouth, he sensed it was some kind of gaff.

"Trying to do something to help fifty thousand children get out of France before it's too late. But, of course, we have something called 'quotas' in this country. And everyone knows 'quotas' are far more important than helpless children or saving people's lives."

"Who says that?" he asked.

"What do you think?" she asked. "Congress, of course."

"And what have we done?"

"You mean the White House? Well, I suppose you've done all you can. Especially Mrs. Roosevelt. She's been so helpful. But time is running out. Before we get the quotas amended, I'm afraid thousands and thousands of innocent people will have been killed."

"I assume you're referring especially to the Jews."

"Why?" she asked. "Do you have any particular feelings about what the Nazis are doing to the Jews?" She was sitting ramrod straight against the back of the seat.

"It's unspeakable," said Jackson. "Any word I could try to use to describe it would be insufficient."

"Did you know I was a Jew?" she asked.

"No, of course not."

"Don't tell me it wasn't obvious to you."

"As a matter of fact, it certainly wasn't. What does your being a Jew have to do with anything?"

"I've had to tolerate a great deal of unpleasantness recently because of being a Jew and having the job I do."

He glanced over at her staring straight ahead into the slow-moving traffic. "You're not supposed to be objective, is that it?"

"So they say."

"Let them," he said. "You have every right to be biased

about the murder of your own people. As a human being, you have an obligation to be biased. Let *them* be objective."

There was a long moment of silence. "Thank you," she said at last. "I suppose this is a fairly serious conversation for so early in the morning."

"Shall we discuss the weather?" he asked.

"Isn't this humidity just the end!"

They both laughed. The tension in the car passed as quickly as it had appeared. He checked the mirror again, turning onto Pennsylvania Avenue. No sign of the DeSoto.

"What is happening with this election, by the way?" she asked suddenly.

"Excuse me?"

"Nobody seems to know if Roosevelt is going to be a candidate again or not. How about some inside information?" She was teasing him, but there was seriousness there too.

"I'm afraid not. I simply don't know," he said. "I doubt if anyone does. With the possible exception of the President himself."

"But he's simply got to run," she said.

They were approaching the massive stone façade of the State, War and Navy Building. He found a gap in the traffic and maneuvered them over to the left lane, arriving in the empty space reserved for government vehicles.

"Let's say I agree with you. But there are a great many factors involved in whatever decision he finally makes," said Jackson. "Here we are."

"Yes, here I am. Thank you so much for the lift, Mr. Jackson." She began to open the door on the traffic side.

"Careful," he said. "And why don't you call me Jack? By the way, what's your name?"

"Oh, dear, I forgot to tell you, didn't I? Rona Silvers. Hey, you'd better watch out!" She gestured at the sidewalk, where a District policeman was walking rapidly in their direction.

"That's okay, Rona. So long now. And good luck with the quotas this morning."

"Good-bye." She slammed the door and hurried around to the sidewalk. The cop began to make frantic gestures informing Jackson he was in the wrong parking spot. Jackson ignored him, wanting another look at her. From the back, she looked very small, a child amidst the grown-ups, hurrying inside the building. Yet that was the Assistant Undersecretary of State melting into the throng at the top of the granite steps.

The policeman was shouting now; people were beginning to stop and stare. Jackson eased the stick into first gear and turned the Ford back into the traffic. Over his shoulder, he looked for an opening.

On the far side of Pennsylvania Avenue, a tan DeSoto was idling. Two men in trilby hats stared hard at his Ford. Maybe they were tourists, thought Jackson. Sure. And he was the Lincoln Memorial.

11

Washington to New York was not the most scenic train journey in America. Especially if, like Jackson, you had taken it hundreds of times before. The open windows let a harsh, gritty blast into the compartment that did little to refresh the passengers on a hot June morning. Delaware and Pennsylvania were mostly low, wooded hills and the backsides of farmhouses, an occasional scrap heap, frequent small towns that flew past in the blinking of an eye. But he found himself drawn into the scenery, and then into a kind of trance.

What was this all about, this problem of Roosevelt and the photographs? Why would the American people be so outraged? He knew they would be, of course. And he knew all the easy explanations for why. But what was the true reason?

Image, he thought. It was so important. The "image" of a President.

Even before he was elected, when he was still a candidate, the press set out to build a man an image that would be as vivid in the people's minds as Old Glory itself. It went with the job. It didn't even have to be a handsome, attractive image. Look at Grant, or Warren Harding, or, for God's sake, Herbert Hoover.

But it had to be an image that could be depended on, thought Jackson. Smash the image, even just change it a little, and you were in danger of a revolt among the voters. Change that image and you were tampering with the people's most fundamental need. The need to feel secure, even sane.

It was like the train. Looking around the compartment, he realized he was the only one bothering to look out the window except for one small child a dozen rows ahead. Everyone else was intent on a newspaper, a book, even preferring to stare at the ceiling rather than look out the window at the rush of scenery flashing past.

Out there was a nation. But you couldn't expect them to look at it from a train window: as a flowing multitude of endless variety and change. No, each had his own picture of what America was, pasted right up in the front of his mind for constant reference. Of course, Jackson knew he was no exception. He, too, carried pictures around inside his head that often replaced the reality in front of his eyes. But less and less, especially since his marriage had gone bad. That had put him off pictures. Like the picture in his mind of standing on Barbara's doorstep in Phoenix; her tight, angry face shouting at him to go away, never to try to see his daughter again. That was only one of Jackson's pictures. Everyone had a set of his own. No wonder it was important to have a President with an image that you could depend on, aspire to, but not change. No, never change.

By the time he came out of his trance, he was in a taxi pulling to a stop under the St. Regis canopy. A doorman dressed like a Napoleonic general in blue and gold stepped up to open the cab door.

Inside the elegant, rather small lobby, Jackson asked for Mr. Leaper and was handed a tiny envelope.

2.45 P.M.

Dear Jackson,
    I'm in the King Cole Bar. Sir Ian would like you to join me there.

Cheers,
G. Leaper

It was a very large and high-ceilinged room. The bar stretched across the back wall under a giant mural depicting the Jolly Old Soul being serenaded by his trio of fiddlers. Most of the room was taken up with square, unadorned wooden tables. At one of them a tall horse-faced man was waving his arm frantically in Jackson's direction.

"How *do* you do, Jackson? This *is* a pleasure."

"Hello, Leaper."

"Please call me Greville. What would you like to drink? I'm having a gin and tonic."

Jackson shook his head. "I think a ginger ale would about do it. I haven't had lunch yet."

"You haven't? I'm sure they can fix us some sandwiches." He turned and began to beckon for the waiter.

Jackson ordered a roast beef on rye and Leaper said he was ready for another gin and tonic. How about a glass of beer? he suggested. Jackson stuck to his ginger ale. Leaper, looking disappointed, said, "Suit yourself, though last time I saw you, you were rather deeply involved with a bottle of port."

"That was last time," said Jackson. "Is Sir Ian joining us here?"

"Sir Ian is upstairs. I'm afraid something came up at the last moment. We'll be joining him at half-past, so I thought it would be more pleasant to wait down here."

"Fine. I needed something to eat," said Jackson.

"Did you drive up from Washington?"

"No, I took the train."

"Were you followed?"

Jackson nearly choked. "Why do you ask that?"

Leaper smiled. "Well, I must confess we were afraid you might not come to 'ow. I asked a couple of my fellows down in Washington to keep an eye on you. I gather you spotted them. . . ."

Jackson started to rise, changed his mind and sat down shaking his head in disbelief. Leaper talked as if it were all some harmless game of hide-and-seek. "Are you crazy? I ought to . . . ought to be furious with you, Greville."

"Why, Jackson?"

"Because you had me followed, for Christ's sake. You put me through a lot of unnecessary heart failure this morning. I had to lose those two punks before I got on the train and . . . would *you* like to be followed, for God's sake?"

"But I am!" cried Leaper gleefully. "Didn't you know that?"

"Of course not."

"Well, I don't know their names, of course, and they change like the tides. But they're all FBI agents, no doubt."

"Are you kidding? Why is the Bureau following you?"

"Not just me. Sir Ian. All of us. As for why, you'd have to ask the Director, as you call him, why. I think he suspects we're foreign agents. Quite correctly, of course. And his job is to tail foreign agents. Absurd, really."

"Knowing the Director as I do, you might be right," said Jackson.

"I know I'm right. Here come your sandwiches."

It was only one sandwich but it was delicious. When Jackson had finished right down to the pickle, Leaper informed him that the time had arrived to go meet Sir Ian.

It was hardly what Jackson had expected to find on the eighth floor of the St. Regis. The room they first entered had been stripped of all furnishings that might in any way suggest a hotel room. Except for the pile carpet and the brocade curtains, it looked just like an office. Which indeed it was, and a busy office at that. At one of the two desks a white-haired woman with tortoiseshell glasses sat pounding away on her typewriter at about 150 words per minute. She didn't bother to glance up when Leaper said, "That's Mrs. Presby-Johns."

"Hello," said Jackson.

A slight shift in the rate of key-pounding told him that his greeting had been acknowledged.

"Now *this* is more like it, isn't it?" asked Leaper as he ushered Jackson into the next room of the suite.

He wasn't sure it was, although it certainly was far more like a hotel room. Two large beds under cherry satin coverlets filled half of it. Then the obligatory pieces of Regency furniture. The wallpaper was floral and the prints on the wall depicted scenes of "Old New York." The bathroom door was ajar and, from inside, there came the sound of running water and then a loud gargle. Followed by an abrupt squeak as the tap was shut tight.

Sir Ian Fraser emerged from the bathroom with his face covered by an enormous red towel. When he'd finished drying his eyes and ears, he looked up and was startled to see them in the room.

"Oh! Forgive me, gentlemen. Just tossing a bit of cold water on my face. You must be Jackson. Won't you take a seat, Jackson? I don't use this room often, and when I do, I'm generally asleep."

There was nothing immediately strange about Sir Ian except, perhaps, for his size. About five-foot-four was

Jackson's guess. But he had compensated for his height by the way he held himself: shoulders back, belly in, head erect, all lending a definite military aura to the man.

But then Jackson gradually began to absorb the man's broad upper lip, his wide mouth and those bulging, sad eyes. There was no doubt about it: he reminded Jackson of a frog. A nice frog or a nasty frog? Time would surely tell. The next few minutes, in fact.

Sir Ian sat down on the edge of one of the beds and crossed one pressed dark gray trouser leg over the other. He looked at Leaper. "Are you going to sit or are you going to stand?"

"Sit, I suppose."

"Then sit."

"Right," said Leaper. He took the chair in the farthest corner of the room.

Sir Ian turned to Jackson. "Please don't look at me like that."

"Excuse me," said Jackson. "Was I . . ."

"Like I was about to have you flogged. What happened in Paris was most unfortunate. But you were only following orders and I can hardly condemn a man for that."

Jackson was not sure what to say.

"Now, look here, Jackson," said Sir Ian, "I've been told you're willing to share the information you got out of Hayward. In return, we have some news you will most certainly find as valuable as it is shocking."

"Go on," said Jackson.

"Would you mind if I asked you to go first?"

"All right. If you wish."

"Very good. Then what did you want from David Hayward that sent you to meet him in Paris?"

"Some photographs."

"Ah?" said Sir Ian. "I can't say I'm terribly surprised to hear that."

"There were twelve of them," continued Jackson. "Hayward had taken them in Warm Springs, Georgia, in March of 1936. They were rather intimate shots of the President together with his personal secretary, Miss Marguerite Le-Hand. She has been the President's closest working companion for twenty years."

"Quite," said Sir Ian. "I understand the historical background behind their relationship. And I have met Missy

LeHand on several occasions. When you say 'intimate shots,' just what do you mean?"

"They were lying on the grass . . ."

"Embracing?"

"Yes."

"Clothed or unclothed?"

"For God's sake," said Jackson. "They were on a picnic. Of course they had their clothes on. In one of the photographs, they do kiss. In others, they are embracing with obvious affection. The pictures aren't pornographic, Sir Ian. They're politically scandalous."

"Oh, I see, is that all?" said Sir Ian. "Tell me, was your mission a success? Did you get these photographs from Hayward before he hanged himself?"

"I received the photographs in print form. But not the negatives."

"Where are the negatives?"

"Hayward claimed to have destroyed them."

"And do you believe he was telling the truth?" asked Sir Ian.

"No."

There was a long silence during which Sir Ian seemed to be studying something out of the window beyond their heads on the far side of Fifth Avenue. He turned back to Jackson. "I should tell you that what you've just said has horrified me, sir. If Roosevelt falls from power in this country, Britain may well cease to exist as a nation. It is as simple as that."

Leaper cleared his throat. "Excuse me, but are you positive Hayward didn't have the negatives with him in Paris?"

"Almost a hundred percent positive, yes."

Leaper turned to Sir Ian. "Then that explains it, sir."

"Yes, Greville, it just might explain it." He turned to Jackson. "I take it you are still interested in finding these negatives?"

"Of course we are."

"I believe Greville mentioned the name Sir Roland Plenty to you in Lisbon?"

"He did."

"Then you might like to know that Sir Roland Plenty arrived on the North American continent on June 20, seven days ago. If anyone has the negatives, I'm afraid it must be Sir Roland."

"He's in the States?" asked Jackson incredulously.

"We can't be sure. When he eluded the Yard in England, they notified all immigration and customs departments in the Empire. But you know how sloppy most bureaucracies are. The customs man in Montreal did not bother to read his notice until just three days ago. He instantly recognized the face. Plenty had come in on a Greek freighter out of Liverpool under a South African passport. Where he is now, we can only guess."

Jackson nodded.

"But our guess is that, yes, Sir Roland is now in the United States."

Jackson looked over at Leaper. "You mentioned in Lisbon something about a 'contact' Sir Roland had in our Senate. . . ."

Before Leaper could reply, Sir Ian said, "Leaper was not more frank with you in Lisbon for a simple reason. He wasn't sure of you yet. He may have mentioned some of the difficulties we're having with your FBI?"

"Yes," said Jackson.

"We are extremely limited in what we can do in this country. The Director resents deeply our presence here in New York. Any actions we may take which seem to him an intrusion on his own territory are bound to have most negative consequences. Not just for ourselves, but for the President. We understand how much he has risked by allowing us to operate in this country."

"Yes, he has," said Jackson.

"The entire operation would be so much easier if you had an intelligence service comparable to our own. One that was distinct from the FBI. But that's neither here nor there. Greville, would you like to finish your briefing on what we know about Plenty for Jackson here?"

"Yes, sir." Leaper rose and walked to the center of the room. "Sir Roland Plenty has an American son-in-law. His name is Anthony Benet. Have you ever heard the name?"

"No," said Jackson. "I don't think so."

"Benet met Sir Roland's daughter while he was on a year's fellowship at All Souls in 1936. Benet himself comes from an old and rich Massachusetts family. Educated at St. Paul's, Harvard, the Harvard Law School. His field is international law. He married Nicola, Sir Roland's daughter, in the spring of 1937. They returned to Boston.

Shortly thereafter, Benet resigned his lectureship at Harvard and went to work in Washington as an aide to one of your senators. A senator with a good deal of foreign-policy responsibility."

"Who?" asked Jackson.

"Senator Borah of Idaho."

"What? Are you saying Plenty's son-in-law was on Senator *Borah's* staff?"

"Exactly. I believe Borah was the chairman of your Senate Foreign Relations Committee?"

"He certainly was," said Jackson. "And one of the most powerful men in Washington before he died." A maverick Republican, Borah might well have been President had he not insisted on fighting the bosses of his party all his life. He'd been one of the founding fathers of the isolationist movement. And Roosevelt's personal nemesis for the past seven years, until Borah had died of a cerebral hemorrhage the previous January. "Did Benet's work take him near the committee?"

"Indeed," said Leaper. "He was hired because of his background in international law."

"This is incredible," said Jackson. "If it's true, it means the Germans had a direct line into the Senate Foreign Relations Committee."

"Benet made two trips to Berlin that we know about," said Sir Ian. "One in 1938 and one in July of last year."

Jackson was on his feet. "You apparently have men in Washington. Is Benet being watched?"

"Oh, yes," said Leaper. "We've had him under surveillance since we heard from Montreal. There's been no sign of Sir Roland."

"We hardly expect a man of Plenty's intelligence to lounge on his son-in-law's doorstep," added Sir Ian. "But I wouldn't be surprised if Benet knows where he is now. It would have been so much better if we could have taken him in Canada."

Jackson nodded, aware that the English would have loved to have arrested Sir Roland on their own ground. Beyond the FBI's reach. "What's Benet doing now that Borah is dead, by the way?" asked Jackson.

"I believe he has gone to work for another senator," said Leaper.

"Who?"

"Senator Wheeler."

"Jesus Christ!" said Jackson, his mind racing ahead. "Sir Roland could be coming over here to deliver the photos to his son-in-law, who works for Wheeler!"

"It is possible," said Leaper.

"Senator Wheeler is making a strong bid for the Democratic nomination. Those photographs would just about guarantee he got it."

"Disturbing," said Sir Ian. "As we have information suggesting your Senator Wheeler is being manipulated by the Abwehr, the Nazi military intelligence group."

"Still," said Leaper, "we have no proof that Benet is acting in league with his father-in-law. He may simply be an American with strong isolationist beliefs . . . and a rather unfortunate choice of in-laws."

"I'll have him immediately checked out," said Jackson. "I still have friends in the Bureau."

"We thought," said Sir Ian, "you might want to have a chat with him. It could prove awkward for one of us, you see."

"I suppose . . . yes, I could talk to him." Jackson was thinking that this was really a job for the Bureau with its machinelike efficiency and unlimited resources. But Roosevelt had been firmly against involving Hoover.

Sir Ian stood up and said, "I don't want to keep you much longer, Jackson. Actually I have a plane to catch this afternoon. But I wanted to make sure you understood the kind of man we're up against. Leaper explained to you what Sir Roland managed to accomplish in England?"

"Yes, I think so."

Sir Ian shook his head. "Blackmail is one of the most odious crimes. Worst of all, the blackmail victim is invariably made to feel as if *he* is the criminal. Sir Roland was a master blackmailer, we now know. So it is not too surprising that suicide frequently creeps up in his past history. Not just Hayward. Even while he was a boy at Eton. One of those older-boys-exploiting-the-juniors-in-the-dormitory type of things. Two boys were sent down. Sir Roland was the prefect on the floor. One of the boys killed himself soon afterwards. And then, much later of course, there is Sir Roland's own daughter."

"His daughter?" asked Jackson.

"Yes, Nicola Plenty Benet. She committed suicide last

summer. They say Benet was completely broken up about it. She'd returned to Oxford after an emotional illness to recuperate in her parents' house. She killed herself there. You might just bear that in mind."

Jackson nodded, wondering where that piece of information would fit into the puzzle which was now scattered all over his mind.

"One final thing," said Sir Ian, reaching into his pocket. "This is a photograph of Sir Roland Plenty which you may keep. On the back I have written his son-in-law's Washington address."

Jackson stared at the photo, at the broad powerful face, the almost invisible eyebrows etched over two deep-set eyes that seemed to dare anyone to meet them. The picture of Sir Roland made an immediate and unpleasant impression on Jackson. In the days to come, he would frequently find that face coming up out of his memory to haunt him. It was a formidable face, an enemy's face.

Sir Ian escorted him to the door. "I'm flying to England for a few days. Not too long, I trust. But please keep Greville informed of any progress you make."

"By all means," said Leaper. "Do keep in touch."

"I'll keep in touch," said Jackson. And this time he meant it.

12

"Lon Chaneys" they had called the disguise artists at the Bureau, although that didn't mean they weren't respected.

Jackson had never been much of a "Lon Chaney" at the FBI. Over the years, he'd limited himself to a small collection of false identity cards which he still kept in a manila envelope in a locked drawer of his desk. The envelope was his equivalent of a shelf in the wardrobe department of a Hollywood studio; those cards were his wigs, false noses, Tudor robes and gorilla suits. One of them proved he was a salesman for one of America's largest insurance companies. Another that he worked for the Internal Revenue Service. A third that he was a member of the Communist party.

The card Jackson removed from his envelope and slipped into his wallet, on the afternoon after his talk at the St. Regis, had been issued by the Boston *Globe*. It listed Jackson's position as "reporter" and bore the raised seal of the state of Massachusetts.

So far his day had led him up a series of blind alleys in pursuit of information about Anthony Benet. In fact, perhaps the only major accomplishment he'd managed yet had nothing at all to do with the illusory son-in-law of Sir Roland Plenty.

Waking on his couch in the rubble of his savaged apartment for the third morning in a row, Jackson had called a domestic agency and arranged for them to send a woman over to clean his place. All their girls were bonded, claimed the voice over the phone. More or less, anyway. It cost six dollars and Jackson guessed the "girl" would be lucky to see two bucks of that after the agency had taken their commission. He'd told them he would leave his key hidden under the milk box. Then he'd driven himself into town, daring to hope that the next few hours would begin to yield some of the answers he desperately needed.

His first move at the office was to call Harry Hopkins and give him a thorough briefing on the St. Regis meeting. As soon as he'd finished, he began to wonder if he'd not made a mistake. Hopkins was stunned, unable to speak at first, and then unable to stop speaking in an alarmed, almost frantic voice of the horrible implications in Jackson's report. "It's like a nightmare come true," he said. "Benet is now working for Wheeler? Oh, my God, didn't I tell you, Jack? Didn't I tell you?"

When Hopkins suggested that Jackson ought to get the FBI onto Benet as soon as possible, Jackson managed to end the phone conversation without committing himself to anything definite.

What about the FBI? Officially, Jackson no longer had any friends there. The Director had declared him persona non grata when he'd "defected" to the White House. Unofficially, there were still men like Orth whom he considered friends but knew he could not really trust anymore. But, friends or no friends, he knew the Bureau was the logical place to go first in any investigation of this kind.

Jackson had not forgotten Roosevelt's remark about having "his man" inside the Bureau: Stan Peddie. He reached for the fat *Directory of Federal Administration Personnel* on his desk and turned to the Bureau's section. Looking down the page, he found it: "PEDDIE, STANLEY J., *Asst. to Dir.: Case Coordn.*" It was a pivotal job, very high up the chain of command. It meant Peddie ought to have full access to most of the files.

Jackson knew the Bureau's number by heart. It took a minute before the switchboard put him through to Peddie's secretary, and another minute before he got the man himself. The FBI official's voice started out friendly but put up a self-protective layer of distance the moment he realized who Jackson was.

"The name is Anthony Benet," he said after Peddie had rather reluctantly agreed to help. "He's currently on the staff of Senator Wheeler. Before that, he was with Borah at the Foreign Relations Committee. We'd like everything and anything."

"You know I'm going to have to check this out with . . . our mutual friend?" said Peddie.

"By all means, sir."

"Okay," said Peddie. "Spell the name for me."

Jackson did so.

"We'll have to see what there is. My access is limited to C files without a prior author. If it's in the P files, I'd have to do some footwork. What's your extension over there?"

Jackson told him. "I appreciate this."

"Sure, but, in future, I'd appreciate it if you called me at home, agreed?"

"Of course," said Jackson.

"I ought to get back to you before lunch. Maybe sooner," said the FBI official.

It was just before noon. There was nothing in either the Criminal or Political files at the Bureau. Peddie said that didn't mean there wasn't a file on Benet. It might be upstairs in D-104, the Director's personal docket. If that was the case, there was nothing Peddie could do. Jackson thanked him and the two men hung up.

At that point, Jackson knew he had no choice but to go outside. The Director wasn't the only man in the District with a private filing system. He took out his address book and looked up the telephone number of Oscar Mikes.

It would cost him something. It always did when you dealt with the crafty Hungarian-born journalist. Mikes put out his own newsletter full of Washington's "inside dope," which was usually a week to a year ahead of what the national syndicates were willing to print. His methods of verification were highly unorthodox. Rather than double- or triple-checking, Mikes went on his instincts. But they were very sharp, honed on a steady supply of information from various disaffected officials or insiders willing to reveal material for a fee, a favor, or, most often, some ulterior political motive of their own.

Jackson wasted the next three hours trying to track Mikes down all over the city. Although his base of operations was an apartment in Silver Spring, just over the District line in Maryland, Mikes did a great deal of old-fashioned legwork. Understandably, since many of his informants were not anxious to be seen entering his apartment. The answering service, of course, had been trained to give out nothing to his callers.

Most of the day was gone and he had nothing to show for it. That was when Jackson unlocked the drawer and reached for his "Lon Chaney" envelope. After mulling it over for ten minutes, he decided there was no other way. He had to go directly to Benet.

Reached at his desk at Senator Wheeler's office, Anthony Benet spoke in a soft, cultivated voice laced with just a hint of English intonation. A certain aloofness disappeared quickly when Benet learned that this was the *Globe* calling him for a personal interview. Boston was Benet's hometown and he even "recalled" seeing Jackson's byline from time to time!

"I was told over in Cambridge that you were one of the three men in Washington I must see," lied Jackson.

"You must be kidding," said Benet, unable to conceal his pleasure. "I thought they'd all written me off since I moved down here to the crude world of politics."

"You'd be surprised," said Jackson.

Benet couldn't resist it. Which made it easy for Jackson to arrange a get-together for five that afternoon. Just a drink and a chance to become acquainted.

"Where are you staying?" Benet asked.

That stopped Jackson for a split second. "Oh, I've shacked up with some of the wife's relatives out in Arlington. Saves the expense money for more important things, you know. Like mortgage payments and shoes for the kids."

Benet laughed. "I know. Don't understand how you newspaper boys do it on your salaries. Why don't you come to my house?" He gave his address. "How about five o'clock, then?"

Jackson assured him five would be just fine. He'd wanted it to be at Benet's house from the start and he was pleased that the possibility of brushing with a brother-in-law in his undershirt and mewling brats at his in-laws' had put Benet right where he wanted him.

Georgetown wasn't a particularly fashionable address for Washington in 1940, although more and more people were beginning to move back into the old houses, some of which dated back to pre-Revolutionary days. Jackson parked at the bottom of the hill. Benet lived on Thirty-first Street. And Jackson was curious if he could spot the British stake-out around Benet's house as easily as he'd seen the tan DeSoto the other morning.

Yes, sure enough, there they were. A black Plymouth

sedan this time. Two of them in the front seat. No trilby
hats. They were parked on his side of the street and Jackson had to pass them as he walked up. He restrained an
urge to say something clever like, "Cheerio, mates, you're
as obvious as two tits on a bull." Both wore light summer
suits. One of them, on the curb side, had his arm dangling
out the window with a cigarette burning between two
henna-colored fingers.

But what was this? Double coverage? Only half a block
beyond, Jackson saw his old friend the tan DeSoto. It was
parked on the opposite side of the street, pointed uphill
like the Plymouth. Two men in the front seat. One of
them wearing a trilby. They paid no attention to him.
Both were gazing at a house four doors farther on. From
the numbers, Jackson calculated that it must be Benet's
house. Of course he didn't need the numbers to tell him
that.

One carload was a shadow. But two carloads was more
like an audience. Jackson began to feel the queasy beginnings of stagefright as he thought about walking up the
steps and ringing Benet's doorbell.

The house had been attractively renovated, with a good
deal of money obviously spent. The bricks were painted a
soft cocoa shade of brown. The wooden trim a glossy
black enamel. You had to walk up three steps from the
sidewalk to the yard. The front door had been painted a
bright fire-engine red and the bell was set into a highly polished brass plate. "Benet" was etched onto this plate in a
dignified script, the kind you'd expect to find on a wedding
invitation.

As soon as Benet opened the door, Jackson had an ink-
ling of how difficult it was going to be. The voice on the
phone had misled him. He was prepared to meet someone
he was sure he would dislike. Someone, he'd assumed,
whom he would be able to open up and read like a book.

"Hi," said Anthony Benet. "Christ, you're right on
time. I only just got back. Come into the living room
while I see if I remembered to fill the ice tray."

Of average height, slender, with brown hair parted on
the left above a noticeably handsome face, Benet looked
like an honest man. As ridiculous as that might be, there
was the Oscar Mikes in Jackson. He rarely made snap
judgments about other people. He'd been around too long

for that. But when they did come, he always found he had a hell of a time shaking them off. Benet looked like an honest man.

Now, what did that mean? That he could have posed for an advertisement for "Your Friendly Banker"? He could have. Did it mean that he looked intelligent, unpretentious, and basically straight? Like he'd just stepped out of a shell after rowing for two hours up and down the Charles River? Like he was kind to animals, an efficient employee, enjoyed softball games on Sundays and clams on the half shell? What the hell did it mean?

Jackson sat down in the narrow living room and made up his mind to be tough. The room was furnished with some style, neither antique nor modern, but very livable. The couch and two armchairs were covered in turquoise hopsacking. There was an attractive fireplace and the carpet was charcoal gray. Above the fireplace hung an oil portrait of a very young, very beautiful woman.

For once, thought Jackson, here was a profile that deserved to be described as "classic." She had long golden hair and extraordinary sapphire blue eyes, a proud forehead, a mouth that was ripe and full. If that was Nicola Plenty Benet, then Jackson had already answered one question.

Benet reappeared and caught Jackson admiring the portrait. He looked away quickly. That was odd, thought Jackson. Almost as if he didn't want to be reminded it was hanging there. Why put it up in the first place? And in the most commanding position in the room?

They had scotch, bourbon or gin, said Benet. Jackson said bourbon would be fine, with ice. If there was ice. There was ice.

When they'd finally sat down facing one another, drinks in hand, and begun to talk, Jackson found himself at a loss as to how to break through the wall. The wall he had himself built with his phoney story about writing a piece on the last ten years of American foreign policy.

Telling himself to be tough was one thing. He'd walked into this meeting with Benet armed only with the most circumstantial evidence. If Benet was in touch with Sir Roland, Jackson certainly didn't want to tip their hand this early. Or else, he wouldn't have bothered with the bogus newspaperman cover story. And he soon began to wonder if the subject he'd chosen hadn't been too clever by half. Benet had done a great deal of thinking on recent American foreign policy and welcomed this chance to let fly his conclusions.

"To me, the whole key to this decade's foreign policy is really to be found ten years earlier, back in 1920," he said. "I'm referring to Congress's rejection of Wilson's bid to take us into the League of Nations. That decision, by Congress, has really set the tenor of every major foreign-policy decision we've fought ever since."

"I'd agree with you on that," said Jackson. "And I had, of course, planned on mentioning it at the beginning of my piece."

"Are you going to follow a fairly strict chronological line in your article?" asked Benet.

"Well, sir, it is a newspaper and we have to make things clear for our readership. Yes, I had planned on that."

"Because early in this decade is a kind of foreign-policy desert, apart from our recognition of Soviet Russia. That was in thirty-three. Now, in thirty-five you've got the original Neutrality Act being passed. Then, in thirty-six we had that naval pact with Britain and France which was the start of our troubles. Then the fight over the Spanish Civil War. And so on, with most of it being our reactions to events that were generated overseas. Thank God. You mentioned Senator Borah over the phone?"

"Yes," said Jackson. "I plan on developing his work at the Foreign Relations Committee into a large part of the article."

"Very, very good. I was with him only the last few years, of course. And privileged to have spent any time at all in association with him. Certainly one of the great senators of all time. We all miss him so much."

"How would you compare him to your new boss? To Senator Wheeler? In foreign policy, that is."

"I wouldn't even begin to try. Although their states happen to adjoin physically, Idaho and Montana you know, they're two very different kinds of men. Both did share a strong isolationist philosophy. As I do myself. I suppose I've been more influenced by Borah. Up to a certain point."

"Oh? What point would that be?" asked Jackson.

"Senator Borah loved this country so much, he came to

regard it almost as a kind of Promised Land. He so much believed in the basic decency and strength of America that he was afraid every time we became too involved with another nation, we were in danger of being corrupted. Almost as if America's greatness could be stolen away or could somehow rub off. I don't go that far myself. I believe America is strong enough to engage in an international dialogue without risking its virtue every time we sit down and talk to another nation. So long as the dialogue is carried out in peace, according to the strictures of international law."

"One thing that interests me," said Jackson. "Speaking of international law, how does the isolationist movement feel about Germany's violation of several major treaties and international agreements? I don't mean to press you, but I rarely hear the isolationists complaining about the German violations."

Benet gave him a searching look. "Well, I suppose there isn't enough said about it, no. But look, Mr. Jackson, Europe is in a turmoil of its own making right now. Many treaties have been broken. There has been aggression. But the isolationists aren't setting themselves up as international judges. All we're doing is trying to keep America from compounding the mistakes, multiplying the bloodshed, and butting into a mess in Europe which really has nothing to do with us."

Jackson could have disputed that opinion until he was red in the face, but he'd already pushed it far enough. "I suppose you're right," he said. "Tell me, are you helping Senator Wheeler with his campaign?"

"I beg your pardon. Senator Wheeler hasn't been nominated yet, so there's really no campaign."

"Perhaps not, but certainly it's no secret that he's trying hard for the nomination."

"I'm not a politician, Mr. Jackson. I'm a policy adviser, specifically foreign policy. As far as Senator Wheeler needs my advice on foreign affairs for his present political aspirations, that's how far I'm helping him."

Benet was becoming defensive but Jackson thought he would try just a bit further. "And how far is that?"

"From time to time, I help the Senator on political speeches when there is a definite foreign-policy message in the text. That's about it." He stared at Jackson coldly.

"Well, let's get back to Senator Borah. I understand you did some traveling as his envoy." He eased into a reassuring smile. "That must have been fascinating."

Was that a dark cloud descending behind Benet's eyes? "I did some traveling for the Senator, yes. And it was enlightening. Very enlightening indeed."

"Yes?"

"Yes. I learned a great deal on those trips, including a lot about myself I may add. Of course travel is always enlightening and . . ." He didn't finish, suddenly confused. Jackson had seemed to strike paydirt there. Whatever Benet had learned about on those trips, it hadn't apparently been all that pleasant.

Benet insisted then on veering back onto the straight and narrow, and boring, path of Jackson's topic. It wasn't all that boring, perhaps, and it certainly wasn't uninformed, but it sure as hell wasn't what he'd come for.

Not until forty-five minutes had passed could he steer Benet back onto the terrain where the stalking could begin again.

"I notice a slight English accent in your voice," said Jackson, interrupting a discourse on Borah's Polish position. "Is one of your parents English by any chance?"

"No." Benet fixed him with a curious stare. "I spent some time in England. But only a year. No one has ever told me that before."

"Oh, well," said Jackson. "But I really detect a bit of that accent. What were you doing in England for a year? That must have been fascinating too."

Benet sensed the irony in Jackson's question, but it merely confused him. He started to explain about his fellowship at Oxford and then Jackson had a sudden insight into the man.

Benet was locked tight. He was one of those men who held their emotions inside them as if in an iron vault. There was pressure in there, immense pressure. Jackson could almost see it, as if it were bulging out the sides. Yet on the surface Benet liked to cruise along as cool and calm as if he were on ice skates . . . as if he had nothing to worry about. Yet these questions were clearly putting him under great strain. It shone through his eyes, all that repression of . . . of what?

"My tutor was E. S. Robel. Have you heard of him?" asked Benet.

"I'm afraid not."

"*The* expert on Anglo-French relations. Incredible scholar and a wonderful character. You ought to read his books."

"Any one in particular?"

"*The Lifting of the Darkness*, try that first. It begins with the Norman invasions."

"I'll look for it," said Jackson. He leaned back on the couch as Benet glanced at his watch. Although it was now past seven o'clock, it was still daylight. The sun was falling through the windows in shafts of orange and red. "She's very beautiful," said Jackson.

Benet looked up sharply. "Excuse me?"

"Her."

He followed Jackson's eyes up to the portrait, then quickly took them away. "Yes." That was all he said.

"Do you live here alone?"

"Yes, I do. My wife died last summer. That is her portrait."

"I didn't realize. I'm sorry."

Benet accepted the apology for what it was, a polite gesture. There was a long silence during which Jackson kept thinking he'd made a mistake in coming here. All he could think of now were the crude, knockout questions. The ones which would get him si. nce and then a fast shuffle to the door.

"Do you think this chat has helped you at all?" asked Benet.

"Oh, definitely. You've been a great help," lied Jackson.

"I'm glad." Benet stood abruptly to his feet. There was no ambiguity; he was telling Jackson to get out.

"Let me give you a telephone number," said Jackson. "My brother-in-law's place out in Arlington. Call me if you think of anyone else I ought to talk to."

Benet found a piece of scrap paper and watched with slight interest as Jackson scribbled down the number. "I might be away for a few days," he said suddenly.

"Oh? This week?" asked Jackson.

"I'm not sure yet. Perhaps. How long will you be in town?"

"Another week at least."

"Well, I'm glad I seem to have been of some help. I don't really know how." He escorted Jackson to the front door, looking very tense.

Benet tried to force a smile onto his face, but it couldn't get past that look of utter confusion in his eyes. In the end, it came out more of a grimace. "Good-bye then, Mr. Jackson."

The door closed quickly behind him. Across the street, the tan DeSoto was parked in the same spot. Jackson looked for the black Plymouth but it was too far down the hill. He began walking back down to his own car.

Anthony Benet might be an honest man. But somewhere in his life was at least one big lie. Perhaps it was only that slight affectation of Oxford in his voice. Or perhaps it had happened on one of his trips, the trips he'd claimed were so "enlightening." Or, and Jackson wondered, perhaps it was hanging over the fireplace in that portrait.

Halfway down the hill, he saw the black Plymouth. The door opened on the curb side as he approached. Out came the man with the henna-colored fingers holding a camera. Balancing it on top of the doorframe, before Jackson could react, the man snapped his picture. He ducked back into the car and slammed the door.

They passed Jackson, fishtailing up the steep hill in second gear, the driver's foot right down to the floor.

Maybe he *was* the Lincoln Memorial.

13

Jackson drove back across the Potomac to Arlington, checking his rearview mirror every few minutes. Traffic was sparse. He was certain he wasn't being followed.

When he turned into his driveway on Woodlawn, he was surprised to see the lights burning downstairs. Considering her track record over the past few nights, he'd been sure Rona would be out Friday night until the small hours of the morning. He wondered if she was entertaining her boyfriend at home for a change. Hell, that was none of his business.

He put the Ford in the garage, closed the doors and locked them with the rusted Yale padlock.

If it hadn't been so late when he left Benet's house, he would have driven up to Silver Spring and tried knocking on Mikes's door. Not that the Hungarian would have minded if you turned up at his house at four o'clock in the morning, so long as you had something choice for him. Something so "hot" it couldn't wait until the light of day. But Jackson had no information to give. Correction, none that he was willing to give. Any approach to Mikes would therefore have to wait until normal business hours.

He snapped on the light in his living room. At once his mood began to lift. A six-dollar miracle. He closed the door, turned around 360 degrees, and walked out to inspect the kitchen. Yes, there too. It wasn't just that the apartment had been put back in order. This was better than it had ever looked. Jackson wasn't exactly the world's most conscientious housekeeper. He'd never seen the rugs looking so clean, the sink so spotless, the bed so incredibly "made." Gone was all the wreckage in the kitchen, the glass in the bath. Six bucks? From now on, those six bucks were going straight to the Walters Domestic Bureau every week.

116

He switched on the radio in the bedroom and found some opera up near the high end of the frequency band. Then he stripped off his clothes, tossing them haphazardly into a heap on the floor. Fresh towels had been laid out in the bathroom. He turned on the water, adjusted it until it was hot enough to scald, and stepped into the shower. He had rinsed his hair, was humming along with *Figaro* on the radio, when he heard the knock.

Cursing, he stopped out onto the slick tiles, grabbed a towel and made a quick pass at his face, then draped it around his waist and emerged into the sudden, comparative coolness of the hall. There was nothing better on a hot, muggy night than a hot shower.

"Who is it?"

"Rona."

He made sure the towel was in place, then opened the door with his free hand.

She took him in, from his face to his bare toes. "First I wake you up. Then I get you out of your bath. You must really love having me around," she said in embarrassment.

"Nonsense," said Jackson. "My shower was finished. What's up? I mean, what can I do for you?"

"Nothing at all, I'm afraid. This was supposed to be . . . well, a social visit. I heard you come in and saw you were alone. Hope you don't think I'm spying or . . ."

"Of course not! Come inside. I'll just be a second, then we can have a drink." He moved aside, made encouraging motions with his head until she'd entered. "Have a seat. I'll throw on some clothes."

The wet towel and the clothes he'd been wearing were quickly dumped on the floor of the closet. The way he was going, the six-dollar miracle wasn't destined to last very long.

When he reappeared in the doorway of the living room, he was wearing an old pair of lightweight slacks and a blue-and-white-plaid summer shirt, no socks and his worn-out moccasins. He'd combed his hair back, still slick from the shower, and his cheeks had a ruddy glow that gave him the illusion of well-rested good health.

"*You* look cool," she said from the couch. "I was just reading this." She held up a small sheet of paper that had been torn out of a pad Jackson kept beside his telephone. "You seem to be having some domestic problems."

"What's that?"

"It was just here," she said, nodding at the coffee table.

He took the paper from her and read, in clumsy block capitals:

DEAR MR. JACKSON,

    IT TOOK ME NEAR SEVEN HOURS TO CLEAN YOUR HOUSE. NEVER SEEN SUCH MESSY HOUSE IN TWELVE YEARS WORKING. IT COST SIX DOLLAR FOR 5 HOURS NORMAL BUT I DON'T SAY NOTHING TO WALTERS THIS TIME. NEXT TIME HOUSE SO BAD COST FOUR DOLLAR EXTRA. UNLESS YOU WANT CALL ME PRIVATE. CALL KL-5-4853 AND ASK FOR RUTH. AFTER SIX.

The signature was "Ruth Maben." He folded the paper and tucked it away in his shirt pocket.

"I had her in today to clean up after the break-in."

"You mean you don't normally have a maid? Or you don't normally live in such a messy house?"

"Both, I guess. Although I'm not the neatest person in the world," he said. "What would you like to drink? Actually, we've a limited selection at the moment. Some bourbon and I thought I saw a little scotch out there. Oh, yes, and some gin."

"What is bourbon like?" asked Rona.

"You mean you've never tasted bourbon?" he said in mock astonishment.

"I'm not a big drinker. I think you could count the times I've had hard liquor on one hand. Sometimes I do drink a sherry, though."

"Sorry, we're all out of sherry," he said. "Let me mix you a very light bourbon with lots of ice. I think you'll like it. It's kind of sweet, in a way. Sort of like cornbread or . . ."

She grimaced. "Sweet cornbread? You pour it and I'll try it, but no more descriptions, please."

He left for the kitchen, wondering if charm was like calculus. Did you lose your talent for it if you didn't keep in practice? Relax, he told himself. After all, she was the one who came upstairs.

In the two years since Barbara had walked out on him, Jackson had spent about as many romantic evenings as Rona had consumed stiff drinks in her lifetime. At first he'd been far too self-absorbed in the loss and the hurt to even think of going out. Gradually that wore off, but it was difficult to go back and begin all over again as if he hadn't been married, as if Margaret hadn't been born. No, with women Jackson had usually depended more on luck than charm. In his job, he could lose himself completely, and be just as tough and aggressive as the situation demanded. But with women he tended to play things for laughs rather than the stronger, more serious emotions.

Yet Jackson was no good at kidding himself. He needed a woman badly. Not just the physical part, although that was definitely there. But in every department of his frenetic, unorganized life, the absence of a woman was slowly but surely doing him in. Yet even if his job didn't demand so many hours of his time, he doubted he could bring himself to prowling the social circuit of Washington in search of a partner like so many other younger, newer men. He spent enough time in his job as one kind of hunter. It couldn't be like that with women: he refused to let it be.

After he brought their drinks back into the living room, he took the chair opposite where Rona sat on the couch. "How did it go this morning?" he asked. "With the quotas?"

She ran her finger down the side of the glass and took a trial sip. When she'd swallowed, she said, all seriousness, "You were right. It *is* sort of sweet. This morning went badly. Just as I expected."

"Sorry to hear that. What happened?"

"There just doesn't seem to be any hope of getting Congress to lift the quotas, or even to enlarge them. But we may get one concession."

"And what's that?"

"The quotas are supposed to function on a monthly basis: so many immigrants from each country allowed entry visas each month," she said. "But they're now talking of suspending the monthly requirement. We could use up the entire annual quota right now, when it's desperately needed. There's not much time left. And there's a terrible transportation problem."

"The blockade," said Jackson.

"Yes, the blockade makes it even worse." She looked at him. "How was your day? I hope it was better than mine."

"My day isn't worth talking about."

"Why?"

"It's a long story."

"You've just contradicted yourself, Mr. Jackson. Why don't you tell me? Seriously, I'm interested in what you do over at the White House."

"Frankly, my day was pretty disappointing, and so, I guess, I'm reluctant to talk about it."

"Was it what you called 'security work' the other morning? Aren't you allowed to talk about it?" she asked.

"Yes and no. In a nutshell, I spent the day trying to obtain some information. But without much success. And then I guess that's partly my fault. I had to interview someone, and instead of being prepared, I walked in cold and made a fool of myself. Actually, the last couple of hours of my day were rather strange."

"Why? How strange were they?"

He laughed at her persistence. "Strange."

She was so beautiful. It was her eyes, he decided. Dark, with flecks of smoky gray in the iris, there seemed no limit to the emotions they could express. Her beauty was nocturnal, the way he'd first seen her on the stairs in the rain. Tonight her hair spread out on her shoulders in a mantle of soft, black silk. She wore no lipstick. Her lips were naturally dark, etched above, a full bow beneath: a sensual mouth which, perhaps, had not yet discovered itself.

"You make it sound dangerous," she said.

"It wasn't dangerous, just strange."

"And you're not going to talk about it, I can see."

He shook his head. "Not tonight. Have you and Millie been friends for a long time?"

"Oh, no. We're not really close friends. I only know her from the office. She heard me complaining about the painters in my apartment and my allergy and offered to let me use her place while she was away. She said she didn't want any money but, of course, I'm going to give her something."

"Where do you live when it's not full of painters?"

"Here, in Arlington. On Cedar Lane. It's just two rooms. Millie said you'd only recently divided this house. Did you have the whole thing to yourself before?"

"Yes, when I was still married." That's what she'd been

looking for; he might as well make it easy. "Did Millie tell you I'd been married?"

She blushed. "As a matter of fact, Millie did mention it, yes."

"I suppose you're curious what happened?"

"Oh, no!" she said. "I wouldn't dream of asking you that. It's none of my business."

"What about you?"

"Do you mean have I ever been married?" She laughed at the idea. "I'm afraid not. I was engaged once, though." The memory of that made her laugh again.

"Was it that funny?"

"Yes, it was. You see, my parents are very old-fashioned, orthodox people. And the world I grew up in was a little like a small village plunked down in the middle of New York City. They were not exactly happy when I told them I was going to college. You see, when a girl gets to be about eighteen where my parents grew up, she's already in danger of becoming an old maid. But I did go to college and they didn't make too much of a fuss. It was when I told them I was planning on going to graduate school that they really hit the roof.

"I used to work in a drugstore on Second Avenue every summer. Well, during the last summer before my senior year at City College, my parents arranged a marriage for me."

Jackson raised his eyebrows.

"Yes, it's true. He was the son of the butcher whose shop was across the street from my father's shop. I suppose he was a nice boy. He'd fallen in love with me and his father had gone to speak to my father. They were also very orthodox Jews. They'd come from Silesia. My parents are from eastern Romania, near the Black Sea. The boy's name was Jacob. He was kind of skinny and nervous, sweet really. His father was a butcher, so he was going to be a butcher. Maybe he was bright, but I don't think he had enough strength to ever break with his parents. We had one dinner with both families. A formal announcement, toasts, and all those nervous stares across the room. Two days later I realized I could never go through with it and ran away to a girlfriend's house in Brooklyn. I got another job and I stayed away all summer. In the fall, I went back to City and, of course, my father came up to find me on the first day. He looked so heartbroken, yet he was so incredibly stubborn. He said I would be forgiven, could come back to live with them, just so long as I was ready to marry the boy. Marry him in three weeks' time.

"I told my father I would never marry Jacob. I was going to finish City, go on to graduate school, and I had kept my summer job working for Bell Telephone. He begged me to speak to my mother. But when I did, and she couldn't change my mind, that was the end. I haven't seen my father in eight years. My mother I visit about three or four times a year. Although she's practically risking her life when she sneaks out of the house to meet with me. To my father, I'm dead. He even held a funeral for me."

There was a long silence. Then Jackson said, "And that's funny?"

"I know it sounds sad to you. And it probably is sad. I cried my share of tears. But not for a long time. When I think about it now, I think about what I'd be like as Jacob the butcher's wife. I'd have three or four kids and be sneaking out to the library to borrow books my husband couldn't begin to understand. His mother would live upstairs and constantly be complaining about the way I kept the house, the way I raised the kids, the way I looked after her son. I also think about my father sitting there with that black band on his sleeve, mourning me, while I was just a mile away! Working my brains out to keep my grade average up, to get the scholarship I wanted, to do all the studying I had to do plus hold down a full-time job. So part of it is sad, part of it makes me angry, but I choose to regard it all as if it's funny. And it *was* worth it. I have no doubts, no second guesses. It just occurred to me that perhaps you're a little shocked by this? You wouldn't be the first man."

"If I'm shocked," said Jackson, "it's only because it seems like a miracle you've made it this far."

"Why? Because I'm a woman?"

"No. Because you're not filled with self-pity."

"Self-pity?" she cried. "Why on earth would I pity myself? I have a wonderful life. When I look at the Jews in Europe, the refugees, all the victims, I know that at least I have an opportunity to try to help them. How very lucky I am! Not just because I'm a Jew who happens to live in America. It's not so easy to be a Jew in America either.

Look at what they call Roosevelt when they really want to curse him: 'Jew-lover.' Do you know how that sounds to someone like me? You're wrong. I *am* bitter. I'm bitter about that."

He nodded, searching for the right words. "It's difficult . . . for me to say anything. Anything I could say would sound cheap, too easy."

"You could tell me about your Jewish friend in college," she said with a scathing edge in her voice. "Or about how much you enjoy reading the Old Testament. Believe it or not, I once heard that."

"See what I mean?" he said.

"Yes. And I know I'm not being fair. Don't think I'm always like this. It's just lately. I'm sorry. Here I am for a so-called 'social visit' and I'm throwing anti-Semitism in your face. The State Department is a funny place. I don't exactly fit in too well with the Brooks Brothers crowd and the old-boy network which can trace itself back to John Adams and Elihu Root. The strange thing is, there's a rumor going around town that the Secretary of State is a terrible anti-Semite. But it was Cordell Hull who appointed me to the job I have now, and despite a lot of opposition. Not very diplomatic of him, was it?"

"Maybe not," said Jackson. "But obviously a wise and well-considered choice."

Suddenly she frowned. "I've been talking too much, I know. You've hardly said a word."

"Haven't I? I thought I'd been doing my share."

"Not at all. What do you have to say for yourself, Mr. Jackson?" She leaned back on the couch, far more relaxed now. Perhaps the bourbon had something to do with it.

"I say this," said Jackson. "Tomorrow is Saturday. Why don't you and I plan on spending it together?"

She closed her eyes, then opened them with a serious expression. "Tomorrow I'm going to be at the office. I would have been there tonight, except they have a stupid rule about forcing everybody out on Friday nights so they can mop the floors. Do you know how many cases, letters and cables I have to read? Thousands and thousands. All of them urgent. Tomorrow I've got to work."

"And Sunday?"

"Ah, Sunday. The official sabbath of the federal government. Sunday the office is locked. But I'll be bringing home tons of work."

"Look, I know every one of those cases is desperate," said Jackson. "And I know you won't like me saying this, but I think you ought to spend Sunday with me. How many of those people will you help by working yourself to death? You're not the only person in Washington who thinks that he can work twenty hours a day, seven days a week. And, excuse me, but you wouldn't be the first person to get seriously ill trying to do so. Enough sermon. Now, you might not believe this, but I happen to own a yacht. It's a little over fourteen feet long. It has one sail. And if there's a good wind, it'll do about four knots. I keep it at Colonial Beach down on the Potomac. You could bring your work along. I don't need a crew. All I need is a pretty audience."

"What's a knot?" she asked. It wasn't "no," and she seemed to be seriously considering the idea.

"A knot is one nautical mile per hour. If we went down early, we could cross over to Leonardtown, have lunch at the Waterman's Inn."

"And you're only suggesting this because of your concern about my imminent death from overwork, is that it?"

"Of course. Why else would—"

The phone rang, cutting him off.

She motioned at the door. "Should I leave you alone to talk?"

."Don't be silly." It rang a second time. "I have no idea who it could be."

It was only two steps from the chair to the phone. "Hello?" he said, while looking at his watch.

"Hello, Jackson. Leaper here." The line from New York was full of static but the Englishman's voice had no trouble getting through.

"Hello, Leaper. What can I do for you this evening? Or is it morning?"

"Sorry about the hour, old man. I understand you had a tête-à-tête with our friend Benet this evening."

"The fellows called you up with that information, did they?"

"Naturally. I don't expect a report at this hour. Unless Benet happened to mention where he was going tonight.

The fellows, as you call them, assumed he was on the plane to New York."

"Hold it, Leaper. Start from the beginning."

"After you left his house—about fifty minutes after, to be exact—Benet came out and got into a taxi. Our men followed him to the airport at a discreet distance. He bought a one-way ticket to New York. They followed him to the departure gate. At nine o'clock Benet boarded American's flight 115 to New York. At that point they rang me. I sent two other men to the airport to await his arrival. The plane landed twenty minutes ago. Benet was not aboard. That's why I'm calling. He seems to have either exited somewhere ten thousand feet over the Atlantic or, perhaps, pulled a swizzle back at the airport in Washington."

"They're sure he didn't get off in New York? They could have missed him in the crowd."

"I don't think so. No one remotely like his description left the plane. Now, did Benet mention a trip to New York while you were with him this evening?"

"All he said was that he might be leaving town for a few days. I had the impression it wouldn't be as soon as tonight. You think they screwed up in Washington?"

"I'm afraid so," said the Englishman.

Jackson glanced across the room at Rona. She was watching his face with fascination, taking in every word.

"You're probably right. I'll look into it myself."

"I was hoping you would. Rather embarrassing to lose Benet just now. I don't know what Sir Ian will say."

"That's your problem, Leaper. And the problem of your men here in Washington. They sound like they could take a few lessons in subtlety from the Marx Brothers. By the way, is one of your fellows a camera nut? Did he decide to take a snapshot of me for his scrapbook this afternoon?"

"Sorry? What do you mean?"

"Somebody took a photograph of me outside Benet's house when I left. Was it one of your clowns?"

"I'd hardly think so. Certainly not on my orders."

"Well, you might have a word with your men, Leaper. Try 'incompetent' for a start. Also you might tell them to find a new car for their operations. That tan DeSoto is about as subtle as a hook-and-ladder truck."

"Jackson, you will call me if you find—"

"I'll call you, Leaper. Don't worry about that." He slammed down the phone, then cursed himself for losing his temper in front of her.

She was already on her feet.

"Where are you going?" he asked.

"Downstairs. I told you about tomorrow. Have to be up bright and early."

"Did I frighten you away?"

She stared at him with obvious amusement. "It would take more than that to frighten me, Jack." It was the first time she'd used his name.

"And Sunday?"

"Let me think about Sunday," she said.

He opened the door for her and she stepped out onto the wooden landing, turned and started to thank him.

"Think about it right now," he insisted. "Come on, I'll give you ten seconds."

"Thank you very much for putting up with me. And for your introduction to bourbon." She put forward her right hand.

"Six, seven, almost eight seconds used up . . ."

"You're awful! How am I supposed to keep you hanging on all day waiting for my decision?" she asked.

"I don't know. Nine . . . ten . . . time's up!"

For a moment he thought she was going to say no. The pushing wasn't like him. But Leaper's call, the news of Benet's flight, had thrown him off balance. Then her face shed its forced composure, her eyes closed for a second, and she said, "I won't be any fun. I'll bring armloads of work, ask you dozens of questions like 'What are knots?' You'll wish you'd never asked me. But I'll go on Sunday."

It was very close, it could have ruined everything, but in the end he resisted the urge to reach out and hug her. Instead, in his sober, experienced man-of-the-sea voice he said, "I don't think you're going to regret this."

An hour later, alone in his bed, Jackson could still hear the sound of her laughter.

14

National Airport occupies what was once a marsh on the Virginia bank of the Potomac. Jackson flashed his White House ID at the uniformed cop at the gate. He was directed to a special parking lot near the arrivals end of the terminal building, reserved for airport officials and government VIPs.

It was a few minutes before nine o'clock when he found his way to American's office on the concourse level. The door was locked and his knocking brought no response.

It wasn't until 9:10 A.M. that a young man with blood-shot eyes and several shaving nicks on his face arrived to open up. The lights took a while to decide to function and the young man muttered "coffee" under his breath, leaving Jackson to admire a view of concrete-block wall.

The coffeepot was on an electric ring inside the closet where the office supplies were kept. Jackson watched over the young man's shoulder as he measured out four shaky spoonfuls, then made a quick run out to the water cooler. While he was gone, a woman walked into the office. In her mid-forties with bleached blond hair and a pair of huge sunglasses perched on her nose like a black butterfly about to take flight, she gave Jackson a cursory glance, then disappeared into the storage closet. The young man returned balancing his pot of water.

" 'Morning, Doris," he said.

"Don't 'morning' me. I feel like you look. God, I hate Saturday mornings. Hurry up with the java, Neal."

"Coming right up."

"Who's that outside?" she asked.

"Don't know."

"You didn't ask him?"

"Just got here, Doris, for Pete's sake. You ask him."

She came out and gave Jackson a severe look. "Can I help you?"

"I hope so." He'd been holding his wallet in his right hand behind his back. Now he produced it, letting it fall open to his White House identification. Doris bent forward, lifted the butterfly sunglasses, and suddenly snapped to attention.

After that, things went very smoothly. As soon as he'd outlined the problem to them, they flew into action. Jackson was given a seat and a cup of coffee.

Exhibit number one was the passenger manifest for Friday's flight 115 to New York City. Down near the bottom, Anthony Benet's name was clearly listed with a notation on the seat number: 16-C. But someone had drawn a pencil line through the name. Neither Doris nor Neal had a ready explanation for what that might mean.

Nothing to worry about, Doris assured him. It was only a matter of a phone call. While she was busy looking up the home number of the supervisor who'd been on duty the previous evening, Jackson asked Neal if he could have a complete list of all the commercial flights that had departed from National on Friday night.

Neal left to get this information from the girls at the central information desk. While he was gone, Doris reached the supervisor. She told him that an "official from the White House" was making inquiries about a passenger named Benet. They'd found his name on the 115 manifest, but somebody had crossed it out. What did it mean? She listened for about three minutes, thanked the man, and hung up.

"He says it caused quite a stir. Benet got on the aircraft, all right. But at the last minute he told the stewardess he'd forgotten something and ran off the plane. Once the doors are closed, it's usually too late. In this case, they let him off. The flight left a couple of minutes late due to the confusion. Without Benet."

"Thanks a lot. So now we know what the pencil line means," said Jackson.

He waited another ten minutes until the young man returned with the Friday schedule.

Jackson quickly flipped to the second page and began where it read "21:00 EST."

The American flight to New York left at 21:15. The

next flight was Trans World Airlines to Los Angeles at 21:25, followed by a United flight to Chicago at 21:30. There were four more flights listed with departures before midnight Friday. Including another to New York at 22:00 and one to Boston a few minutes later. That made six possible airplanes Benet could have boarded after he ran off flight 115. He thanked Doris and Neal, said that somebody would probably be back in touch with them, and left the office.

On the main floor, Jackson found a phone booth and dialed long distance. "That's right, operator, I want this both person-to-person and reverse the charges."

When he finally got through to Leaper, he told him what little he'd learned. Now it was going to be a simple matter of legwork, questioning the various airline personnel at the gates where planes left after 9:15 P.M. on Friday and showing them Benet's picture in case he'd used a false name.

Leaper assured him that his men would get right on the job, and that they'd been suitably chastened for their slipup the previous evening. Jackson dictated the numbers and departure times of the six possible flights. "With any luck," he said, "your men should know where Benet went by midafternoon."

Leaper agreed and they hung up. Jackson dropped another coin in the pay phone, got a different long-distance operator, and gave her the Silver Spring numbers. Person-to-person again, but this time Jackson would pay.

Oscar Mikes had a very soft, unflappable phone manner which went along with his job. If Joseph Stalin had called him up direct from the Kremlin and said he had some off-the-record information he'd like to pass along, Mikes would have taken it with the same serene composure that greeted any other caller. Like a fisherman, first he had to get you on the line and delicately set the hook. Later, very slowly, he'd reel you into range, where, suddenly, he'd stick in the gaff.

It had been over a year since they'd last spoken. Mikes acted as if it had only been yesterday. Jackson wondered if he could stop by for a little talk in, say, forty-five minutes? But of course, said Mikes. Did he even have to ask?

The quickest route to Silver Spring was back across the

Arlington Memorial Bridge, right through the center of downtown Washington, then out Fourth Street through the northwestern section of the District. Traffic had picked up. The suburbs were rushing into town to do their Saturday-morning shopping. It took Jackson longer than he'd expected, almost an hour, before he pulled into a parking space outside Mikes's building.

There was a doorman to screen visitors, one of the chief reasons Mikes had chosen the place. When Jackson told him where he was going, the doorman nodded and said, "Apartment Six. Go right up, sir. You're expected."

The dogs began to bark even before he'd hit the bell. A moment later, he heard Mikes calling them in Hungarian, then the sound of a bolt being thrown and the door opened.

A wiry little man in his early sixties, Mikes had each German shepherd by the collar before Jackson got his foot inside. They were enormous dogs, a matched pair with black and silver coats. Rows of sharp white incisors were displayed for Jackson's benefit while the dogs made that ominous gnarr deep in their throats.

Knowing the routine, Jackson bent low and gave each brute a nice long sniff of the back of his hand while Mikes said incomprehensible but apparently complimentary words of introduction. Suddenly the growls ceased and the heavy tails began to thump.

"How are you, Jack?"

"Not bad, Oscar. And yourself?"

The little man made an enigmatic gesture. "Not so bad, not so good. In other words, Jack, much the same. Perhaps a little older. Perhaps a little weaker in the . . ." He patted his stomach. "But up here"—his finger touched his temple—"I think perhaps just a little more wise."

This too was standard routine with Mikes, and Jackson played along. "You live and learn, is that it, Oscar?"

"Never enough to make a perfect wisdom perhaps. But if you live you must learn. Come into the other room, Jack. I have something for you."

It would have been a spacious apartment if it wasn't crammed from wall to wall with the cheap cardboard file boxes in which Mikes stored his life's work. In those boxes was a vast reservoir of data: incriminating secrets and innocent statistics, hard facts and dubious rumors, worthless gossip and highly valuable intelligence. Taken as a whole, it added up to a vivid picture of Washington, D.C., over the past thirty years. Not the kind of picture you'd find on a postcard; more like the kind they took in a hospital casualty ward. An X ray of the official corpus.

It occurred to Jackson that what motivated Oscar Mikes was not too far removed from whatever it was that compelled some men to collect old bits of string until they'd rolled up a ball of the stuff which weighed six hundred pounds and could fill the back of a large truck. Mikes's newsletter, which had a private circulation of no more than three thousand and brought him only a very moderate income, never ranted with moralistic indignation. It simply delivered the news, most of it very new indeed, in a somewhat awkward prose that owed far more to the Sears, Roebuck catalog than it ever would to the Washington *Post*.

"Sit down, Jack, and make yourself relaxed," said the Hungarian, directing him to a table covered with a flower-patterned oilcloth. He did as he was told. Mikes ducked out into the kitchen.

Several minutes later he was back with two steaming white china bowls. He set one down in front of Jackson, gave him a fork and brought the other around to his own place across the table.

"Eat and then we talk," said Mikes. He immediately proceeded to do just that, ducking his white-haired head and rapidly filling his mouth with forkfuls of the food. Jackson paused for a moment, watching, thinking that Mikes reminded him of a strange sort of white heron. Long ago he'd forsaken the blue skies and the shallow rivers for this cluttered, document-stuffed set of rooms.

The bowl contained a kind of pasta, actually egg noodles, covered with a creamy pink sauce redolent of garlic, tomato and caraway. It was delicious.

Halfway through their meal, there was a shrill whistling from the kitchen. Mikes rose and went out, came back a few moments later with a pot of strong tea and two small, fluted tea glasses.

"This is great," said Jackson.

"You should only have to eat it in Kisvarda to know how delicious, Jack. It is the wheat for the noodles which makes the difference. This is so-so. In Kisvarda you are almost in the Ukraine, with wheat as sweet as crushed almonds."

When they'd finished, and Mikes had cleared the table, he returned to sit facing Jackson. "I find it interesting to see you here in my home, Jack. When only two days ago I heard your name mentioned in this very room."

"Oh?"

"Yes. But please do not ask from whom, for you know I cannot tell you. The rules are the same for everyone who talks to me. And how would you feel if I broke them for you? To walk away wondering to whom I would break *your* confidences?"

"I understand," said Jackson. "But I wish you hadn't told me."

"Perhaps it was a mistake. But then again"—he smiled—"I consider you a friend. You and I have helped one another in the past. Anything I tell you, perhaps it is some kind of help. If I heard your name two days ago, it can only mean you are near the center. The center of what? That is, of course, what I wish to know. But you, Jack, were the one to call. Do you have good news for me?"

Jackson knew perfectly well that by "good news" Mikes did not mean amusing human-interest stories or advance word on a drop in the rate of unemployment. By "good" he meant news that was sufficiently savory, unusual or shocking.

"I'm afraid not, Oscar. This time I've come to ask a favor. One I hope I'll be able to repay sometime in the future."

Mikes held up his hand. "Let us not worry about repayment before you have even asked your favor. If I can help, I will."

"I'm looking for all the information I can get on a man named Anthony Benet. And I don't have time to go out knocking on doors, doing my own digging. Anthony Benet, I'll spell it for you." He did so. "He was Senator Borah's aide. Now he works for Wheeler. He's a young man, personable, not a fanatic. I gather he's a fairly important wheel in the Washington isolationist machine. Not a headline grabber, but one of their bright young men. Do you know him?"

"Not personally, no," said Mikes.

"But you've heard of him?"

"Wait one moment." The Hungarian rose and disappeared down a hall. Jackson heard the sound of boxes being shifted and the rustle of papers. Mikes reappeared with two thick folders cradled in his arms. He tapped the top one. "Brown, that is for Republicans. My Democrats are in blue. This one"—he tapped it again—"I took from my back bedroom, the cemetery room. Everyone dead or retired, gone from Washington. This is Borah's file for his last five years. The other one: Wheeler's file for the past ten months. That one I keep in my own bedroom."

"And those?" Jackson nodded at the stacks of file boxes in the living room.

"Alive but not so very alive," said Mikes. In his lexicon, "alive" was synonymous with "in power," so that those men whose files were confined to the living room were not necessarily the victims of wasting diseases. Just those who occupied the lower slopes of the Washington alp, either on their way up or slowly slipping downward.

"Now, let us see where he is," said Mikes, opening the brown folder. It took him some time searching through the papers. "Ah, yes, Anthony Benet. I have found him. Wait while I read to remind myself of all details."

"July 18 of last year," he said looking up a few minutes later. "You remember?"

Jackson shook his head.

"Perhaps you were away. A meeting at the White House. The President and the leaders from both parties in Congress. Also Secretary Hull and two of his aides. No?"

Jackson shook his head again. "I haven't the slightest clue, Oscar. There are meetings like that every week and they don't brief me unless it's something in my area."

"No matter. I will tell you. What was the big question on the Hill all last summer? The repeal of the embargo sections of the Neutrality Act, yes? A dozen bills proposed, all of them defeated."

"What happened on July 18?" asked Jackson.

"Roosevelt tried a last-minute appeal to the Congress leaders. Germany was on the verge of invading Poland, according to every one of our diplomatic reports. Roosevelt insisted that by repealing the embargo, we would warn Germany not to think we would just sit idly by. I believe

Roosevelt regarded the meeting as his last chance to convince Congress."

"I have heard something about that meeting," said Jackson. "It didn't work."

"No, certainly not. The embargo was not repealed until *after* Germany invaded Poland, until November. But this"—he tapped the page with his finger—"tells why the meeting failed. According to my source, a very good source, it was Senator Borah who defeated Roosevelt, refuted everything the President said. There would be no war in Europe, Borah claimed, and certainly not before January. There was no truth in the reports of German mobilization. 'I don't give a damn about your dispatches,' Borah said. 'We all have means of acquiring information. I myself have gone to great effort to secure information from different sources. I tell you confidently, my sources are far more reliable than those alarmist reports from some embassy dandies.'"

Mikes looked up from the paragraph he'd been reading. "That was, Jack, the end of Roosevelt's hopes to repeal the embargo. Borah's colleagues were not about to call the Senator from Idaho a liar. For Roosevelt, a big defeat. Congress adjourned a few days later. Of course, the President was very angry. You recall his press conference?"

"No."

"He said the Republicans and some Democrats had placed a bet that their President was wrong. He sincerely hoped that they would win their bet."

"So did the Poles," said Jackson.

"True, Jack, and perhaps a repeal at that time would have discouraged the Germans from their invasion. But what interested me at the time was the idea of Borah's secret European sources," said Mikes. "Naturally I made it my business to investigate a little further. Borah was not an untruthful man. If he said he had sources, it must have been true. I wondered just *who* these sources might be, no?"

"Okay," said Jackson. "Who?"

"It was not difficult to discover there was only one source. You must be able to guess his name by now."

"Anthony Benet?" said Jackson. "Of course! He was in Berlin last July."

"So he was. And sending back long telegrams full of reassuring good news. All Germany wanted was peace. There was no mobilization. There would be no war. I have never myself seen these telegrams. But I have spoken to a man who had access to them."

"How many telegrams in all?"

"Five, I believe," said Mikes.

"And Borah believed them? He took Benet's word over the word of the entire State Department?"

"A natural occurrence in this city. Benet was no doubt a trusted aide. And," said Mikes, "not the first man to have been misled by the clever propagandists of Berlin."

"*If* he was misled."

"You believe he deliberately sent telegrams with false information?"

"One never knows," said Jackson.

"Perhaps you are giving this too much of a sinister shade. Perhaps the young Benet was only telling his master in Washington what he wanted to hear."

"Perhaps," said Jackson. "Or perhaps his true master wasn't in Washington at all."

"You think Benet is a German agent, Jack?"

"I don't know. I honestly don't know. But I don't like what you've just told me."

Mikes placed the Borah file aside and opened the blue file on Senator Wheeler. "I know this one as well as I know my own name."

"You have quite a bit on Wheeler, do you?"

"Are you interested in Wheeler?"

"Why not?" said Jackson. "Especially if Benet's working for him."

"Many people are working for Senator Wheeler these days."

"You mean like John L. Lewis?"

"Yes," said Mikes. "And there is a German named Hertslet in the embassy here who furnishes the Senator with an unlimited supply of unflattering things about Britain. Did you know that too?"

Jackson put on his poker face. "Perhaps."

"It's all right, Jack. Senator Wheeler has many helpers these days, it is difficult to keep up. Are you going to this party on Monday night which Wheeler has organized?"

"What party?"

"It is for raising funds. In Virginia, at the home of the woman called Fabri."

"Kitty Fabri?" Jackson recognized the name of one of Washington's most famous hostesses. "You mean she's opening her house to Wheeler for fund-raising?"

"Yes, for the America First. And it will be very amusing, no doubt, to see what they have to say to each other. Lindbergh and Hull, that is."

"What?" cried Jackson. "This is getting fantastic. Secretary Hull is going to be there?"

Mikes nodded, a devilish grin on his face. "Yes, it is surprising. I think it will not be a formal debate. But apparently Secretary Hull could not resist the chance to face Colonel Lindbergh in person. These speeches of Lindbergh must have offended the Secretary very deeply. A proud man, but perhaps it would have been wiser not to lend his presence to such an affair. No?"

Jackson said nothing. He didn't want Mikes printing rumors of White House dissatisfaction with the Secretary of State's performance. All he said finally was, "This party should make amusing reading for your readers."

"Yes, it would be amusing to attend. But, of course, Oscar Mikes is not likely to receive an invitation. However, I will have friends who will no doubt tell me all about the evening."

"No doubt," said Jackson.

"Ah, Jack," he said with a broadening smile, "I must now look into this Benet much more carefully. You see, already you have begun to repay me."

"Begun?"

"There is one other thing." Mikes scratched his chin as if he hated to ask the question. "But perhaps it would be too much to ask."

"Or to answer," said Jackson. "But by all means ask, Oscar."

"It is only a few weeks until the convention in Chicago . . ."

"That's right," said Jackson.

"But the President says nothing. The Democrats are like chickens when they see the farmer pick up his ax. Yet Roosevelt says nothing to calm the party."

"I suppose it does look rather confusing from outside," said Jackson.

"So confusing that you were in Paris a few days ago, Jack?" asked Mikes. "Instead of making arrangements for Chicago?"

"I've made the arrangements for Chicago. And I can't talk about the Paris trip, Oscar."

"I am not the only one who is interested. No, Jack, not in the trip. In this thing they are saying all over Washington. But so far there is not one who can give me the answer. I don't know, but perhaps *you* are the one?"

"The answer to what question?" asked Jackson.

"Why is Roosevelt afraid?" There it was. Jackson had been hooked and played. He could see it as clearly as if it were a polished steel hook, with the sharply pointed spar on the end, and Mikes leaning out over the rail, with that deceptive look of the white heron, looking to gaff him and lug him aboard.

"Sorry," said Jackson, "but I'm not the one."

15

The passenger in seat 16-C had not fastened his seat belt despite the lighted sign at the front of the cabin. He sat with a leather briefcase across his lap, staring out the small window at the engine.

In the flashing red beams of the utility trucks, Anthony Benet saw the dull silver blade begin to turn. That was it. In one eruptive movement he thrust himself to his feet and out into the narrow aisle. He was halfway to the front when the first stewardess turned and spotted him. Thinking to remind him of the seat-belt sign, she started in his direction. But just before they collided, she saw the intent look in his eyes, stepped back from her rump pushed into a passenger's shoulder and heard Benet shout, "I can't afford to leave it! I must get off!"

At the cabin door, the other stewardess was too surprised to say a word. The man who brushed past her looked well-dressed and obviously important. As he went down the metal ramp, she managed to call at his back, "We can't wait for you, sir."

There was no reply.

Inside the airport, the immediate area around the departure gate was almost deserted. Everyone had either gone home or upstairs to wave off the plane from the observation deck. He turned and asked the airline clerk for the nearest men's room.

Safely inside the locked stall, Benet sat down on the toilet and waited for fifty minutes to pass.

At ten P.M. he emerged from the men's room and walked directly to the United ticket counter. He purchased a one-way first-class seat on United's flight 34 to Boston, giving his name as "Robert Martin." Departure was at 10:25, and they were due to board very soon, said the ticket agent. Benet went straight to the gate and was the first passenger to board the aircraft a few minutes later.

Safely buckled into his seat and climbing to an altitude of 8,500 feet, he had the row to himself. His briefcase stowed beside him, his legs stretched out in front, he tried to relax. But relaxing was out of the question. When the stewardess came by, he ordered a double scotch, thinking he ought to nurse it for the rest of the flight. But ten minutes later he was already ordering his second double.

As soon as he'd gotten Jackson out the door, Benet had made a long-distance call to Boston and the *Globe*. They'd never heard of a John Jackson on their staff. His worst fears confirmed, Benet had begun to literally shake. It took two drinks to calm him to the point where he could call Duxbury. As soon as Sir Roland came onto the line, Anthony blurted out what had happened.

Sir Roland had been as solid as a rock. In a few seconds he began to give Anthony very detailed, careful instructions. The brilliance of the man was always a shock.

As the airplane cruised in steady flight high above the Eastern seaboard, Anthony found himself thinking of Senator Borah. It was Jackson's questions, of course. They'd sparked it off again. That memory of Borah's expression when they had all gathered in his office as soon as the news came of the German invasion of Poland. How had it been possible?

Borah had tried to force the same confident fire into his eyes, the defiant awareness of his own rightness. But it just wouldn't work. There had been no accusations that afternoon. Anthony, sick to his stomach, simply could not grasp it at first. How had he been so completely misled? Or had he been? Everything he had seen in Germany, everything they had told him, had made an invasion of Poland seem out of the question. Should he have looked more closely, listened more carefully? Had it been a treacherous game of deceit or his own incompetence?

The fire had gone out in Borah that afternoon, although the man refused to back down. He'd staked his word as a gentleman and a Senator on the Germans' peaceful intentions. On Anthony's telegrams. In the end, when the hemorrhage in his brain occurred a few months later, Anthony had not even been surprised. He'd known the terrible conflict raging inside the old man ever since that afternoon.

And what of his own conflict? Anthony just could not be sure. Had he been tricked by the Germans, or were there factors in their decision to invade which occurred after his visit? Had it been their deception, his own naiveté, or something else entirely? In the end, when Wheeler's offer of a job had come, Anthony had decided to accept it. Despite what had happened in Poland, and now the entire Continent, his isolationist beliefs remained unshaken. Even if Germany was as monstrous as her worst enemies claimed, Anthony still knew that America could only lose by entangling itself in Europe's mess.

In the early hours of Saturday morning they rolled to a stop outside the terminal at Boston's Logan Airport. Inside the building, he caught a glimpse of Frank's white hair and dark suit. His grandfather's butler-chauffeur for as long as Anthony could remember, Frank had driven up from Duxbury to meet the plane.

The drive down through Boston and along the south coast took them an hour.

Suddenly they were turning off North Ocean Road onto a cracked-shell drive. It was a five-minute run across the estate before their headlights picked out the front of the house. The moon had already disappeared. It was too dark to see more than an outline, the lights blazing downstairs. But Benet didn't need the moon to know what it looked like. The house sat on the edge of a high bluff, its back overlooking a private beach and miles of Cape Cod Bay. The building was oversize, white clapboard, with green shingles and two giant dormers. Half a dozen brick chimneys were ranked along the spine of the roof like sentries.

Martha, Frank's wife, opened the great front door just as he reached the top step. "Hello, sir. Your grandfather couldn't wait up any longer. He's gone to his bed. Mr. Plenty is waiting . . . excuse me, sir. Sir Roland is waiting for you in the library."

"Thank you, Martha. And why aren't you in bed?" He peered down into the pale gray eyes that he had known all his life.

"Frank made me get up, sir. Thought you would want a bite to eat."

"No, Martha, I'm not hungry. Now, you get right back upstairs to bed. I can take care of myself."

"Yes, sir. There's beef and cheese in the icebox, just in case, sir."

"I'm sure I'll manage, Martha. Now scoot."

He paused to watch her hurry around the corner of the dining room in the direction of the back stairs, which would lead her up to their attic apartment.

The hallway in which he stood had not changed one iota in the thirty years that Benet had known it. Lighted by a brass chandelier which reflected Benet's face in the polished bowls of eight gaseliers, the entrance to his grandfather's house was like the door to his own childhood. Its confluence of stained woods, white enamel woodwork, ancestral portraits, a captain's mirror, the Isfahan carpet, always gave him a heady feeling. It recalled a father he had never known, a father who had somehow disgraced himself and then been swallowed up by a mysterious West. And a mother whose home this had been all her life, a life which had ended with pneumonia when Benet was seven years old. The home of Clarence T. Elliot, his grandfather.

He walked down to the last door on the right.

The library was a long, high-ceilinged room with a formal hearth and, during the day, a sweeping view out over the Atlantic. Tonight the lamplight glinted off the cracked spines of the thousands of books which lined its walls. There was a slight breeze billowing the gauze curtains at an open window. And above the backrest of a dark red leather armchair, Benet glimpsed the pink eminence of Sir Roland's hairless scalp.

"Hello," he said.

Sir Roland did not bother to rise or even to turn. "Hello, Anthony."

"I think I'll make myself a nightcap. Want one?"

"No, thank you. I've had my limit tonight."

Anthony went to the drink cabinet and took a tall crystal glass out of the cupboard, then poured two inches of the finest malt scotch into it. A short pull of siphon, and he moved over to where the chairs and the leather Chesterfield divan were arranged.

Sir Roland was wearing his maroon silk dressing gown over a pair of worsted trousers. The gown emphasized his ample girth, well over two hundred pounds of it. As always, his expression was an extraordinary combination of geniality and ferocity.

Sir Roland was annoyed. Annoyed with these obtuse Americans, the foolish old doddard of a grandfather, the inept servants, but most of all with this young man standing before him. Annoyed at his phone call, his traumatized reaction, so predictable, to what had happened, but more than anything simply annoyed at his existence. Once upon a time, even as recently as a few hours ago, he had seen fit to make use of Benet. But now only one final use remained for him, and that was, appropriately, a most menial one.

"Well . . ." said Anthony.

"Well indeed! Did you follow my suggestions about the airport?" asked Sir Roland.

"Yes."

"Do you think you were followed?"

"I don't think so. But I'm really not sure."

Sir Roland nodded patiently, concealing his anger.

"Has it been all right for you here?" asked Anthony.

"Most pleasant. Your grandfather is a fine host and a most engaging conversationalist."

"He does run on these days," said Benet.

"Not at all. We'll all get to be his age one day. The least we can do is lend a sympathetic ear."

Anthony nodded.

"I'll be quite sorry to leave here," said Sir Roland.

"You've decided to leave, then?"

"There's no choice, is there? Now they've approached you, it will only be a matter of days before they come here. I'll be far away by then. You'll be back in Washington." He smiled, his great benevolent Caesar smile.

"Where will you go?" asked Anthony.

"Dearborn. You've heard of it?"

"Dearborn, Michigan? Of course."

"What is it like?"

"It's an industrial city. Really part of Detroit, but with a different name."

"And Henry Ford owns it?"

"A lot of it, I suppose."

"Like Coventry, perhaps?"

"Perhaps," said Anthony. "Why Dearborn, or shouldn't I ask?"

"I have a friend there."

It wasn't much of an answer, but Anthony willingly accepted it. Just as he'd accepted his father-in-law's explanation of his sudden bewildering appearance in the United States the previous week.

Sir Roland had turned that explanation into a lecture. It should be a lesson for Anthony and his isolationist friends, he'd said, what was happening in England since the start of the war. Law itself had been tossed out the window. They were hunting down men like himself and throwing them into jail because of their private beliefs. To believe in peace, in the coexistence of nations, that had become a criminal offense. Let the American isolationists take heed and redouble their efforts.

Of Sir Roland's relations with Germans, Anthony knew very little. He dared not let himself suspect more. Sir Roland was a great man, a brilliant man. A man who had been what his own father never had: solid as a rock. In Anthony's moment of deepest guilt, Sir Roland had stood staunchly at his side. More than that, far more. Sir Roland had offered him unconditional forgiveness. It was a debt from which Anthony could never free himself.

He had been the one who had failed Nicola. Even if he did not understand the precise nature of that failure, he knew it must be his. Her illness, withdrawal, the madness, her suicide: they all could be traced back to Anthony, to their marriage. Even the doctors said so. When he'd met her, she had been the most beautiful, most wonderful woman he'd ever encountered. And she had clung to him with a passion and a joy that eclipsed all the lonely years of his own childhood. It was only after they'd settled in Georgetown that her illness had begun. Why, the doctors could not seem to agree. And there was no possible explanation for her death. An unspeakable tragedy for which Anthony had to hold himself responsible. A death for which Sir Roland, her father, had never once blamed him.

"How will you get to Dearborn?"

"By automobile, I think," said Sir Roland. "If you will agree to drive me."

That surprised him. "Drive you to Dearborn?"

"Yes. If you would, Anthony."

It was a long drive, almost a thousand miles, and he had no desire to go.

"You see," said Sir Roland, "we don't know how efficient or determined they are. The English want me very badly. To make an example of me, you understand. Roosevelt and Churchill . . ." He held up two fingers, pressed tightly together. "Like that, of course. They will be watching the airports and the railways. I thought an automobile would be safest. You know, Anthony, I have no license to operate an automobile in this country."

"I understand. The problem is," said Anthony carefully. "I absolutely have to be in Washington on Monday evening. Senator Wheeler is depending on me."

"So you shall be," said Sir Roland, smiling generously. "We'll leave in the morning, early. What time is it now?"

Anthony checked his watch. "Past two o'clock. What about a car? I doubt I can drive all the way to Dearborn, then back to Washington by Monday evening. Look, I don't want to sound as if I'm trying to make excuses. But it seems to me that it might be better for you to wait a few days. Then I could—"

"It must be this weekend," declared Sir Roland. "As for a car, your grandfather has already agreed to let us have the Hudson. And you can fly from Dearborn to Washington in plenty of time for your meeting."

"But the Hudson is Frank and Martha's car."

"Your grandfather did give it to them, didn't he? I'm certain Frank won't object. He rarely uses it. This is quite inconvenient for you, I know. Will you forgive me, Anthony?"

These last words triggered a spasm of anxiety in the younger man that was evident from his sudden change in expression. "No, please don't say that. You're . . . of course, you're right. You must leave here very soon."

"This man who came to see you, his name was Jackson?" asked Sir Roland.

"So he claimed."

"You should check on it. Tomorrow, while we're on the road, you can call some of your friends in Washington. Perhaps they'll know who he is."

"Is it really important? He's probably just a policeman."

"Do policemen usually go to the trouble of pretending to be journalists? No, I think not," said Sir Roland. "You must have friends who could help you find the truth. And it could be very important to me."

"All right, I can try."

"That is all I ask." Sir Roland pulled himself to the edge of the chair in preparation for the considerable feat of standing all his bulk erect. "You said it was gone two. Perhaps we should think of retiring."

"Yes." Anthony drained the last of his scotch and set the glass aside.

"Tell me the truth, Anthony."

"Yes?" He looked into Sir Roland's small, bright blue eyes but found himself unable to hold the stare.

"Do you really mind doing this favor for me?"

"No," said Anthony. "Not at all. Please don't think that—"

"Good!" said Sir Roland. "Really, this is awfully good of you. Especially considering how much you've already done for me, Anthony."

He sensed something hidden in Sir Roland's words, an implication that annoyed him yet somehow eluded him. It continued to bother him after they'd said good night, and all the way upstairs to his old bedroom, where, mercifully, sleep took him quickly.

At 8:15 the next morning Martha entered his bedroom and put down a heavily laden tray. Anthony had slept deeply, but hardly enough. The whiskey was still with him, making him feel more than a little ill. He managed his coffee, forced down some of the eggs and bacon, then took a long shower.

Downstairs in the library, his grandfather was waiting with all his usual questions about Washington, about "that cripple" in the White House, and about this trip they were planning. Sir Roland was working very hard at implanting in his grandfather's mind the necessity for keeping the trip secret from anyone outside the family. To Anthony's surprise, Frank seemed quite cheerful about having his Hudson taken away from him. However, Martha did seem in rather a bad mood this morning.

Frank had brought his collection of road maps up from the garage. After examining them for a few minutes, Anthony said he thought the quickest route would be via Niagara Falls into Canada, then crossing back into Michigan from Windsor. That would lead them straight into Detroit.

Sir Roland took him aside a few moments later and hissed, "Canada? Absolutely out of the question, Anthony. We don't want border checks. Pick the route where we're least likely to encounter problems. Michigan can't be *that* difficult to reach, Anthony."

After another inspection of the map, he settled on U.S. Route 6. They could drive across Connecticut, take the bridge over the Hudson at Poughkeepsie, and link up with U.S. 6 about twenty miles west of Bear Mountain. The highway wound a circuitous, out-of-the-way route across the northern edge of Pennsylvania, giving Scranton a miss, leading them to the shores of Lake Erie. They'd follow the lakeshore all the way around through Cleveland and finally straight up to Dearborn.

This plan was approved by Sir Roland and there were no further protests. Frank carried their luggage out to the car, then returned to stand beside Anthony's grandfather to wave them off. This festive farewell grated on Anthony's nerves. His stomach had not been right since he'd woken. And he knew it was absurd for him to resent Sir Roland's predicament. Forcing himself to smile, Anthony put the Hudson in gear and accelerated, crunching them forward over the white shells of the drive on their way west.

III

RIVER ROUGE

JUNE 30, 1940

16

Neither Anthony nor Sir Roland was prepared for his first glimpse of Dearborn late on Sunday afternoon. From one end of the horizon to the other, the River Rouge plant of the Ford Motor Company challenged the eye to a battle from which there could only emerge one possible victor. Under a sky that seemed to hold a perpetual thunderstorm, the towering chimneys of the blast furnaces belched their black tornadoes.

At the River Rouge slip, freighters from the Great Lakes were being emptied of their iron ore, coke, limestone and zinc. Elevated railroads carried the crude material forty feet in the air to enormous bins by the side of the furnaces. Molten, fiery ore gushed out into great tubs on wheels that rolled to the largest foundry in the world for the casting of the engine blocks. Another vast building contained the rolling mills, attached by conveyors to the nine-acre installation where the presses constantly stamped out body panels, fenders, gas tanks, doors, radiator shells and hoods. Next door was the forging plant, where such components as springs, wheel drums, crankshafts and transmission gears were produced. In the center of it all, like a low, boxed concrete plateau sprawling for hundreds of yards, continuously fed by moving conveyors from every corner of the 1,096-acre plant, was the final-assembly building.

Many Americans believed that Henry Ford had invented the first automobile the way his friend Thomas Alva Edison had invented the electric lightbulb. That was not true, and Ford himself never claimed otherwise. What Henry Ford had invented was *mass production*. As the greatest businessman the world had yet known, Ford's true genius was not as a tinkerer, an inventor, but as an organizer. And the River Rouge plant was his lightbulb.

Anthony had to stop and ask directions to Michigan Avenue. Twenty minutes later he and Sir Roland pulled into the gravel drive of a modern Colonial house which stood on two acres of its own grounds. There they met Thomas Holtzer, one of the two or three men closest to Henry Ford.

Tall and severe-looking, he reminded Benet of a Prussian hawk. His hair was cropped very close to his skull and his sharp, beaklike nose bisected two intense, almost predatory eyes. He was tall and powerfully built, with a tiny waist in contrast to shoulders and a chest that would have suited a Córdoba bull. He dressed to accentuate the effect of his build.

When he opened his mouth, however, the man was curiously inarticulate. He was obviously not a shy man but he had difficulty in simply telling them that two guestrooms had been prepared for them. Would they like to take baths and change before dinner? Drinks would be on the patio. Later, Anthony would conclude that Holtzer was rather intimidated by Sir Roland, and hence his initial reticence.

When Anthony came downstairs forty-five minutes after their arrival, he found Sir Roland and Holtzer deep in conversation on a flagstone terrace overlooking a grove of apple trees. They stopped talking the moment he appeared.

It was like that for the rest of the evening. After drinks, Mrs. Holtzer led them inside, where they sat down to a dinner of pork roast, boiled potatoes, applesauce, green beans and blueberry pie. A delicious Moselle was served with the food and Anthony drank more than he intended. The uniformed maid kept coming back to refill his glass and he had no idea how many bottles they went through.

As far as Anthony could tell, Thomas Holtzer was utterly devoid of charm. Once he'd found his tongue, he spoke in a gruff, even crude voice, never laughed, and certainly never said anything which made the rest of them laugh. On the whole, the conversation was carried by Sir Roland, who had decided to subject Mrs. Holtzer to a full blast of his flattering wit.

After dinner they returned to the patio. A young moon hung in the east like half a golden egg. The maid brought out coffee and Holtzer poured brandy.

It was then Anthony raised the subject of his return

flight to Washington and the problem of getting Frank's car back to Massachusetts.

Nothing to worry about, said Holtzer. Sir Roland had already explained the problem. A plane would be waiting at the airport at nine the next morning to fly Benet home. As for the Hudson, the company shipped thousands of automobiles all over the country every day. Holtzer would arrange to have the Hudson back in Duxbury in forty-eight hours at the latest.

It had been a long drive and Anthony was exhausted, the brandy having obliterated the last of his stamina. After another fifteen minutes, during which no more than ten polite and strained sentences were spoken, Anthony made his apologies and retired to his room on the second floor.

In the few moments of remaining consciousness as he lay under a starched sheet on a thick sprung mattress, Anthony puzzled over the fact that if Thomas Holtzer was Sir Roland's friend, why was it so patently obvious that the two men had never met before?

Downstairs, Thomas Holtzer had sent his wife off to bed. A few words about discussing business and not wishing to bore her: she knew the code. And she knew the consequences if she disobeyed it. The code was common to many marriages; the consequences were not.

As soon as she had hurried from the patio, her husband turned to Sir Roland and began to speak in a low, emphatic voice. He talked without pause for nearly five minutes, jamming one of his fingers into the arm of his chair for effect from time to time. Sir Roland quietly absorbed the onslaught of words, his face an impassive mask. But all the time, his eyes were absorbing Holtzer's fervor. Until, by the end, Holtzer could no longer look him in the eye.

Holtzer seemed to consider himself a vital German resource within the United States. No doubt Berlin had told him he was one of their most important agents. All agents were told the same; it was standard espionage practice to keep their operatives' morale high. But in Holtzer's case, such importance was highly exaggerated.

Holtzer lacked both the discipline and the caution necessary in a true agent of the highest grade. He was listed by several Berlin intelligence agencies, including both Admiral Canaris' Abwehr and General Heydrich's S.D.

But on both lists his classification was low. A man to be manipulated, usually for propaganda exercises, he had never been given the full briefing due a first-class agent. But now General Heydrich wished to use him.

Before dinner, while Anthony had been upstairs, Sir Roland had produced his envelope containing the small prints of the Roosevelt pictures. Holtzer had been greatly impressed, even amazed. The plan itself had been partially revealed to Holtzer weeks before by one of Heydrich's most trusted operatives secretly based in the United States. But now that Sir Roland had arrived, Holtzer said he had thought of some new "refinements" of his own.

Was it cowardice or simply a rare instance of caution in a man who usually flaunted his pro-Nazi sentiments? wondered Sir Roland. The gist was simple. Holtzer thought that instead of publishing the photographs in the *Independent* and involving Ford personally in the affair through a broadcast on the *Ford Sunday Hour* radio program, they ought to consider passing the pictures to a friend of Holtzer's who worked for the *Chicago Tribune*.

Sir Roland had no intention of explaining exactly why Holtzer's suggestion, with its hint of cowardice, was absolutely out of the question. The fact that there was currently a great power struggle taking place in Berlin between Canaris and Heydrich was none of Holtzer's business. Nor was the fact that the outcome of this struggle between the Abwehr and the S.D. probably hinged on what happened in the next American election. Canaris' efforts were being focused on groups like America First and Senator Wheeler's campaign. While Sir Roland had given Heydrich the ace card over four years ago. Correction: made it available to him. Sir Roland had known from the start that he could not actually give the Night Letter to Heydrich without simultaneously making himself obsolete, a threat.

Sir Roland had never given up the negatives, despite all of Heydrich's entreaties and subtle threats. Now he would reap the benefits of that decision by being the one to personally deliver the Night Letter. He, Sir Roland, would play the ace which would effectively establish the S.D. as the premier intelligence agency in Berlin.

He chose his words to Holtzer carefully. "Excuse me,

but what you have just said leads me to believe you either have a poor memory or a weak liver."

"What do you mean?" asked Holtzer. "I resent the implication that—"

"Resent it," cried Sir Roland. "By all means, resent it. And prove it is not so."

"What do you mean?"

"I mean that you are acting under strict orders issued by the highest Berlin authorities. General Heydrich himself has formulated the details of this operation. It carries the highest priority, the greatest secrecy. You have been allowed to partake of this operation from the very beginning. It is a great honor, sir! You should realize that."

"Of course. Of course I understand that," said Holtzer. "Don't think I'm not aware of the secrecy involved. I've never had any problem on that score. They know what I've done for them in Berlin. Believe me, what I've done is—"

Sir Roland cut him off. "Your past service on behalf of the Reich is well-known in Berlin. Do you think General Heydrich would have chosen you otherwise?"

"Well, I'm just glad they realize," said Holtzer.

"Of course they do. But what you have just suggested to me would hardly be understood in Berlin. Do you think that after all the careful planning that has gone into this operation, you can now substitute a plan of your own? Just how do you think General Heydrich would react to that?"

Holtzer said nothing, staring sullenly at the floor.

"I don't wish to threaten you!" said Sir Roland. "Certainly not. But I must caution you that Heydrich would hardly understand if I were to repeat what you've just said to me. He would take it as disloyalty. Perhaps even worse, as betrayal."

"That's ridiculous," protested Holtzer. "All I was saying was that we might want to cover our tracks a little deeper. If anything went wrong, it would certainly be traced back to me. And I don't think Berlin wants to risk losing one of their most important friends here in America just because—"

"Just because?" cried Sir Roland. Holtzer's self-importance was unbelievable. He had no idea he was the most expendable part of the entire operation. "Just because of the Night Letter? Good God, man, don't you realize how important this is to Berlin? You've seen the photographs."

"I just don't know," said Holtzer, squirming in his chair. "Look, you have to understand that I've got my own difficulties at the plant. And now you tell me about this White House guy who was poking around your son-in-law. He *was* White House, you're sure?"

Sir Roland nodded. "According to Anthony's source, Jackson is a minor staff member, political, at the White House. Which I take as a reassuring sign under the circumstances. I suspect the English simply said something to Roosevelt and he sent one of his functionaries to take a quick look at Anthony. No need to get upset. I would be far more concerned if Jackson had been FBI." Sir Roland wasn't at all sure he believed this, but it was necessary to calm Holtzer.

"Yes, well, I still don't like having you here in my house. That's why I want you to go up to the camp I told you about. You'll be safe there until the freighter arrives on Friday."

"How far is this camp from here?"

"Only about eight hours' drive north."

"And you're sure it's secure?"

Holtzer nodded. "You'd be as safe there as you'd be in Berlin, believe me."

"Then, if you insist, I will agree."

Holtzer looked relieved. "You could even leave the pictures with me if you were afraid they might—"

"My orders," snapped Sir Roland, "are quite clear. I am to personally retain possession of the negatives until the moment I hand them to the journalists. Your orders are also clear. You are to arrange the meeting and to accompany me. I cannot overemphasize the importance of the timing. General Heydrich, the *Amerika Insitut* and myself have all agreed. It must be this Friday, the fifth of July. With the national holiday, the newspapers will be hungry for things to print. From the *Independent*, the story will quickly be picked up across the country. We will have a bored, captive audience. And on Sunday, they will go to their churches and hear their minister preach against immorality in the White House. Followed, as you know, by the broadcast."

Holtzer frowned at the mention of the broadcast. It had

been his idea in the first place, suggested to Heydrich's
agent a few weeks before.

"You anticipate no trouble with Ford about the broadcast, do you?" asked Sir Roland.

"No, of course not."

"And you've arranged the meeting for tomorrow?"

"Yes. Nine-fifteen. Then you can go straight up to the
camp."

"This broadcast," said Sir Roland. "You believe it will
have the wide-ranging effect you initially predicted?"

"Look," said Holtzer irritably, "if Henry Ford gets on
his own radio show and says Roosevelt is morally unfit to
be in the White House, you're going to have millions of
Americans agreeing with him. The *Ford Sunday Hour* is
the third most popular show on the radio. They'll have to
dig the White House out from under all the telegrams sent
by outraged listeners."

"Ah, I see," said Sir Roland, barely concealing his skep-
ticism. "General Heydrich, as you know, was quite
impressed with your idea. But I had the fleeting impression
just now you might have had second thoughts yourself."

"No, no, I still think it's a great idea," said Holtzer.
"Look, please forget what I said before. I just started
thinking these last weeks. Now that you've finally arrived, I
can see that I was thinking too much."

"A bad habit," agreed Sir Roland. Especially for someone with Holtzer's intellectual capacity, he added silently.

"Tell you truthfully, I can't stop worrying a little about
this guy." Holtzer nodded toward the ceiling.

"You mean Anthony? He is not to be worried about, I
assure you."

"No, this guy from the White House. Jackson or whatever his name was."

"You have absolutely nothing to worry about, Herr
Holtzer. Especially now that you will have me safely hidden in this camp to which you're so anxious to dispatch
me."

"Nothing personal in that," protested Holtzer.

"Of course not. Just let me emphasize the importance of
bringing me back here on Thursday, on the fourth. We
will go to the journalists together on Friday morning. They
will take the negatives and you will then escort me straight
to the *Freiburg*. No doubt you will never see me again.

Now, tell me something about Ford. I am looking forward to meeting him."

"Don't expect too much," said Holtzer. "He's pretty old these days."

"Senile?"

"Call it what you want."

"Is this generally known?" asked Sir Roland with some alarm.

"Don't worry. He's regarded like some kind of saint in this country. Except by the unions, of course."

"A folk hero?"

"Like I said, call it what you want. Anyway, you'll meet him soon enough." Holtzer looked uneasy, not used to being bullied as Sir Roland had just been forced to bully him. "You're sure these pictures will make Roosevelt resign?"

"We can't be sure about resignation," said Sir Roland patiently. "But one thing is certain. A third term will be out of the question."

Holtzer nodded. "You want another brandy?"

"Thank you, but I think not. I will retire now. It will be a long day tomorrow."

"Yeah, sure." Holtzer stood up, and Sir Roland slowly did likewise. A few minutes later the two men parted at the top of the stairs and went to their rooms at opposite ends of the house.

One by one the lights downstairs were being extinguished as Harriet Mullins went about her final chores. She had already cleared the two snifters from the patio and put the brandy bottle back in the cabinet.

Mrs. Mullins had been the maid in the Holtzer residence for the past twenty-one months. She and her husband, who worked in the Ford glass factory at River Rouge, lived on the eastern edge of Dearborn in a district called Fordson.

It had not been long after she'd arrived in the Holtzer house that Mrs. Mullins had discovered the peculiar acoustics of the kitchen. Although the patio was some forty feet from the kitchen wing, the way it was set into the back of the house, under an overhanging roof, made its acoustics like one of those band shells out at Ford Twin Lakes.

Mrs. Mullins could stand in the kitchen on a warm night and hear almost everything that was spoken outside.

And since the Holtzers' cook, Ida, usually left for home as soon as dessert was served, it was Mrs. Mullins who stayed to wash the dishes. In the summer, with her hands in the suds and the window open, she had heard many things from the patio. As neither Mr. Holtzer nor his wife ever came into the kitchen, they had no idea how audible they were outside.

Nor did they have any idea that Mrs. Mullins' husband, Lloyd, was an undercover organizer placed inside the River Rouge plant by the executive committee of the union.

17

The long beige Lincoln-Zephyr which Holtzer had ordered began to move over the gravel drive. In the back seat, Anthony sat alone staring at the house and Sir Roland's back disappearing through the front door. A moment later the car turned onto Michigan Avenue for the short drive to nearby Ford Airport.

Anthony believed that Sir Roland would be staying with the Holtzers for an indefinite period of time. Depending on how things progressed with the war and American politics, Sir Roland had said, he would either return eventually to England or, perhaps, take up permanent residence in America.

Sir Roland had shaken hands with Anthony believing that it was the last time he would ever see him. He gave no hint of that to his son-in-law, of course. But he was not at all sorry to see the last of Anthony Benet.

Some minutes later, Sir Roland and Holtzer were themselves pulling into the traffic on Michigan Avenue in the back of Holtzer's personal Lincoln.

"We're meeting him at the Rotunda, but we'll be passing his house soon. Up here, on the right," said Holtzer.

Set on seven thousand acres, bounded by the River Rouge on the south and Michigan Avenue on the north, the Ford estate occupied roughly a third of Dearborn: the entire central district of the city. Sir Roland caught no more than a distant glimpse of Fairhaven, as the house was called, across manicured lawns and elaborate gardens. It was a gray stone mansion, crouched low on the horizon.

They turned down Schaefer Road in the direction of the smokestacks and the sprawl of the plant.

"You said last night he was senile," said Sir Roland. "Can you give me a better idea of what to expect?"

Holtzer shrugged. "Expect Henry Ford, that's all I can tell you. He's full of contradictions. He carries a pistol, for example, but is opposed to capital punishment. At the same time, he thinks prisons are a waste of the taxpayers' money. He won't touch alcohol or tobacco. And I should warn you"—he gave Sir Roland a curious glance—"he has a peculiar thing about fat men."

"I beg your pardon?"

"Fat men. He always says that he's never met a fat man he could trust. I've seen him fire men off the plant for being overweight."

Sir Roland looked down at his substantial girth but chose to say nothing. No doubt Holtzer was having him on.

A mile down the road, Holtzer nudged him and said, "That's the Rotunda."

"My God," said the Englishman. "It is . . . something." At first glance it resembled nothing less than a huge concrete toy. But then he realized the architect's intention. Ten stories tall, without a window, the building was designed to look like four enormous gears of diminishing size stacked one on top of the other.

The chauffeur let them off at the main entrance, where a line of noisy schoolchildren stood awaiting entrance.

"Usually opens at nine," said Holtzer. "They close it when he comes. For God's sake, act impressed."

Holtzer had a word with the guard, who whispered something back in his ear and opened the door for them.

They entered a great circular hall. The light came from a skylight high above. Around the walls, twenty feet tall and minutely detailed, photographic murals depicted every aspect of the River Rouge plant: the docks, blast furnaces, men on the assembly line, nurses in the hospital, drivers testing the latest models, engineers bent over their drawing boards. But Sir Roland had only a brief chance to take it all in. Holtzer was guiding him quickly past a huge globe on which Ford's international empire was clearly marked, toward a doorway underneath a sign reading "North Wing Exhibition Hall."

Holtzer came to a sudden, abrupt halt as soon as they'd entered the doorway. "Christ, I should have known," he said.

"What is the matter?"

"He's got Bo Pawker with him."

"Bo Pawker?"

"Ford's bodyguard. Chief of the goon squad. Be careful of him. He's smarter than he looks, and Ford listens to what he says."

Across the polished granite floor of the museumlike chamber, Sir Roland saw two men leaning over a large glass display case. One of them was tall, white-haired, with a lean, shriveled face, dressed in a black suit that hung loosely off his bones. The other was much younger, brawny with an arrogant assurance in his stance; his head was cocked back above enormous shoulders, his hands jammed into the pockets of his dark blue suit jacket. As they approached, he glared at them, then spoke to the older gentleman, who just shook his head, intent on his examination of the display case.

Henry Ford waited until they were just a few feet away before he glanced up. Very slowly he raised himself to his full height. He looked from Holtzer to Sir Roland, and quickly back to Holtzer.

Sir Roland felt there was something unreal about the old man. Almost as if he were one of the wax exhibits in his own museum.

" 'Morning, Thomas," he said to Holtzer.

"Good morning, Mr. Ford."

Ford slowly turned to Sir Roland and squinted his eyes. "What's wrong with you?"

"Excuse me?" blustered Sir Roland.

"Mr. Ford, this is Sir Roland Plenty. The man I was telling you about," explained Holtzer.

"The Englishman, I remember," said Ford. "He's fat as a sow in season. What's his name again?"

"Sir Roland Plenty." Holtzer was extremely nervous, while Bo Pawker had a nasty smirk on his face.

"Are you feeling all right, boy?" Ford asked Sir Roland.

"Why yes, fine. Quite all right, thank you, Mr. Ford."

"It's a miracle. Did Holtzer tell you I didn't take to obese men?"

"As a matter of fact, he did mention something about that. You see, I . . . that is . . . actually, I am rather large."

Never in all his sixty-two years had Sir Roland been so affronted and yet so helpless to correct that affront. "Ah

. . . I assure you, I have not been called a boy in quite a number of years, Mr. Ford. Very flattering that, of course. You see, I'm sixty-two. Perhaps if we could talk about the matter which has brought me all the way from—"

"I'm seventy-seven years old and you won't find an ounce of fat on my body. The way you look, you're either filthy rich or a sick man. I'm filthy rich but I'm not fat. If your heart hurts, you ought to stop eating. And if you can't control yourself, how can you call yourself a man? Thomas, you said there was something you wanted to show me, isn't that right?"

"Sir Roland has come all the way from England to show you some photographs of Roosevelt, Mr. Ford."

"Is that so?" Ford turned to Bo Pawker, who shrugged his shoulders. Then back to Sir Roland. "Come over here. I've got something to show you, too."

The Englishman approached the edge of the display case. It was at least six feet by ten feet and contained perfect mock-ups of all the buildings and conveyors at the plant. Ford tapped his finger on the glass over a particular model. "Know what that is?"

"I'm afraid not," said Sir Roland.

"My soybean plant. You ever heard of soybeans over in England?"

"Oh, yes, I believe we know all about soybeans over in England."

"Oh, no you don't. If I was a gambling man, I'd wager Winston Churchill never heard of a soybean in his life. He came to see me here, that Churchill. Few years back. I told him the problem with England was not enough food. He laughed in my face. An island ought to grow all its own food. Forget about trying to manufacture. Vegetables and livestock, that's what I told Churchill. Make England self-sufficient. They can leave the manufacturing to us. He laughed at me. What do you think of that?"

"I think Churchill ought to be hanged," said Sir Roland.

Ford raised his eyebrows and peered closer into this stranger's face. "You do?"

"Yes, I do."

"Well, that's English thinking. I wouldn't go that far. Look here. My soybean plant. I do everything with soybeans. I make paint, the meal in the hot tops, bind the charcoal, make the compound for steering wheels and distributor caps. That's my soybean plant. Winston Churchill never thought of that, did he? You bet your butt he never did. Now, look over here." His finger tapped the glass above another model.

"Yes?"

"My tire plant. It's not finished yet. When it is, I'll be turning raw rubber into finished tires in three hours. You ever hear of that in England? Of course you didn't."

Holtzer cleared his throat loudly. "Sir Roland dislikes Churchill just as much as you do, Mr. Ford. That's why he's come to see you."

"Well, Thomas, I'm glad he's here so I can show him a few things. Like my soybean plant." He turned to Sir Roland. "Do you believe in reincarnation, mister?"

"Well, I am a Christian certainly," said Sir Roland, desperately looking for Holtzer to assist him on this. "Reincarnation has always fascin—"

"Of course you're a Christian. We're all Christians here. But I'm talking about reincarnation," insisted Ford, his eyes sparkling. "When I brought out my first Model T, people used to drive down the country and those dumb chickens would get knocked all over the road. All the farmers in Michigan were after me. Because those chickens had never seen an automobile before. Model T must have killed a million chickens in its time. But look what happened. By 1923 the chickens had got smart. When they heard an automobile coming, Lord, they cleared off fast. Now, how do you account for that? Everybody knows a chicken is too dumb to get smart. Can't train a chicken the way you train a dog. No, sir, those chickens in 1923 had learned the hard way about what an automobile could do to them. Those were dead chickens come back to life. And that's reincarnation, mister. I believe in it. By the looks of you, you ought to believe too."

"Of course I believe," said Sir Roland softly. He'd begun to perspire heavily.

"You believe those chickens had been hit in the butt in a previous ilfe?"

"Yes."

"I'm guided," said Ford. He tapped the side of his head. "Do you think I could have done what I've done if the Lord didn't speak to me?"

"No, of course not," said Sir Roland.

"Produce like hell, keep prices down, and the wages high. That's what the Lord told me. They call it capitalism, but I call it Henry Ford's message from God."

"It certainly seems to have worked for you."

"You can tell that to Churchill, but he won't listen. The same with soybeans. The same with growing enough food. It's only common sense. Now, what did you want?"

"Show him," said Holtzer.

As Sir Roland reached inside his jacket pocket, Bo Pawker suddenly stepped in front of him. What on earth did the man think he was going to do, draw a gun? Ford looked on impassively over Pawker's shoulder as Sir Roland pulled the envelope with the three-by-five photographs out of his pocket.

"I also have the negatives," he said. Bo Pawker opened his hand and Sir Roland reluctantly placed them on the thick, leathery palm while staring at Ford.

"Please, Bo," said Holtzer. "Let Mr. Ford see them."

Bo Pawker paid no attention. He took a long look at each print.

"What is it, Bo?" asked Ford.

"Pictures of Roosevelt with some minx."

"Let me see." Pawker turned and handed the photographs to his master.

Ford held each print about a foot from his eyes, studying it. They might have been diagrams of a new manifold gasket for all his face gave away.

"Who took these pictures?" he finally asked.

"An Englishman by the name of Hayward," said Sir Roland. "He felt it was his duty."

"That sure as hell isn't Eleanor. What do you mean *his* duty? Is that an Englishman's duty? Going snooping with a camera in somebody's backyard?"

"Under the circumstances," said Sir Roland, but he wasn't allowed to finish.

"Who is this woman?"

"Her name is LeHand. She's Roosevelt's mistress and has been for almost twenty years. Of course, the public is supposed to believe she's only his secretary."

"I don't like this," said Ford. "I don't like this one damn bit."

Sir Roland flashed Holtzer a desperate look.

"What do you think, Bo?" asked Ford.

"The woman ain't Eleanor, like you said, boss." '

"It just looks bad," said Ford. "Bad for the institution and bad for the people. The people ought to see these pictures."

"That's exactly what we thought," said Holtzer. "And why we knew you would want to see them first of all."

"Do you think his wife knows?" asked Ford. "Hell, I've been married fifty-two years. People aren't going to like this. Not one little bit. What do you think, Bo?"

"Good for the Republicans," said Pawker. "Lots of hay."

"Is that the actual President down there with that woman? You're sure that's no camera trick?"

"No, sir," said Holtzer. "That's the President, all right."

"How I hate that man. Trying to shove the unions down my throat. And this National Recovery Act. Just a cover for the unions. Now this . . . this adultery. So that's what he does in the White House? I wouldn't want my Clara to see this picture. Bo?"

"Like you said, Mr. Ford, it looks bad for the institution."

Ford turned to Sir Roland. "Why'd you bring them to me?"

"Well, knowing how the American people look to you, Mr. Ford, with such deep respect, I thought you would know best what to do with such scandalous information."

Pawker was growing increasingly annoyed at something. "Holtzer, what's up your sleeve? What do you want Mr. Ford to do?"

"Now, Bo, don't start this again. We can settle our personal differences at an appropriate time," said Holtzer. "As for the photographs, it occurred to me that we ought to release them through the *Independent*."

"So that's it," said Pawker. "Why didn't you say so straight off?"

Ford was frowning. "Not like last time. We can't be repeating the same mistake we did in 1920. Thomas, you published those Protocols of Zion and got me sued by the Jews."

"This is very, very different, Mr. Ford," Holtzer assured him.

"Bo?"

"He's probably right, Mr. Ford. Those Protocols were

nothing but hot air. These pictures are the real thing. I don't see how you could get sued."

"We also thought Mr. Ford might want to make a personal statement," said Sir Roland cautiously.

Pawker turned and glared at him. "A personal statement?"

"On the *Ford Sunday Hour*?" said Holtzer quickly. "These pictures are going to create a hell of a disturbance." He turned to Ford. "The people, sir, will be very upset when they see their President is nothing but a . . . a gigolo. They'll need guidance. Someone above the political level. Someone whose moral standards have always been an example to the nation. Who else but yourself."

"What do you think, Bo?"

"Boss, publishing these photos is one thing. This personal statement is another." He gave Holtzer a long hostile stare. "I can't help but remember your last one, Holtzer. That Nazi medal you convinced Mr. Ford to accept. That one hit us right in the face."

Ford nodded solemnly. "Sales down nineteen percent for three months. What did I need a medal for, I ask you?"

"Or a personal statement," said Pawker.

"But this has nothing to do with the Germans," said Sir Roland. "This is the President of the United States caught in an unspeakable betrayal of his moral obligations. A domestic matter which, Mr. Ford, you are fully entitled to speak out upon. And, I hasten to add, the political repercussions can only be favorable to your own interests."

"You mean Willkie," said Ford, as if talking to himself. "We'll put Willkie in next November if it's the last thing I do. But no more Germans."

"Somehow everything Holtzer comes up with always has a kraut attached to it somewhere," said Pawker. "Maybe because he's a kraut himself." He turned away, then looked at Sir Roland. "And you, what's your angle? When did you join Holtzer's gestapo? You talk like a guy with plenty of class. And you're English. I don't get you."

"There's very little to get," said Sir Roland, attempting a genial smile. "Besides what has already been said."

Pawker nodded, entirely unconvinced. He turned to Ford. "Maybe you should be getting along back to the office. We have those people coming in at ten o'clock."

Ford was taking another look at the photographs, paying little attention to what they were saying. He looked up and said, "I don't own the *Independent* anymore, Thomas. Only the name. Sold the paper after those Jews sued."

"I know there's nothing to worry about on that score," said Holtzer. "I'm sure I can convince the *Independent* to print these pictures. Any newspaper in the country would be hungry to print them. And the *Independent* could make a fortune on the syndication rights."

"Is that so?" Ford looked at the photographs with new respect.

"Knowing Holtzer," said Pawker, "he'll be getting a big chunk of that money. As for the personal statement, Holtzer, let's put it this way. Mr. Ford will consider it."

"I'm sure you will, Bo."

"Now, we better get moving. Mr. Ford, are you ready?"

"Yes, Bo, get me back to my office. What about these?"

"I'll take those, thank you," said Sir Roland, reaching for the photographs and quickly returning them to his inside pocket. "It has been a great privilege meeting you, sir."

"What?" asked Ford.

"A great privilege to meet you."

"Well, for a fat Englishman, you know your manners, that I do say. Take good care of those pictures. The people ought to know. And Willkie. Maybe I'd better call Willkie."

"Gentlemen," said Pawker. He guided Ford past them and on out of the hall with the slightest touch at the elderly man's elbow.

As soon as they'd gone, Sir Roland turned to Holtzer with a look that would have melted glass.

"Before you say a word," said Holtzer, "remember that I warned you. And we didn't count on Bo Pawker. But I have a few days to work on him. We have a fifty-fifty chance of getting the statement. And the go-ahead on the *Independent*. That's all set."

"I must say you operate under rather peculiar handicaps here, Holtzer," said Sir Roland.

"What did you expect? This is Dearborn. Not Berlin."

"And thank God for that," said Sir Roland.

Less than an hour later, he was sitting in an automobile surrounded by four men on his way to northern Michigan.

The men were all auto workers, Holtzer had said. But under his tutelage, not Pawker's or anyone else's at River Rouge. Silver Shirts, Holtzer had called them. Highly disciplined, he said, trained in weaponry and hand-to-hand combat. They were an elite force who hoped one day to take their rightful place in the international fascist movement beside their brothers from Germany, Italy and Spain. Sir Roland would be safe with them until Thursday, the Fourth.

18

The breeze was out of the northeast. The sky without a trace of cloud.

It was a little before ten o'clock in the morning when they pulled into the lot at Carson's Bait and Provisions. An unpainted wooden jetty hung out over the quiet Potomac with perhaps twenty small boats roped to its mossy timbers. The river was over two miles wide at this point.

At first Rona had been a bundle of hesitancy and self-consciousness. Her only previous nautical experience, she'd warned him, was on the Staten Island ferry. Dressed in heavy twill slacks, a long-sleeved blouse and a light green cardigan, she carried a six-inch-thick folder clasped to her bosom. He'd insisted that she wear a bathing suit under that outfit and had waited an extra fifteen minutes in Arlington while she went back into the house to change.

Dinghy was as modest a vessel as Jackson had claimed. But Rona was genuinely impressed with it. While he cast off, she sat huddled in the open cockpit hugging her documents, trying to absorb what he was doing while nervously checking the receding shoreline.

After several difficult moments, luffing on the edge of control with the sheet snapping loudly overhead, he had them on a decent tack headed across the river. Leonardtown was on the opposite bank in its own narrow inlet, where the sailing, under these wind conditions, would not be all that easy. Jackson, looking forward to the small challenge, settled down at the tiller.

Rona opened up her folder of papers and made a show of beginning to read, but her eyes kept glancing at the shore. "It's so quiet," she said. "It's hard to believe we're moving."

As the sun rose higher and they sailed farther out into the river, it grew increasingly hot. He wondered how she could stand being buttoned up in all those clothes. Finally he suggested she might be rather warm.

"Now that you mention it," she said, "I think I'm about to turn into a piece of toast."

"Then by all means why don't you . . . you know?"

"Yes, I know. Forgive me for being such an idiot." She began to climb out of her sweater, blouse and slacks. Finally she was in her bathing suit, a powder-blue strapless model, and he was once again surprised at just how tiny she was. Perfectly contoured but tiny, with small firm breasts and a bottom he could have covered in the span of one of his large hands. Her skin was very white and he knew it had been a long time since she'd last been exposed to the sun.

"You'd better be careful," he said. "You don't want to burn."

"That's a funny thing," she said. "I never get sunburned. Or almost never."

"Well, if you say so. I'll keep an eye on you just the same."

"Oh, you will, will you?"

"You bet I will."

"Why don't you just take care of your job?"

"And what's that?" he asked.

"To make sure we get out of this alive."

He couldn't help himself, the laughter came up and forced his head back so that his eyes took the full blast of the sun.

"What's so funny?" she demanded.

"Are you really that scared?"

"What do you think? This water is definitely over my head and the shore looks about twenty miles away. I hope you're a good swimmer."

"You mean you're not enjoying it? Not one little bit?"

"I didn't say that." She was trying to hide her smile. "I . . . I'm enjoying it. At least, I think I am." She started to rise, unsteadily, still holding her big folder of documents.

"Well, why don't you stow those papers in the dry locker for a while?"

"Perhaps I should," she said. "But just for a little while."

When he had her folder put away safely, he pulled her gently next to him beside the tiller. For the next few

minutes he proceeded to explain the basic principles behind sailing.

It took them two hours and fifteen minutes to reach
Leonardtown. The last part, tacking up in the inlet, she enjoyed as much as he did. For he kept up a running com-
mentary on the problems of sailing into the wind with
only a very limited space to maneuver.

The Waterman's Inn sat on a small hill at the head of
the inlet. Founded in 1793, it had been run by the same
family for over 150 years. Since its founding, it had been
a favorite Sunday retreat for people seeking a breath of
fresh sea air and a delicious lunch.

There was a special buffet on Sunday: all you could eat
for a dollar. They filled their plates with crab salad, baked
Virginia ham and other local specialties. Rona was amazed
at her own appetite. It must have been all that fresh air
after months of sitting cooped up in the State, War and
Navy Building.

On the way back, with the wind at their stern, they flew
across the swells. It had picked up several knots since
morning and the waves were just beginning to break into
white crowns. They reached the Virginia side of the river
in less than an hour. Then tacked leisurely up the coast to
the jetty.

Rona had apparently forgotten all about her folder and
lay on her stomach near the bow with her head cradled on
her arms. He thought she might have fallen asleep. But after a while she rose and carefully worked her way back to
sit beside him.

Traffic on the Potomac had picked up considerably in
the past few hours. Dozens of sailboats, of all classes, rode
the easy, whitecapped swells, including one great ocean-
worthy ketch whose spinnaker billowed like a huge white
squab out in the center of the channel.

Rona helped with the tricky business of landing and
then tossed the bowline to one of the young Carson boys,
who tied them fast. While Jackson began to clean up,
stowing the sail and washing out the bottom of the cockpit, she climbed up on the jetty and put on her slacks and
blouse.

"Why don't you go get us a couple of cold beers?" he
suggested. "Need some money?"

"Of course not. Two cold beers coming up." He stopped

to watch her walk down the narrow dock. The change that had come after only a few hours out on the water was incredible. It had all been new to her and so she had no way to prepare her defenses. The Assistant Undersecretary of State had become a young and beautiful woman again. There was fresh color in her cheeks, a new sparkle in her eyes, and a hint of accomplishment in her walk.

It was then Jackson noticed the two men. One was leaning on the fender of a black Buick parked near the front of the bait store. The other was striding in his direction. He stopped and let Rona pass him, tipping the brim of his hat with one finger in a curiously ironic gesture.

Both men stuck out in their formal suits and their almost identical fedoras. Hardly Sunday-afternoon attire around Carson's boatyard.

"Hello, Jack," said the man when he'd reached the place where *Dinghy* was moored. "Have a nice sail?"

"Hello, Malcolm."

The FBI man reached into his pocket for his Viceroys. "Surprised?"

"Should I be?"

"I guess you're wondering what I'm doing down here."

"Considering the last time I saw you was sitting behind a desk in the Paris embassy, yes, I guess I am wondering what you're doing here."

"Can I come aboard?"

"No. I'll come up there." Jackson went to the bow and pulled himself up onto the rickety dock in one smooth effort. Over Orth's shoulder he saw Rona come out of the bait store followed by old man Carson and the two of them approach the soda cooler on the porch. "What's this all about, Malcolm?"

"I've been transferred back to Washington for a while. After the surrender, there was no point in my hanging around Paris."

"So you came down here to tell me that?"

"Not exactly."

"And how the hell did you know where to find me?"

"Come on, Jack," said Orth. "You know how things are."

"Do I?" asked Jackson, increasingly enraged. "I don't like it, Malcolm. Not one little bit."

"Sure, I know. It wasn't my order, if that makes it feel any better."

"Why should it? Why should I give a damn who gave the order? You bastards followed me down here on Sunday morning and . . . Jesus! What is this?" He moved closer to Orth, holding his arms rigidly at his sides, truly furious.

Orth stepped back as casually as he could. "Come on, Jack, you're smart enough to know I came down here for a reason. Let's get it over with. Then you can get back to your friend. Not only that, but I promise you the surveillance stuff is all over now."

"Oh, yeah? How about the interior-decorating stuff? How about the amateur-photography stuff? How about you start giving me some very straight answers, Malcolm, otherwise I may just lose my temper!"

"The time has come to share, Jack. We know half of it, maybe more. You know how the Director is. Well, this time I tend to agree with him. When Roosevelt has the entire Bureau at his disposal, why the hell does he have to approach the British? We know about the photographs, Jack. We know what a spot he's in and, believe me, we want to help him."

"What are you talking about?" snapped Jackson. His ransacked apartment, the black Plymouth outside Benet's house, Orth's questions back in Paris: none of them added up this far. There had been a leak somewhere, higher up the echelon.

"We *know*, Jack. So cut it out. We know about the negatives and about this Sir Roland Plenty. And we know you've been running with the British on this. Your little meeting up in New York, we know the whole score. I came down here to tell you that we knew. So we can start out right tomorrow."

"What's happening tomorrow?"

"The Director goes to see the President. Afterwards you and I will be working as a team again. Like the old days, Jack. Just like in New York."

"Is that what you think?"

"Jack, it's what *has* to happen."

Rona had started toward them with two bottles of beer. But the other man stepped up and blocked her path, detaining her in a conversation which, as far as Jackson

could see, had succeeded in thoroughly confusing her. She
kept looking from where Jackson stood to the man, shaking her head, protesting.

"Tell that asshole to let her alone. Anything you want
to say to me, she can hear."

Orth shrugged and shouted, "It's okay, Dunne. Let her
go." Turning back to Jackson, he said, "Very attractive
young woman."

"And an Assistant Undersecretary at the State Department. So watch your manners, Orth."

"For real?" asked Orth, doing a quick double-take.

"You're damn right she's for real. Now, listen to what
I'm going to say." Jackson took a deep breath, then let it
out in a harsh rasp of angry words. "You bastards
wrecked my apartment, snapped funny pictures of me on
the street, followed me all over town and, no doubt, have
been plugged into my phone since I got back. I'm not
some punk who folds up the second he gets a look at your
shiny FBI badge, Malcolm. Did the Director send you
down here himself? It must be killing him, poor bastard.
So he's going to have a talk with the President. Afterwards
you and I are going to be a team just like the good old
days? So why don't I just open up and . . . Hi there."

He stopped talking as Rona arrived, and gave her a
wide smile. She held out one of the beers and looked curiously from Jackson to Orth. "That man over there said
this was some kind of official business. Maybe I should—"

"Rona Silvers, this is Malcolm Orth. He's an FBI agent
and used to be an old friend of mine. Thanks for the
beer." He raised the bottle and let the ice-cold liquid refresh his parched throat. "As I was saying, Malcolm, I can
read a bluff as well as the next guy. If tomorrow I am told
that I'm working with you, then I'll probably manage to
swallow my pride and do that. Until then, you're wasting
your time, pal. If you know what you *say* you know, then
you only know about a third of it."

"We know the limey boys lost Benet at the airport. And
we know where he actually went. Boston, that's where he
went," said Orth. "What I don't understand, really I don't,
is when the problem is this serious, why the President
thinks he can cut the Bureau right out of it."

"I know about Boston," said Jackson.

"Yes? The British didn't come up with those answers

until hours after we did. They're playing Sherlock Holmes over here. They don't have the resources, and you know it. Now, if Benet has gone to meet Sir Roland, and Sir Roland has the negatives, then we've got it locked up. While the limeys are still knocking around trying to pick up his trail up north."

"Good for you," said Jackson sarcastically.

"Can't you see, Jack, how this has hit the Director? He feels betrayed. He thought Roosevelt was his friend. Believe me, he doesn't want the Republicans in right now. He's no isolationist, that I can assure you."

"Hell," said Jackson. "Isolationism is hardly the Director's style, is it? The more enemies we've got, the fatter his budget. I'd be interested in anything you could get on Boston, Orth. On Benet, for that matter. But don't give me this sob story about the Director's feelings, okay?"

Orth laughed. "You're damn right you'd like our information on Boston. Okay, Jack. Maybe they did mess you around this past week. What did you expect? You know how tough this game can get, and you know the President wasn't leveling with Hoover. But tomorrow we start out all new. Bringing the British in was a terrible mistake. The Director will sit down with the President tomorrow and, believe me, the President will feel much better once he realizes he just can't go this one alone."

"Malcolm, let's wait until tomorrow before we continue this conversation."

"Fair enough." Orth turned to Rona. "Jack tells me you're an Undersecretary over at State, miss."

"*Assistant* Undersecretary," said Rona. "Why?"

"No reason. I guess I'm just impressed, that's all."

"The way I look has nothing to do with how I perform my job, Mr. Orth. Nor, believe it or not, does the fact that I'm a woman."

"No, sir. I mean, ma'am. I'll bet it doesn't hurt, though."

Jackson stepped forward. "Malcolm, as I said, if there's anything for us to talk about, it will be tomorrow. Why don't you get along back to the office now. We have some cleaning up to do here."

"Oh, sure, I understand perfectly. I guess we'll be meeting tomorrow. It will be interesting to hear what they've come up with in Boston."

That hurt Jackson but he said nothing. There was truth in what Orth had said. The Bureau was a superb police organization.

Suddenly Orth stopped and turned around to face them. "You know, Jack, what puzzles me is your attitude to all this."

"How's that?"

"I mean, they could decide to release those photos at any minute. But here you are holding a diplomacy seminar with the Assistant Undersecretary out on your boat. Like I said, it puzzles me. See you tomorrow." Orth turned and continued walking down the jetty. Jackson stared after him, his fists half-raised, unable to answer the insinuation although it infuriated him. Yes, there was more truth in Orth's comment than he cared to admit.

Rona must have sensed his mood, for she stood aside, silent, and eventually followed him to the car, holding her beer bottle almost as if it were a candle.

When they were about two miles north of the jetty, he turned to her and said, "Excuse the language, but I feel like I deserve to have the shit kicked out of me."

"You look like somebody just did."

"You haven't asked me for any explanations."

"Should I?" she asked.

"No," he said. "You don't have to. I'm going to tell you."

"Is that wise?"

"It might be," he said, not really knowing what he meant. But as he began to tell her the story, from the start in Paris, up through the previous day with Mikes, he sensed that Rona was a very good listener. He could feel her body begin to go rigid with anger and, as he sensed her reaction, two things happened. He felt for the first time, as if it were an ache inside his own body, the terrible threat of what they might do to Roosevelt.

And he realized that the woman on the seat beside him was a woman he could dare to love.

19

On the following morning, Monday, July 1, the Director of the Federal Bureau of Investigation arrived at the White House to confer with the President. The meeting, hastily arranged over the weekend, was scheduled for 8:45 A.M., but the Director arrived, as was his habit, ten minutes late.

At nine o'clock, on the third floor of the executive wing, Jackson picked up the phone and called Steve Early.

"Do you know about this America First party Wheeler has put together at Kitty Fabri's tonight?"

"You bet I do," said Early. "The whole town is talking about it. I'm taking the missus to see the main attraction."

"Lindbergh and Hull?"

"Yes, sir, a ten-rounder between Colonel Lone Eagle and the Secretary, I wouldn't miss it."

"What does Hull think he's going to accomplish?" asked Jackson.

"Don't ask me, Jack. That Lindbergh has really got his goat."

"I want to go. Can you get me in, Steve?"

"Hmmmm," said the press secretary. "We were only given four invitations. And we had to pay for them, too. Can you believe it? A hundred bucks apiece. But I reckon you could sell them for twice that with no trouble. What's on your mind, Jack? I didn't know Kitty Fabri parties were quite your style."

"They're not. But I understand there will be a lot of heavyweights from the Hill present. You know, there's been concern that Wheeler might have a lot to gain from these . . . from the pictures, Steve. Tonight might just be the time he decided to start showing them around."

"Are you serious?" asked Early with alarm. "You think Wheeler might have latched onto the negatives?"

176

"We don't know that. We only know that there's a member of Wheeler's staff who is connected, in a very loose way so far, to Hayward."

"Jesus Christ! So you want to try to keep Wheeler from passing out any free pictures tonight?"

"I don't know if it will come to that, Steve. But I thought I ought to go, just in case."

"I've promised one of the invitations to Hersken over at the Treasury Department, but I guess you'd better take it. It's for two, so take a lady if you want to be less conspicuous."

"I'll see about that, Steve. By the way, do you know if Hoover has set up an appointment to see the Boss today?"

"He's in there with the Boss right now, Jack. Why?"

"Nothing important. Just confirming something. Thanks, Steve, for this ticket. I'll send Norma down for it."

"Anytime. You know the booze flows hard and heavy at Kitty's parties. And lately these America First meetings have been getting kind of wild. It'll be good to have you there. At least Cordell will have a couple of friends in the place. So long now." He hung up.

* * *

Shortly before ten A.M. the Director rose from his damask-covered Monroe armchair, bobbed his head curtly at the man behind the large desk and said, "Mr. President, thank you for your time." He turned and strode in an unwavering line to the door, where he let himself out into the corridor.

Behind his desk, Roosevelt was momentarily distracted by the observation that the Director never seemed to walk anywhere. When he moved, it was always at full charge. Yet, unlike the apocryphal bull in the china shop, he was surprisingly nimble. He wasn't a blind force. On the contrary, the Director moved with a quite elusive, always careful grace.

Roosevelt reached for the intercom and buzzed Missy, asking if she would come up.

Three minutes later Missy let herself into the room with her notebook in one hand and a binder full of letters for his signature in the other.

"Sit down for a moment," he said. She recognized the

troubled tone in his voice but said nothing. Roosevelt leaned back in his chair, clasped his hands behind his head, letting his eyes wander along the walls covered with his naval prints, the shelves full of the best examples of his stamp and model-ship collections.

She wanted to ask him how his meeting with Hoover had gone. But she knew better.

"What would you say if I told you I was thinking of resigning?" he asked.

Her mouth dropped open but she caught the cry of dismay. He was depending on her for a considered, unemotional response. Taking her time, composing herself, she went over each word of his question in her mind.

"First, I think I would say 'Why?'"

"All right. If I were being less than honest, I could tell you a number of reasons. But I want to be as honest as I can. So all I can say is that I can't tell you. That is *awful*. Can you forgive me?"

Missy thought for a moment she might cry. But that would only make things far worse. She bit down hard inside her cheek, then said, "I'll always forgive you, you know that."

"Dear Missy, I know. Which is why I ask your forgiveness in the first place."

"Do you mean resign, Franklin? Or do you mean not run for the third term?"

"I'm not sure," he confessed.

"If you were to resign, Garner would move in here. Could you live with that?"

He closed his eyes for a brief moment. "It would be difficult."

"Have you . . . have you talked to Eleanor?"

"No, dear."

"Or Harry?"

He shook his head.

"Is there anyone else you could talk to?"

"No, I think perhaps this one is all mine."

She nodded, not really understanding. For twenty years she had trusted him and for twenty years he had repaid her in kind. Suddenly, on this warm, beautiful July morning she felt a terrible premonition uncoil in her body like a hideous snake suddenly come to life after a winter's hibernation.

"Franklin, does this . . . is this in some way my fault? I feel frightened, as if it had something to do with you and—"

He laughed. That rich, sonorous laugh. "Dear, dear Missy. Your fault? No, never," he said. "How wonderful you are. And how silly at times. Wonderful and silly. I love you very much. Come here."

She rose and walked around the side of the desk, to his outstretched hands. He drew her face down and their lips met. She held him tenderly and pressed her face against his. He felt the cold tear trace a line down her cheek.

Then she quickly straightened and wiped her eyes, smiling at him, self-conscious and relieved. "I am silly," she said. "A silly woman."

"A wonderful woman."

"Whatever you decide . . . I know it will be right."

"If only there were 150 million Missys in this country, I'd never have to worry about a thing."

"You'd hate that," she said.

"Perhaps I would."

"Well, should I get back downstairs? Or do you have any more terrible questions to ask me?"

"Should I not have asked you?"

"Of course you should have. I only wish there was something I could do to—"

"You already have," he assured her. Missy forced herself to smile, not completely convinced, and started toward the door. "Oh, would you call Jack Jackson and ask him to come over?"

She stopped. "Is Jack somehow—"

"No more questions, my dear. Just tell Jack I'd like to see him as soon as possible."

Leaper had called from New York with what he termed "prodigious tidings."

He'd just received a cable from London. Would Jackson like it read to him over the phone? Jackson said he would indeed.

ARRIVE NEW YORK MONDAY NIGHT STOP NEW SEARCH ABINGDON OPENS BENET DOOR STOP EVIDENCE IN HAND STOP SIGNED FRASER

Wasn't that wonderful, asked Leaper. Sir Ian had turned up some new information on Benet. He would be arriving that very evening. Did Jackson want to come up to New York?

No, said Jackson, he didn't think he could make it. If the evidence was truly important, he could fly up to New York the following morning.

A short while later, Missy called and in a strange, subdued voice told Jackson the President would like to see him in the Oval Room as soon as possible. It was the call he'd been waiting for since late the previous afternoon. Now that it had come, Jackson felt curiously unnerved. He tried asking Missy several questions, but she ducked each one.

When things began to go badly in the White House, thought Jackson, you could almost taste it in the air.

It took him exactly eight minutes to get from his office through the executive wing and up to the central corridor on the second floor of the residence.

Roosevelt was behind his desk with his back turned to the door, staring out across the South Lawn. He swung around abruptly when Jackson entered, and beckoned him toward one of the chairs.

"I just had your old boss in here," he began.

"I know. Look, before you tell me, to save you time, why don't I tell you what I already know?"

Roosevelt nodded.

Jackson gave him a full report, including his talk with Orth at the jetty and a description of the FBI's "search" of his apartment, their surveillance outside Benet's house, and finally what he'd learned from Oscar Mikes. He concluded by saying, "I've thought it over very carefully. Somebody here in the White House has been talking. I don't know who else you've taken into your confidence. But I can assure you that I've only discussed this matter with you, Steve and Harry." Not strictly true, but he'd only told Rona after the fact.

"I know about the leak," said Roosevelt. "And thank heavens it's not a sinister one. You can probably guess it yourself?"

Jackson shook his head.

"Harry Hopkins. He's awfully upset about this whole thing," said Roosevelt.

"I suppose he didn't think I could handle it by myself," said Jackson.

"Not at all. Don't take this personally. Harry just wanted what he thought would be best for me. He's had very little personal experience dealing with Hoover these last years."

"So what did you tell him?"

"Hoover? What *do* you tell him? No matter what you say, Edgar always has a way of finding out what he wants. So this time I told him just what he wanted to hear. It saves a great deal of aggravation later."

"Does the Bureau take over the operation?"

"Yes, at least officially. I've put you in as my chief liaison. Hoover wanted to report directly to me. But I told him it had to go through you first. All of it. Whatever they come up with."

"I'm not very popular with the Director."

"So I gathered," said Roosevelt. "Quite frankly, I'm beginning to feel like an awful fool, Jack."

"What makes you say that?"

"I'm the President of the United States. But this is basically a personal problem. A very private and nasty business. I should have foreseen something like this years ago. Now I've got the Bureau involved, and you, and the British. Any minute the whole problem could become public. Thursday is the Fourth of July. We're going up to Hyde Park on Wednesday with Eleanor, some of the kids, Missy. I'm going to give it a good long think. It's either resignation or a statement unequivocally turning down the possibility of a third term. I suppose I'd hold the press conference on Monday. That would leave me one more week until the convention opens in Chicago. I don't have to tell you what a mess the party is in right now. All my fault, of course. I simply can't allow it to go on any longer. No, next week at the latest, I must make a statement. Hardly time enough, but I'd see what I could do to smooth a path for Wallace or, maybe, Cordell. This Wheeler bid must be defeated."

"I agree. But I don't see how your resignation could ever do that. And . . ." He paused, thinking it out.

"And what, Jack?"

"And suppose we get the negatives? What if we get

them on, say, Tuesday, the day after you'd gone in front of the press?"

"I'd feel like a pretty big fool then, wouldn't I? But they're clamoring for me to declare my intentions. Wheeler and the rest are at each other's throats. No, I've got to set a time limit on my own delaying tactics."

"What if we got them this weekend? Before Monday? Would you change your mind?"

"About a third term?" He stared up at the ceiling as if the answer lay embedded in the ornate moldings. "Perhaps. It's such a confounded business. Do you know what Hoover is really up to? What is the crux of the Director's problem?"

Jackson shook his head.

"It's not the British and it's not that I tried to outflank him. The real problem is this foreign-intelligence question. The time has come when we've got to consider establishing our own version of what the British call their Secret Service. Hoover, of course, *wants* all of it. He wants to expand the Bureau so that it has both a domestic and a foreign responsibility. The power of such an agency would be quite incredible. I don't think any President could hope to control the Director once he had that kind of power. The Bureau would become a law unto itself. A monster. Do you see what I'm driving at?"

"Yes, of course."

"Then what would you do if you were in my shoes?"

"Not resign."

"Perhaps I should fire the Director. But how could I explain that to the press? He has an enormous following. And he is one hell of a good policeman."

"And you're one hell of a good President," said Jackson. "But suddenly you're talking about firing yourself. I'll play along with the Bureau. And there may be something new from the British side. Sir Ian is arriving back from London tonight. He's sent a cable saying he has new information on Benet. Give it one more week. Think it over while you're up in Hyde Park, but give me this week."

"All right, Jack. One week."

"We'll do it," said Jackson, amazed at his own confidence. "I promise you." He rose from his chair.

"There's one thing, Jack, you *must* promise me. If the time comes that you do get your hands on those negatives, *keep* your hands on them. I don't care who it is, don't pass them to anyone else. Especially not Hoover or any of his agents."

"I understand."

"Then good luck to you, Jack."

If it had been a pep talk, thought Jackson, it hadn't been necessary. But if it had been a warning, he'd be damned if he didn't pay it careful attention.

As soon as he returned to his office, he called Malcolm Orth over at the Bureau.

Orth was happy to hear from him. If you could call a voice fat with gloating "happy." Orth had more information from Boston. They'd traced Benet from the airport to his grandfather's estate in Duxbury, Massachusetts. The grandfather himself was a stubborn old goat who had not been at all responsive when he heard they were from the FBI. But one of the servants, an old woman, had opened right up.

She said that Sir Roland' had been staying at Benet's grandfather's house for over a week. On Friday, Benet arrived and the two stayed up half the night talking. Early the next morning, they drove off in a 1936 Hudson which had been given to her husband by his employer. It was the way they'd just taken her husband's car which made her talk, she'd said.

When the grandfather was questioned again, he'd broken down and admitted all of it. But he still refused to state where his grandson and the Englishman had gone.

The Bureau had the license number of the Hudson out on a forty-eight-state alert, said Orth. It shouldn't be long.

Jackson reminded him that all new developments in the case were to be immediately relayed to him at the White House. He turned down Orth's invitation to come over to Bureau headquarters and ignored Orth's hint that he might welcome an invitation to Jackson's office. If they were going to be a "team," it would be on Jackson's terms alone.

After he finished with Orth, Jackson knew the time had come to fill Leaper in on the Bureau's involvement. It took a while to get the Englishman on the phone. Apparently he was having his hair cut in the basement of the St. Regis. When Jackson finally reached him, he kept the story short and straight. After all, the bad blood between the British and the FBI was really none of his business.

When Jackson had finished, there was a long pause on ʟeaper's end. "I suppose I shall have to tell my fellows up in Massachusetts to give up the hunt," he said at last.

"Yes, I suppose you should," said Jackson. "But look, Greville, this doesn't mean you're out of it. Let's see what Sir Ian has first. And, in the long run, this may work out for the best."

"Oh, I know, those FBI men are awfully efficient," said Leaper. "It's simply that, well . . ."

"Yes?"

"They're such bloody sods, that's all."

20

Under a tented pavilion of apricot silk, three hundred guests were seated at thirty round tables on Kitty Fabri's back lawn.

It was nearing ten o'clock. During the past several hours they had worked their way through cocktails and assorted canapés, coquilles St. Jacques, chateaubriand with sauce bearnaise, pommes Anna, braised celery, a salad of fennel and watercress, very ripe Brie, and finally fresh strawberries with Chantilly cream. Coffee had just been served, along with trays of petits fours. Now the waiters were beginning to circulate with an assortment of liqueurs. A tall black man dressed in a ruffled shirt and long gray tailcoat like a Colonial footman was wheeling a trolley on which were displayed a dozen different boxes of Havana cigars. He stopped at their table, and Jackson, despite Rona's frown, found himself pointing at the box of Montecristos.

Rona leaned over and whispered in his ear, "I didn't know you smoked cigars."

"Neither did I," said Jackson.

"It will make you look like one of them."

He winked at her. "That's the general idea."

They had been seated near the rear of the sea of tables, a long way from the small stage with its patriotic bunting, polished walnut lectern, and the banner which read "AMERICA FIRST" in giant blue capitals.

"I don't believe you," she said. "I think you *like* cigars."

"There are cigars and then there are cigars. This one happens to belong to the latter category."

Rona looked lovely in a white gown with an embroidered bodice of fine red and gold threads, a design that accentuated her dark beauty.

At first it had been difficult to convince Rona to come to an affair sponsored by the America First Committee.

185

But when he told her that Secretary Hull would be speaking and suggested that he needed all the support he could get in front of such a biased crowd, she finally agreed to go.

A full complement of strings had played Strauss waltzes during the dinner. When they weren't consuming the rich courses, Jackson was quietly pointing out some of the personalities at the surrounding tables. There were Congressman Fish of New York and Congressman Karl Mundt of South Dakota. And Governor Philip La Follette, who'd flown down from Wisconsin for the evening. There were a number of other ranking senators and congressmen. And then the big money: Colonel Sosthenes Behn of ITT, Edsel Ford, Mr. Eberhard Faber, Jim Mooney, who worked for General Motors, and even Cap Reiber, the swashbuckling friend of FDR who headed Texaco.

The Strauss melodies had stopped and something was happening at the front. A man had risen and was walking up to the stage. Dressed, as were most of the guests, in a white dinner jacket, Jackson recognized Senator Burton K. Wheeler even before he'd turned around to face the crowd. He gave Rona a gentle nudge. She followed his eyes and at that moment Wheeler tapped the microphone twice, began to count to five, while someone hastily turned down the volume, which had been far too loud.

"Who?" asked Rona, taking the fingers out of her ears.

"Wheeler."

"Ladies and gentlemen, my fellow senators, distinguished members of the House of Representatives, most honored guests, *friends*," said Wheeler, "welcome."

There was a great shout of approval from the crowd.

"Before we go one bit further, there is something we must do. It behooves us, after such a grand and elegant supper as we have just enjoyed, to say our thanks to a truly great lady. A lady whose generosity and graciousness are only exceeded by her legendary beauty. Ladies and gentlemen, when I ask this lady to stand up, I want you to let her know just exactly what we feel about her. Kitty?"

In the front row, Kitty Fabri rose to her feet in a blaze of emeralds and platinum-blond hair.

The audience responded with passionate applause, whistling, table-pounding and somebody even tried to start a chant of "We love Kitty."

Kitty Fabri's exact age was a well-kept secret, but from what he was able to glimpse before the crowd rose for a standing ovation, Jackson guessed she would not see fifty again. What he knew about her was limited to what he'd read in the papers and the occasional piece of gossip he'd overheard. She'd had four husbands, including a senator and a Supreme Court justice, all of them well into their seventies before she'd married them. At the moment, she was a widow, which meant that the rumors linking her with various eligible codgers around the District were again in full force.

"Speech!" shouted her guests.

Jackson caught sight of her as she went to the platform, dressed in a skintight tube of dazzling green. He had his first view of what an old congressional wag once had dubbed, "Washington's answer to the Sierra Nevadas." Kitty's bustline was almost as famous as her parties, and they had no doubt heard about her parties as far away as Tokyo and Leningrad.

"My dear, dear friends," she murmured into the microphone. "You all know Kitty's no speaker. All she can say is she hopes you enjoyed your dinner. And she knows we're all looking forward to hearing from Secretary Hull"—there were a few boos—"and Colonel Lindbergh. So no speech from little old me. Just"—she put her hand to her lips and smacked out a big kiss to the throng—"know that Kitty loves you all."

Rona tugged on Jackson's sleeve. He turned. Eyebrows raised high, she asked, "Do you think Kitty ever heard of the Depression?"

"Sure," said Jackson. "It was the guest of honor at her last banquet."

Then Wheeler took the microphone to explain the evening's ground rules.

It was not going to be a debate, he said. Rather, Colonel Lindbergh and Cordell Hull were each going to speak for twenty minutes on the agreed subject of "American Ideals and the War in Europe." In deference to his position, he said, Secretary Hull would speak first. Immediately after the Colonel's speech, the orchestra would return and there would be dancing. The guests were welcome to stay all night if they wished, for Kitty would be serving a country breakfast round about three A.M. And all donations to the

America First Committee would be accepted anytime after the speeches.

Jackson admired the slickness of the operation, with the blank checkbooks and the boxes already on the tables, where all could see what you gave. Then something caught his attention in the front and made him nearly jump out of his chair.

Wheeler had been on the verge of introducing Secretary Hull when a man rose and approached the small platform.

Wheeler came out from behind the lectern and bent down. The man whispered in his ear; when he turned to go back to his seat, Jackson realized it was Anthony Benet.

"Friends, I have a correction to make on tonight's program," said Wheeler. "Colonel Lindbergh is extremely anxious to get back to his family in New Jersey tonight. So he has asked if he could speak to us first. Secretary Hull has kindly agreed to this change in plans." Wheeler looked upset. Obviously they'd been saving Lindbergh, the star attraction, for last in order to hold the audience until they could collect the donations.

"What's wrong?" asked Rona.

"Nothing," Jackson said. "It's all right."

"Are you sure? Do you want to leave? I certainly don't mind," she whispered.

"Leave? Of course not."

"What *is* it?" she insisted.

"Benet's sitting up there in front. The man we've been looking for since Friday."

"Oh." She could think of nothing else to say.

Wheeler had finished his introduction and Lindbergh was coming onto the stage.

All through his speech, Jackson kept his eyes on Benet, and it was difficult for him to pay attention to what Lindbergh was saying. Fair and slender, with that impossibly handsome face known to millions around the world, Lindbergh was having an obvious effect on the women in the audience. From what Jackson heard of the words themselves, it sounded like a sermon. Every once in a while there was a key phrase like "the international banking concerns" or "war profiteers" that made Jackson wonder if Lindbergh had any idea who the hell he was talking to this evening.

The self-righteousness was the astonishing thing, to Jackson at least. Didn't anyone else under the orange canopy wonder what made this man speak as if he'd only just returned from a conference with the Almighty himself? Lindbergh gave the impression of an attractive, rather spoiled rich kid. What had happened to the quiet, self-effacing Lone Eagle?

No wonder this audience seemed to adore him, Jackson thought. The aviator-turned-isolationist must have reminded them of one of their own children.

After twenty-five minutes, Lindbergh concluded his speech, saying: ". . . as alone, strong and free of foreign entanglements, America moves bravely to secure a future as prosperous and as peaceful as she herself must always remain. I thank you."

Thunderous applause erupted as Lindbergh took a long swallow from a glass of water and began to leave the platform.

"Wait here," said Jackson. Rona looked up at him, started to speak, then just nodded. He left the pavilion and walked down across the dark lawn toward the front. Forty feet away, Benet was standing in the midst of a crowd that was trying to shake Lindbergh's hand.

Jackson waited in the shadows for the next ten minutes until Lindbergh had left the pavilion and he saw Benet sit back down. Only then did he return to Rona.

Cordell Hull was an impressive speaker, but the crowd was obviously not with him. He was dignified, elegantly handsome, with thinning white hair, and his mouth had a permanently sardonic expression. There were deep creases under his eyes from overwork. His large aquiline nose gave him a kind of nobility which, curiously, was reinforced by his soft Tennessee drawl. Not a matinee idol, perhaps, but not a spoiled rich kid either.

His speech was as different from Lindbergh's as English from Gaelic. Where Lindbergh had been emotional, Hull was logical. Where Lindbergh had asked them to look at the horrors of War, Hull requested them to take a glance at the facts of this war.

Lindbergh had never once condemned the aggression of Germany, let alone the atrocities the Nazis were committing in Europe. Hull asserted that so long as a totalitarian Germany persisted in attacking the democracies of Europe, no democracy in the world was going to be safe. Of course, he did not come right out and urge entry into the war. But he made it clear that he believed America ought to help her English brothers resist the tyranny of a Germany which, unlike Colonel Lindbergh, Hull did *not* regard as "invincible."

All seemed to be going on well, despite Steve Early's apprehensions of that morning. Hull was winding to his conclusion when suddenly a man in a dinner jacket stood up and shouted, "I've never heard such a pack of lies in my life. Come on, Hull, who do you think we are? You just want to get us into this war to cover up your New Deal fiasco."

"Sir, I have three more sentences," said Hull through the microphone. "I would request you to have the courtesy to allow me to finish."

"Finish? You were finished before you even started, Hull," shouted the man.

"Sir . . ." But Hull did not continue.

The original heckler had been joined by several more among the crowd. Other guests were telling the hecklers to sit down and let the Secretary finish. The vast majority was confused, distracted from the speech, watching a series of shouting matches begin to spread under the canopy.

Cordell Hull was having no more of this. He folded his speech and walked off the platform. Some of the more polite among the crowd began to try to get some applause going. At various tables, fierce arguments were in progress.

At that moment, the bedlam turned to slapstick. Kitty Fabri's parties were famous for her original, climactic touches that sent the guests home chattering about how Kitty had done it again.

Above their heads, two giant flaps dropped open in the apricot-hued canopy, revealing a compartment out of which spilled three hundred white doves, terrified out of their wits. The ensuing confusion as the birds flailed their wings, trying to escape, was not to be believed. Some of the birds fluttered right down onto people's heads before they remembered that they could fly. Others were beating against the canopy trying to claw their way out.

Rona clung to Jackson's arm. He looked at her, expecting her to be frightened or upset. Instead, she was laughing so hard tears rolled down her cheeks. "Come on," he said. "I want to see where Benet goes."

She followed, clinging to him, finally able to gasp, "Can you believe it?"

Secretary Hull and his wife, escorted by Steve Early on one side and an undersecretary on the other, were marching up the lawn outside the pavilion. Jackson caught Early's eye and the two nodded curtly. Hull looked ready to explode.

They reentered the pavilion down near the stage. Various America First officials were trying to comfort some of the women who had become hysterical and to separate a few men who were threatening to rip off their dinner jackets and engage in fisticuffs. Kitty Fabri was sitting beside a spellbound septuagenarian, fanning herself, oblivious of the chaos around her. Jackson recognized her elderly companion as a recently widowed senator.

A crowd had gathered by the lectern around Wheeler. Benet was there. Jackson stood about fifteen yards away, Rona holding his hand.

Wheeler was directing some men to run fetch the collection boxes and cover the exits before too many guests got away. He overheard Wheeler say, "I'll settle them down. For God's sake, Tony, tell those musicians to start playing."

Wheeler turned for the platform steps and Benet left the group and approached the lawn. He suddenly halted, and looked into Jackson's face.

"What do you know?" said Jackson. "I didn't realize you were here tonight, Mr. Benet."

"Excuse me but—"

"I tried to call you several times this weekend," said Jackson, stepping up to block Benet's path. "I was hoping we could get together again. Our last talk gave me so many new ideas. Photographs, for instance."

"Photographs?"

"Yes. I thought you could help me with some photographs."

Benet looked confused. "I don't know about that. This is hardly the time. This is a hell of a time, in fact. Why don't you . . . uh, call me tomorrow?"

"About the photographs?" asked Jackson, with emphasis on the last word.

"I don't think I have any photographs that have anything to do with . . . with your article," said Benet. He looked genuinely puzzled. "But if you have more questions, perhaps I can—"

"You won't be going away?"

"How did you know I went away?" asked Benet sharply.

"I just assumed. You never answered your phone."

"I had to go to New York unexpectedly. Look, I must get those musicians started. This is no place for us to continue our . . . uh, interview. I'm very busy. Try me tomorrow if you wish."

"I sure will," said Jackson. "And those photographs, I think—"

"Excuse me, will you?" Benet pushed past him and out onto the lawn.

After watching him stride to the small bandstand, Jackson turned to Rona with a disappointed expression. "Let's get the hell out of here."

"You mean you don't want to dance?" she teased. "Not with all these nice people and these pretty birds?" There was a new look in her eyes.

"I want to dance," said Jackson, "but not here. Not with these clowns. Let's go get the car."

* * *

Fifteen minutes later he pulled into a Mobil station in downtown McLean, told the sleepy kid to fill it up and went inside to use the pay phone.

He had no idea of Orth's home number, or even where he was staying now that he was back in the States. He called the Bureau switchboard and told them to relay the message to Orth immediately. The Bureau had a forty-eight-state alarm out for Benet: so where was he? At Kitty Fabri's goddamn fund-raiser. The big machine could use a little oil. And if the Director wanted this one so badly, his agents could damn well work for it. He returned to the car, paid the kid and started the engine. Rona sat close to him, her dark hair falling on his shoulder.

"So you'd like to dance," he asked softly.

"Would you?"

"If you . . ."

"No ifs," she said. "Would you?"

"Yes. Very much."

"I seem to remember you have a radio at your house."

"A Zenith. Very good for dancing," he said.

"Then let's."

It took Benet nearly forty minutes to reach a telephone. First he had to start the musicians. Then help supervise the fund solicitation. That proved to be a disaster. Kitty's terrified doves and the bedlam at the end of Hull's speech had convinced about two hundred people that there was no point in hanging around for more Strauss waltzes and a country breakfast at three A.M. Only about sixty guests lingered under the apricot pavilion.

When he finally placed the call in one of Kitty's guestrooms, the long-distance operator was stupider than usual. It took him ten minutes to get through to Holtzer's house in Dearborn, only to hear that Sir Roland was no longer there. But Holtzer assured him the message would be passed along.

Benet didn't like Holtzer but he felt certain Sir Roland would want to know what had happened. So he carefully reported his conversation with Jackson, brief as it was. The mention of the word "photographs," which Benet had not understood at all, sent Holtzer into a paroxysm on the other end of the wire. Finally he recovered himself enough to thank Benet for calling so promptly.

"It'll be taken care of, don't you worry," said Holtzer. "We're going to settle this real soon."

21

Jackson awoke in a room full of ghostly light, dawn looming outside his window, with Rona pressed warmly against the cambers of his naked back. Her arms encircled his chest and he felt her breath, slow and regular, on the nape of his neck.

He looked at the clock and read ten minutes past six. Gently he lifted her arms and moved to a sitting position on the edge of the sheet. Despite having had only a few hours' sleep, he felt totally refreshed and wide awake. He stood and watched Rona stir slightly in her sleep as she sensed his absence. She was different. A woman in his bed, that alone was quite a change from the past couple of years. But Rona was . . .

He smiled to himself, shaking his head, and left the room. In the kitchen, he poured himself a glass of orange juice, drank it in one long gulp, poured another and drank that. He went to the john and splashed cold water on his face.

What else, he thought, was different? It was tickling his mind just out of reach and then . . . Of course. He'd seen Benet last night.

Benet was back in Washington and, if Orth had received Jackson's message, things might already be moving very fast. This was not a morning he could afford to lie in bed. No matter how much he might like to do nothing else.

When he returned to the bedroom, Rona's eyes were open. She shook her head slowly, holding out her arms, looking as if she were still half in a dream.

The sight of her body stirred him profoundly. She was so small yet so full, with breasts that held their firmness even in repose against her flared rib cage. Her nipples were erect, her tapered legs thrown casually apart on the white

194

linen. Breasts and flat belly and the dark triangle between her thighs: he approached her and knelt on the sheet, naked. Their lips met, open and moist, and he ran his hand up the soft length of her. She reached out and lifted his manhood in the cup of her palm. That one caress sealed it. His hand slipped to her waist as, in a single fluid movement, she swung herself under his body and raised her legs so that her heels locked around the small of his back. Lifting her bottom in one hand, he found her at once. So tiny, yet there was a way for him. He fought the urgency as she moved on him as if in the possession of a thousand currents. There was no need for proving, for all the intricacies of acquaintance, arousal, the smoothing reassurances. They had been there. They had won that in the pitch-black hours so recently past. This was the proof. Filling, stretched, quivering, she was not ashamed to cry out with her victory. He responded with a cry and a convulsion, a series of brutal thrusts, his letting go and the final spasm. Not a word had been spoken. Good morning. Good, good morning. . . .

The telephone rang in the living room.

"No, goddammit," Jackson groaned into the pillow. "No!"

She giggled.

"I'm not going to answer it." It wasn't fair.

"You've got to," she said.

"How do you know?"

The insistent ringing again.

"I know," she said. "Go ahead."

He reached the living room just in time to cut off the fifth nagging electric bleat.

"Sorry to disturb you, old man," said Leaper in a brisk, excited voice that was not a bit sorry. "We've just checked in at the Mayflower Hotel."

"Who?" asked Jackson. "What?"

"Sir Ian and I. We've just now arrived, you see. Sir Ian has brought the most important news, Jackson. Really you must—"

"I've got some news for you too," said Jackson. "I saw Benet last night. He's back in town."

"Really?" cried Leaper. "Now, that *is* very good news indeed." He repeated it in an aside to Sir Ian, who must have been standing next to him in the hotel room.

Suddenly Sir Ian's voice came on the line. "Jackson, Fraser here. You say Benet has returned?"

"He certainly has. I saw him last night."

"Do our friends in the Bureau know this?"

"Yes, as a matter of fact, they do," said Jackson.

"Do they have him in custody?"

"I don't know. I could find out. What brought you two down to Washington so suddenly?"

"I'll tell you, Jackson, the moment you arrive here. Now, if there is any way we could get to Benet before . . . Do you think it possible?"

"Maybe," said Jackson. "This is really that good?"

"On the contrary, it is disgraceful. But quite helpful from our point of view, yes. Provided, that is, we can get to see Benet alone before he's hauled away by Mr. Hoover's agents."

"Can't you give me any idea what . . .?"

"Not on the telephone," said Sir Ian. "We're in room 1814 at the Mayflower. You'll come now?"

"Twenty minutes," said Jackson. "Give me twenty minutes."

"And the Bureau?"

"I'll think of something," Jackson assured him. And as he hung up the telephone, he did, amazingly, have an idea that just might work.

Returning to the bedroom, wondering at the mystery of what had caused Sir Ian and Leaper to suddenly fly down in the middle of the night, he found Rona sitting up in bed with the sheet tucked across her bosom and a smile on her face.

"I know you have to go. It's all right. I don't mind," she said. "I don't mind at all."

Christ, four minutes before, he'd been willing to let the telephone ring itself out of existence. Now he'd suddenly forgotten he wasn't alone. If the morning was just a sample of things to come, this was going to be quite a day.

He moved to the bed and sat beside her. "Something really impor—"

"Important has come up," she said, finishing for him. "Of course, and I understand."

She reached out and cradled his face in her hands, then pulled it to her own. They kissed; his hands took her gently by the shoulders and pulled her to him, and that was when it happened. Something broke inside him and he found himself suddenly lying beside her on the bed locked in a kiss that went on and on.

It wasn't fair, but she had said she understood, and finally Jackson realized it was true. He had to go. Yet how could he leave her now?

He leaned back, staring into her eyes, so full of the words but hardly daring to speak them. Finally he said, "Do you . . . do you think you could ever love me?"

She smiled, kissed him very softly and said, "Yes."

"I know that sounded bad," he said.

"Bad?"

"It wasn't very brave."

"Yes it was."

"I think I could love you."

"Good," she said.

"I do love you."

"I love you," she said.

"Good. Because . . ."

"Because?" Her eyes widened, her lips parted slightly.

"Because I love you. Oh, Christ, and I have to go right now, too. This is terrible."

"No." She shook her head. "You go. I understand."

"I'll call you at the office later."

"Please do," she said. "I won't be there until ten or so. Today is the day Millie comes back, remember? I'll be moving back into my own apartment this morning."

"That's right. Look, maybe I can pick you up after work. But leave your phone number here before you go." He pushed himself up off the bed. "This is just rotten."

"Why? I don't think so. I think it's wonderful," said Rona.

He dressed very quickly and she watched him without saying a word. When he was ready, he came back and gave her a final kiss.

"You will call me?" she asked. "You're sure?"

"I love you," he said.

"And I love you."

A trolley laden with the egg-stained remnants of an early breakfast sat outside Leaper's room in the Mayflower. Jackson stepped around it and knocked on the door.

Sir Ian opened it. Leaper was hovering just inside. "I'm sorry," said Jackson. "I'm very late."

"Come, come," said Sir Ian. "No apologies necessary. Now, what do you have in mind?"

"About the Bureau?"

"Exactly."

"It's all taken care of. That's partly why I'm late. I stopped in the lobby just now and called the agent in charge, Malcolm Orth. He wasn't in his office yet but I left a message. He's expecting to meet me at his office at ten o'clock. I said we'd go over to pick up Benet together."

"And it's only half-past seven now," said Leaper. "Jolly good. That gives us a good deal of time."

"Indeed," said Sir Ian. He waved Jackson to a seat and picked up a light tan mackintosh. Fishing in one of its pockets, he came up with a package wrapped in heavy brown paper.

"This is Nicola Benet's diary," said Sir Ian. "As far as we know, neither her husband nor her father was aware she kept a diary. It was found after I ordered a second thorough search of the Warden's Lodge at Abingdon two days ago. Hidden in the bathroom adjoining her own room. Evidently the young woman placed it there shortly before she took her life, as the final entry is dated on the day of her death."

Sir Ian shook his head. "What she has written about her father and Reinhard Heydrich is monstrous. Absolutely monstrous. I suspect Benet had no knowledge of it. I believe the effect of this diary will convince Benet to tell us everything he knows. It is a shattering document."

Jackson started to reach for it. Sir Ian shook his head. "I have not shown the diary to Greville. And I shall not allow you to examine it either. But Anthony Benet must read it. In fact, by law, it is his property."

Jackson looked at his watch. "We should hurry."

"Indeed we should. But there is one more thing I must tell you. Through our agents on the Continent, we now believe the Germans are preparing a massive bombing assault on the British Isles. Not as cover for an invasion, but something far more frightening: a terror bombing campaign launched against civilian targets. You see, the Nazis would prefer not to invade. They believe the Luftwaffe can destroy Britain's will to resist without putting a single man on the beach. The campaign is scheduled to begin within the next two weeks."

Jackson waited for him to continue, wondering just what this had to do with the problem immediately at hand. "Yes, that sounds terrible."

"I believe," continued Sir Ian, "the blackmail attempt against Roosevelt is directly related to the air attack I have just mentioned. The Germans want to strip Britain of its most powerful international friend at the same time that they try to bomb the civilian population to its knees and surrender. I believe the German plan could succeed."

Jackson nodded solemnly, anxious to get moving.

"And so does Mr. Churchill," said Sir Ian. He looked from Jackson to Leaper, who was also examining his watch, and back again. "Enough said. Shall we go?"

22

"The Bureau will have a stakeout," said Jackson as they neared Benet's Georgetown home. "I'm going to try to con them. Otherwise they'll get nervous and call Orth."

He made the turn and began the climb up Thirty-first Street. About fifteen yards below Benet's house, he spotted a light blue Chevrolet with two heads silhouetted in the back window. Jackson drew up beside them, stopped and rolled down the window on Sir Ian's side. The startled agent in the driver's seat looked up. In his mid-twenties, blond, wit' a pug nose, Jackson took him for a rookie.

" 'Mor..ng," said Jackson, handing over his wallet, which was opened to his identity card.

The agent finished looking it over and passed it to his partner.

"You boys had a long night?" asked Jackson.

"Came on at six," said the agent.

"Quiet?"

"Dead. They picked him up out in Virginia, I think, and followed him back here. Said he went straight in the house and turned off the lights about twenty minutes later. He's sacked out."

"Not for long," said Jackson. "We've come down to babysit until Orth can make it."

"You mean you're relieving us?"

The other FBI man, ten years older and obviously the officer in charge, finished checking Jackson's White House credential and handed it back to his partner. He turned and studied Sir Ian and Leaper carefully. "Who are they? White House?"

"Colonel Fraser and Major Leaper," said Jackson. "War Department. You want to see their cards?"

200

The senior agent paused, then shook his head. "That's okay. What's the story on our boy in there?"

"That's what we've come to find out. We're not here to relieve you, sorry. Just to start talking to our friend in there. Orth will be down in an hour or so, soon as he can make it."

"Okay," said the agent, "He's all yours. We'll be out here in any case."

"Right," said Jackson, and started the car moving on up the hill.

The doorbell woke Anthony from a drugged sleep in his bedroom on the second floor. He'd taken one of the barbiturate pills as soon as he'd arrived home. But even after he'd undressed and climbed under the sheets, the tension of the past few days seemed almost unbearable. As he lay in the quiet darkness waiting for the drug to work, his leg muscles twitched uncontrollably and he had to gulp for his breath as if the anxiety was smothering him.

Now the drug was still very much in effect. He somehow managed to climb out of bed and drifted through the habitual motions of drawing on his robe, moving down the corridor to the stairs as if sleepwalking, yet somehow conscious of the doorbell ringing again.

"Who is it?" he asked before opening the door.

Jackson nudged Sir Ian. The Englishman nodded, then said in a booming English accent, "Ian Fraser here. I have something of the utmost importance for you, Benet."

Benet struggled to open the top latch, barely able to keep his eyes open. It was only when he'd swung open the door and seen Jackson that the adrenaline kicked into his bloodstream in an attempt to counteract the drug.

Sir Ian had already taken charge. In a move as graceful as it was rude, he'd pushed Benet straight back into the hallway and stepped inside the house. Jackson and Leaper were right behind him. The door slammed shut.

"How do you do, Benet? May we come in and sit down?"

"What the . . . what is this?" said Benet, staring at Jackson. "Do you think you can push into my . . . ?"

"Now, now, Benet. We're going to give you a full explanation," said Sir Ian. "Leaper, perhaps you might locate the kitchen. I'm sure Benet would appreciate a cup of strong coffee."

"I don't understand what you think . . ."

But Sir Ian kept on pushing, gently but firmly, until Benet was tripped up by the edge of the couch and toppled backward into a sitting position. "What on . . . what the *hell* do you think this is?"

"What do *you* think this is?" demanded Jackson. "What does it look like?"

Suddenly Benet's confused and indignant expression dissolved. Jackson's words, perhaps just the sound of his voice, had penetrated the stupor. They watched as fear caused his mouth to collapse.

"You have no right," he said, almost a whimper. "I know who you are, Jackson. You'll never get away with this."

"Is that so?"

"Quiet!" ordered Sir Ian. "Please sit down, Jackson. I will do the talking. Mr. Benet, I want you to know that I represent His Majesty's Government and I am here on official business. I apologize to you for the manner in which we've just intruded into your home. But this is a matter of great urgency."

"What . . . what time is it?" asked Benet. The drug was coming and going in waves, alternating indignation and sleepy languor.

"It is half-past seven in the morning," said Sir Ian. "I shall wait until Leaper has brought you a cup of coffee. However, I will tell you outright that we are here with regard to your father-in-law, Sir Roland Plenty, a fugitive from British justice whom we know to be in this country."

Benet stared at him, started to reply, then decided to say nothing. They sat in silence for perhaps five minutes listening to the sound of Leaper banging about in the kitchen. Finally he emerged through the far end of the dining room with coffee and cups for the four of them. "Quite a marvelous cooker you've got there, Benet. Lights itself. After I spent five minutes hunting down your bloody Vestas."

"Thank you, Greville," said Sir Ian.

"Not at all, sir. Shall I play mother? You'll each have to tell me how you like it. Cream, sugar, Benet?"

When Benet had received his black coffee, he stared at

it for a long moment before he said, "You have no legal right to be in my house. You forced your way inside. I am telling you to leave. If you do not leave at once, I will call the police."

"I'm afraid," said Sir Ian, "that is not quite possible." He smiled apologetically.

"Oh, no? I'm afraid that is possible," said Benet. He put his coffee on the side table and abruptly rose to his feet. Before he could take a step, Leaper had moved across the room with surprising speed and was blocking his path.

"You ought to sit down, Benet," advised Sir Ian. "Or I shall have Leaper sit you down."

"Oh, really?" Benet shoved Leaper backward and stepped past him.

To Jackson's amazement, Leaper's next action was performed with the quick, spare lightning of a professional. Some sort of judo, he guessed. But nothing Jackson had ever been taught. Leaper had reached out and taken hold of Benet's right wrist, given it a delicate wrench against the tendons, and suddenly Benet was on his knees, his arm straight out behind him in the Englishman's almost casual grip. A gasp of pain escaped his lips, his face went white. An instant passed, then Leaper released the wrist and said, "Truly sorry, old man. But won't you please sit down? Please listen to what Sir Ian has to say."

Rubbing his forearm, muttering something about "kidnapping," Benet returned to the couch. He was not a brave man and that secret had just been revealed to all of them. Jackson felt embarrassed.

"Anthony," began Sir Ian, "we simply wish to know where we can find Sir Roland Plenty. Tell us, and we shall leave your house at once."

"I suppose you're going to beat me until I tell you," said Benet. "Is that the way His Majesty's Government operates?"

"Most certainly not," said Sir Ian. "If you had not pushed Leaper first, he would never have touched you."

"What about the photographs?" said Jackson. "Did Sir Roland give you the negatives, Benet? Have you given them to Wheeler?"

"What?" Benet looked confused, then angry. "What is it with you and these photographs, Jackson? I don't have the slightest idea what you're talking about."

"I'll bet you don't."

Benet shook his head. "You're wasting your time. I'm not going to help you, or Roosevelt, make an example of an innocent man. Pick somebody else to make an example of."

"Example?" asked Sir Ian.

"You know what I'm talking about. When you leave here, I'm calling the police. And the press. What jurisdiction do you have in this country? And you." He turned to Jackson. "You're nothing but a hired thug, aren't you? A White House thug."

"Benet!" snapped Sir Ian. "I ask you one more time to tell us where Sir Roland is hiding in this country. We know you were harboring him in your grandfather's house. We know you drove him somewhere this past weekend after you spoke with Jackson. I assure you, if you call the police, they will bring you very little satisfaction."

Sir Ian paused. "Sir Roland is wanted in England on counts of multiple blackmail, espionage and treason. For the past eight years, he has been an agent of the *Sicherheitsdienst* branch of the Nazi S.S., under the direct command of Reinhard Heydrich."

"That's preposterous," said Benet. "Are you willing to go to such absurd lengths just to—"

"Just to what?" asked Sir Ian. "Crucify an innocent victim? A true believer in the fellowship of all r :tions? Is that what you believe? I'm terribly sorry, my boy. But you yourself are the victim of Plenty's monstrous deceit."

"Of course I am. Anyone who doesn't agree with you is a Nazi, is that it?"

As he reached into his mackintosh pocket, Sir Ian's face grew extremely somber. He had no taste for this. But, as expected, it had proved necessary. Benet himself had seen to that. He was living a lie. A lie he had built upon, covered over, refused to exhume.

Sir Ian began to untie the string around the brown paper parcel. Jackson could see he dreaded what he was about to do.

"This is a copy of your late wife's journal. The only copy, so far as I know."

Benet's head jerked around, his eyes dropped to the parcel. "What are you talking about?"

"Nicola's journal."

"She never kept a journal," said Benet. "Never."

"Journal, diary, I don't know what she might have called it. Very possibly she never called it anything but kept it strictly to herself."

"It can't be. . . ."

"I'm afraid it is," said Sir Ian. "We've checked it against the handwriting in letters found at Abingdon Lodge. This is most certainly your late wife's journal. Evidently she kept it secret even from you. It was found by Scotland Yard but, of course, now it belongs to you."

"Let me see that. I know her handwriting."

"Just one moment. First I want to assure you that only two other men besides myself have read this. Both of them work at Scotland Yard, one a senior officer and the other their handwriting expert. I have not permitted Jackson or Leaper here to look at it. Now, I have marked certain passages which I think you ought to read. Which you *must* read or I shall read them to you aloud, in the presence of these two gentlemen. That is something I have no desire to do, so please do not force me."

"I want to see that!" insisted Benet, reaching out for the book.

A medium-sized, thick volume bound in fine-grained vellum, there were six little white tags stuck between the gold-edged pages. Sir Ian opened the book to the first. "This entry is dated December 18, 1933. I believe your wife was sixteen years old at the time. It was written in Bavaria, at the Plentys' holiday cottage in Murnàu."

"I know all about that," said Benet. "Give it here." Sir Ian let him take it.

In the tight, feminine script that he immediately knew as Nicola's handwriting, Benet read:

12/18/33—Dichtershaus, Murnau. They are having dinner now downstairs and I am alone, after waiting for Greta to bring up the tray. Arrived back at four P.M. in Reinhard's car, but alone. Neither Daddy nor Mummy asked many questions. Only the usual things, "Was it pretty?" or "Who did you meet?" That's Daddy's, of course. I was at Reinhard's house for five days. Endorf is, I think, not as pretty as Murnau but the Heydrich house was absolutely gorgeous. Many rooms, scads of servants, the old "hunting" style. I like Reinhard very much but can't imagine why he puts up with me. He says he would like to take me to Berlin one day. I said I would love that. At first, I thought he might have some kind of fancy for me. He told me that I was more beautiful than any German girl. But he was always very correct and I always called him "Onkel Reinhard." Several times he held my hand in the sleigh, and there was a kiss every morning and before retiring in the evening. Very formal. I must say I enjoyed myself and was treated as a grown-up lady. There were three other couples and a woman I suspect is Reinhard's mistress who rarely came downstairs before dinner. His wife is in Berlin. I must say that R. is a very handsome man. If I were older, it would be difficult not to fancy him. It was very good of Daddy and Mummy to let me accept his invitation. But then Daddy and R. are such dear friends. I wouldn't be surprised if Daddy hadn't suggested the whole idea because of our disagreement before leaving England. I do miss London this Christmas. Especially W. and Roselyn. I shall go to sleep now and let myself dream of Berlin. But instead of "Onkel" it will be W. How silly I am! But more happy tonight than any time since we arrived.

Benet looked up sharply, first at Jackson, then at Sir Ian. He was doing his best to hide his feelings but the panic was evident on his face. "I don't understand. It *is* her diary. But so what? I never knew . . ."

"I chose that entry because it is the first substantial reference to Reinhard Heydrich. The passage speaks for itself. Now will you please turn to the next place I've marked. August of the following year, 1934."

8/29/34—Dichtershaus, Murnau. The astonishing thing is that I could face them without breaking to tears. I was gone for ten days. From München Reinhard and I went to Mannheim and the castle at Pfungstadt. I have never felt so important. We actually had six soldiers with us when we were on the train. And the private car was just as I thought when I read about King George last spring on his way to

Scotland. It was exactly as it was at Christmas until
we reached Pfungstadt. The castle, I thought, was
beautiful but very gloomy. On an island in the middle
of the river. "Onkel Reinhard"—he laughed about
that and seemed to like it.

We arrived late the first night, almost dinnertime,
in the car. I was in my room changing when Reinhard knocked and came in. He suggested we have
supper in his rooms rather than in the downstairs hall
which I had said reminded me of King Arthur and
was rather spooky. His rooms were across the hall
and there was a balcony with a view down the river,
as if you were on a ship rather than in the great house.
We had a lovely dinner, served by Reinhard's personal
man, Horst, with champagne. A very funny dinner
because Reinhard imitated so many of the people we
had met the previous night at Baron Feustel's party.
Then it began. First many words about how beautiful
and intelligent I was. I was tipsy, too, I think. I cannot
tell you how frightened I was because of the change,
so suddenly. I tried to laugh at first but that only made
him laugh. Then I grew angry, and he laughed more.
Finally, I had some sort of fit and that was when he
hit me. Only once but it left a mark for two days. I let
it happen then, too frightened to say a word. It was
very painful. Afterward, he went out but he wouldn't
let me leave and I must have cried for several hours.
When he returned he was more drunk than before and
forced me to have him two more times. I did not sleep
all that night but lay there afraid to move.

In the morning, he was absolutely different. I was
allowed to go back to my room. But in the evening
he came again and said many things about how he
loved me, the wrong that he knew he had done, but
the madness of his feelings with the wine. He called
me many sweet names in German and stroked my
hair. In the end, he carried me to the bed. That time
I was very sore but I could feel something had
changed in my mind. Three more times that night.
The next day we went out in the car and there was a
lunch by the Rhine. That night I went to his rooms
for supper as he asked.

It was never again the terrible way it had been the

first night, never again the madness. It became something as in the cinema, watching myself and R., and each day was different, less frightening, and only the thought of Daddy and Mummy prevented me from perhaps giving in with my whole mind. We spent five days in the castle. R. swore that he loved me! I never said I loved him. Yet I am sure that I do. Of the first time, I think I will one day be grateful. How little I knew and how much I still have to learn. In the end, I wept for hours on the train after he left me at Mannheim. Now I am alone and in two days we return to Oxford. Tomorrow I will speak to them about my plan (our plan), for studying in Berlin this winter. I am alone and truly a woman and I think that is the loneliest thing one can ever be. He has a wife, I know he has other women. And I wonder what will become of me?

There were tears in Benet's eyes and he did not look up this time. With difficulty he turned the pages to the next place Sir Ian had marked.

1/3/35—Abingdon. I am alone in the lodge, having arrived back from Germany yesterday night. Mummy and Daddy will not arrive until tomorrow but all the servants are here now. Since I stayed on in Berlin for the New Year's Eve celebrations, it was decided I would return alone via the Hook of Holland.

Berlin! How to begin to describe those twelve days? I stayed in Reinhard's large flat overlooking the Tiergarten and R. was with me every night. He has divorced his wife, he says. So many balls, grand dinners, luncheons, the two days we went to Bad Lausick and the adorable inn. One night we even met the Fuehrer at the palace they call the Chancellery. It was the last night before Hitler left for his home in Bavaria. There must have been two thousand people at the ball but we spent at least half an hour alone with Hitler in his private library. He seems to me a very shy man. He obviously likes Reinhard very much. He said not a word directly to me after we'd been introduced and seemed not to want to look at me. But after we'd left, Reinhard said the Fuehrer had thought me exceedingly beautiful, and with beautiful manners. "Why are the English women the most beautiful?" he had asked R.

Another night R. introduced me to Leni. He is difficult to describe. My age or perhaps a little younger. R. said he was his "nephew." But Leni himself later told me this is not true. R. is very fond of Leni but acts toward him in a manner that puzzled me. Sometimes he is so very kind and affectionate; other times, he was quite cruel. Three times I saw him strike Leni. Leni and I got on rather well. He is a most handsome boy, blond as I am, and very slight. He said his home was Frankfurt but did not speak of his parents. R. told me to treat Leni as my brother. Since I have never had a brother, I did not quite know what that meant. But sometimes I had the feeling that when Leni and I were talking, Reinhard was watching us with jealous eyes. But he seemed to *want* us to become good friends. It was on the last day that he asked me, "How do you feel about Leni? Do you like him very much?" I was not sure how he wanted me to answer. Of course I said Leni was a very nice boy and I quite liked him. "Good," said R. "I was afraid you would perhaps be jealous." I assured him that I was by no means jealous of Leni, whom I had come to regard as I might a brother or a very close friend.

But I did not see Leni again, although he was supposed to have come to the station to see me off with R. The New Year's party was very tiring for me and R. did agree to leave early. But I'm afraid neither of us got much sleep. It is so hard to have these times with R. and then return to England where I am treated once again as a little girl who cannot take two steps without danger of falling down and drowning in a mud puddle. I will speak to Father again about studying in Berlin when he returns. Now I must finish my unpacking and then to bed. It is always good to be back in this house. I wonder if I could ever stay away too long?

The next marked passage came a few pages later. While Benet read, Leaper had cleared away their cups and saucers and retreated to the kitchen. Looking up, Benet saw

Jackson studying the portrait of Nicola over the mantel. Unwillingly, his eyes were drawn to it. All of what he had read was absolutely new to him. She had never spoken of Reinhard Heydrich except in passing, as someone her father knew.

Nicola's portrait captured a pose that Benet had seen many times when she had been alive. It was the way she had looked before her "illness" had begun. She was in one of those very quiet, faraway moods. Sometimes he had suspected she was unhappy with him when she was like that. And how many times had he asked, "What's wrong, dear?" only to be told, "Nothing. Nothing's wrong," in a voice that could barely conceal some profound distress underneath? If he pressed her, begged her to explain, she would end up weeping with what, to him, seemed quite inexplicable grief.

After the "illness," when each day seemed to draw her farther and farther away, and the times she had disappeared for a night, once even for three days, claiming to have no memory of where she had been, it had been difficult for him to control his temper. And yet everything only made him love her more. The times when she was hardly coherent, her rages, the men who called on the telephone after her disappearances, only to abruptly hang up when he answered, the wretched way she had looked when she was brought back by the District police that last time: all had made Anthony love Nicola with the passion of a drowning man trying to cling to a scrap of floating timber in a wild sea. He had refused, time after time, to believe her when she said she must leave him and return to Oxford. For what reason? She had never given him a single reason he could understand.

Only when the doctors prevailed upon him, describing the progressive nature of the schizoid disease, had he consented. And after he had sent her to England and begun to receive her letters, those terrible garbled child's words that accused him of being in some awful conspiracy which he could not begin to understand, he had let himself harden to the situation. *He* was responsible, she'd said, over and over. For what? For loving her and marrying her? For her illness? The doctors had assured him that it was all part of the disease. And Sir Roland had written him at least once a fortnight: warm, understanding letters that offered hope and went out of their way to absolve his son-in-law. It was enough to make him feel terribly ashamed.

Anthony had carried on well enough after she had gone: working hard for the Senator, taking no time off for his own. He was secretly relieved to be able to come home to an empty house for a simple meal by himself. It was an orderly life and he was an orderly man. But a life built around an empty space that he did his best to pretend was not there.

4/5/35—Murnau. Arrived and went straight upstairs. Daddy away but Mummy took one look at my face and spent an hour trying to make me talk. I could only respond in the coldest, worst fashion until, I'm afraid, she became very angry. Perhaps if I had poison now I would drink it. So many times in the car coming back I thought of jumping out, as we were going very fast along the mountain curves, to fall on the rocks. If I could have only had the courage.

When I left England, I was to go to Berlin. But in Hannover the train was stopped to take on passengers and two to R.'s men in their uniforms came to my compartment and told me there was a change. Reinhard would meet me at the castle in Pfungstadt. I saw nothing unusual with this change in plans and went with the men to a private room in the station until the next train to Mannheim. At Mannheim, late that evening, I recognized the Mercedes from before and the same driver. But when we reached the castle, R. was not there. Leni was there. He greeted me warmly. There was a telephone call from R. later that afternoon saying he would be delayed several days. But to have a pleasant time and to do anything I wished. There were many servants and the car was always at our beck and call. Leni and I stayed in the castle four days before R. arrived.

We got along very well together. Each night I went to my room and Leni to his and he kissed me good night, saying, "Sweet dreams, little English princess." I must say I was in agony at not seeing R. It had been so long since Christmas. I could barely stand to go to bed alone in that place without him.

Then R. arrived. He did not come and see me for several hours. I couldn't understand, but one of his men was sent to keep me company. Both R. and Leni were nowhere to be found. However, at nine o'clock R. entered my room and swept me up in his arms. I shiver to think of how wanton I was. He took me downstairs then. Waiting there were a number of guests he'd brought from Berlin, men from the S.S., and several young women, very beautiful. A great table had been laid and I sat on R.'s lap during the final part of the meal because it had been very drunken and the men were singing, the women allowing themselves to be touched quite openly.

At about midnight, R. picked me up and carried me upstairs to my room. He left me there and said he would return in a few minutes. Instead, sometime later, Leni entered my room, naked and ashamed. He explained that R. was drunk and had pushed him into my room. That R. wanted Leni and me to make love. I could not understand this at all and felt a great panic. But Leni wrapped a sheet around himself and sat down on the far side of the room and tried to tell me that R. did become quite mad sometimes when he was drunk, but it would pass. Then R. came into the room and he was really quite mad. The sight of Leni sitting in the sheet seemed to infuriate him. He picked up Leni and began to beat him terribly, calling him vile names, and then he dragged him over to the bed. I was pleading with him but this had no effect. In seconds, R. had ripped off my dress and my knickers and then was holding me with one hand and Leni by the neck with the other and slapping our bodies together on the bed. He wanted Leni to have me but Leni could not, physically could not. So R., while still holding me, dragged Leni to him and bent down and took Leni's small sex into his hand and moved it back and forth until he had Leni hard. Then he held me down as I wept and Leni took me. After this, I was weeping so hard I thought I would never be able to stop. But R. had quite forgotten about me. He had removed his clothes. He began to

have Leni from the back. R. is very large and I could
not see how Leni could stand it but he seemed to
have become a different person. Then he made Leni
have me again. This time I submitted but R. went
into Leni from the back as he was having me. Then
they stopped and changed so that it was R. having me
and Leni in him. And then he made me take Leni
and him into my backside, and then into my mouth,
both at the same time. And it went on and on. We
must have slept.

The next thing I knew was the explosion. I sat up
and there was R. at the side of the bed with a
revolver in his hand. I smelled the powder and then,
O God, I looked down and there was Leni's head all
smashed on the sheet with blood all over me and the
bedclothes and bits of hair and teeth and blood everywhere. It was too much to even scream. "He's a
Jew," shouted R. "Stinking little Jew, did you know
that? Get up and wash that Jew blood off yourself."
Then he left, walked out of the room. I was so terrified and sick and I ran out into the corridor and, God
forgive me, I ran to him and threw my arms around
him. But he pushed me out of the way and repeated
that I should wash. And I could not go back into that
room but lay down on the cold stone floor in the hallway until one of R.'s men came and made me stand
up, threw a blanket around me and took me to another room. And I was told to wash myself, some of
my clothes were brought, and then I was in the
strange room by myself all day and evening. About
eight, a servant came in with supper on a tray. I
asked about R. and he told me R. had left, that I
would be driven back to Murnau in the morning. I
did not sleep at all that night. I began to suck on the
towel in the bathroom. Just lay on the bed and
sucked on it until it was too wet, then sucked an another part. And in the car all the way I sucked on another towel I had found in the bath. But before we
reached Dichtershaus, I forced myself to put the
towel away. Still I have a terrible feeling that I want
to suck on a towel, or any piece of soft cloth, and
that I am losing my mind. And of course I must be. I
could not tell Mummy because I have never told her

anything; not even when I first bled did we discuss such things. But I think I must tell Daddy when he returns. I have to leave Germany as soon as possible.

Benet was unable to finish the passage, which went on for several more agonized sentences. He closed his eyes, slumped back against the couch, one leg bent up on his lap as if he were about to curl into fetal position. It was not grief. But an actual physical pain wracking his body.

Jackson shot a questioning glance at Sir Ian, who shook his head.

"Steady, man," said the Englishman to Benet. "There's only one more passage I must have you read. The last one marked. It's shorter than the others."

"How could you?" asked Benet in a hoarse whisper. "Doesn't anything have any meaning . . . any value to you?"

"Anthony," said Sir Ian in a gentle voice, "you are quite correct. That is a question each of us must ask himself. A question I would very much like to ask such a man as your father-in-law. Now, please read the final passage or I shall be forced to read it aloud."

Benet forced himself to pick up the book from where it had fallen beside him on the couch. In this journal, between these two leather covers, were all the answers Nicola had never been able to give him.

He remembered a Christmas four years past, the first Christmas after their engagement. She had gone off to Germany with her parents as she had every Christmas since she'd been a little girl. This time, however, she hadn't wanted to go but her father had insisted. The afternoon before her departure, she had broken down and wept so pitifully but wouldn't tell him why. Anthony had flattered himself, thinking she simply couldn't bear to be parted from him. The wedding wasn't until May. And what a miserable three weeks he'd passed during her absence: spending the "Joyous Season" alone in a strange country in his drafty room at All Souls. He'd listened to Welsh choirs on the BBC, written her long letters and torn them into little bits, gone down to the library and found himself beside the river instead. He couldn't read a line in any book. And he received three letters and five postcards from Nicola in Murnau. And one from someplace called Endorf.

It was the final entry. The date was the same as her death. The day he sailed out of Southampton on the almost-new *Queen Elizabeth*, aboard which, on his first morning, he received Sir Roland's cable. It was dated July 26, 1939.

7/26/39—He was here for three days. Daddy's friend. Just like R., Daddy's friend. Left an hour ago and sails at six. Daddy's friend spent all his time in Daddy's study. Talking about Daddy's friend. Not Daddy's little girl. Not Leni. Wanted to talk to me but I won't talk. Talk to Daddy. Even Mummy can talk to Daddy, but not me. I won't ever talk again. Daddy told me not to talk. So I won't talk. When he's far out to sea, I'll sink in the bath and open veins like red violets like Leni's blood on my breasts all quiet, never talk, never again. But I won't tell what Daddy did. Only to Leni and he knows, Leni knows. I see him knowing. When he's far out to sea, I'll sink in the bath. All Daddy's friends, do they think he's pretty? Leni knows.

Daddy's friend. Just like Reinhard Heydrich. His host for ten days during July 1939. Who had raped his wife. Far worse than that. Daddy's friend. *He* was Daddy's friend. And Heydrich. And Leni. And Nicola:

TOOK HER OWN LIFE AT NINE THIS EVENING STOP LETTER AWAITS YOU ON ARRIVAL IN NEW YORK WITH FULL DETAILS TRAGEDY STOP DO NOT BLAME YOURSELF STOP GOD'S WILL. . . .

Her Daddy, Sir Roland: unspeakable. Pimp. Much too clean a word for what he was: his own daughter, only daughter, how old? Sixteen? A monster like Heydrich. Sir Roland had known all along, from the start, encouraged it. Panderer. Whoremonger. Pimp. What could words do? Murderer. Traitor. What was he? Daddy's friend.

Jackson saw it coming long before Benet actually left the couch and started for him. He'd seen a few men that far gone before in his life: drugs, booze, emotional shock.

In this case, it was the latter. All circuits fired at once, the insulation burned off, the breakers blown wide open. Benet came at him with no expression in his eyes, just the blank killing look. Yes, and Jackson had started it. The wrenching free of the mandrake lie that shrieked like a bloodstuck pig on a cold October afternoon.

Jackson stood up quickly and administered the only effective therapy: a clean right to the jaw.

Benet dropped on the carpet at Jackson's feet. Sir Ian ordered Leaper to bring up some whiskey, and then they set about gently slapping Benet awake. Jackson knew it had not been all that much of a punch.

Once he'd come to and they had got the whiskey down him, he was a very different man. They got him up on the couch and Sir Ian wasted no time in asking the questions. Anthony told them everything he knew then: Dearborn, Holtzer, and the disturbing news, at least to Jackson, that Benet had called the night before and not been able to speak directly to Sir Roland. Just Holtzer, and Jackson knew Holtzer from 1936. One of Jackson's first "special assignments." Holtzer and Bo Pawker and the River Rouge. That had been quite a little job: the unions and Henry Ford, and Ford's refusal to accept the National Recovery Act with its provisions for collective bargaining between management and workers. Not a very successful job from Jackson's point of view. Ford had never been persuaded to join the NRA. Let's hope this time it went better. Goddamn it. Sir Roland had picked some lovely allies in America. Dearborn wasn't a city, it was a battlefield. One of the toughest towns Jackson had ever seen. He'd rather go up against Wheeler and John L. Lewis any day than the River Rouge. One thing was certain, they'd need a friend up there.

They left Benet at 9:15 A.M. The agents in the Chevrolet were still parked outside. Jackson gave them a wave. It was returned. They walked up the street and climbed in Jackson's car and started back toward the White House. He had to call Lester vanKamp at once. Lester was the friend they would need in Dearborn: the president of the auto worker's union and an expert, if that was the right word, on the River Rouge. Lester vanKamp was Henry Ford's archenemy and, thank God, Jackson's friend.

Sir Ian, sitting beside him on the front seat, had been

very quiet since leaving Benet's house. Finally he turned to Jackson and said, "I simply cannot make up my mind."

"Make up your mind, sir?" asked Leaper from the back.

"Yes, about Benet. Was it his father-in-law's brilliance or simply Benet's own stupidity?"

"He didn't strike me as a stupid man, actually," said Leaper.

"Then weakness. Call it what you will. It seems clear that Benet was utterly in the dark about Sir Roland. Jackson, what do you think?"

"Perhaps he preferred it that way," said Jackson.

"In the dark?"

"Guilt," said Jackson. "You said it yourself about blackmail. Guilt often makes the victim feel as though he's the criminal. And that was Sir Roland's specialty, wasn't it?"

"So it was," said Sir Ian. "So it *is*."

23

Rona had told them to expect her an hour later than usual at the office on Tuesday. She would be moving back into her own apartment that morning. But if she would have risen with Jackson, she would easily have managed to pack her things downstairs at Millie's and call a Yellow Cab to take her over to Cedar Lane. That way she could have been at the office right on time.

She was just being lazy and she knew it, lingering in that delicious slumber following their lovemaking. The sheets held his heady, masculine smell long after he'd gone. Jackson was only the fourth man Rona had ever made love with in her life. And the previous three had all been carefully planned, one in graduate school, two since she'd gone to work at State. They had all come after lengthy, complicated courtships. And each had proven to be a detour off a course which she had long ago set down for herself. If Jackson was a detour, at least he was an honest one. At least it had been spontaneous.

Rather than continue the debate inside her own mind, she'd surrendered to sleep. A deep sleep that somehow began to go wrong. There was something smothering her, dark and furry and inhuman, pressing her head down into the pillow. She woke up with a start.

A cat. A shaggy black-and-white cat with a long bushy tail and an insouciant expression. Not a nightmare at all, but Basil, Millie's cat, whom she'd been feeding for the past week.

"Hello, Basil," she said. "You naughty cat, what are you doing up here?"

It looked at her with a bemused tolerance and then shut its eyes.

Rona got up then, took a quick shower and put on her

218

evening gown to walk downstairs to Millie's. She was just smoothing the bed when the doorbell sounded.

Perhaps he had forgotten something? But surely Jackson would have his keys.

"Yes?" she called through the front door. "Who is it? What do you want?"

"Western Union, Missus Jackson. We have a telegram here for your husband."

"Oh! Just a minute." Rona began to work the unfamiliar lock.

Luther and Demby had played shotgun poker for kitchen matches until a little after midnight. Then Sue Ann, Demby's wife, arrived haggard and smelling of fried bacon and burned potatoes from her job down at Perky's, the roadhouse diner on the outskirts of Smoke Hole, West Virginia.

When Sue Ann saw the bottle almost empty on the table, she started right off shouting. But Demby was in a pretty good mood. He'd been winning most of the worthless pots and the bourbon had been hitting his soft side that evening. Not his crazy, mean side. So instead of getting up and starting one of those godawful riots that Luther could hardly stand, Demby had gone over and put his skinny arms around Sue Ann's lardy body and kissed her mouth closed, wet and sloppy, in the middle of her cussing him out. He'd led her straight into the bedroom of the cabin, winking over his shoulder at Luther, who was damn glad to see them go.

Almost immediately, Luther heard the shudder of the old bedsprings and Demby's boots scudding across the pine floor. Soon the monotonous creaking of the bed as Demby began one of his marathon humps. Luther had never known a man who could hold himself back as long as Demby could. And living in the next room these last fourteen months, Luther knew all about it. So, too, for that matter, did most of the women around that part of the mountains, who didn't seem to be able to get enough of Demby.

After a while Luther got up and cleared the table, taking the last two pulls left in the bottle. Then he went over to his bed against the wall. He shucked his boots, pulled off his clothes and lay down on the cot. Twenty seconds later, thanks to the bourbon, he was asleep.

When the telephone began to racket on the wall near the door, he sat bolt upright, thinking for a second he was back in prison. Then he heard the tree frogs and crickets outside and lunged drunkenly to his feet. He hit the telephone with the side of his hand, trapped it with his belly, and managed to get it up to his ear by the time he realized where he was.

Five minutes later, after copying down the exact address, Luther hung up.

He dressed quickly and went into the back room without bothering to knock. Leaning over the bed in the dark, he easily picked out Demby's lean body next to Sue Ann's hummock-shaped figure. Luther dug his fingertips into the back of Demby's neck and lifted the younger man off the pillow.

"Get up, Demby. That was Holtzer on the phone. He's got another job for us, heah? Get up, now, move!"

While Demby was kicking and cussing around in the back room getting dressed, Luther made coffee. They would need it to make the 120 miles from Smoke Hole to Washington by morning, crossing almost the entire range of Shenandoah Mountains on the way.

Outside, Luther's old Plymouth was parked under some low boughs at the edge of the clearing. The moon was still up and the pines shone with an eerie silver light. Demby let the screen door slam shut behind them.

When Rona opened the door, she saw a man in his late forties with a severely weathered face full of crow's-feet and tiny, etched wrinkles. He smirked at her, revealing a mouthful of crooked yellow teeth. His right hand was tucked under his left armpit. He looked like a tramp, she thought. But she had no idea what Western Union boys looked like these days.

"Could I speak to your husband, ma'am? He has to sign for it, you know?"

"I'm sorry," said Rona. "My . . . Mr. Jackson has already left. I can sign for it, can't I?"

Luther looked sharply over to his left. Following his glance, suddenly Demby stepped forward holding the gun. A sawed-off twelve-gauge Remington shotgun, the stock had been cut down so that it could be wielded in one hand. The barrels were two yawning black holes pointed directly at Rona's face.

"Inside!" ordered Demby.

"Do just like he says, lady," said Luther. His right hand came out of his armpit now, holding one of those bulky regulation-issue Army .45 automatics. With his other hand, Luther pushed Rona back into the room.

Taking her upper arm in his massive hand, Luther jerked his head toward the door to the kitchen. Demby grunted and moved quickly in that direction, holding the shotgun in front of him as if it were a torch and he was compelled to follow its beam.

"Sit!" ordered Luther, pushing her into one of the arm-chairs. "And keep your yap shut or you'll be goddamn sorry."

A minute passed before Demby called from one of the bedrooms: "He ain't here, Luther."

"Shit," said Luther. He looked down at Rona. "Where'd he go? Work, huh?"

She nodded, hugging her arms to her breasts.

Demby came out of the kitchen. She turned and looked at him, a much younger man than Luther, perhaps in his mid-twenties. Handsome, in a sunken way. His features were very sharp and he was so thin she wondered if he wasn't suffering from some kind of disease. But he moved with an animal grace that frightened her badly. Especially when he immediately began to size her up so that she felt as if his eyes were stripping her naked.

"What we going to do?" he asked Luther, leaving his eyes fixed on Rona.

"Shit," was all Luther would say at the moment. He moved over and pulled the curtain aside, looked down into the driveway at the garage with its open door. "What time does your man come home here?"

She shook her head, unable to speak until she'd swallowed. "I . . . I'm not sure."

"What do you mean *not sure?*" asked Luther. "I asked you what goddamn time he gets home." He took a step toward her, gesturing with the .45, "Don't you see we ain't playing games?"

"Please, I *don't* know. He didn't tell me. It could be anytime."

"Look at her," said Demby. "Will you *look* at *her*, Luther?"

The older man shot a glance at his companion. "So that's it, boy?" He laughed a short, bestial laugh. "So that's it? Always the same, huh, boy?" Luther turned on Rona. "You don't know what time, is that right?"

She shook her head, biting her lip.

"Then we'll just sit down and wait," said Luther. "And guess what, lady? You're gonna set right in that chair and not make any noise. Not even when we hear your husband come home. 'Cause my friend here"—he nodded at Demby—"he has a hankering for you. Don't you, Demby?"

"Damn right I do."

"But if you're a good little lady I won't let him do nothing to harm you, understand?"

"Ah, Luther, what the hell?"

"You shut your mouth, boy!" snapped Luther. "I won't let him, see? Not if you do everything we say. We ain't here to kill nobody. Just to take you and your husband on a little vacation up to the mountains. You know?"

Rona looked from one to the other. "I know," she said softly.

Luther laughed. "Sure you know."

"Luther?" asked Demby.

"I told you to shut up! Get out in the kitchen and find what there is to eat. See if there's any whiskey." He turned to Rona. "Reckon I'm gonna set down here"—he backed onto the couch—"and we'll all just relax a spell. Have us something to eat and drink. Wait till your husband comes home. What time is usual for him? Five? Six o'clock?"

"He could be very late," said Rona. "He doesn't work regular hours."

"Neither do we, lady. So where's your whiskey?"

"In . . . the kitchen," she said, remembering the other night when Jackson had introduced her to bourbon.

"Good. And don't worry about Demby. He can hump like a Kentucky Derby winner but he does what I tell him. And you, a nice married lady and all, I won't let him. Unless, that is, you want to give us trouble."

"I won't give you any trouble," promised Rona.

"That's real good. Real good. We'll all just set here and,

in a little while, I'll let you cook us something real nice to eat. How about that?"

"I'd be glad to," said Rona.

An hour later, she did get up and, under their close scrutiny, fry up all the eggs that were in the icebox. Along with two cans of sardines, a package of soda crackers, and half a jar of pickles, this was a meal they seemed to enjoy. They washed it down with Jackson's scotch, finished that, then started on a new bottle of gin.

About 10:30, Demby decided it would be a good idea to search the house for whatever he could find. Money, jewelry, guns, whatever. He disappeared into the other room while she sat at the kitchen table listening to Luther, half drunk, telling her about a trip he'd once made down to Mexico. Suddenly Demby appeared with a furious look on his face. "You ain't got one dress in that closet and there's nothin' in the drawers," he accused Rona. "What the hell is going on?"

"What you mean?" asked Luther.

"I mean this bitch ain't his wife. There's only one person living here. And that's a man. What are you, lady? His whore, that's what she is, Luther."

"You mean"—he turned to Rona—"you ain't Missus Jackson?"

Rona didn't know what to say.

"Why didn't you tell us?" asked Luther.

"Well, I . . ."

Demby began to laugh. "You're his whore. Jee-sus! And Luther here . . . Luther was being so damn careful about . . . Luther!" It was too hilarious for Demby to continue.

"Luther here what, jackass?"

"You got right sentimental about this little piece of chicken tail, didn't you?"

"Makes no difference. Married or not, she's done okay by us so far. So don't start thinking I'm going to let you start." He turned to Rona. "Don't you worry. He listens to me."

"I want to show her my hog, Luther. Come on now."

"You shut up!" hollered Luther. "I told you. She done us right so far. Now, Demby, get back there and see if you can't find something worth stealing around here."

Laughing to himself, Demby did as he was told. But not before he'd given Rona a look that seemed to say that sooner or later Luther would be powerless to prevent him having his way.

Two minutes later Demby found her purse and was back with it. They had her name then, her job, some old letters from her mother and about nine dollars in cash. Rona Silvers. It sounded, said Demby, like she was Jewish.

"What the hell difference does that make?" Luther wanted to know.

"Well, she might be communist too."

"Shit! Your old man was a communist, Demby, weren't he? And he sure weren't Jewish. Nine bucks and change. You still ain't found nothing. Get back there." The truth was, Luther was enjoying telling Rona about his woman down in Tampico and she was doing a very good job of pretending to enjoy it too.

At 11:35 A.M. Jackson turned the Ford into his drive-way and pulled to a stop beneath the outdoor stairway. "You want to come up?" he asked Leaper. "I'll only be a minute."

"No point really," said Leaper. He smiled and stretched out his long legs in the front seat. "Go ahead, old man. I'll wait down here."

"Right." Jackson got out of the car and slammed the door. They had come straight from the White House and were on their way to the airport.

It had taken Norma twenty minutes or so to reach Les-ter vanKamp in Michigan. Jackson had explained the situ-ation to the union leader, leaving out only the specifics about the negatives. He said they badly wanted the En-glishman called Sir Roland Plenty; that it was of vital im-portance to Roosevelt; that there was some friction with the FBI on this matter. When he mentioned Holtzer's name, vanKamp had let out a long sigh on the other end of the wire. They were bitter enemies, Jackson knew.

"If the Englishman is staying at Holtzer's house, I can easily check that," said vanKamp.

Jackson said he would be very grateful. He told the union leader what flight they planned to take, and van-Kamp said he would have someone meet them at the air-port.

After Jackson had briefed Sir Ian and Leaper on the phone call, Sir Ian did something that surprised him. He stood up in the cramped office and said, "I believe you are well on your way to resolving this problem. I shall now say my farewells."

"Your what?" asked Jackson.

"Good-bye, as it were. I have not had any sleep in almost forty hours. And I do not have to remind you that I am hardly as young as yourself or Leaper here. No, I shall return to the Mayflower and try to sleep. Failing that, I shall return to New York this afternoon. I leave Sir Roland to you younger men. Greville, might I have a word with you in private?"

Greville stood up and the two men walked out of his office. Jackson thought there was something strange about Sir Ian's behavior, but perhaps he, too, was just suffering from the fatigue of the previous few days. When Greville returned, alone, he said that Sir Ian had gone off to the Mayflower.

Their flight to Detroit was scheduled for 12:30. That left plenty of time for Jackson to stop off and get his revolver. Knowing the River Rouge as he did, and not really knowing Sir Roland at all, Jackson had decided it would be foolish to arrive unarmed.

As he walked up the staircase to his apartment he noticed nothing unusual. In fact, his thoughts were far away. For when he'd arrived at his office after Benet's house, the first thing that had caught his eye on the desk was an envelope with his lawyer's address in the upper-left-hand corner. He'd opened it and read that his lawyer had received a letter from Phoenix. Barbara's lawyer had said that as far as Mrs. Muller was now concerned, there were no plans to have Jackson's daughter adopted by Carl Muller. Furthermore, Mrs. Muller was willing to allow Jackson's daughter to visit her father that coming August.

It was a beautiful morning, with a Delft-blue sky flecked with scattered wisps of cloud, and Jackson was still savoring the news in that letter as he bounded up the stairs. He was just about to insert his key in the lock when the door was flung open.

Luther was standing in the entrance with his .45 automatic pointed at Jackson's face. In the background, he saw Rona staring at him, terrified, as Demby held the sawed-off shotgun to her temple with his right hand. His left hand was wrapped around her head, squeezing her mouth shut.

"Mistah Jackson, don't fucking move!" he whispered. Jackson froze.

"Keep your hands away from your pockets," ordered Luther. "Step in here. Slow and easy now." Jackson did as he was told.

"Cover me, Demby," said Luther. "Now, you turn around there, Jackson. *Raise* those hands. I'm gonna look you over."

Luther patted him down with an unprofessional but thorough zeal. "You don't carry no gun, Jackson? And I was told you was some big government agent."

"You must be joking," said Jackson. "I don't work for the government. You must have the wrong man."

"Shit!" said Luther. "You don't lie too good, boy. Your woman here works for the government. And she already told me you did too. Turn around now."

Jackson's eyes met Rona's. She was very frightened, but she seemed to be in control of herself.

"Set down. Over there." Luther pushed him and Jackson landed on the center of the couch, watching as Demby removed his hand from Rona's mouth and let it run slowly down her side, over her breast.

"Don't like that, do you?" asked Demby, leering. Jackson gave him a look that could have, was meant to, flush a toilet.

"Shut up," ordered Luther. "And keep your paws off her. Jackson, don't get the wrong idea. All we gonna do is take you and her up to the mountains for awhile. A week maybe. Nobody's gonna touch your old lady or you so long as you keep things real easy. Just a real nice vacation for you two lovebirds, hear?"

Jackson nodded. It was pure chance. They could have told him to sit anywhere. He hadn't thought of moving the gun since the night he came home from Paris, the night he met Rona on the stairs. His hand was resting casually on the edge of the cushion, having found the smooth metal flange that separated the two wooden palm grips.

"It's your party while it lasts," said Jackson. "Just tell your cockroach friend here"—he nodded at Demby— "next time I see him get even close to her, I'm going to step on him so hard his guts come out his asshole."

If he could, Jackson wanted to start them going. So far, everything had been far too smooth to give him an opening.

"Mistah!" shouted Demby. "Just for that, I'm gonna make you *watch* when I show your woman my big old ugly hog."

Luther shook his head sadly. "You won't get far if you push on Demby, Jackson. He listens to me, but only so much. For your own damn good, keep your mouth shut."

"Too late, Luther," said Demby. "He cut his slice. Now he's gonna have to watch me eat it, once we get 'em home." He laughed hard at that.

"Enough of your bullshit," said Luther. "I'm going down and put his car in the garage. Demby, you stay here and keep them on the couch. I'll bring my car around and we'll load them up. Won't do to be walking them up the street. You," he said to Jackson, "give me the keys to your car."

Jackson reached carefully into his pocket and took out his ring of keys, than held them out to Luther.

"Why don't we take his car, Luther?" asked Demby. "I could drive it back."

"Because, you stupid jackass, we ain't got no other plates for it."

"Oh," said Demby, covering them with his shotgun. "I guess maybe you're right."

"Git over there now, woman, and set next to your old man," ordered Luther. She did as she was told, easing onto the far end of the couch. Jackson thought she was handling herself very well, but worried that something might suddenly shatter the trancelike state she seemed to be in now.

He knew it was time for him to make his move, but he certainly didn't want Rona sitting next to him when he did.

"Can I have a drink?" he asked Luther, who was going out the door.

Luther stopped. "No, sir. You can have your drink later. Demby, you keep your distance from that man, hear?"

"Why?" sneered Demby. "He ain't nothing big."

"You do like I tell you." Luther turned and strode out the door, his boots clumping loudly down the wooden staircase.

"Well, now," said Demby, standing in the center of the room with his shotgun on Jackson, "you two sure look like a happy couple. You got yourself a right fine little woman there, Jackson. I sure am gonna enjoy showing her my big old ugly hog." He laughed uproariously.

Jackson paid no attention, waiting for a shout, a scuffle, the first distraction from outside. Luther should have been almost at the bottom of the stairs by then. Far enough to have spotted Leaper sitting in the Ford. He was afraid Leaper might be so tired that Luther would be able to sneak up on him without any chance of resistance.

The seconds became minutes. There was still no sound from outside. Finally, even Demby noticed the silence. "What's that Luther doing? He should have had that Ford in the garage by now."

Jackson shrugged.

Another two minutes passed. Demby began to edge sideways over toward the open door. "I'm gonna look," he said, "and I don't have to tell you how dumb you'd be if you made me use this on you." He flipped up the barrels of the twelve-gauge for effect. "So just sit real still like you been doing."

When Demby reached the doorway, he glanced down quickly at the car and the garage. "Luther? Hey, Luther?" he hissed.

Jackson had his fingertips around the grip of the .38 underneath the cushion. He'd carefully felt his way so that he knew exactly at which angle it was lying. But Demby kept checking them every other second. The man was careful—stupid, but exceedingly dangerous.

"Luther!" he called. "Goddamn it, answer me." Still watching them on the couch, he put his right foot onto the landing above the driveway. "Luther!"

There was a faint whistle from the street. Just enough, it jerked Demby's head around suddenly.

Jackson drew the .38 out from under the cushion and brought it up to get off his shot, simultaneously moving to his right to block Rona from the shotgun.

But as he fired, aiming for the center of the chest, another shot sounded from the driveway. It hit Demby in the right shoulder, spinning him back into the doorway as Jackson's bullet entered a little low in the skinny chest. As he fell face forward onto the floor, his shotgun went off into the doorframe. Demby landed with a fatal thud on his belly in an explosion of wood splinters and plaster.

Jackson moved quickly to the body and stared down at the gaping exit wound in the lower back and the gash in the back of the shoulder from the first bullet. He moved the shotgun away with his foot, then turned to Rona. "Are you okay?"

"Yes. I'm all right," she said.

He stepped out onto the landing. "Leaper?" he called.

Leaper was already underneath the landing. "Down here, old man. Are you quite all right up there?"

"I think so," said Jackson. He looked back into the room at Rona on the couch. Her eyes met his. She seemed unable to move, frozen in shock. "Where's the other one?" he asked Leaper.

"Around back. Unconscious, but I ought to check on him." Jackson suddenly realized Leaper was holding Luther's Army .45.

"Do that," he said. "And by the way, I didn't know you could shoot like that."

Leaper stopped and smiled up at him, that deceptive eight-year-old's smile. "Oh, yes, Sir Ian insists that we all—"

"Jack!" she screamed behind him.

The explosion filled the room, shaking the landing on which Jackson stood. Demby had somehow got his hand on the shotgun. Jackson looked from the shredded couch to Rona to the man on his belly with the sawed-off weapon in his hand. He emptied the .38 into Demby's back.

Then his killing rage abruptly left him and he stepped over the body and into the room. Demby's second shot had pulverized the near end of the couch, the end Rona was not seated on. She seemed to be fine.

It was only as he approached her that he saw her eyes were closed, her head slightly lilting to the right. Her hands lay unfolded in her lap, her white gown immaculate and spread out around her small figure. He knelt beside her on the couch, whispering her name, taking her hand.

Rona did not respond. He looked in vain for any sign of a wound. Perhaps she'd fainted. He checked her pulse but could find none. Then he lowered his head to her bosom.

Very faintly, he could detect the flutter of irregular heartbeat. Behind him, he heard Leaper enter the room. With his head against her breast, he felt almost as if he was standing on a mountain trying to make out a distant echo from across a deep valley.

"We've got to call a doctor."

Then he saw it. The thin red line suddenly dropped down across her left cheek. Leaning forward, he gently lifted Rona's hair. Just below the hairline, there was a dark red gash on her perfectly white skin. The shotgun had sent a stray pellet that had caught her just by fluke. No fluke, no fluke, not with a weapon like that. He fought to push back his rage: there was no time for that now.

Leaper had already picked up the phone and was asking the operator for an ambulance when Jackson took the receiver away from him. In a level voice he told the operator his exact address and what he wanted her to do. Fortunately, she understood him the first time.

Twenty-three minutes later, they heard the sirens coming around the corner onto Woodlawn.

Leaper ran out to meet them, leaving Jackson with Rona. His cheek pressed to hers and his hand covering her breast, he was telling himself it couldn't be too deep. God, not too deep.

24

Sitting on the couch in the warm morning light, Benet found himself staring at her portrait. Hideous. He had not been able to look at it for a year, not since her death. But now he suddenly found himself unable to ignore the revulsion, the gagging nausea in his throat, and looked at her. Why was it so hideous? Nicola herself was beautiful, in the painting as in life. The artist had done a magnificent job of capturing her beauty. Yet now it might have been a bloodsplashed carcass hanging on an iron hook: that's how it made him feel.

The anger swept over him like a heavy tide. He felt much too heavy to float on its surface. His intellect had shut off. His body, full of the anger, had been taken over. So strong, it was like being drunk. Except there was nothing fuzzy about how he felt. Only an awful clarity.

Daddy's friend. The words had become a litany that replaced the need for thought. Daddy's friend. If anger could be expressed in words those were the words. Daddy's friend. A cadence of breakers on distant cement. Not surges, but an irrepressible rising tide of anger.

He suddenly remembered the diary and wondered if they had taken it with them. No, he was sure it was still in the room. He rose and found it hidden behind the curtain on the interior windowsill.

He began to leaf through the gold-edged pages, reading a sentence from one page, a paragraph from another, feeling her handwriting as if it were being scratched onto his mind with a sharp steel point. Suddenly he closed the diary.

It was beyond endurance. He uttered a soft, helpless cry and fell to his knees in the narrow carpeted space between couch and wall. Crawling on all fours, he wailed as he dragged himself out into the hall. There was a mirror there. He recalled the many times Nicola had glanced into it, checking her golden hair and her lipstick, before they went off into the evening for a dinner party or a concert. Now, sniffling, he rose and looked at his own swollen red face. How disgusting he was.

Only when he gave himself completely to the anger did the clarity return.

He remembered his grandfather's words that afternoon up in Duxbury three years before. Nicola had left the room and his grandfather suddenly brought out the package. "I know you'll think this foolish of me, Anthony," he'd begun. "But you have something to hold on to now. A wife and a home and, God willing, a family soon. That city is not safe. It's your constitutional right to carry a gun. Even if you pack it away in the bottom of a drawer someplace, I want you to take it. You never know. There might come a time. Dammit! Just take it to make your foolish old grandfather feel better."

Anthony had taken it, hidden it in the car without telling Nicola. No need to upset her. His grandfather thought it was 1864 or something. But, in a curious way, Anthony had been flattered by the gift. It was a fairly powerful-looking revolver, although he certainly knew nothing about guns. A Colt something, his grandfather had called it. Brand-new, oiled, dark gray steel. A box of twenty-five cartridges packed along with it: his grandfather was always thorough. Anthony had stowed it away in the bottom of a drawer in his tool bench down in the cellar the day after they returned to Georgetown. Never thought of it again except on two occasions: both when Nicola was so ill, he feared she might find it and take her own life. Something had told him to get it out of the house, but he never had. Funny. How clearly he could see it now.

"Now, what the hell is he doing?" asked the younger FBI man as Benet's door opened.

"Dammit, Budge," said his partner. "Where is Orth?" He had no idea Orth was still back at Bureau headquarters waiting for Jackson. It was 10:37 A.M. and Orth had been trying, without success, to get some word out of the White House switchboard. But when he finally reached Jackson's secretary, she had said she had absolutely no idea where he was or when he'd return.

Anthony Benet had come out of his house, closed the front door and locked it. He was dressed in a light green summer suit, a raincoat draped over his left arm. He set a small valise down on the porch as he fussed with his keys.

"Should we collar him?" asked Budge.

"How can we do that?" said the older agent. His name was Hal Griese. "We're a surveillance, not a pickup. Christ, I thought the White House guy said he was going to wait until Orth showed up. Why the hell did he take off?"

Benet had finished locking the door and was approaching the sidewalk. His car, a gray Pontiac, was parked just up the hill, He made straight for it.

"Looks like he's taking a trip, doesn't it?" said Griese.

"What do we do?"

"We've got no choice. Follow him."

"Follow him? Orth is supposed to be down here any minute now."

"You want to wait for Orth? You want to tell him, 'Sorry, but the guy came out of his house and drove away about ten minutes ago. We thought we'd wait for you.' Look," said Griese, "we can call Orth at headquarters the first chance we get." As they looked on, Benet put his valise in the back seat, then climbed behind the steering wheel.

"Where do you think he's going?"

"Jesus, Budge, how would I know? Maybe he's going to get a haircut. Maybe he's going to Hong Kong. All I know is we're on surveillance. Our orders are not to lose him. Now, watch it. Here's your chance to show me what they taught you. I don't want this guy to know we're on his tail."

"Don't worry," said Budge. "He won't know a thing."

"For Christ's sake, just don't lose him," said Griese. "Or you'll be driving a typewriter in Clerical for the rest of your life."

It was 10:44 A.M. when the two cars, separated by sixty yards, made their way toward the northern border of the District. Benet stopped for gas outside Rockville. There was no chance for Griese to get to a telephone. Not until Chambersburg, Pennsylvania, when Benet stopped to eat at a diner, did the FBI agent manage to get a call through to his office in Washington.

Orth had been to the house by then and known the worst. At first, he was furious. But finally he calmed down and told them to stick with Benet and call in every chance they got. "You driving?" he asked Griese. "I don't want that kid driving. I don't want any chance of losing this character."

"Of course I'm driving," lied Griese. "What do you think?"

"Good. This is very important to us, Hal. Keep me informed every chance you get. The minute he settles, I want to know."

It didn't occur to Griese to mention Jackson's visit to the house with the two War Department brasshats. If he had, he would have solved at least one of Orth's problems. Jackson's disappearance. Orth's initial discomfort had turned into the beginnings of a full-blown temper tantrum. The Director had told him to keep Jackson fully informed. He would have thought Jackson would want to take full advantage of whatever he could get on this. Instead, Jackson had suddenly vanished. Could he have something that Orth didn't yet know about?

The next time they called Orth, they were across the line in Ohio. And the time after that, they'd just passed the northern outskirts of Toledo. It was after nine P.M. and both agents were exhausted. They had been subsisting on candy bars all day.

"How does he seem to you, Hal?" Orth wanted to know.

"You mean is he running?" asked Griese. "It doesn't seem like it. Never breaks the speed limit and he sure doesn't know we're on his tail."

Quite true. Benet had no idea he was being followed. The miles were dropping away with the hypnotic precision of a strip of film projected on the horizon for him alone. In a way, he'd never really come out of his barbiturate fog. Even doing sixty across the hills of western Ohio, it was as if he were still sleepwalking.

As he drove, two recurring nightmares took turns in his mind. One was the diary passage about Leni. Knowing Nicola as well as he did, it was impossible for Anthony not to think of this without imagining that it was he, not Nicola, in the bed. Not his body, but his mind that was being violated, exploded, covered with gore. The scene struck him as vividly as if it were his own memory, his own life.

The other nightmare *was* his own. It dated back just over a year to a night in Berlin, July 1939. They were sitting under the high arches in the dining room of the Hotel Metropole: Benet, an American journalist, two other Germans, and Heydrich. Benet had just returned from a two-day tour of the Ruhr. What a farce that tour must have seemed to his guides. He hadn't seen a thing that remotely resembled an armament, a weapon or a bomb. Heydrich was their host. By then, he and Anthony had met at least half a dozen times. Sir Roland had arranged that with his letter of introduction before Anthony's first Berlin trip.

The orchestra was playing and the dance floor was full of uniforms and pretty young women. Heydrich was in his black uniform, his high brow and long nose shining with a pale brilliance. Heydrich's skin was so white, it always made Anthony uncomfortable, as if the man were translucent. His eyes, however, were a cold, very restless azure.

Suddenly Heydrich put his hand on Anthony's wrist. Not a friendly movement, but a grip that was tight enough to cause pain. He had been drinking heavily. They all had that evening. "It is a pity your wife is not here to share this," he'd said.

Anthony had mumbled something about how, yes, it was a shame Nicola wasn't there.

"Next time you visit Berlin," said Heydrich, "please bring your wife. You know we are old friends. I am an 'onkel' to her, did you know?"

No, Anthony had not known that. Nor did he know why Heydrich was digging into his wrist with fingers like steel cables.

"Oh, yes. From when she was a little girl, we were very good friends. Please bring your wife, Herr Benet, next time you come to Berlin."

And Anthony had promised to bring her!

It was something he'd forgotten as quickly as the next morning. Now it tormented him as he drove west. The nightmare fed his anger as the miles passed, focusing his vision with the clarity he dared not lose.

"Well, I'm going to take a chance and fly up to Detroit," said Orth the last time Griese called. "I want you to stick with him. Use the field office in Detroit for your next report. I'll have them waiting for your call."

"You're flying out tonight?" asked Griese.

"Right now. As soon as I can get a plane." Orth slammed down the phone. There was no reason to be angry with Griese. He and the rookie had been doing a first-class job. What was getting to Orth was Jackson. He'd given up trying to locate him hours ago. But he'd expected Jackson would be the one anxious to keep in touch. Not so, and it was slowly burning Orth up.

Benet reached the outskirts of Dearborn at 10:15 in the evening. It was the same road he'd taken with Sir Roland only two days earlier. As he crested the low ridge, the River Rouge spread out below him, enormous shadows on a darkened plain, the outdoor security lights flickering like scattered stars beneath the dim outlines of the furnace stacks. Orange flames danced against the night sky. Was it a city, a factory, an armed camp? Even at night, its energy was intimidating. Benet could make out the outlines of the freighters unloading in a blaze of floodlight, the conveyors snaking into the huge shape of the blast furnace. Beyond, it was too dark to clearly distinguish the various plants, the assembly giant, the rolling mills. Just a spread of security lights glinting like splintered glass on a black horizon.

It was a warm night. The wind coming through his windows had been some relief as he drove that afternoon. Here in Dearborn the wind was harsh, with a stench of burned ore and a grit that bothered his eyes. But relief was not something he was looking for in the wind anymore.

Not as he slowed down before the gates on Michigan Avenue that marked the entrance to Holtzer's estate.

IV

WHITEFISH
POINT

JULY 2, 1940

25

In the end, Jackson and Leaper flew to Detroit aboard a
small Navy plane. It was far too noisy to hear themselves think, let alone talk, and for that Jackson was grateful. Leaper had done his best all day to keep out of Jackson's way, to help whenever he could. Now, as they taxied
to a stop outside the commercial terminal at Detroit Airport, he stood up in the narrow aisle and put his hand on
Jackson's shoulder as if to remind him that they still had a
long way to go. It was just after ten o'clock on Tuesday
night.

Jackson was okay now. He hadn't been, not at all, when
the police arrived with the ambulance. The Arlington sergeant had tried to question him as they were putting Rona
on the stretcher. Jackson had shoved him out of the way.
At that point, he was so angry and unstrung that he would
have hit the cop if he so much as said another word. But
the officer backed off.

Jackson helped the ambulance attendants with the delicate business of getting Rona down the stairs and out to
the street. As they were loading her carefully, skillfully,
into the back of the ambulance, he suddenly realized what
a miserable job they had. What a sad, thankless bitch of a
job. Carrying the sick and dying all day, six days a week,
fifty weeks a year, from their homes to the hospital, from
the hospital to their homes, on that wretched strip of canvas with its two wooden supports.

Something inside him closed down then, and suddenly
he was okay. He realized that it wasn't going to do any
good to hit someone, to shout or kick the walls.

He told the cops exactly what had happened and
watched while they cuffed Luther and shoved him into the
back of a patrol car. Another ambulance came to collect

Demby's body. Jackson and Leaper got back into the Ford and drove to the hospital without exchanging a word.

Rona was taken straight into the emergency operating room. Twenty minutes after Jackson and Leaper arrived, a doctor came out into the corridor. They were calling in a specialist, a brain surgeon from Maryland, and Rona would be moved upstairs for the operation. It looked like the small steel missile had penetrated the interior wall of her skullcase at a point approximately two inches above her left ear. Until the specialist arrived, they wouldn't know the degree of cerebral damage. He advised Jackson to relax and take it easy. It would take some time yet.

While they were waiting for the surgeon to arrive, Jackson decided to call the State Department. He eventually got through to someone in the Immigration Department, who was horrified to hear the news. When he hung up, Jackson called Norma and told her what had happened. She wanted to rush right over, even though she had never met Rona, but Jackson asked her to stay at the office and not to tell anyone what had occurred.

At 2:14 P.M. Rona was wheeled into the large operating room on the fourth floor of the hospital.

Leaper seemed prepared to sit next to him on the bench in the antiseptic dull-green corridor for as long as Jackson remained there. Finally, it was Jackson who said, "I don't think we can wait any longer."

Rona had been on the table for three hours and, as far as they knew, she might be there many hours more. Time was extremely critical. It was posible the FBI might have already arrived in Dearborn and taken custody of Sir Roland. For the past hour, Jackson had been putting off the phone call to vanKamp. Finally he went to the booth and had the long distance operator put it through.

VanKamp told him that Sir Roland had not been seen in Holtzer's house for over twenty-four hours. VanKamp's informant did not yet know where Sir Roland had gone, but was attempting to find out. When was Jackson coming?

Jackson said they would be leaving very soon. He explained what had happened at his house, and left no doubt in vanKamp's mind that he believed Holtzer had been responsible. That was one thing that had been tearing up his insides: the thought of Holtzer sending those animals after him.

Upon hanging up with vanKamp, Jackson placed several more phone calls. After some White House string-pulling, a Navy plane was ordered to stand by for the flight to Detroit. He also now consented to Norma's offer. She would come to the hospital and keep vigil outside the operating room. He still couldn't get a word out of any of the doctors or nurses. Christ, how he hated hospital corridors.

What made it possible for him to agree to leave was his absolute confidence that Rona would recover. It didn't matter how serious a head wound, how long she was on the operating table, he knew she would be all right. He had closed his mind to any other possibility.

As soon as they entered the terminal in Detroit, Jackson saw Stan Wicks, one of vanKamp's bodyguards. Jackson had gotten to know him fairly well the last time he was out at River Rouge.

Wicks was in his late thirties, short and stocky. His face had been badly disfigured in one of Henry Ford's mills when he was seventeen years old. Soft-spoken, gentle, without the obvious signs of bitterness, he always struck Jackson as a potentially dangerous man. All you had to do to provoke Wicks was to prove yourself a threat to Lester vanKamp. Wicks worshiped the soil on which vanKamp trod, like tens of thousands of others in that part of Michigan.

The two men shook hands and Jackson introduced Wicks to Leaper. VanKamp had gone home to his house in Ray Center thirty miles north of Detroit, and Wicks had come to drive them up. Jackson hesitated for a moment. He had a strong urge to go straight over to Dearborn and knock on Holtzer's front door. But Leaper must have read his mind, for he suddenly said, "I do think that's best, don't you, Jack?"

There turned out to be very little to the town of Ray Center except wooded hills. They passed one small general store with two gas pumps outside, closed. Then Wicks turned off onto a dirt road and took them through a number of confusing turns until Jackson had lost all sense of direction.

Lester vanKamp had not chosen to live in the woods because he was a country boy at heart. VanKamp had grown up in a Cleveland slum. Living in the country was something he did because his life might well depend on it.

Lester vanKamp had a great many friends and only a few enemies. But his friends were, for the most part, poor men, auto workers, immigrants who'd come to the Detroit area to make their "fortunes" in the mammoth plants of the three major automobile companies. Lester's enemies, on the other hand, were very rich men. Men who intended not only to keep what they had, but to increase it. By organizing the auto workers, vanKamp had put his life on the line. There had been three assassination attempts during the past nine years alone. It did not help his chances of survival that his enemies had branded him a communist, which he was not, or that there was at least one standing offer of twenty-five thousand dollars for the man who could prove his bullet had ended vanKamp's life.

Wicks suddenly slowed down before a modest but comfortable-looking house. As soon as he pulled inside the garage, Jackson started to get out of the car.

"Just a second," said Wicks. A door opened and Bill Sarnton, another of vanKamp's bodyguards, came down into the garage. He greeted them, then went around to the back of the garage and opened what had at first appeared to be a solid wall.

The headlights picked out another road leading off into the woods. Wicks explained, "This here is Bill's and my house. Lester lives back here another hundred yards. We've got the whole place, forty acres, fenced in with electric wire. Only way you get inside or out is through our garage."

By this time, they had reached vanKamp's house. It looked like several log cabins joined together into one rambling place. Wicks pulled to a stop in a floodlit gravel yard.

The kitchen door opened and Lester vanKamp stepped outside in jeans and a short-sleeved shirt. In moments, Jackson and Leaper were inside a large, cheerful kitchen saying hello to Mrs. vanKamp, who had stopped washing the dishes and come over, wiping her hands on her apron, to greet them.

Lester was as close to smiling as Jackson had ever seen him. He was a tall man with surprisingly narrow shoulders and the beginnings of a belly, no doubt the result of all the time he had to spend behind a desk and at the conference table. His wife was also tall but very thin, with graying hair and pale green eyes that looked at Jackson with concern. He guessed vanKamp had told her what had happened, for she immediately asked if he wished to use the phone. He certainly did.

When he reached Norma at the hospital in Virginia, she was sorry to report that Rona had still not left the operating room. Nor were the doctors being any more communicative about her condition, which was listed as critical. Jackson thanked her and told her he would call again in an hour. Although that meant Rona had now been on the operating table for over nine hours, the fact made no dent in Jackson's confidence. He simply refused to register it.

Jackson returned to the dining room, where Mrs. vanKamp had set out coffee and pie. It was summer, and all the windows had been replaced by screens. Jackson could hear rushing water outside in the darkness. He asked vanKamp about it. "That's a little branch of the Clinton River. We've dammed it off for swimming."

Mrs. vanKamp asked if there was anything else they would like.

"I would love a beer if you have one," said Leaper.

Lester vanKamp shook his head. "I'm afraid we don't keep alcohol in this house, Mr. Leaper. If you would really like a drink, I could call up the men at the other house and ask them to run something up."

Oh, no, said Leaper, he'd just as soon have coffee. Jackson wished he had warned Leaper about the vanKamps' strong views on temperance.

To change the subject, Jackson asked how vanKamp had learned about Sir Roland. The union leader explained that he had a maid planted in Holtzer's house and said that when the Englishman was leaving on Monday afternoon, she had heard the word "camp" used to refer to his destination. What camp it was, she didn't know, but was going to try to find out. Now, however, they had to wait until her husband picked her up after work tonight.

This elaborate espionage between union and management surprised Leaper. "It sounds as if you're fighting a war up here," he said. "I must say I didn't realize industrial relations were quite like this in America."

"We are fighting a war, Mr. Leaper," said vanKamp

sternly. "And from what I know of England, I doubt it is really much different there."

Leaper confessed that he knew little about the American labor movement, or its British equivalent for that matter. And nothing at all about Ford or Holtzer.

VanKamp nodded and proceeded to explain just what they were up against in Dearborn.

No matter how enormous, how diversified and far-flung his empire grew, Henry Ford insisted on running the Ford Motor Company as a one-man operation. All decisions of any importance fell to him alone. Of course, Ford had to have some associates to whom he could delegate a certain amount of responsibility. But the Ford bureaucracy was a most peculiar one. There was no clear chain of command. Instead there was a feudal system in which the executives were like barons vying with one another for the ear of King Henry. Ford didn't even allow his executives to take titles. So it was hard to say exactly what Thomas Holtzer's position was in the Ford empire.

"Ford is strongly antilabor," said vanKamp. "But he is a loyal American. Holtzer, on the other hand, is extremely proud of his German background. Obsessed, in fact. There is no question but that he has strong links to the Nazi regime. It was Holtzer who talked Ford into accepting the Grand Cross of the German Eagle, which raised such a fuss in the newspapers.

"Holtzer's biggest rival in the Ford Company is Bo Pawker," vanKamp continued. "Pawker handles the River Rouge problems on a day-to-day basis. He's really Henry Ford's right arm, his chief source of intelligence within the plant and his main enforcer. Pawker is a very tough customer. He and Holtzer hate each other's guts.

"The problem with Henry Ford these days is that he's simply getting too old to maintain his previous iron control. For a time, Holtzer tried turning Dearborn into a little Berlin, the fascist capital of the United States. He encouraged all sorts of extremist groups to organize there, including Father Coughlin and the Bund. They actually had Fritz Kuhn, the so-called American 'fuehrer,' on the payroll over at River Rouge as an engineer. Fortunately Bo Pawker is as anti-German as Holtzer is anti-Semitic. Kuhn tried to rape some nurse in an elevator over at the Ford hospital, and that gave Pawker his chance to kick him out. Right how Holtzer is heavily involved with a home-grown fascist outfit called the Silver Shirts. It was founded by a man named William Dudley Pelley. You see, Bo Pawker had *his* goon squad, so Holtzer has found one of his own."

"How medieval of him," said Leaper. "It sounds like a marvelous firm to work for: goon squads, Silver Shirts. My word!"

VanKamp turned to Jackson. "How are you doing?"

"I'm okay."

"We ought to hear something soon." He looked at his watch. "It's after midnight now."

Jackson nodded.

"You haven't really told me much about this, Jack. But if you say it's of critical importance to the President, I guess that's all I need to hear."

"I'm sorry, Lester. I'd like to tell you more but I have orders from the President himself." That was not strictly true, but he had no idea how the union leader might react to the Missy question. Basically, Lester was a very rigid, conservative man beneath his reformer's exterior. "I can tell you this. If we can't get our hands on Sir Roland, there won't be a third term for Roosevelt. The President made that clear."

VanKamp absorbed this news with a dark frown. The last thing he wanted was for a Republican to get in and start dismantling the New Deal.

Jackson excused himself to make another phone call. It took them longer to track Norma down this time. When he finally reached her, she said in a breathless voice that she'd just come from the fifth floor. Rona had left the operating room twenty-five minutes before. She was not conscious yet and the doctors were still not committing themselves. But it was a good sign, wasn't it, that she was out of the operating room? It was wonderful news, said Jackson, assuming Rona was still unconscious due to the anesthetic. He urged Norma to go home then and get some sleep. She said she would probably leave soon, but would come back first thing in the morning.

Leaper was yawning when Jackson returned to the dining table. "You'll be my guests tonight, of course," said vanKamp.

"We don't want to impose on you, Lester," protested Jackson. "There are plenty of hotels in Detroit."

No, he insisted, they should stay with him. And then he asked, "How is the girl?"

Jackson told him that she had just left the operating room and was not yet conscious, but he hadn't yet heard the doctor's report.

VanKamp nodded. His eyes were full of sympathy but he refrained from speaking to Jackson about the matter.

At one o'clock there still hadn't been any call from Harriet Mullins or her husband. Finally, vanKamp insisted they all go to sleep. He led them to a bedroom on the east end of his house, rough-hewn log walls and two narrow beds, a pair of cheerful gingham curtains on the window. The moment the door closed, Leaper flopped backward onto the cot and, in seconds, had begun to snore softly. Jackson turned off the light.

Jackson did not remember hearing the phone. The first thing he recalled was a sudden flash of light in his face and then vanKamp's soft voice urging him to come out to the living room. They let Leaper stay where he was.

"Mullins just called," said vanKamp. "The Holtzers had guests and the party didn't break up until nearly two o'clock."

"What time is it now?" asked Jackson.

"Almost three."

"What's the story, Lester?"

"The young man who arrived with the Englishman on Sunday showed up again tonight."

"What?" said Jackson.

"Yes. He arrived right in the middle of dinner. Holtzer called him Anthony, she thought. Do you know him?"

"I certainly do," said Jackson. He'd forgotten all about Benet.

"Yes, well, he was looking for the Englishman. Holtzer took him into another room away from the guests. But Mrs. Mullins managed to eavesdrop. Holtzer made a telephone call to Sir Roland, and then Anthony spoke. He said he needed urgently to see him and couldn't explain over the phone. It was agreed, and they told him how to get to the camp. I was afraid of this, Jackson."

"Afraid of what?"

"I didn't want to bring it up until it was confirmed. It

looks like Holtzer has put the Englishman into a place called Whitefish Point. It's a Silver Shirt camp. Wait, I'd better get you a map."

He went out into the kitchen and returned a few moments later with a well-worn map of the state, which he spread out next to Jackson on the couch. He pointed to a spot at the northeast tip of Michigan bordering on Lake Superior. Slightly above the town of Sault Ste. Marie was a peninsula which ended in a place called Whitefish Point.

"It's a rundown Methodist camp the Silver Shirts bought three years ago, Jack. They've turned it into a fortress, a training camp. There could be as many as a hundred men up there. They handle all the Silver Shirt chapters in the Midwest. There's another camp someplace down South and one out in California. But this, I believe, is the largest."

"What do you mean by fortress?" asked Jackson.

"Look, these men are lunatics. They think America is only months away from a fascist takeover. Pelley wants them to train to take on the U.S. Army if necessary. We did a thorough check on Whitefish Point last fall. We make it our business to know what these men are up to."

"Are they well-armed?"

"Hell yes. Apparently they've even got some automatic weapons now."

"Have you had trouble with them, Lester?"

"Not so far. Most of them are young, too young to have been in the World War. But apparently they have a couple of veteran ex-Army people supervising the training."

"So Sir Roland is hiding out in this camp," said Jackson. "And Benet went after him. Dammit!" Jackson brought his hand down hard on the edge of the couch. "I just remembered. When we left Benet this morning, there were two Bureau men sitting outside his house. I'm willing to bet the Bureau has been on his tail all this time. I wonder if Orth . . ." He didn't finish, realizing vanKamp couldn't possibly understand what he was talking about.

"You said on the phone you'd prefer not to have the Bureau involved in this, isn't that right, Jack?"

"Yes, I'm afraid so."

"Well, if you're thinking of going up to Whitefish Point I'd like to caution you. Those men are not boy scouts, Jack. You could use all the help you can get."

"I'll take your word for that, Lester. But if the Bureau is up there already, I'm afraid outside help is the last thing I need."

"You go in there shooting, you're going to have a battle on your hands," said vanKamp. "I'd like to offer you some of my men if you want them. Just say the word, Jack."

He shook his head.

"What are you planning, then?"

"I don't know. I'll tell you what. If you could loan us a car and someone who knows the roads, I'd like to leave as soon as possible. I'd be grateful for just that much, Lester."

"How about Stan Wicks?"

"Stan would be fine," said Jackson. "I'll want to leave in fifteen minutes or so."

VanKamp stood up, a grave expression on his face. "I can only wish you luck. Let me call Stan."

Twenty-five minutes later, they were pulling out of the garage onto the forest road, with Wicks at the wheel and Leaper slumped in the back seat, sound asleep again. Jackson wondered just where the hell they were going. A Silver Shirt picnic at Whitefish Point?

The camp had come alive in the night. Sir Roland stood on the porch watching a dark circle of men. Two terrified fighters stood in the center with their ax handles raised stiffly like bats. Nance's voice was screaming: *"Get on it."* The ax handles flashed white as bleached bone, thudding, cracking flesh, the two men battering each other in the torchlight. Was this a dream? Minutes before, he'd been in his bed and Nance had appeared in his doorway: "I thought you'd want to see this."

See this? The man was unhinged, thought Sir Roland. The hideous sound of ax handle on rib cage, the choking gasps. Nance had his pistol raised in the air: "We're going to make men out of you two pussies." And the sound of wood on the skull, lethal. Nance was barking to finish it.

Sir Roland slumped against the porch rail for support. "We caught these two queers down in A barracks." Nance called himself a captain: washed out of the Marine Corps, by his own admission. "On your knees, Rogers." The younger one nodding in dumb obedience beside the dark shape on the grass. "You tell this dead pussy you're

sorry for beating his brains out, Rogers." A breathless
whisper: "I'm sorry." "Louder!" The circle of men holding
its breath around the kneeling man beside the body under
Nance's torch. "I'm—" Nance discharged his pistol into
the back of the young man's head, tumbling him forward.
"Johnson, take three men and bury this garbage."

For what? wondered Sir Roland. He watched Nance
walking toward him, a barely concealed smile on his face.

26

Somewhere around Grayling, north of Flint, Anthony thought he heard a motorboat racing beside him in the dark woods. Then he felt the resistance in the steering and knew it was a flat tire. In the middle of nowhere, on a country road at four A.M., he pulled off onto the shoulder.

It was much cooler this far north. He found himself shivering as he opened the trunk. Then he had the jack out and the spare and got down on his back on the rough ground. It took him ten minutes to lever the Pontiac up to where he could remove the useless tire and begin fitting the new one in its place.

After the lugs were tightened and the jack lowered, everything replaced in the trunk, Benet hesitated before climbing back in the car. He'd been there about twenty minutes, and just one car had passed him, a Chevrolet going very fast. Despite the cold, he walked about ten yards from the car and lay down on the soft needles at the edge of the forest, his hands under his head, his eyes closed for a moment. For the first time since that morning, he felt a tremor of doubt. He forced his eyes to open. Up through the branches, he saw cold bright stars.

They had been married on August 2 in the chapel at Abingdon by the Bishop of Cranebourne. There was a hired Rolls-Royce waiting after the reception in the Lodge. They drove down to London in midafternoon; it was raining. But they were dry and warm once they reached their rooms high in the Savoy overlooking the dark brown Thames. They had dinner up there, another bottle of champagne, and even the rain mottling the windows began to seem special, a good sign. The next morning they took the boat train to Southampton to board the *Île de France*. Yet the honeymoon didn't really begin until they arrived in New York. They spent five days at the Plaza, and then went by Pullman to San Francisco. He wanted to show her his America.

Everyone they met was charmed by her beauty, her accent, and she was ecstatic in her praise for all of it. He'd even dreamed that they made a baby in one of those Pullmans shunting over the Great Plains under a canopy of stars.

Anthony forced himself up off the soft pine needles. If he slept, his anger would pass. Anger was his only chance for redemption; it was exalted. The temptation to sleep had passed, and it would be the last time he would look back. A moment later, the Pontiac was moving northward.

He had to wait forty minutes for the next ferry. Once aboard, he went out on deck where the wind blew chilly and a hundred feet below the waters of Huron and Michigan merged in the darkness. And then he was in upper Michigan and following the signs.

Dawn broke not long afterwards: a pink and violet plateau on the eastern horizon. It gave him the feeling of driving inside a vast cathedral.

At a town called Emerson, Lake Superior suddenly came into view through the pines on his right. The water was jet black and cold-looking. There was no traffic, only the hushed whine of the Pontiac's tires on the blacktop. He reached for the map as he drove, and found that he was very close, only twenty-five miles from his destination.

Three towns lay along the eastern side of the peninsula: Paradise, Shelldrake and Whitefish Point. He passed through Paradise about 6:30 A.M. A sleepy little lakeside resort where the only sign of life was a pair of young boys with fishing poles on their shoulders, waiting for him to roar past. Even the gas station was closed, but he had almost a quarter of a tank left.

The road hugged the shoreline. He passed an occasional summer house built over the water on piers, the first wisps of breakfast smoke beginning to curl out of a stone chimney. Once he saw a fisherman far out on the lake. Alone in his rowboat, motionless, all patience concentrated on a tiny metal barb turning on the current far below in the shadowy depths.

Holtzer had not told him the name of the camp. Just Whitefish Point. From the map, Anthony could see the peninsula ended very sharply, shaped like a kind of thorn stuck into the southeastern flank of Lake Superior. He guessed it would be no problem to locate the camp.

Whitefish Point was almost identical to the two previous towns he'd passed through. Bungalows along the shore, a dozen stores, and a tiny movie theater. The marquee drooped out over the sidewalk and advertised *"Snow White and the Seven Dwarfs*—TWO SHOWS SAT." A few more people were up and about. He considered stopping and asking for directions. But what would he ask for: "The camp?"

There were more houses north of the town center and several dirt roads leading back into the woods. One mailbox said "The 3 Lil Shavers" and another read "Frisconte." He guessed neither was likely. The blacktop suddenly ran out. Ahead lay a dirt road. He was going to drive on when he saw the sign nailed to a tree. In faded paint, he read, "Camp Missinaibi," and in smaller letters, "United Methodist Synod of Michigan, All Inquiries to UMSM, 428 Beeton Avenue, East Lansing." Over this, in crude black letters, someone had painted: "PRIVATE—KEEP OUT."

He took his foot off the clutch and eased forward onto the dirt. About twenty-five yards into the woods, he could go no farther. Two metal posts were driven into either side of the narrow track and, slung between them, a metal chain blocked his way.

He got out of the Pontiac and was just lifting the chain when a voice shouted, "What the hell do you think you're doing?"

Looking up, Benet saw a young man dressed in military-style fatigues holding a rifle on him. He was less than ten yards away.

"Excuse me," said Benet. "I didn't see you."

"You see me now, don't you? Get back in your car and get the hell out of here. You know this ain't a public road."

"Look, my name's Anthony Benet. They're expecting me here. Sir Roland Plenty?"

"What do you mean 'expecting' you?" The young man began to approach through the underbrush, holding his rifle on Anthony. He couldn't have been over twenty, with a severe overbite and a scrawny neck. His ugliness was almost comic. "You mean Captain Nance? No one told me that."

"Isn't there an Englishman staying here? Sir Roland Plenty? I called him last night and he—"

"Hey!" shouted the young man. "Who's that?" He was looking over Benet's shoulder back up the road. "They come with you?"

A light blue Chevrolet with two men in front was visible. As they watched, the driver of the Chevrolet suddenly reversed and the car went rapidly backward until it was out of sight.

"No," said Benet. "They're not with me." It didn't occur to him that he might have been followed. "They just made a mistake, you see?"

"Maybe," said the young man. "So you're here to see the fat Englishman, huh? Nobody told me last night when I came on duty. You sure they're expecting you?"

"Positive. I told you, I called last night."

"Okay, but you better not be bullshitting me. I'll ride with you. They're in Headquarters Barrack. You wouldn't know that. Get in your car, mister."

Benet climbed into the car as the young man dropped the chain, then came around and got in beside him. "You just drive straight on, mister."

After a small bend in the woods, the road proceeded for another fifty yards, then suddenly came out into a clearing. The peninsula was only two hundred yards wide at this point and Benet could see the lake on either side. The clearing looked like a playing field, with several tall old oaks near the sides and a cluster of brown tents close to the woods on the right. Directly in front of them, atop a tiny rise in the terrain, stood the camp buildings.

They looked like the kind of temporary sheds thrown up at a construction site. Unpainted, long and narrow, they looked incredibly shabby. As the car reached the camp center, he saw they were arranged in a loose circle around a flagpole that stood on a small wood platform. A modest two-story house with a peaked roof and a small porch, tilting slightly on its foundation, was the only thing in the camp that wore a remotely fresh coat of paint.

"Headquarters Barrack," the young man said, pointing at it. "And if you ain't telling the truth, I'm going to be in a hell of a bad way. So you better be. Otherwise I'm going to make sure you get yours just the way I get mine."

"I'm telling the truth," said Benet. "Just find Sir Roland and he'll explain."

"Come on, then."

They got out of the Pontiac. "You wait here," said the young man when they'd reached the porch.

"All right." He watched him slip hesitantly inside the house, closing the screen door quietly behind him. What was this place? Certainly it wasn't a Methodist camp. Although the air was warming as the sun rose, fatigue made him shiver. He'd been on the road for nearly twenty-four hours.

He heard muffled voices and then the sound of footsteps on a flight of steps. He pushed his right hand into his pocket and closed it around the revolver grip. The screen door opened and a man in his early forties wearing striped pajamas and slippers stepped out onto the porch. "Get back to your post, Moriarty," he hissed. "Now!"

The young sentry who had guided Benet clattered down the steps and began to double-time across the grass.

"What's your name?" asked the man.

"Benet. I'm looking for Sir Roland Plenty. I called last night from Dearborn and—"

"I know," said the man. "My name's Captain Nance." He stuck out his hand. The moment Anthony touched it with his own, the hand withdrew. "You're the Englishman's son-in-law. Come inside."

He followed Captain Nance into a dim hallway, down to a parlor badly furnished with bits and pieces of worn-out junk. What brought him up short was the enormous photograph on the wall. He didn't recognize the man in the photograph. But he recognized the fascist salute and the silver uniform, complete with leather crossbelt, high boots and the insignia on the shoulder. Behind the figure was a huge banner on which three bolts of lightning and the initials SS were emblazoned. A smaller replica of this banner hung on the opposite wall.

The man who called himself Captain Nance smiled and said, "Field Marshal Pelley. Too bad. You just missed him."

"Oh?" said Benet.

"He left Sunday. Have a seat. We had some night exercises until about four this morning. That's why the place is so goddamn quiet."

"I see."

"I suppose you want to see Sir Roland right away, huh?"

"If I could," said Anthony.

"I'll get him." Captain Nance nodded at the ceiling.

"This place . . . you're the Silver Shirts, is that right?" asked Anthony.

"You bet we are," said Nance. "Didn't Holtzer tell you?" Benet shook his head.

"We've got sixty-four men in training at the moment. Come next month, we'll have a hundred and fifty, maybe even two hundred. You going to stay around for awhile?"

"I don't know," said Benet. "I don't think so."

"You look beat. You drive all night?"

"Yes."

"There'll be breakfast at eight-thirty. After that we can fix you up with a bed."

"If I could see Sir Roland now . . ."

Nance gave Benet a cautious look, then turned and went out. A moment later, Benet watched the stripes on his pajama trousers going up the stairs.

His nerves were so badly frayed that he couldn't keep his left hand still. His right hand was wrapped tightly around the gun in his pocket. There were voices upstairs, footsteps, then a door closed. And silence.

He turned and looked out the window. From the back of the house, he could see the rest of the point. It was all pines for another thirty-five yards to where the land ended abruptly, with a path leading down through the middle. Off to the left stood a small dock where a few boats looked like they were rotting slowly into the lake.

"Anthony?"

Benet jumped and turned to stare at Sir Roland.

"What's this all about, Anthony? I must say your call has put me in a state."

This was the man whose patronage he'd found so flattering? This pompous fat pig? The eyes which had always intimidated Anthony in the past now seemed like pitiful dark smudges. Empty holes in a pig mask. Behind which not a spark of true feelings, no recognizable human emotion, save perhaps some form of bestial greed, was evident.

"Why don't you shut the door?" said Anthony.

"If you wish, of course." Sir Roland complied. "Did you really have to drive up here in the middle of the night? Couldn't you simply have told me what you wanted on the telephone?"

"Sit down."

Sir Roland could no longer pretend not to notice his son-in-law's strange manner. "I say, Anthony, what is the matter with you?"

"I told you to sit down," he said, bringing out the revolver and pointing it at Sir Roland's stomach.

Sir Roland's eyes flashed for an instant, but that was all. He nodded, as if this were really quite ordinary, and took a seat on a wooden chair near the door. "Anthony, perhaps you could explain. And I assure you there is absolutely no need to point that weapon at me."

"Shut up!" ordered Anthony in a loud voice. "Just shut up."

"Of course, Anthony."

He reached into his jacket pocket and removed the diary. "You see this? Yesterday they gave this to me and made me read it. Thank God they did. Now you're going to read it."

"I'd be happy to read anything you wish me to. But don't you think you owe me an explanation for this . . ." He waved at the gun.

"When you read this, you won't need any explanations," said Anthony. He took two steps forward and tossed the diary into Sir Roland's face. As the older man bent to retrieve it, Anthony said, "That's your daughter's diary."

Sir Roland looked up, his mouth open to reveal a nervous pink slug of a tongue licking his bottom lip. "I beg your pardon?"

"Pick it up! Pick it up or I'll blow your head off!"

"You must be mad!" cried Sir Roland. "Nicola's diary? Nicola never kept a diary."

"Pick it up!"

"You *are* out of your mind."

Anthony laughed, high, unreal laughter. "Am I? I'm not so sure. Now, pick it up and read it. Read all about your daughter and your friend Heydrich. Oh, you were so helpful, weren't you?"

"What *are* you saying, man?"

"You filthy pig. You pimped for your own daughter. Now *pick it up!*"

Sir Roland reached down and picked up the diary. "I don't have my reading glasses," he said.

"You don't have your reading glasses?" roared Anthony. "Jesus Christ! Do you think I'm actually going to let you leave this room? I thought you were so brilliant. So distinguished. And what marvelous friends you have here. These Silver Shirts. For God's sake! Listen, you don't even have to read it. I'll tell you what she wrote. And all these years you kept telling me not to *feel guilty*. Jesus! *My fault?* Oh, my God."

"Please use your common sense, Anthony. Look at where you are. These men are not going to let you walk out of here if you do something to harm me. These men: have you seen them? Savages . . . no, I can't even find words to describe them. What I saw last night. They killed two of their own men just for—"

"Shut up! I want to tell you exactly what Heydrich did to your daughter. To my Nicola."

"Heydrich? Anthony, what are you saying? You met the man yourself. He was like an uncle to her. There was never any—"

"Any what?" screamed Anthony. "Any filthy pimping? Oh, Jesus, you were so happy to have her marry me, weren't you? And I was stupid enough to be of use to you. I was, wasn't I? You even convinced me it was all my fault. I was just a whore to you too, wasn't that it? The only problem . . ." He couldn't finish. He wept openly, his head erect. What did he have to hide from this man? "The only problem was that we loved each other."

"Of course you did," said Sir Roland soothingly. If only the gun could be gotten away from him. But Anthony was too far away and Sir Roland didn't dare move. "*Of course* you loved each other. And whatever they've told you, this clumsy faked diary, nothing can change your love. Can it, Anthony?"

"Would you shut your mouth!" shouted Anthony. "Because just to hear you say that word makes me want to—"

"Sorry, Anthony. I'm terribly sorry. Please, I can see you have been misused. But do you know why? It's Roosevelt, Anthony. He's fabricated this diary. Do you know *why?* Please let me show you. Let me show you what I have. Anthony, he's only using you to protect himself against the truth. The filthy truth. Because of what I have on Roosevelt."

"What do you have?" Anthony was in a million pieces. Shattered. If only he could collect enough of himself to pull the trigger and finish it. Yet part of him, the years of legal training, perhaps, forced him to listen.

"Oh, Anthony, you talk of filth! Do you know why they've done this to you? Because I have photographs, Anthony. Proof of Roosevelt with his whore. Tomorrow, Anthony, tomorrow we will give them to the newspapers. It will mean the end for him. Everything that you've worked so hard for will be possible. They'll never get into the war after this. There'll be no war, Anthony. These photographs will make it clear."

The word "photographs" echoed in Anthony's mind. "They told me about your photographs."

"Did they?" cried Sir Roland. "Oh, I doubt that, Anthony. *I doubt that.* You must see them for yourself."

"I'll see them. But not here. I want you to stand up, pimp."

"Of course, Anthony. Anything you say." Sir Roland stood up quickly.

"We're driving out of this place, and if there's any trouble, you'll get a bullet through your head. Understand?"

"Certainly I do. I can show you the photographs. I'll look at this beastly fraud they've given you and prove, Anthony, I'll *prove* to you it's a lie."

"I don't want you to say a word. Not a word. We're going out and getting in my car, and you don't say a word, understand?"

"Yes, of course, Anthony. I won't say—"

Sir Roland did not finish. At that moment, the door opened, hitting him squarely in the back, with enough force to knock him on his knees.

Captain Nance stood in the doorway in his pajamas, holding a Thompson submachine gun in both hands.

In his bedroom above the parlor, Nance had heard every word through the thin wooden floor.

"Put down that gun!" shouted the Captain.

Anthony looked at him, then down at Sir Roland on his knees. Whether it was simply fatigue or a conscious decision, the order did not immediately penetrate. As his eyes swung to Sir Roland, the gun in his hand swung too. Not very far. Perhaps only an inch.

Captain Nance pulled the trigger. A shattering burst of fire raked the room where Anthony stood. As it did so, there was a vaguely sad look in the eyes of the maniac Nance. He hadn't really intended to kill Anthony. At least, not yet.

27

A mile north of Paradise, two Harley Davidson motor-cycles blocked the lakeshore road. The state troopers were checking driver's licenses, turning away anyone who didn't live farther up the peninsula.

Jackson produced his White House card. The young trooper's suspicion suddenly changed to friendly deference. "If you're looking for the FBI, you'll find enough of them up there all right," he said. "Just keep going to the end of the Point. You can't miss."

There was another roadblock on the southern outskirts of Whitefish Point. Again Jackson's White House card eased their way. He didn't bother to ask what was going on. The fewer questions you asked, the more they assumed you knew. And Jackson thought he already had a fairly good idea of what was happening up ahead.

All the troopers they saw were heavily armed with shot-guns or 30.06 rifles. As if they were expecting an assault force to come roaring up the road at any minute. But in the village of Whitefish Point, there was more of a festive atmosphere. Groups of citizens were clustered on the side-walks talking it all over. They stared with curiosity as Wicks drove up the center of the street.

It was nearly noon. A bright, warm day, it should have been perfect for swimming and boating. But nobody was swimming at Whitefish Point and there wasn't a boat in sight out on the lake.

As they entered the woods north of the village, they be-gan to pass many green-and-white Fords, trooper squad cars, abandoned at the side of the road. Up ahead, they could see more vehicles parked haphazardly in the center of the road. They could go no farther. Wicks pulled onto the pine needles under the trees and killed the engine.

Although there were perhaps forty vehicles in the im-

mediate area, they didn't see a single human until they'd
walked up to where the metal posts and the chain had
stopped Benet earlier that morning.

This was evidently the command post. There were four
cars, two of them unmarked, and about twenty men in
trooper uniforms and plainclothes.

The sound of sporadic gunfire had been with them since
they got out of the car. It was coming from the woods farther out on the peninsula.

Jackson picked Orth out of a circle of five men from a
distance of forty yards. Some of the men were obvious Bureau types, others ranking trooper officers. Orth looked like
a retired middleweight boxer in their midst; a puncher
gone fat and losing his hair.

When they were about fifteen feet away, Orth suddenly
looked up and saw Jackson. He quickly said something to
the others and left the group. There was a thin smile on
his face but his eyes were furious.

They shook hands in the center of the dirt road. Orth
looked at Leaper and Wicks. Jackson didn't bother to introduce them.

"Hey there, Jack," said Orth with an attempt at jollity,
"we seem to be making a habit of this. Don't tell me
you've been at the Ritz these last two days?"

"Afraid not. What's going on here, Malcolm?"

Suddenly Orth's face darkened. "Just a second, Jack.
First I want to know where the hell you've been. What
were you doing at Benet's house yesterday? And why the
hell haven't you called me?"

Jackson shrugged. "I wanted to ask him a few questions, that's all."

"Oh yeah? We were supposed to do that together,
remember? You've been grandstanding, Jack. And it hasn't
done you a fucking bit of good. Has it?"

"Is Benet up there?" asked Jackson, nodding in the
direction of the gunfire.

"You bet your ass he is. And he's not the only one."

"Oh?"

"They've got one of my agents, a rookie named Budge.
He's shot up, we don't know how bad, and these lunatics
are holding him hostage."

"How about Sir Roland?"

"Yeah. We know he's in there. You really think you're

pretty cute, don't you, Jack? Showing up like this, asking me what's happening, not bothering to say a fucking thing about what you've been doing while my men are out here getting their heads blown off."

Jackson looked at him without a trace of either resentment or remorse. "Save your breath, Malcolm. Tell me what's been going on."

Orth shook his head, still furious, but began to tell him. His agents had followed Benet all the way from Georgetown up to this godforsaken spot in the woods. Been on the road for nearly twenty-four hours, he said, with hardly enough time to stop and pee. Benet arrived early that morning. His agents had taken a quick look to make sure there were no other exits, then gone back into the village and called him. Orth had flown up from Detroit in a seaplane.

But too late, as far as he was concerned. On the phone, his agents hadn't been at all sure what this place was. There was a sign out front saying it was a Methodist camp, but that looked way out-of-date to them. Orth had told them to do a little quiet checking while he was on his way up.

"Griese is getting some sleep now, but he can tell you the whole story later. In a nutshell, they were walking up through these woods when suddenly all hell broke loose. I mean shooting. Griese figures there were at least six of them. Budge got hit. In the leg and then a chest wound. We don't know how bad. All Griese had was his .38 against these maniacs with their carbines. He tried to carry the rookie out. But they were coming down on him like a son of a bitch. Finally he had to drop the kid and run. He's lucky to be alive."

"No warning shots? They were just fired on?" asked Jackson.

"You've got it. These are Silver Shirts. They think they're the regular Dawn Patrol. We've had two of these troopers wounded already this morning. You can hear it, huh? I can't keep these cowboys under control. And the Silver Shirts are taking orders from a real lulu who calls himself Captain Nance. We're getting a line on him from Washington right now."

"Can we see?"

Orth looked at him as if he were crazy. "You want to see? By all means, Jack, follow me, then."

They followed him up the road past the officials with their maps and radiotelephones. Orth suddenly veered off into the woods. They walked for about thirty-five yards under the pines before he stopped and said, "From here on, they can see us, so keep low."

Crouching, moving behind Orth from one stand of pines to the next, they approached the edge of the clearing. Now it was quite obvious where all the troopers were: strung out at the edge of the woods on their bellies, forming a line that faced, some eighty yards away, the camp buildings on their small rise. Jackson could see occasional movements up in the camp, in the corner of the windows, underneath the raised floors, behind makeshift barricades. Occasionally there would be a shot, then an answering volley from the trooper-infested woods.

"Isn't this sweet?" hissed Orth.

"I don't get it," said Jackson.

"Don't ask me, pal. This Captain Nance is out of his little mind. We've offered them a fair deal. If they hand over Budge and the guys who shot him, we'll go easy on everyone else. They turned us down flat."

"When was this?" Jackson asked.

"About an hour ago one of the trooper officers volunteered to go out there with a white flag. Took a lot of balls, I can tell you. Anyway, he went in for a talk with this Nance. We offered our deal. Nance came up with, get this, his own set of demands."

"Is that why you're sure Sir Roland's in there?"

"Right. The trooper was taken onto this house. He said there was a fat Englishman sort of advising this moron Nance."

"Sir Roland is no moron," said Jackson.

"Well, Captain Nance is. You know what he told the trooper? That he's called for reinforcements and that by six o'clock tonight this whole place is going to be swarming with his Silver Shirt brothers." Orth guffawed. "There aren't more than 350 Silver Shirts in the whole country. And they sure as hell aren't going to get up here in time to help out their buddy Nance. Do you want to know what Nance's demands are?"

"I guess so," said Jackson.

"He wants us to have Bernard Baruch, Henry Morgenthau and Felix Frankfurter up here by six o'clock tonight. If we hand them over, he'll agree to give us Budge. He also wants either fifty thousand dollars in cash or the equivalent in guns and ammunition. I mean, he actually gave us a list, a shopping list, of the arms he thinks we're going to hand over."

"What are you going to do?"

Orth nodded at the surrounding woods. "Right now we've got about seventy troopers here. By tonight we'll have over two hundred. The state is sending in men from all over. The idea is to show Nance that he's got zero chance of keeping up this insanity. But I tend to think it won't work. So do the troopers. There was some talk of bringing in the Army. But the Director wouldn't buy that, of course. We've been lucky on the press. But it's only a matter of time before some reporter gets his nose in here."

"So?" asked Jackson.

"So we figure . . ." But something caught Orth's eye. "What the hell!" he said. "Shit, another hero."

Jackson followed Orth's line of sight to a place about fifty yards to their right. A trooper was out of the woods crawling toward some mud-colored tents on his belly, rifle cradled in his arms infantry style. He'd already been spotted by the Silver Shirts up in the camp. Their bullets were kicking up the dirt.

They had to watch helplessly as the firing from the camp increased in deadly frequency and the trooper suddenly changed his mind. He began to inch his way back in the direction of the woods, the bullets sending up small fantails of earth all around him. He had about ten feet more to go when his body suddenly lurched, his legs came up, and he curled on his side. His back was facing them. Jackson could see the stain rapidly enlarging on the back of his tan shirt, down over his buttocks.

"The stupid fool's got hit," said Orth.

All along the edge of the woods, the troopers had been watching the advance and then the perilous retreat. Now they opened up in a thunderous mass reply to the bullet that had wounded their fellow officer. The noise was deafening and the woods stank of gunpowder. "Get down," Jackson yelled to Leaper and Wicks.

Orth fell beside him on the pine needles. "Jesus, it's getting worse. A lot of these troopers are no better than the lunatics in that camp. We've told them twenty times to avoid drawing fire."

"And you're going to keep this up all night?" yelled Jackson.

"No shit!" said Orth. "Come on. Let's get back." They started to crawl back out of direct range of the camp's guns.

"Wait," said Jackson. He'd just seen another trooper break cover at the edge of the woods. The officer ran straight to his wounded friend, bent down and lifted him in a fireman's carry. Miraculously, he managed to hustle back into the woods without being hit. The rest of the troopers sent up a tremendous din, increasing their heavy fire. Jackson could see the bullets hitting the old wood of the camp barracks. They seemed to smoke as they hit.

"These are cowboys," said Orth. "Real cowboys. You can't tell them a thing."

They reached a point where Orth felt it was safe to stand. "You've still got to be careful," he said. "They're pumping enough rounds in here to hold off a company of regular Army."

When they'd come back near the road, Jackson said, "What about the lake? Have you thought of taking them that way?"

Orth looked at him with eyebrows raised. "Do you really think I'm stupid, Jack? Look, we've had a Coast Guard patrol boat up here for the last two hours. One of those boats that used to chase the bootleggers. They tried to go in close for a look and they nearly got ripped to pieces. This Nance has a Browning machine gun. Where he got it, I don't know. But when he saw the boat, he had them put it over on the north shore. The Coast Guard are lying about a mile off now."

"Does Nance have any boats?"

"No, a couple of rowboats, that's all. We estimate there are more than sixty men in the camp. You're not going to find sixty men piling into a few crappy rowboats."

"So what the hell *are* you going to do?" asked Jackson. They had all stopped at the edge of the command post, Leaper and Wicks standing just behind Jackson. Orth was ignoring the searching glances of several of his fellow Bureau men.

266 *Paul Spike*

"You know there's nothing to get upset about in the long run, Jack," he said. "We'll come out of this okay. It'll take a little time, but that's all. As soon as we get enough men up here, we'll move on them."

"When?"

"There's talk of going just before dawn. That way we can move across that open field in the dark. And as soon as it starts to get light, we'll hit them. In the dark, we'd shoot up too many of our own people. But right at dawn . . . here, let me show you." He motioned at a trooper sitting in one of the cars. "Hey, bring me that map, would you?" The trooper nodded and was soon walking toward them with a map in his hand.

Orth unfolded it and Jackson held one side. It was a surveyor's map of the entire township. The camp area was laid out in detail in the upper-right corner, filling the end of the Point. Orth described how he thought the troopers would probably make the raid, pointing at the various small rectangles that marked the camp buildings.

"Where is Sir Roland?" asked Jackson.

"In here," said Orth, putting his finger beside a tiny square located near the tip of the peninsula itself. "This is the main house. We figure they've got Budge in there as well. That's their headquarters. As you can see, it's the hardest to get at."

From the land, perhaps, thought Jackson. But it was exposed to the lake on three sides, with only about forty yards behind it and the end of the Point.

This really was fine for the Bureau. They had the troopers to do the dirty work. They were certain to take Sir Roland before too long. Of course, Orth was genuinely concerned about his young agent, the hostage. But Jackson couldn't forget Roosevelt's words at the end of their last meeting. "If the time comes that you do get your hands on those negatives, *keep* your hands on them. I don't care who it is, don't pass them to anyone else. Especially not Hoover or any of his men." The way things were now, the negatives were as good as in the Bureau's hands. As Orth said, it was only a matter of time.

"So you'll probably go in at dawn?" asked Jackson.

"I think so. Unless this bastard Nance gets some sense, which I doubt."

"Then I guess I have time to go into town and make a phone call."

Orth grinned. "Jack, you've got all the time in the world."

Jackson looked at Leaper and Wicks, then turned back to Orth. "So I guess we'll see you later."

"Knowing you, Jack, I wouldn't bet on it. By the way, how's your Assistant Undersecretary these days?"

Jackson's face suddenly went livid. He forced himself to speak in a slow, quiet voice. "Could I speak to you alone for a moment, Malcolm? Something personal?"

"Why not?" Orth followed him over to the side of the road and into the forest. When Jackson turned, his lower lip was caught between his teeth and his eyes raging.

"You see this tree, Malcolm?" he asked.

"Yeah?"

"How would you like me to take your face and push it through this tree? You have a big fat mouth, you know that?"

Orth was stunned, trying to understand what had suddenly come over Jackson. "Jack . . . what . . . the . . . I . . ."

"Remember this, Malcolm. You and I were friends once, but no longer. I don't ever want to hear you say another word to me that doesn't come strictly in the line of duty. The next time you make a personal remark to me, I'm going to take your face and smash it. I don't care what it is, you shut your mouth when I'm around. You got that? I mean it, Malcolm." His neck muscles were stretched taut, his arms hung loose but ready at his sides. "Malcolm?"

Orth managed to nod. He knew he was no match for Jackson. Perhaps fifteen years ago, but no longer. He hadn't the faintest idea what he'd said.

Jackson walked off and left him beside the tree. Leaper and Wicks followed. Five minutes later, they were in the car on their way to the nearest telephone.

28

I t was an old-fashioned drugstore, dark, cool, smelling of
soap and spearmint. Leaper and Wicks waited at the
lunch counter while Jackson used the telephone in the
back. The owner, an elderly man in white shirt and clip-
on bow tie, took their orders. Since neither man had eaten
in many hours, they ordered cheeseburgers and french
fries.

Jackson's face was pale and strained when he left the
phone booth twenty minutes later. He took a seat next to
Leaper at the counter, wiped his eyes on his hands, then
rested his forehead on his palms for a long moment. Looking into the owner's expectant face, he ordered a cup of
coffee and a bacon sandwich.

"How is she?" asked Leaper.

"She's in a coma. They don't know much," said Jackson. "Until she comes out of the coma, they won't know if
the operation did any good or not. There could be . . .
permanent damage to the brain."

"But they don't know that," said Leaper. "Not yet."

"No."

His coffee came and it helped. So did the sandwich a
few minutes later. He knew that his mind was divided between the situation at hand and what was taking place in a
hospital a thousand miles away. It couldn't continue like
that. He felt the two men waiting patiently for him to take
charge. He could not live in two places at once. He wasn't
doing any good for Rona, certainly, and he wasn't going
to begin to solve the problem out at the Point like this.
No, he would have to try to forget the hospital and get on
with his plan.

He'd begun to see the plan while Orth was showing
them the map back in the woods. Ever since, he'd been
developing it without really being conscious that it was in

fact "the plan" he was working on. Now, as the coffee went to work, he suddenly pulled it up out of the murky part of his mind and began to concentrate on it in earnest.

After a few minutes, he turned to Leaper and Wicks and asked, "Do either of you have any sailing experience? Have you spent any time around boats?"

Wicks shook his head. But Leaper cocked one eyebrow skeptically and said, "My uncle used to keep a boat down at Monte. I spent an unfortunate number of holidays providing him with inexpensive deck labor when I was a boy."

"Monte?" asked Jackson.

"Yes, Monte Carlo."

"Oh. And did you ever handle a small boat by yourself?"

"From time to time, yes."

"Good." Jackson turned and beckoned the owner, who was hovering just within earshot behind the counter. When he'd come closer, Jackson asked, "Is there anybody in this town who rents boats?"

"Man you want to see is Tom Steinmuller," said the druggist. "Down at the White Bear Cabins. You probably saw his place as you came into town."

Jackson nodded, vaguely recalling having seen the sign. "Thanks."

"You boys with the government?" asked the druggist.

"You could say that."

"That's a crying shame what they're doing out at the Point. If we had a decent sheriff around here, he'd have cleaned those Nazis out long before it came to this. You boys FBI, aren't you?" He looked like he wanted to settle down for a long, folksy chat. "I reckon you're going to clean them Nazis out now, but good, aren't you? Never seen so many troopers in—"

"How much do we owe you?" asked Jackson, cutting him off. When the druggist had figured it out, Jackson reached for his wallet and paid.

The three men emerged onto the sidewalk a few seconds later. "Let's take a little walk," said Jackson.

Wicks nodded, evidently willing to follow his lead in all things. Leaper came along too, but he wore a particularly skeptical expression on his face. On their way down the small main street, Jackson stopped for a moment in front of the local hardware store. He carefully examined the window display of hunting and fishing supplies. Finally they went on toward the southern edge of town.

The White Bear Cabins stood under the pines between the main road and the lake, about ten small rough-hewn log cabins. Jackson noted the neat little dock down by the lake and the five or six boats tied there.

They entered the cabin marked "Office." A bell tinkled as Jackson opened the door. Tom Steinmuller came out of his back parlor into the knotty-pine foyer and stood behind the desk. His smile began to fade as soon as Jackson told him they weren't really interested in renting a cabin.

"Actually we were told you might have a boat we could rent."

Steinmuller looked the three of them over, his eyes lingering for an extra moment on Wicks's disfigured face. "You men with the police?"

"Not exactly. But we are with the government in Washington."

"I thought so," said Steinmuller. "I tell you this trouble up on the Point has shot me all to hell. Fourth of July weekend and I'm completely empty. Had three parties take off this morning. And they're not letting anybody up here, even the folks that reserved with me months ago."

"We don't have anything to do with that," explained Jackson. "That's the State's decision. But we are interested in renting one of your boats."

"Well, I do have a couple of boats I rent out from time to time. What exactly were you looking for, mister?"

Jackson told him. It turned out that Steinmuller had something he thought would fit the general description. They followed him outside and down to the dock.

It was a converted lifeboat salvaged from one of the old lake steamers, a sixteen-foot wooden skiff. Not only did it have a fifteen-horsepower Benson outboard mounted on the stern, but Steinmuller had rigged up a small mast midships. He said he used it mostly for overnight fishing and camping trips, and usually didn't rent it out.

Jackson could see that it was in good condition, recently painted, dry as a new cork. It had a pleasing gull-like shape to the hull, which he guessed could absorb anything the lake might offer in the way of stormy weather.

But when Jackson said they wanted to rent it for

twenty-four hours, Steinmuller became anxious. Was Jackson planning on taking the boat up around the Point? Didn't he know they were shooting like crazy up there and might get themselves killed? Not to mention getting his boat blown full of holes.

Jackson finally overcame Steinmuller's reluctance with an ancient remedy: hard cash. The normal rent was a dollar an hour plus fifteen dollars security money. Jackson offered him fifty dollars, plus fifty more as security. He would also pay Steinmuller to fill up the tank with gas for the outboard. All in advance.

The cabin owner was still mulling it over when Jackson said, "And I've changed my mind about the cabins. We'd like three of them for the night."

That was the clincher. It added another eighteen dollars to the total and Steinmuller was glad to have it. A young man in his early thirities, square-jawed with very fine blond hair, he shook hands with Jackson to seal the bargain. They went back to the office and Jackson gave him the money, part in a check, but the bulk in cash.

Then Jackson asked if he could use the phone for a long-distance call. He would, of course, get time and charges from the operator. Steinmuller told him to go ahead.

Jackson called the hospital in Virginia and told Norma he could be reached at the telephone number of the White Bear Cabins. She had nothing new to report on Rona's condition.

After he hung up and counted out the money for the call, Steinmuller asked him, "When do you think you'll be wanting to take it out?"

"In about half an hour. As soon as I do a little shopping up in town."

"That's fine. I can run up to the Sunoco and get your gas then," said Steinmuller.

The three of them were walking back into town when Leaper suddenly cleared his throat and said, "Excuse me, Jack, but are you seriously considering what I think you are considering?"

"I suspect so."

"Didn't you hear that man Orth tell you about the Coast Guard?"

272   *Paul Spike*

"Yes. But that was the Coast Guard. And they tried to go in broad daylight."

"Good God, man. Are you thinking of going in there at night?"

"No," said Jackson. "Closer to morning."

Leaper shook his head, exasperated but struggling to control himself. Finally he said, "But we're not equipped for this, are we? I mean, just look at what I'm wearing."

Jackson glanced at his linen suit and dark brogans, then laughed. "I don't know. I think you're rather well-dressed, Greville."

"He said there were over sixty armed men in that camp. Now, really, Jack, those are hardly sporting odds."

"In the first place, I haven't told you my plan. But I *will* tell you right now that I don't plan on fighting sixty men from a converted lifeboat. Let's wait until I find out a couple of more things. Then I'll let you know exactly what I have in mind. Okay?"

Leaper started to reply, then simply shrugged.

Jackson's destination in town was the hardware store. Inside the cluttered shop was a glass-fronted case full of hunting rifles. At Jackson's request, the owner came over and unlocked the case.

Fifteen minutes later the three of them left with Jackson carrying a long brown parcel. Inside was a new Remington twelve-gauge shotgun, a pump-action model, and a box of twelve double-O buckshot shells.

They drove back to the White Bear Cabins in Wicks's car. Steinmuller had assigned them three cabins side by side along the lake. Since there was no luggage, except for Jackson's new parcel, there was no unpacking to be done. They were down at the dock a few minutes later.

The combined weight of Jackson, Leaper and Wicks lowered the skiff considerably in the water. Wicks sat in the bow and pushed them off. There was a mild breeze out of the northeast, just enough to ripple the dark blue lake. Jackson assured himself that Steinmuller had filled the five-gallon portable tank. He started the little Benson on the first pull. It made a harsh, rancorous noise that took some getting used to at first. The lake was very quiet otherwise. Jackson realized that he hadn't heard any shooting from the Point in a long time. Perhaps there was a truce.

They went out in a southeasterly direction, leaving the

village and the Point behind them. About half a mile off shore, Jackson cut the engine.

He asked Leaper to hoist the sail.

Jackson had two immediate objectives. The first was to see whether Leaper in fact knew anything about sailing a small boat. That was immediately obvious as soon as he saw the confident ease with which Leaper handled the sail. So on to Jackson's second objective: to see just how well the skiff handled.

Leaper and he took turns at the tiller, running ahead of the wind, then tacking in long diagonals off the green line of the shore. It was not all that Jackson would have hoped for in a boat. It was rather clumsy and the rigging was too loose, but it would do, he thought. Certainly they wouldn't ever get much speed out of it, but then again, his plan didn't really call for speed. No, if the time came that they had to make a quick getaway, it would mean that the plan had probably failed anyway. He pushed his doubts out of his mind as they ran leisurely down the coast until they were opposite Shelldrake, then turned and made their way back north.

On the return run, Jackson said to Leaper, "You know, I was surprised by the way Sir Ian took off so suddenly in Washington. I was certain he'd want to be here when we took Sir Roland."

Leaper suddenly looked a little sheepish but he nodded. "Yes, well, Sir Ian is a very busy man. You must realize that he has a great number of operations to supervise."

"Sure," said Jackson. "But I had the feeling there was a little more to it. Come on, Greville. I see that look in your eyes again."

"I beg your pardon, old man. What look is that?"

"The look I first saw in Lisbon. The look that makes me suspect you're not telling me everything you know."

Leaper glanced at the shoreline, as if he'd prefer to swim there rather than continue this conversation. "I suppose you might be right. I certainly would have, though . . . when the time came."

"The time?"

"When we had successfully apprehended Sir Roland."

"Which I hope will be sometime in the not-too-distant future. Like tomorrow morning," said Jackson. "Do I have to wait until then?"

Leaper shrugged. "I suppose I might as well tell you now, if you insist. Sir Ian is not in New York, as he led you to believe."

"Oh? Where is Sir Ian?"

"In Canada. Windsor, to be exact."

"Across the border from Detroit?"

"Yes, I believe so. You see, Jack, *you* want the negatives. But *our* main objective has always been Sir Roland Plenty himself. When we do get him—I assume you believe that will be tomorrow morning—I was going to ask you . . ."

"Ask me?"

"Yes, ask you if I might possibly take Sir Roland off your hands. That is, deliver him across the border into Canada."

"So that's it," said Jackson. "Sir Ian is waiting for you to deliver the goods to him in Windsor."

"Well, yes."

"And you were going to 'ask' me? What if I said no?"

Leaper produced his boyish smile. "Why on earth would you say that, Jack? I mean, really, it's the negatives you want. Sir Roland is British. He's our property, as it were. What good could he possibly do you people?"

"I'm just wondering what your orders were in case I did say no."

"Please, Jack, let's not talk of outrageously hypothetical questions. Of course you would have agreed."

Of course, thought Jackson. And if he didn't agree? But that was hardly the problem. Not what would happen *when* they took Sir Roland. The problem was *how* they were going to take him and, in one sense, Leaper was right. There was no point in pursuing this question any further.

It was just after six in the afternoon when they returned to the dock beside the White Bear Cabins. Steinmuller wandered down to ask how they'd liked the boat. Jackson told him it was just fine.

The trip had worked up their appetites and it was Wicks who turned to Steinmuller and asked, "Is there any place around here where a man can get a good steak and a couple of drinks?"

"There's the Mooney Lodge. Just south of Shelldrake. They've got the best steaks in this part of the state."

"What do you say?" Wicks asked Jackson. "I don't know what you've got in mind exactly. But I could sure use a decent meal before we do whatever the hell we're gonna be doing."

"Of course," said Jackson. "I'm not going to argue with that. Leaper?"

"A bit of meat would do me nicely, yes," said the Englishman. "Not to mention the considerable thirst I seem to have developed out on the water."

"Then let's drive down to the Mooney Lodge," said Jackson. "By all means."

Steinmuller had been rubbing his jaw thoughtfully, staring out over the lake at the distant Canadian shore. "Can I ask you something, Mr. Jackson?"

"Sure."

"Are you planning on taking the boat out tonight?"

"Frankly, yes."

"I thought so. Look over there," said Steinmuller. "See that?"

There was a gathering mass of dark cloud in the sky above Canada, a stormhead that had not been there even an hour before. It was still far off in the distance but the fact that it had happened so suddenly indicated it was moving, and in their direction.

"Storm coming," said Steinmuller. "This time of year we get them every four or five nights."

"How bad?" asked Jackson.

"I don't know what you mean by bad. This lake can get pretty wild. Lots of electrical stuff. From the look of that, I'd say it'll hit us about eleven or twelve tonight."

"Thanks," said Jackson. "But we won't be going out until much later, until close to morning. Let's hope it'll have blown over by then."

"Maybe," said Steinmuller.

They left him standing on the dock still staring at the distant storm and went up to the car. The drive down to the Mooney Lodge didn't take long; they passed quite a few trooper patrol cars going in the opposite direction.

Steinmuller had been right. The large T-bone steaks were prime and they each had a couple of drinks with the meal. Over coffee, Jackson began to explain his plan.

He took pains not to sound too obviously persuasive. Neither Leaper nor Wicks was the kind of man who could be cajoled into following you. In the end, Jackson left the decision to go completely up to them. Of course, the plan hinged on there being three of them. If one man decided it was too risky, and refused to go, then Jackson would have to scrap the entire operation.

Both Leaper and Wicks, each in his own style, soon made it clear that they hadn't come all this way only to back out now. Of course, Leaper still felt uneasy about it all. But he admitted that he could see no other possible alternative to Jackson's proposal, short of surrendering the entire mission to the FBI and the troopers. And that was unthinkable.

By the time they returned to the White Bear, the sun was just disappearing behind the trees. Both Leaper and Wicks said they would like to get all the sleep they could. Jackson had told them he would be knocking on their doors at four-thirty A.M. But there was one more thing he had to do before he could think about getting some sleep.

He'd borrowed Wicks's car keys, and now he drove back through the empty town and up into the woods on the Point. The last mile of the road was lined on both sides with parked trooper cars. Jackson had to show his identity card three times before he could reach the improvised command post.

There were several dozen heavily armed men milling about in the dimly lit stretch of road just beyond the chain posts where he'd last talked to Orth. From the sound of it, the woods were full of troopers, although no actual gunfire now. A few cars had been pulled up so that their parking lights could give some illumination for the men in charge to read their maps by.

He was looking for Orth and thought he'd spotted him in a group of about ten self-important-looking officials, some in uniform, others definitely Bureau men. They were clustered at the side of the dirt road in the shadows, and Orth seemed to be talking most of the time, the others paying rapt attention.

Jackson approached the edge of the group, then suddenly froze. That wasn't Orth's voice. The group had parted as he neared them, and suddenly the voice stopped too.

In the half-light, the Director's eyes fixed on Jackson's face. The Director's expression did not change, not one iota, yet Jackson felt the sudden blast of hatred directed through those two cold eyes.

He returned the stare.

Not a word passed between the two men, neither willing to speak first. The others in the group shifted uneasily, not sure what was taking place. Jackson glanced around to see if Orth was there. Then turned an his heel and strode away as quickly as he could.

The Director had taken personal control of the operation at Whitefish Point!

He finally found Orth sitting in the back of an unmarked Plymouth drinking a bottle of soda pop and taking bites out of a sandwich. Orth looked up, startled to see him. But he didn't say a word until Jackson started asking the questions. No, said Orth, no real truce had been worked out with that lunatic Captain Nance. The firing had only ceased when they'd finally been able to keep the troopers from exposing themselves to fire from the camp. Yes, the Director had flown up from Washington that afternoon to take over the operation. Yes, that was highly unusual. Not since Prohibition days had the Director insisted on taking direct responsibility over an operation in the field.

Budge was still a hostage, said Orth. And Nance's "deadline" had come and gone. The dawn raid was still in the works.

For the first time, it truly dawned on Jackson just how badly the Director must want those negatives. He'd heard all he wanted to from Orth. Turning away, he started to walk off when Orth called his name.

"What is it?" snapped Jackson.

"I want to . . . Jack, I owe you a big apology. When I spoke this afternoon, I had no idea about the girl."

Jackson went very tense, but said nothing.

"You ought to know, Jack, that the guy they arrested at your house, his name is Luther Miller."

"So what?"

"This Miller has talked. He says he and his buddy were hired by a man named Thomas Holtzer to kidnap you. Now, Holtzer is the man who—"

"I know who Holtzer is. Conspiracy to kidnap, is that it? What's the Bureau going to do about it? Send a telegram of congratulations to Holtzer, I'll bet."

278 Paul Spike

"Jack, please," said Orth. "The Bureau went to pick up Holtzer as soon as they got the information from the District police. He's left his Dearborn house, taken his wife and cleaned out two wall safes that were hidden in the house. There's a nationwide alert on him. You know we're doing everything possible to . . ."

Jackson walked away without bothering to hear any more of it. They'd gotten enough to pick up Holtzer, to put him away for the rest of his life, and what had they done? He didn't care if he was being fair or unfair. All that mattered was that Holtzer had escaped and the Director was now issuing the orders at Whitefish Point.

He was so angry he had to sit and grip the steering wheel as hard as he could for five minutes until he felt able to start the car. But by the time he had driven back to the White Bear Cabins, the anger had been replaced by another equally unpleasant emotion.

Jackson was afraid. Not of danger, not of Silver Shirts, not of a clumsy boat and a stormy weather forecast, not even of the Director. Failure, that was what he feared. Failure and what it would mean for Roosevelt, for all of them.

His only hope was to throw himself completely into the plan. There could be no failure.

He found Steinmuller reading a newspaper in his parlor just off the office foyer. Jackson asked it he'd mind answering a few questions about the lake out near the Point.

Tom Steinmuller said he had been fishing around the Point all his life. He proceeded to draw a map for Jackson. It looked like a large V lying on its side. From the tip, he drew a thin line to the paper's edge. That, he explained, was where the Point extended under the lake surface. It was an underwater ledge. On the southern side, it was extremely shallow. There were many submerged rocks that left only a few inches clearance for a boat. But on its northern side, the ledge dropped off sharply and the water was very deep. How deep, Jackson asked. Steinmuller said that the entire northern shore of the Point was deep enough so that a man couldn't take more than three steps off the beach before he was up to his neck in the water.

Jackson thanked him and went out, taking the map. When he reached his cabin, he turned on the light and picked up the parcel from the hardware store. He unwrapped the shotgun, took out the shells and loaded five of them. Then he undressed down to his shorts and climbed between the sheets on the narrow cot.

Lying in the dark, he wondered if he would be able to sleep. He concentrated on the plan rather than letting his mind wander back to Arlington, to those two hired animals, the shout and then the explosion as he stood on the landing. From time to time, he suddenly saw the Director standing in the shadows, surrounded by his group of loyal subordinates, staring fiercely at Jackson. God, how the man must hate him!

No, he clung to the plan, imagining it over and over in his mind. Norma had not called, so nothing had changed at the hospital. If only he could sleep. But each time he would start to doze, the plan would merge with his dreams and he would suddenly be living through it. Then he would snap awake, wondering if it was all finished, realizing the illusion, and then start the process all over again.

Just before midnight, true to Steinmuller's prediction, the storm hit. Where there hadn't been any sound at all, suddenly a ferocious wind was shaking the pines, rattling the windows and the shingles on the roof. Lightning flashed outside, exposing the interior of the cabin with a weird bluish brilliance. Then the huge detonation of thunder overhead. He could hear the lake being whipped to a frenzy. Great splintered charges of electricity ripped out of the darkness and it sounded like bombs were exploding twenty feet above the roof. And then, confronted by the wild energy of a Canadian storm, he knew it was hopeless. Hopeless and beyond control. Not a thing he could do, not a single thing.

29

His name was being shouted and he sat bolt upright in the darkness. That wasn't the wind hammering on the cabin door. Jackson moved quickly and got it open, to find Steinmuller, dressed in a poncho in the squalling rain, come to tell him there was a phone call up at the office.

He dressed quickly and plunged outside into the storm, up toward the one lighted window near the road.

The storm made it almost impossible to hear over the wire. Norma had to shout. Through the static, Jackson heard that Rona had regained consciousness. She was out of the coma and he tried to get more details, but the poor connection made it impossible. Norma just kept repeating the same thing over and over. She was awake. Rona was awake. Finally he shouted "Thank you" into the phone and gently replaced the receiver.

Steinmuller stared at him with wide eyes, his dripping poncho still over his pajamas. Jackson just smiled and shook his head. He was far too happy to know what to say.

Back in his cabin, he fell asleep at once. Some hours later, he suddenly found himself awake in the dark looking at his wrist. The faint greenish-blue radium hands stood at twenty minutes past four.

It took him several minutes to realize the change. The lightning and thunder had gone. The steady torrent had finished. All that remained was the wind, rattling the window frames and brushing the pines together. But the heart of the storm had moved off the peninsula, farther inland. He slipped out of the sheets and began to pull his clothes on, then put the extra shells in his pocket. Lifting the shotgun, he went out to wake the others.

It was 5:10 A.M. when Jackson cut the motor. In pitch

blackness, they were tossing on choppy water 350 yards off the village of Whitefish Point.

"Okay?" asked Leaper. He was crouching in the center of the boat, waiting to pull up the sail, his blond hair blowing wildly in the wind.

"Okay," said Jackson.

They would try the sail, although the wind was very strong. He wanted to use the motor as little as possible in order not to alert them on the Point. The wind was out of the northeast still; the waves were not very high but seemed to be hacking at the boat from all directions, with Wicks in the bow taking most of the spray.

The plan had been to move under power, if you could call the fifteen-horsepower Benson "power," straight out from shore. Now that they arrived, Jackson wanted to tack up parallel to the coast, pass the Point about two hundred yards off, and keep sailing north until they heard the first signs of the troopers' assault. At that moment, he planned on turning the skiff around sharply in the opposite direction. With the wind at their backs, they ought to move quickly back to the Point, aiming for a landing near the tip itself.

There were two things that worried him. First, that they might encounter heavy resistance even before they could land on the Point. Jackson was gambling on the troopers, who would be approaching overland from the other side of the camp, to draw all the Silver Shirts away from where he intended to land.

The second thing that worried him seemed increasingly less likely. He'd been afraid that Sir Roland, sizing up the hopelessness of his position within the camp, would try to run. Orth had said there were boats in the camp. Would Sir Roland attempt to sail across twenty-five miles of open water to Canada? Now that the storm had come, and the water was still quite rough, Jackson tended to doubt it. No, if Sir Roland was going to run, he would likely wait until daylight.

The moment Leaper raised the sail it began to luff so badly that Jackson told him to take it down. It was impossible to sail into this wind, the rigging was much too slack. This wasn't a real sailboat at all. They would have to take their chances with the motor, hoping that its noise would not alert the camp. Perhaps the wind would muffle the noise.

Off to their left, they could see lights flickering near the end of the Point. Jackson guessed they were lights in the main house, the headquarters. He wondered if Sir Roland was awake there, giving orders, advising Nance, perhaps plotting his own escape.

The wind was gradually slackening as the outboard took them north, beyond the Point and into the eastern head of Lake Superior. He didn't want to go too far north. Timing was so crucial. He had to coincide their own landing so that they would beat the troopers, and Hoover, to that house. What if Sir Roland wasn't in the house? Jackson didn't even want to think of such a possibility.

He desperately hoped the rigging would hold so that they could use the sail for the final approach. By no means did he want to go in under power with that raucous Benson.

He had given Wicks his .38, keeping the shotgun for himself. Leaper would not have a weapon. Hopefully, he wouldn't need one as he stood watch over the boat, their getaway man.

It happened so quickly that it took all three by surprise. Where they had been moving in thick and total darkness, suddenly there was a thin edge of incandescence across the east. There was a horizon, just a thread of light that began to rapidly spin higher into the sky, leaving an ashen glow beneath it.

"Look!" said Wicks.

Jackson turned at the tiller, following Wicks's pointed finger. It was still all darkness to the west, but behind them, on the Point, they could see specks of pinkish light. It must be making a tremendous racket, but the wind was carrying the sound away from them. The troopers' assault had begun at the first sign of dawn. What they saw were the flames leaping out of the muzzles of a hundred guns.

"Let's turn it now," he said to Leaper. "As soon as we're around, set the sail. Then I want you to take the tiller and bring us in."

"Aye, aye, Captain."

Jackson pulled hard on the outboard, pulling against the thrust of the wind and waves. It was impossible to make anything but a wide turn. But then they were coming around full, nosing to the south, and he shouted at Leaper.

Once the sail went up, they began to skim over the water. The choppy waves suddenly became helping fingers tossing them onwards, from crest to crest, flying back toward the Point. He cut the engine and moved aside as Leaper came to the stern.

When they were a hundred yards off shore, they could pick out the roar of the guns, muffled but constant. Mixed in with the firing were shouts, human and frantic. Jackson felt himself go hollow in the pit of his stomach. There was too much time before this one, too much thinking time.

The dawn was growing increasingly bright. As they neared the Point, the trees on the shore stood out distinctly in the grainy light. Jackson could make out the top floor of a white house beyond the trees. Two upper windows glowed with a yellow interior light. Ahead, the extreme tip of the Point was now only thirty-five yards away. He waved at Leaper, indicating that he wanted to go in a little closer to the house.

Wicks was poised in the bow, waiting to jump as soon as they were close enough.

"It's very deep here," whispered Jackson. "Wait until we're right on top of it."

Wicks grunted his affirmation. He was holding the .38 in his right hand, scanning the pines for any sign of resistance. The din was increasing in volume the nearer they got: constant gunfire, shouts and cries of pain. Jackson could distinguish the steady bursts of submachine-gun fire from the rest of the shooting.

He dropped the sail.

Wicks jumped off the bow. It was too soon. He landed in water over his waist, holding the .38 at shoulder level, pointed at the line of trees. He found his balance, then reached back for the bowline and began to haul them closer.

There was some mud and, beyond, the soft carpet of pine needles began. They were about five yards from the end of the Point. Jackson looked back at Leaper. He signaled for him to turn the boat around. Leaper nodded and hissed, "Get on with it, you two."

They had been lucky. There wasn't a single sentry on the far end of the Point. Jackson quickly located the path which led straight up through the trees to the back of the house. He went first with the shotgun, Wicks just behind and off to his left.

The house sat on top of a small rise. Its ground floor was stone, a cellarlike foundation built into the ground. Above rose two stories of plain wooden house: the kind of house that could have been taken straight out of a six-year-old's drawing, complete with windows, divided into four panes and a crooked chimney on the roof.

Where the pines ended, there was a small clearing. Jackson was about to step into this when he saw the flicker of movement at the back door. He suddenly froze, Wicks beside him.

A dark figure came out of the lower door and moved quickly off to the right in the direction of the shore.

Jackson waited a full minute and then moved forward. In three running strides he and Wicks were pressed up against the stone wall beside the door.

Wicks suddenly stepped around him, went straight to the door and disappeared inside. With no flashlight and no lights evident inside, it took incredible guts to move into the cellar of the house like that, thought Jackson. He followed in Wicks's footsteps.

They were in a dark musty storeroom or root cellar. Ahead of them, light fell from above, illuminating a flight of wooden stairs. Wicks led the way, then suddenly halted as heavy footsteps resounded on the floor above. The footsteps moved down toward the front of the house, then disappeared. Whoever it was had gone out the front door. Very cautiously now Wicks began to edge up the stairs, holding the .38 into the light above. Jackson wished he had gone first. It would be impossible for him to use the shotgun on the stairs without Wicks getting in the line of fire.

At the top of the stairs, they were in a narrow lighted hallway. Immediately to their left was a kitchen, empty. Across the hall there was a room with a door almost closed, with light spilling through the cracks. Wicks looked at Jackson, then suddenly kicked it open and stood ready to fire at anything that moved inside.

The room was empty. There was a large photograph on the far wall of someone giving the fascist salute, glaring straight ahead with maniacal intensity. The room was cluttered with worthless furniture. One of the walls was covered with disks of exposed and broken plaster: large-caliber-bullet scars. They looked at each other, Wicks shrugged, and they returned to the hall.

Outside the battle was raging, but the house was silent, seemingly empty. There were two more small rooms at the front. And a stairway leading up to the top floor. "I'll go up," Jackson told Wicks. "You check these two and cover the door."

Jackson moved upstairs as quickly and silently as possible. There were four bedrooms, all done up with the same cheap wallpaper on which fat pink roses seemed to laugh at him with his shotgun. From one of the large windows, he took a quick survey of the area beyond the front of the house: panicked men in silver uniforms running across the grass in the dawn.

He started back toward the top of the stairs. Suddenly he heard a footstep below him. Someone called, "Captain? Hey, Captain . . . hey!"

The sharp report of the .38 cut off the voice. The explosion seemed to echo around the interior of the house like a frantic bird seeking escape. Then it was silent. Jackson took the stairs three at a time. Wicks stood over the body looking up at Jackson. The man had fallen on his belly, his face wedged against the bottom step.

"He was coming in to—"

"Don't worry about it," said Jackson. "This place is empty. Let's start figuring out what hell we're going to do."

There was nothing, nobody, not a damn thing in the house. Just one less Silver Shirt, bleeding his life away in the hall. Jackson was afraid Wicks's shot would draw more of them. And their "luck" couldn't hold much longer. Not that he needed any more of this "luck," with Sir Roland nowhere to be found.

Wicks led the way, clambering down the stairs into the cellar. Suddenly they heard heavy footsteps back near the front door. "What the . . . Plenty? What the goddamn hell is going on here?"

Wicks crashed against something metal as he left the stairs, causing a loud noise as whatever it was hit the floor. The footsteps suddenly began to run toward the rear of the house just above their heads. They made their way to the backdoor. "Halt!" shouted a voice above. "Halt!"

Wicks broke into the clearing, Jackson right behind him. As they did so, Jackson happened to glance left toward the lake. Just a glimpse. . . .

The man was standing in the stern of the small rowboat about five feet off the end of a rotting dock. The rowboat did not look very happy with its burden, large as the man was. Jackson had never seen him in the flesh until this moment. But he had seen the photograph and he instantly recognized Sir Roland, who was trying hard to get the little outboard started, winding up the starter cord furiously for another yank.

There was a splintering crash above and behind them. A window had been broken deliberately, followed by the hideous staccato of a Thompson firing at them. They dived for the cover of the pine trees. The path was too far away. Jackson went straight in on his belly, hit and rolled, came up firing the shotgun in the direction of their attacker. As he did so, he heard the gasp four feet away, the great in-suck of air, as Wicks was hit by the submachine gun.

Jackson moved to his side. Wicks's legs were still in the clearing. Jackson suddenly threw himself back as a round nearly pierced his head. He had to watch helplessly as the Thompson continued to throw round after round into the already-dead man. The body lurched with the impact of each slug. It was insane. Suddenly the Thompson ceased firing. Jackson had no doubt it was coming for him now. He turned and ran beneath the low boughs in the direction of the boat.

He almost tripped over it. Wrapped in a filthy, paint-spattered tarp, it had to be a body lying there on the ground. Jackson had no time to stop and see whose body.

He broke cover about eight feet from where Leaper was standing anxiously in the stern of the skiff, its bow pointing out into the lake. He hadn't started the outboard. "There he is!" cried Jackson, pointing at where Sir Roland was now moving north in the rowboat. "Get it started, Greville. Come on, man."

Jackson heard the footsteps running down the path as he heaved himself over the side of the skiff. It took him a moment to get his balance. Leaper was struggling with the Benson's starter cord. "Where is Wicks?"

"He's dead. Hurry!"

When the figure suddenly emerged from the pines with the Thompson in his hands, Jackson was waiting with the shotgun braced against his shoulder. He didn't give Captain Nance a moment to set himself up for another deadly burst of fire. The shotgun discharged its load of double-O at a range of fifteen feet. Nance was torn up in front, torn to shreds, with the first round. The second and third rounds were unnecessary. Jackson pumped them up and fired them into the fallen man as if they were the most necessary things in the world.

"Steady there, old man," said Leaper.

"That's what he did to Wicks. Come on, Greville, let's get on with it."

As if in answer, the little outboard ignited into action on Leaper's third pull of the cord. "I'll take it," said Jackson. "We'll catch him with the sail."

The rowboat was already about seventy-five yards in front of them and steadily increasing its lead. The wind had eased somewhat with the dawn, and was coming around more from the east. The outboard on Plenty's rowboat was smaller than their Benson, but then so was Plenty's rowboat compared to the heavy wooden lifeboat. With the sail, Jackson thought they ought to be able to catch him in a matter of minutes. Leaper was struggling to get it raised when Jackson suddenly saw the other boat coming in from the west.

Light gray and low in the water, the deep-throated roar of its engines carried clearly now over the water. It was still perhaps three-quarters of a mile away. But it had all the speed they lacked. It was heading more toward them than Sir Roland. Of course, Jackson realized, they were being attracted by the sail. Perhaps they hadn't even noticed Sir Roland's tiny rowboat yet.

Leaper had trimmed it as well as he could and they were now beginning to make up some of the distance. They could see Sir Roland constantly looking back at them. He must have seen that it was hopeless. Suddenly a slug hit the water two feet from where Jackson sat in the stern. Sir Roland was armed. He was firing at them.

The Coast Guard patrol boat was coming on like a

sleek gray shark. Another bullet sent up a geyser of spray near the side. And another. "Keep down," he yelled at Leaper, who was standing in the middle of the boat.

"Right," said Leaper. But he leaned out to gather in a bit more of the sail to increase their speed. As he did so, Jackson looked on helplessly as the bullet hit him below the left armpit. Leaper grunted, falling onto his face beneath the mast.

"Christ!" Jackson dropped the tiller handle and moved to him. He rolled him over gently. Leaper's eyes were open. The bullet had entered four inches below the shoulder: a lung shot. He was moving his lips, trying to speak but getting nothing but pink sputum. It was a serious wound. "Stay still. It's not so bad, Greville. Stay still and don't try to talk."

Jackson moved back to the outboard, holding the line that controlled the sail which Leaper had dropped. Only forty yards separated them from Sir Roland now. But the Coast Guard patrol boat had suddenly altered course. Now they were moving to cut off Sir Roland, thinking they'd get both boats. From the sound of it, Jackson realized the Coast Guard were firing carbines at them. Had they been the ones to hit Leaper?

Less than thirty yards now, with the Coast Guard still three hundred yards off Sir Roland's bow.

Suddenly Sir Roland stood up in the rowboat. He emptied his revolver at Jackson. The Coast Guard bullets were sending up waterspouts all around his boat. Jackson quickly looked down at Leaper. The man actually winked at him.

"Keep your head down, will you?" said Jackson, amazed at the Englishman's spirit.

Now he was closing faster and faster. Sir Roland must have gone off his head. He was staring at the gun in his hand, and then hurled it furiously at the oncoming skiff. As he did so, his body suddenly sagged and he lost his balance. He'd been hit. He tumbled headfirst into the lake, clutching at his back as he fell. The rowboat heaved high in the air, glad to have rid itself of all that bulk. It came splashing down on the water, and Sir Roland disappeared.

In another minute, Jackson was there. The Coast Guard were shooting at him, less than one hundred yards away now. The rowboat had drifted a bit. But Jackson was certain he'd kept his eyes on the spot where Sir Roland had gone into the lake.

He searched the water, desperate for a sign of him. A bullet cracked the air inches from Jackson's body. He was furious, beyond control, and suddenly the frustration hurled him into the water. He began to swim. With his head scanning the top of the waves, he swam around and around in a circle. He could feel the pulsing of the Coast Guard engines inside his head. Then he began to dive, in his suit and shoes, again and again. Diving down into the cold, dark water with his eyes open. Diving with his hands reaching into the murk, grasping into the depths for the man who just wasn't there.

V

THE OVAL ROOM

JULY 10, 1940

30

The President was seated behind his desk in a navy-blue summer-weight suit, his cigarette holder in his right hand, his left drumming lightly on the polished walnut. His necktie was a bright arrangement of regimental stripes on silk, alternating reds and yellows, in contrast to his serious, almost dour facial expression.

The Director sat opposite the desk in a high-backed Monroe armchair, dressed as always in a conservative dark suit. However, a kelly-green necktie lent an unusually dapper note to his appearance this morning. His short, thick hands, the backs of which were tufted with dark brown hair, lay neatly folded in his lap. He was speaking and, from time to time, punctuating one of his remarks by bringing his fist down lightly on the arm of his chair. At his feet, leaning against the chair, was a calfskin briefcase.

The Director's words bore the unmistakable imprint of a formal report, an official summary. He picked each word with extreme care, as if he were selecting precious stones from an invisible jeweler's tray. Much to Roosevelt's annoyance, the Director's taste ran to the larger, rarer, utterly impractical sparklers among the English language. He was showing off this morning. The President had to restrain himself in order not to interrupt with a request to, for God's sake, get on with it.

The Director had just begun to list the results of the FBI investigation which followed the successful raid on the camp. Part of this involved the press and how they had been effectively "neutralized." A total of thirty-four Silver Shirts and eleven Michigan state troopers had lost their lives in the dawn assault. Another seventy-four men sustained injuries serious enough to require hospital treatment. The Director beamed as he reported that not a single FBI agent had been killed, including the rookie named Budge who had been held hostage. In fact, there were only four agents from the Bureau on the injured list.

During a thorough survey of the camp area, FBI agents had uncovered a burial ground behind the main house in a grove of pines. Nine bodies, in shallow unmarked graves, in various stages of decomposition, were found.

The body of the young Senate staff aide was nearby. Presumably the attack on the camp had begun before his remains could be buried. Anthony Benet's body had been claimed by one Clarence T. Elliot of Duxbury, Massachusetts, the man's maternal grandfather.

"What do you make of these other bodies?" asked Roosevelt.

The Director frowned. "Four of them were over a year in the ground. The others were all interred without personal effects or identification of any kind. We are in the midst of laboratory classification of all state missing-persons lists. I estimate at least seven more days until we know for certain who some of these men are."

"But what's your guess?" asked Roosevelt.

"From our interrogation of the surviving Silver Shirts, we are certain at least three of the bodies belong to kidnap victims. Perhaps members of the Jewish faith or antifascist activists. Perhaps just drifters abducted under the orders of Thomas Nance."

Roosevelt nodded, thinking that the Director had a fondness for pinning the "drifter" label on anyone he couldn't immediately classify who was involved in a violent crime.

"One of the bodies is definitely Negroid. Two others were only in the ground for a matter of hours. Apparently they were the victims of some sort of crude execution in the form of a duel with blunt weapons which Nance conducted on the night of the second. In other words, Silver Shirts who somehow fell afoul of their leader."

"I take it Nance died during the raid," said Roosevelt.

"That is correct."

"Didn't you have any record on this man?"

"Previous to his joining the Silver Shirts?" asked the Director. "Nothing outside of his military record. He received a dishonorable discharge from the Marine Corps in November 1937. Apparently he was directly involved in the death of three recruits during training exercises at Camp Pendleton, California."

"He sounds like a homicidal maniac," said Roosevelt.

"No doubt he was. But there was nothing in his file subsequent to his dismissal from the Marines."

"I wish there was some way we could keep track of these men before . . ." Roosevelt didn't finish. Realizing to whom he was speaking, he thought better before he completed what had been an ill-considered remark to begin with. "Let's get on with it. Tell me about the Englishman."

"Certainly," said the Director. "As you know, we did not recover the body until Sunday."

Roosevelt nodded, thinking that if it hadn't been for the poor fisherman, the FBI probably would never have recovered the body.

The Director enumerated the FBI laboratory conclusions regarding the death of Sir Roland Plenty. According to the lab report, the bullet had struck him in the left hip, splintering the coccyx and catapulting him into the lake. The bullet was certainly one of those fired by the Coast Guardsmen, who were using Winchester rifles on the foredeck of the approaching patrol boat. In itself, it was hardly a lethal wound.

What had happened, surmised the lab, was that the boat had hit Sir Roland in the head once he was in the lake, rendering him unconscious. An X ray of his skull revealed a deep abscission in the anterior skull area. The forensic experts believed he must have swallowed a great deal of water when he fell into the lake and, once unconscious, a good deal more. Death was due to drowning. Because of the rapid intake of water into stomach and lungs, the body had gone to the bottom like a stone. It took twenty-four hours for sufficient gas to develop in the internal cavities in order to bring a body back up to the surface. The corpse was floating with the current when it was discovered 250 yards off the village of Paradise.

By that time, said the Director, the FBI had already spent one day with the Navy divers out north of the Point. They had been flown from New London with the cooperation of the Navy Department in order to search the lake bottom.

Less than an hour after the body's recovery, the Bureau

had taken custody of it from the Michigan authorities. It was quickly moved to the Bureau field office in Detroit via ambulance, where it was stripped. All articles of clothing, including everything in the pockets, were carefully documented. The Director paused, unclasping his hands and reaching down to lift his briefcase from the pile carpet.

"In the inside left breast pocket of Sir Roland Plenty's suit jacket, we found an envelope containing twelve photographic prints, three by five inches in size. After three days in the lake, they were in an almost unrecognizable condition." He unzippered the briefcase and reached inside with his right hand. Out came a brown government envelope. The Director leaned forward and placed this on the desk directly in front of the President. "The twelve photographs are there. As you will see, they would not be of much use to anyone in their present state. I am happy, Mr. President, to be able to put an end to this potentially tragic episode now and for all time."

Roosevelt nodded without expression. He glanced down at the envelope, on which was typed in capital letters: "THE PRESIDENT OF THE UNITED STATES." It was even underlined. From the size of the envelope, it was obvious the Director was telling the truth about the size of the prints. Roosevelt did not bother to pick it up or touch it in any way. He lifted his head and met the Director's eyes.

"I appreciate this a great deal," he said. "There's just one thing. You did mention, unless I'm mistaken, when you called me on Sunday evening, that some negatives had been found."

"That is correct," said the Director.

"As you know, there has been some concern about these negatives since the problem came to our attention a few weeks ago."

"I am aware of that, yes. Which is precisely why I took the initiative of destroying them."

"I see," said Roosevelt. "You destroyed the negatives on your own initiative, is that correct?"

"That is correct. I personally destroyed them on Monday afternoon, two days ago, in my office. I don't know if you were informed, but the negatives were found in a secret compartment in the leather belt worn by Plenty around his waist. At first glance, it appeared to be a perfectly ordinary fine leather belt. One of our lab men in Detroit noticed, however, that it was slightly wider than usual."

"I'm sorry," interrupted Roosevelt, "but I am not concerned with where he had them hidden."

"I see," said the Director.

"What does concern me is why you felt it your duty to bring me these"—he nodded down at the envelope on the desk—"but to destroy the negatives."

"I felt certain that would be your wish, Mr. President. Considering how potentially inflammatory they were, I was certain you would want them destroyed at once." The Director did not feel it necessary to add anything to this.

"Mr. Director, I would like your personal assurance, your word, that you destroyed those negatives."

"You have my word," said the Director. He was sitting very erect, with his hands folded, looking directly into the President's eyes.

He was lying and Roosevelt had no doubt of it. As surely as Roosevelt was the thirty-second President of the United States, the Director was lying.

Roosevelt gave a little chuckle, almost a kind of apology. "Well, that's fine, then," he said.

"Yes, sir." The Director looked at his watch as if he had urgent business across town.

"Speaking of Englishmen, how is this fellow Leaper doing? The one who was with Jackson?" asked the President.

"I believe he is recovering satisfactorily. University Hospital at Ann Arbor is a fine institution. Could I make one statement for the record?"

"But of course," said Roosevelt. "What is it, Mr. Director?"

"I would like to comment on Jackson's part in this entire operation. I hold him personally responsible for the disastrous final days, including the considerable expense of the Navy divers. He had no right to attempt what he did in that boat. Worst of all, he is directly responsible for the loss of a life, not counting the injury caused to Miss Silvers and Leaper. If Jackson had obeyed orders, I have no doubt that Mr. Wicks would still be alive today."

Inside, Roosevelt was as angry as he had ever been in his life. But his voice sounded cooler than usual as he said,

"I want to thank you for your assessment, Mr. Director. I have already spoken to Jackson."

The Director would not leave it there. "I simply fail to understand what Jackson thought he had to gain by acting as he did."

"I suppose we could write it off to youthful enthusiasm," suggested Roosevelt with a thin smile.

"I would call it insubordination. A clear refusal to obey orders. As you know, Jackson worked for the Bureau prior to coming to you. In reviewing his file, I have found he has a long history of incidents bordering on almost psychopathic negligence. The man is an extreme egoist," said the Director. "Not simply headstrong, but seriously disturbed. I think you might reconsider the intimate role he plays on your staff."

It was already starting. The Director was informing Roosevelt, in no uncertain terms, that he wanted Jackson dismissed from the White House staff. The arrogance of it was truly astounding. Unless you knew what they both knew.

"Do you?" asked Roosevelt, his voice rising to a fine edge. "You should know, in that case, that Jackson submitted his resignation to me yesterday afternoon. I accepted it. But only with the utmost regret. In fact, I have told Jackson that he is welcome to return and work for me anytime in the future."

The Director looked startled, and then just smug. As Jackson was gone, he couldn't care less. He looked at his watch again. "I think perhaps I have taken enough of your valuable time," he said. "Once more I would like to say how gratified I am to be able to bring this entire episode to such a benign conclusion."

He began to rise. "Just a moment," said Roosevelt.

"Of course." The Director sat back down.

Roosevelt reached for one of his cigarettes and smiled at the Director, as if to erase his sharp tone of voice in the previous exchange. "You know, of course, that the Democratic convention opens in five days in Chicago."

The Director nodded.

"I suppose you're wondering, like everybody else seems to be, if I'll be a candidate."

This surprised the Director. As far as he was concerned, there was no doubt whatsoever that Roosevelt was now free to run for a third term and would, of course, do so. But he forced himself to say, "Yes, I suppose I am."

"Well, I've decided I will allow myself to accept the nomination, should it be offered, Mr. Director. I tell you that all confidence, of course. But I won't be going out to Chicago. Nor will I actively seek the nomination. That will be made clear to the delegates through the good offices of Senator Barkley when he gives the keynote address on Tuesday night. However, I think it's probably a safe bet to say the nomination will be offered to me on Wednesday."

The Director allowed himself one of his rare smiles. "I am sure that is a safe bet, Mr. President."

Roosevelt returned the smile, overcame it with a flash of his great white teeth. "What I wanted to tell you was simply this. If I am nominated, and then reelected, I will want you to remain as my Director at the Bureau."

The Director's eyes clouded for a moment. How could danger lurk in such welcome words? Was this Roosevelt's way of saying that it was all understood between the two of them now? He managed to put unction into his voice as he said, "That is good to hear, Mr. President. Thank you very much for your loyal . . . your confidence in me. I only hope I can continue to merit such—"

"Not at all!" said Roosevelt. "You see, I understand now, especially now, how vulnerable we are. Men like ourselves, men in positions of high trust in this government. Always walking a kind of tightrope between our private lives and the lives the public demands of us. Isn't that true?"

"Very true," said the Director.

"Our most innocent, and sometimes not-so-innocent, activities can suddenly be opened up to public exposure at the drop of a hat. The public is a curious beast, as you well know. The people want to look at us as a species of gods. They put us up on a level they themselves would never dare to aspire to, but can never refuse to believe in either. It makes it rather difficult for us. Because we both know how the press can distort things, don't we?"

"Oh, yes," said the Director. He was growing increasingly uncomfortable. "The press are wolves."

"Sometimes they are. But there are all kinds of wolves in this city, wouldn't you say, Mr. Director?"

The Director did not like the implication, not one bit, but he nodded.

Roosevelt leaned over to the left and opened a drawer in his desk. He brought out an envelope, plain white, unsealed, unmarked. He held it up in his hand and let the Director look at it for a moment before he said, "One of those wolves seems to be on your trail. I wish I could tell you his name. But I gave my word I would not. This came to me only days ago. I want to give it to you now."

"Excuse me?" asked the Director. "I don't quite understand."

"I think you will," said Roosevelt. He passed the envelope across the desk to the Director's outstretched hand. "It is all perfectly innocent, I know. But you and I understand how the press can distort things. In this case, the wolf came to the wrong man."

The Director's hands slowly opened the flap of the envelope and drew out the object inside. It was a single photograph, a three-by-five-inch snapshot showing himself and another man. From the look of it, it had been taken with a high-powered lens on a beach. There was very little to it. Just the Director in his swimming trunks standing with his arm thrown casually around the bare shoulders of the younger man, also in swimming trunks. They were both smiling, the rather blunt features of the Director contrasting with the handsome, chiseled features of the man beside him. The Director knew that it had been taken only ten days previously on a Sunday when he had driven down to Virginia Beach with several of his closest friends in the Bureau, including the young West Coast agent he was particularly fond of recently. He knew that it had been taken from at least a distance of one hundred yards, probably from the dunes.

He knew far more than that.

"I want to thank you," was all he could say.

"You are very welcome," said Roosevelt.

With enormous effort, the Director forced himself up on wavering legs. He could not smile, let alone speak. The rage inside him was all-powerful, all-consuming, all-futile. He forced himself to look at Roosevelt once more directly in the eyes. Neither smiled. The message that passed between them was like a cold flame. No win, no checkmate, but a draw. Negative for negative. No matter what each thought of the other, each now held the other's future securely in his grasp. Two masters. Shackled to one another as tightly as two convicts on an Alabama chain gang. If they were going to move forward, backward, to move at all, they would have to move together. Negative for negative.

"Oh, one more thing," said Roosevelt when the Director was nearly at the door.

He turned and waited.

"If I am reelected, I am going to put Colonel Donovan in charge of establishing a new intelligence-gathering agency for this country. Strictly foreign intelligence, it shouldn't infringe on your activities in the slightest. Do you have any objections? If so, please tell me now."

"No," said the Director. "So long as you keep it out of this country, I'll accept it."

"Good enough," said Roosevelt. He watched the Director turn and walk to the door. In an instant, he was gone.

But he would be back, thought Roosevelt. Many times with many different motives, and some of those times, it would be Roosevelt who would have to say to the Director: "I'll accept it." It occurred to him that the Director was still a relatively young man, a healthy man, who might live for many years. Who could predict how many Presidents he might eventually serve? Negative for negative.

Image for image.

EPILOGUE

APRIL 11, 1945

The USS *Foreman* was standing two and a half nautical miles off the southeastern coast of Okinawa in a moderate sea.

It was 21:30 hours and Lieutenant Commander Jackson had just finished his supper. He had been on duty since 07:00 that morning. The invasion, which had begun eleven days earlier, was bogged down now with the Japanese extracting maximum casualties from the Americans in return for every inch of terrain they were forced to yield. It had been a long day, but Jackson was very accustomed to long, exhausting days.

The news was not all bad. Five days earlier, the American Navy had delivered a crushing defeat to the Japanese fleet at Kyushu. But the invasion of Okinawa was proving to be a bloody and interminable affair.

The *Foreman* was one of the three U.S. destroyers shelling that sector of the island. For the first five hours of his duty, Jackson had been on the bridge in constant communication with a Marine captain who was directing the destroyer's two forward gun batteries to various fixes in the enemy-occupied jungle.

Early in the afternoon, the Marines had pushed the Japanese back to a point where they were no longer in range of the *Foreman*'s guns. At that point, the destroyer was only a quarter of a mile off the beach. They had been about to move out to deeper water when an urgent request came from the Marines to take a load of wounded.

Jackson had gone down on deck to help supervise the

unloading as the two LST craft came alongside. It was a delicate operation. Not the least of their problems was where to put the wounded soldiers once they'd been winched up to the deck. These men were critically wounded and all of them came up flat on their backs. Young, shattered, eyes clouded with morphine: Jackson was having to leave most of them out in the harsh sunlight on deck while his men made room for them below.

They had almost finished unloading the second LST when the alarm sounded. The sailors had to scramble across a deck crowded with stretchers to reach their battle stations.

Jackson was halfway to the bridge when he saw them. Just two dark specks edging out of the corona of the sun. Too far away to hear the drone of their engines yet. Quickly, Jackson calculated the odds in his head. Two planes for three destroyers. From their shape, the way they were approaching, he had little doubt they were the suicide planes.

As they began to dive, he knew he would never make it to the bridge in time. He stood watching the graceful looping descent, watching the two black specks grow larger, grow wings, and separate in a rising crescendo of hideous noise. One veered off to the stern, no doubt aiming for the *Stockton*, which was some 150 yards south of the *Foreman*. The other plane kept on diving straight at Jackson.

The destroyer's anti-aircraft guns filled the air with their staccato outrage, lacing the sky around the diving plane with puffs of flak. He could see the sun glinting off the pilot's canopy. It was diving at a steep angle, aiming for the bridge and a midships hit. A lethal hit.

Jackson was unable to breathe, sure that it was going to hit. Perfectly resigned yet furious as the pilot opened up with his machine guns to rake the deck full of wounded soldiers. Only a few hundred yards away, it moved through the brown flak puffs as if they were harmless, disintegrating moths.

It was going to hit. Bullets penetrated the steel only feet from where he stood. Jackson would not move to cover. He knew it was going to hit. And he was transfixed by the spectacle of it, the certainty of it. It was madness. Yet it had its own logic, and its own beauty.

At first it was just an orange fringe around the nose, and then suddenly it was a mass of lobster-red flame: one great scarlet-and-canary-and-tangerine flame stuck between two black wings. They had hit it! The *Foreman*'s gunners had hit the plane!

The arc of the dive was broken as, in a surreal picture, it began to drop straight down less than sixty yards off the port rail. What had been their death suddenly became a fiery jungle blossom falling into the dark blue ocean.

Now, many hours later, Jackson drank the last of his coffee. He stood up with the tray in his hands and crossed the bright, empty officers' mess. After dropping his tray off, he stepped out into the corridor. His tiny cabin was up one deck directly below the bridge. But he paused at the bottom of the stairs, then found himself going out on starboard deck instead.

On the rail, he had nothing to look at but ocean and stars. It was enough.

They would win the war. That was clear now. And all the lives that had perished, all the blood wasted: none of it would ever convince Jackson that it hadn't been necessary to fight. Yet he knew the isolationists had also been right. Everyone had been right: those who wanted to fight and those who wanted to hide. Everyone had his own point and it was valid. Just as it was deadly.

He lingered at the rail for about forty minutes. The occasional sailor who passed left him alone. They were used to seeing him standing there at this hour. Jackson was a good officer, popular with his men, but he was not a mixer. Never had been. Most of the serious talking he did was in his own mind or to Rona, to her letters in his mind.

Finally, with another endless day ahead of him in a few hours, he forced himself to leave the deck with its warm breeze, splendid night sky and illusion of peace. He made his way back up to his cabin, where he stripped off his uniform and lay down on cool sheets in the close darkness. Sleep was not long in coming to him. And with it came one of his best dreams, a restorative dream, a dream of cruising on a sea where the swells were like glass mountains and the depths unchartable.

𝒟

Buy them at your local
bookstore or use coupon
on next page for ordering.

SIGNET Books You'll Enjoy

☐ **BEDFORD ROW** by Claire Rayner. (#E8819—$2.5*)

☐ **JO STERN** by David Slavitt. (#J8753—$1.9)

☐ **SAVAGE RANSOM** by David Lippincott. (#E8749—$2.2)

☐ **FURY'S SUN, PASSION'S MOON** by Gimone Hall.

(#E8748—$2.5)

☐ **RAPTURE'S MISTRESS** by Gimone Hall. (#E8422—$2.2)

☐ **THE LONG WALK** by Richard Bachman. (#J8754—$1.9)

☐ **DAYLIGHT MOON** by Thomas Carney. (#J8755—$1.9)

☐ **MAKING IT** by Bryn Chandler. (#E8756—$2.2)

☐ **THE CORAL KILL** by Bryn Chandler. (#E8347—$1.7*)

☐ **ON THE ROAD** by Jack Kerouac. (#E8973—$2.)

☐ **THE DHARMA BUMS** by Jack Kerouac. (#J9138—$1.)

☐ **FLICKERS** by Phillip Rock. (#E8839—$2.2)

☐ **EMMA AND I** by Sheila Hocken. (#E8694—$2.2)

☐ **THIS HOUSE IS BURNING** by Mona Williams.

(#E8695—$2.2)

☐ **THE MESSENGER** by Mona Williams. (#J8012—$1.)

* Price slightly higher in Canada
† Not available in Canada

Buy them at your local bookstore or use this convenient coupon for ordering.

THE NEW AMERICAN LIBRARY, INC.,
P.O. Box 999, Bergenfield, New Jersey 07621

Please send me the SIGNET BOOKS I have checked above. I am enclosing
$_____ (please add 50¢ to this order to cover postage and handling).
Send check or money order—no cash or C.O.D.'s. Prices and numbers are
subject to change without notice.

Name _____

Address _____

City_____ State_____ Zip Code_____

Allow 4-6 weeks for delivery.
This offer is subject to withdrawal without notice.